Tor Books by Jerry Oltion

Abandon in Place
The Getaway Special
Anywhere But Here

Anywhere Bu

BLOOMINGTON, ILLINOIS
PUBLIC LIBRARY

Anywhere But Here

Jerry Oltion

A Tom Doherty Associates Book
New York

This is a work of fiction. All the characters and events portrayed in this novel are either fictitious or are used fictitiously.

ANYWHERE BUT HERE

Copyright © 2005 by Jerry Oltion

All rights reserved, including the right to reproduce this book, or portions thereof, in any form.

This book is printed on acid-free paper.

A Tor Book
Published by Tom Doherty Associates, LLC
175 Fifth Avenue
New York, NY 10010

www.tor.com

Tor® is a registered trademark of Tom Doherty Associates, LLC.

Library of Congress Cataloging-in-Publication Data

Oltion, Jerry.
Anywhere but here / Jerry Oltion.—1st ed.
p. cm.
"A Tom Doherty Associates book."
ISBN 0-765-30619-0 (acid-free paper)
EAN 978-0765-30619-7
1. Wyoming—Fiction. 2. Imperialism—Fiction. 3. Space ships—Fiction. 4. Citizenship—Fiction. 5. Space flight—Fiction. 6. Pickup trucks—Fiction. 7. Married people—Fiction. 8. International relations—Fiction. I. Title.

PS3565.L857A84 2005
813'.54—dc22

2004058050

First Edition: March 2005

Printed in the United States of America

0 9 8 7 6 5 4 3 2 1

For the United States of America

"Our country, right or wrong.
When right, to be kept right; when wrong, to be put right."
—Carl Schurz

May we never forget the second half of that quote.

Acknowledgments

Thanks as always to the Eugene Wordos for support and inspiration, especially Ken Brady, Aurora Lemieux, Eric Witchey, Dave Bishoff, and Blake Hutchins, who made sure I sat down and wrote when I said I would by the simple expedient of coming over to my house and doing it with me.

Thanks to Elba Solano and Françoise Beniston for help with my Spanish and French. The parts I got right are theirs; any mistakes are my own.

Thanks to Jack McDevitt for the title, which he found languishing unused in my previous book, *The Getaway Special.*

Anywhere But Here

Trent Stinson just wanted to get some cash. It was Friday evening, and he and Donna were headed downtown for their traditional "start the weekend right" dinner out. He had enough cash in his wallet for fast food, but Donna wanted to go to the brew pub tonight, and two burgers and a couple of pints of ferny beer would just about clean him out. A weekend in Rock Springs without money was about the dullest prospect Trent could imagine, so he swung by Southside National on their way downtown and parked across the street from the ATM.

"Be back in a sec," he told Donna as he stepped out and down to the pavement.

It was a long reach. His pickup was standard equipment for a Wyoming native: three feet high at the running boards, with knobby off-road tires too big for the fenders, each wheel individually powered by a General Electric 150 superconducting motor modified with a bank of ultracapacitors for even more torque on startup.

Trent's had been modified a bit more than most. Besides painting the body panels a deep pearlescent red and chrome-plating practically everything else, he had replaced all the glass with half-inch Lexan, oversized and set inside the frames so no amount of pressure could blow it out, and he had sealed every seam with industrial-strength adhesive. He had added extra latches to the doors to hold them tight against the extra seals he had also installed, and he had reinforced all the body panels with angle-iron to keep them from flexing. He'd welded three chrome roll bars across the outside of the cab for extra support, incidentally giving him a sturdy anchor for the two army surplus cargo parachutes packed in separate carriers on top. In back, a homemade camper built of diamond-plate aluminum looked a little like the top half of the Lunar Module that had taken Aldrin and Armstrong to the Moon half a century before. It was sealed just as tight, and he'd tested the whole works to 30 p.s.i.—two full atmospheres of pressure—before he had trusted his and Donna's lives to it.

Those modifications had eaten up most of their bank account, but Trent figured he could take out a bit more without risking next month's house payment. If there *was* a next month's house payment. He didn't want to stiff the loan company, but the way people were jumping off into space lately, you couldn't give away real estate on Earth anymore. When Allen Meisner had dropped the plans for a cheap hyperdrive engine on the world, he probably hadn't considered what it would do to the housing industry, but people were defaulting on their loans right and left, and the banks had yet to foreclose on any of them. They didn't want to get stuck paying the taxes.

That was just the tip of the iceberg. A hyperdrive engine that cost only a couple hundred dollars in parts had changed a lot more than that. Trent's job, for one thing. He was a construction worker, but the only houses being built these days were on planets orbiting Alpha Centauri and Tau Ceti and places farther out. There was plenty of work to be had if he wanted it, but he'd never been excited about commuting, especially when it involved a multi-light-year jump and a parachute landing. And now commuting was impossible anyway, because the federal government had made it illegal to possess a hyperdrive engine. That didn't stop anyone, of course, but it cut down on casual trips, and it killed the one other source of income that Trent could have done: retrofitting other people's vehicles for space. Even though it wasn't illegal to seal up a truck, at least not yet, most people didn't want to make themselves targets for the police, and the ones who were willing to risk it were also generally capable of doing it themselves.

The only decent prospect for work was the new civic center, which had been in the planning stages for over a year and was up for a final yea-or-nay vote at the next city council meeting, but with so many people bailing out of town, Trent didn't expect the council to go ahead with it.

Donna still had her job at the Mall, but it was only three days a week, and they couldn't live on just that. They could relocate, but neither one of them were quite ready to let go of their home town. They'd made one trip out to a sun-like star about fifteen light-years away in Cetus, found some friendly aliens, and gone fishing with them, but that was just a weekend lark before the government had cracked down on such things. They'd had no intention of staying. But if Trent couldn't find work on Earth . . .

The bank's parking lot was deserted. It would normally be quiet this time of day, but there weren't any cars on the street, either. It seemed like half the people in town had headed for the stars in the five months since Allen had made it possible, and the rest of them weren't getting out much. The economy was in the dumper because nobody with a dead-end job was sticking around to work at it, and even though the Galactic Federation had stopped the world war that had flared up when the lid came off the pressure cooker, everybody was still afraid of terrorist bombs materializing overhead. There had been suicide bombings a couple times a month for as long as Trent could remember, but now they were coming in from overhead, and the laser satellites couldn't stop them. Rock Springs wasn't much of a target, but it still put a damper on people's spirits when world tension was so high.

Trent stuck his card in the ATM and keyed in his code. He didn't need to get a balance; he knew there were only a few hundred bucks left. Better just take out sixty or so. Not that saving some for later was all that smart, either, the way inflation was killing the value of the dollar, but Trent figured it was better in the bank than spent.

He whistled softly while he waited for the machine to cough up the dough, and wished he'd put on his jacket. It was springtime by the calendar, but the evening air felt downright wintry.

A van pulled into the parking lot, its headlights sweeping across Trent and the ATM. The driver didn't go for a parking spot right away, and Trent snatched his cash as soon as it poked out of the slot. He couldn't see inside the van over the glare of the headlights. It could be a little old lady in there, but it could be a half dozen out-of-work trona miners looking for an easy mark. If that was the case, they'd get a rude surprise the moment they tried something—there was a .45 colt revolver in the pickup's glove box and a laser-sighted .270 in the gun rack behind the seat, and Donna was a crack shot with either one—but Trent didn't want that kind of trouble if he could avoid it.

The van didn't move. Nobody opened a door. Trent shoved his cash in a front pocket and walked back toward his pickup, and then the van pulled sideways across two parking spots. Not near the ATM, but farther toward the back of the building. Now that its lights weren't blinding him, Trent saw that it was tricked out for space, too. The owner of this rig didn't care for show; he had just welded angle-iron across the wide spans of metal and wound the whole works with steel cable to hold it together against air pressure. It looked like a moving junk pile, but it wasn't the ugliest ship Trent had seen.

The driver was a big guy with a round head. Streetlight glow glinted off his bald—no, that wasn't right. He was wearing a bubble helmet, already sealed up and inflated. It looked like he was just about to take off for somewhere, and was stopping off for some last-minute cash first.

Trent took a couple steps toward the van, thinking he

would ask where the guy was off to, then thought better of it. This wasn't a good time to be walking up to somebody in a bank parking lot. He might have a wife with a gun, too, and she might not wait to see if Trent was friendly.

The van moved ahead a few feet, angling in closer to the building. That was odd; the driver looked like he was trying to get as close to the wall as he could. He drove right up over the curb and crushed one of the juniper bushes in the two-foot dirt strip.

"Hey!" Trent yelled at him, but if the guy noticed, he didn't let on. Probably couldn't hear a thing inside that spacesuit. But what the hell was he doing?

Then Trent figured it out. The vault was just on the other side of that wall. Most people drove out into the desert when they jumped into space, because the jump field was spherical and it made a lot more sense to take a bowl of sand with you than a bowl of pavement, but the hyperdrive didn't care. It would take anything that was inside the field, including a bank vault.

And Trent as well, if he was too close when the driver of that van pushed the "go" button. Calibrating the size of the jump field was more of an art than a science; this guy could take half a block with him if he wasn't careful. And Trent could already see the blue glow from the screen of the laptop computer that controlled the jump. It was up and running, probably set to go with just one keystroke. The van diver could take off any second now.

Trent ran for his pickup. It wasn't provisioned for a trip, but he and Donna might at least be able to survive long enough to call for help if they couldn't get out of the jump field in time.

He got three steps before the bank robber pushed the button. There was a clap of thunder loud enough to make his ears ring, and a gale of wind snatched off his hat and slapped him backward. It didn't just knock him off his feet, but whisked him like a leaf into the air, blowing him head over heels across the maybe ten feet of parking lot that was left and carrying him right out over the huge crater that had been carved into the ground.

A blizzard of papers met him from the other side. Pens and pencils pelted him, and he did a little mid-air dance with a desk chair before they both hit the ground and tumbled to the bottom of the crater.

The guy in the van had set his jump field pretty tight after all: it was only fifteen feet deep or so, and it had only taken that much of a bite out of the bank, too. The part of the building that wasn't halfway to the Moon by now groaned under the sudden shift in load, but it didn't collapse into the pit. Trent didn't know why not; part of it actually hung out over the hole.

Water poured in from half a dozen severed lines, and it was *cold*. Trent rescued his hat before it got soaked and shoved it back on his head, then tried to climb up the side of the crater, but he could only get a few feet before it grew too steep. The surface was slick as glass, sliced smooth down to the molecular level by the jump field. He could dig his fingers into it, but it just crumbled when he tried to climb.

He heard the door of the pickup slam, and footsteps as Donna raced toward him. "Trent!" she shouted. "Trent, where are you?"

"Down here," he hollered back at her. "Get a rope!"

Donna appeared at the edge of the pavement, her blonde hair lit up by the streetlight behind her like a halo around her head. "Oh, thank God you're still here," she said. "When that van jumped, it looked like you just disappeared with it. Are you all right?"

"Yeah," he said, not actually sure yet. His right leg hurt something fierce, but not as bad as it would hurt if the damned bank fell in the hole on top of him. "Don't get too close to the edge. It could cave in any second." The smooth surface was already slumping, and dirt sifted down from a loose layer a couple feet under the blacktop.

"Jesus. Don't go any—I mean—just wait right there. I'll bring the truck up close and tie the rope to it."

"Not too close!"

"I know." She ran off, and he dodged the rocks and dirt that kept trickling down into the pit with him while he waited. The puddle of water was growing fast; his cowboy boots were already ankle-deep, and he could feel it seeping in through the stitching around the sole.

He heard the whine of the wheel motors and the slam of the driver's door, a few seconds of silence after that, then the camper door slammed and he knew she'd gone for the rope in their survival supplies rather than the one he kept behind the seat for towing, but before she could toss it down to him the air filled with the sound of squealing tires and slamming doors. Red and blue light flashed into the open building, and someone shouted "Step away from the pickup and put your hands in the air!"

"Hey, you idiots," Trent yelled up at them, "She's trying to save my sorry ass! Why don't you give her a hand instead of giving her shit."

A face poked over the edge of the hole. "Hey, we got us another one down here," said the cop.

"And I'd rather be up there," Trent said as another shower of debris rained down from the loose soil layer. "Give me a hand out of here."

"Right." There was some muffled conversation overhead, then at last the rope sailed down and hit him in the face. He grabbed it tight and walked his way up the curved bowl until it was too steep for that, then let his feet drop out from under him and hand-over-handed it up the rest of the way. Two cops met him at the rim and hauled him out to stand on the pavement.

Donna just about knocked him back into the hole when

she grabbed him in a hug and buried her face against his chest. He was a muddy mess, but she didn't seem to care. He wrapped his arms around her and rested his bearded cheek on the top of her head. "It's all right," he said. "I'm okay." The cops stood behind her, embarrassedly looking away.

"I thought I'd lost you. Just like that, I thought I'd lost you."

"It'll take a lot more than some piss-ant bank robber to—wait a minute. I know who that was."

"Who?" Donna said, just as both cops asked the same thing.

Trent hesitated. He'd never met the guy, but he knew him by reputation, and he was apparently a pretty good sort, for a thief. But Trent didn't owe him anything, and the guy had damned near gotten him killed. Besides, Trent had already opened his mouth. So he said, "Dale Larkin. The guy who bankrolled Allen Meisner and Judy Gallagher's first spaceship."

One of the cops, Bill Tanner, was an old high school buddy of Trent's. He said, "The same spaceship you helped 'em build in your garage?"

"Yeah." Trent grinned sheepishly. He had never been much of a science geek, but he and Donna had been in the right place at the right time and they had wound up in the middle of things.

Bill said, "Well, what goes around comes around, doesn't it?"

"I didn't have nothing to do with the money," Trent said. "I just hid 'em out when the whole damned country was after 'em for no good reason, and—"

"No good reason?" the other cop said. "You call handing dangerous technology to every malcontent in the world no good reason? People have died because of that damned hyperdrive." He waved a hand at the diamond-plate camper in the back of Trent's pickup and added, "And by the looks of that thing, I'll bet you've got one of your own right here, don't you? You know you forfeit the entire vehicle if you get caught with one. Too bad; it's a nice looking truck."

Trent had to consciously force himself not to clench his fists. Nobody was going to take his truck without a fight, but there was nothing to fight about this time. Trent had a hyperdrive, all right, but it was in three pieces back home: the electronics built into an old CD boombox that still played music, the field coils in a spare wheel motor casing in the garage, and the laptop computer that controlled it sitting in plain sight in the living room where Donna used it to write letters and surf the Internet. The cops could even search the computer for a hyperdrive control program, but they wouldn't find one. The program was everywhere on the Internet; Donna would just download a copy when they needed it.

"Go ahead, search all you want," Trent said, "but you won't find anything. I just like the look." He stared the cop straight in the eye, fully aware of how menacing he looked with a full beard under a black Stetson.

"I just might do that," the cop said, sticking out his chest and glaring back at him. The blue and red lights from the cruiser glistened off his badge.

"Oh, give it a rest, Tom," Bill said. "We've got bigger fish to fry tonight." To Trent, he said, "He's been kinda touchy about hyperdrives ever since he drove his four-wheeler into a launch hole out by Quealy."

"Ah." Trent looked into the hole he had just come out of. "I understand how you feel about that. But that don't make it right to ban 'em. We've given up too much freedom in this country already."

"So says the man at the scene of a bank robbery," said the cop named Tom.

"People have been robbing banks for years," Trent said. "You're not gonna stop 'em by bannin' shit."

Donna let go of him and said, "We got to get you into some dry clothes before you freeze to death."

"That sounds good to me."

"Not until we get your statement," Bill said.

Trent nodded. "Come on up to the house, then. We can kill two birds with one stone."

"Yeah, right, and leave the bank unguarded with a big hole in the middle of it." Bill went over to the edge of the crater and looked down again. "We better call the utility guys to shut all that off before it turns into a swimming hole. How'd you wind up in the bottom of that, anyway?"

"I'd just got some cash when he drove up and took off. The backdraft blew me in."

Bill whistled softly. "That must've been a moment."

"Yeah." Trent's leg was still hurting. He looked for blood, but didn't see any. It couldn't have been broken, or he wouldn't have been standing on it. Probably just a hell of a bruise.

"All right," he said, "if you need a statement, let's get started. It was a dark brown General Electric van, couple of years old, with Wyoming plates. Didn't see the number. It was definitely beefed up for vacuum, and the guy inside was wearing a spacesuit . . ."

It was a couple of hours later before they finally pulled up in front of the brew pub. They had gone home for a change of clothes after the cops were finished with them, and Trent had nearly said to hell with it and just stayed there, but Donna still wanted to go out, so here they were.

You could tell where the pub was just by looking down the street. There were more cars parked in front of it than anywhere else along the five blocks of downtown Rock Springs. Even when the economy was going down the tubes—maybe especially then—people could always find a few extra dollars for a drink.

Apparently they could always find a few extra dollars for a gallon of gas, too. Trent scowled at all the gas-powered pickups and SUVs parked side-by-side in the wide diagonal slots that lined Main Street. Some of them were old, from back when that was the only form of fuel available and everybody thought the Arabs would keep selling it forever, but some of them were new, and those were the ones that particularly chapped Trent's ass. A person could maybe be excused for driving a gas-guzzler if that's all they could afford—and the used ones were definitely cheap if you didn't count the operating expense—but a new one cost just as much as a new electric, and it still burned a gallon of gas every ten or fifteen miles. There were a few fuel-efficient cars around—Volkswagens and Toyotas and the like that people restored for fun—but most of the people who liked those kind of cars also cared about the environment, so they generally converted them over to electric anyway.

Somebody in a flat-black Suburban was just leaving as Trent and Donna drove up. His exhaust pipe belched a blue cloud of smoke when he started up the engine, and the noise was like machine-gun fire. If he had a muffler at all, it was just a glass pack. He revved the engine a couple of times just to make sure everybody knew he was an obnoxious bastard as well as a selfish one.

"Must have a little teeny dick," Trent said as the guy backed out of his spot and roared away. "If the government wants to ban something, they ought to go for those damn things."

Donna laughed. "What, little teeny dicks? I'd be for banning those."

"You know what I meant, woman." He poked her in the side, an easy move since she was sitting right next to him on the pickup's bench seat.

She poked him right back. "Don't go calling me 'woman.' "

"What should I call you, then? 'Girl?' 'Sweetie?' Or how about 'honey bunny ducky downy sweetie chicken pie li'l everlovin' jelly bean?' "

"Chicken pie?" she asked dubiously.

"Hey, I'm quotin' literature here. Don't blame me if it don't make sense." He pulled into the vacant parking spot and the two of them climbed down to the pavement. Trent almost never locked his pickup, but this time he waited until Donna was right in front of it, then he clicked the remote. The sharp squeal of the alarm activating was almost as loud as her squeal of surprise.

"Beast!" she said.

"I'll take that as a compliment." He held out his arm and they strolled into the brew pub like royalty.

The place was busy, but there were a few tables free in back. Their waitress sat them down next to one of the big stainless steel brew kettles that stood in a row down the middle of the pub. Trent picked up the beer menu and tried to remember which beer was closest to Budweiser. Most of the stuff they served here was way too thick and dark for his taste.

A bright yellow flyer fell out of the menu. It showed a picture of a stream running out of a forest, and the caption said, "The fishing is excellent, too." He flipped it over and saw the title: "Alpha Centauri, Land of Opportunity."

"Samizdat," Donna said.

"Gezundheit."

"I said 'samizdat,' dummy. That's what it is."

"I know." The Russian word sounded strange coming from a blonde Wyoming girl, but Trent supposed it was the the best term to describe the recruitment ads and political tracts that people kept passing around in defiance of the United States' ban on all things interstellar. The Russians had developed an entire industry around banned literature back when they were trying to get the truth out past the socialist stranglehold on the press. Trent was embarrassed to think that such a thing had come to the U.S., but the government pissed him off on such a regular basis anymore, it was hard to work up much of a lather over it.

"Let me see that," Donna said.

Trent slid the flyer across the table, glancing up to see if anybody was watching. He didn't suppose the people in the bar would rat on him or Donna, but it was a two-hundred-dollar fine if somebody did.

Donna held it up to the light. "Looks pretty out there. We ought to go check it out."

"Here," Trent said, handing her a regular menu, but another flyer dropped out of that.

She giggled at his obvious discomfort, but she took the menu and covered both Alpha Centauri flyers with it. "I'm serious," she said. "We're running out of money, and all the jobs are on other planets nowadays. We should at least go have a look."

"Yeah, I know we should." He looked at the beer menu

again and decided to try the India Pale Ale. If the name meant anything, it shouldn't be one of the dark ones. That and a bacon cheeseburger might salvage the evening.

There was a sign over the archway that led to the bathrooms: Make Beer, Not Bombs. Trent agreed with that sentiment, even if it was ferny beer like what they served here. He agreed with Donna, too, that they should go look for a better place to live, but he wasn't ready to pack up and go just yet. For one thing, now that it was illegal, they couldn't simply take off for a weekend. The hyperdrive would take you *away* from anywhere, so long as you were jumping into vacuum, but it couldn't put you back onto the ground, or even into the atmosphere. You had to pop into orbit just above the atmosphere and fall the rest of the way under a parachute, which meant that the U.S. would blast your chute with its laser satellites before you even came close to the ground. That's what had happened to Trent and Donna the first time they tried it. It was an automated shot from the missile defense net, and they'd managed to jump back into space and call for help before they'd hit the ground, but rather than apologize and reprogram the lasersats to let parachutes pass, the government had instead made shooting at them official policy. That meant any trip a U.S. citizen took had to include a stopover in Canada on the way home, and it was getting harder to get back across the border. Trent had heard that you needed a visa nowadays even if you had a U.S. passport, and of course the government wasn't handing out visas to interstellar travellers.

The waitress came by and took their order. Donna slipped one of the Alpha Centauri flyers into her menu when she gave it back, but she stuck the other one up between the salt and pepper shakers like a flag. "So when are we going to go?" she asked.

Free land! the flyer promised. *Emigrate now.*

"I don't know," Trent said. He wasn't just being evasive, either. He honestly didn't know, and there were a million reasons for his indecision, starting with the word "emigrate." He didn't like that word. It sounded funny, and not funny ha-ha. It made him think of people dressed in ragged clothes pulling carts full of chickens and pigs. It practically screamed "defeat." The construction industry might have tanked, and the country might be going to hell in a handbasket, but Trent wasn't defeated.

"We've got a whole galaxy to choose from," Donna said. "Shouldn't we at least see if we can find someplace better than Rock Springs?"

Trent snorted. "Hell, we could probably find places better than Rock Springs a hundred miles up the road."

"I'm serious."

"All right." He drummed his fingers on the table, wishing the waitress would get back with their beer, but she was nowhere in sight, so he said, "I certainly don't have much love for the government, but this is still my country. And this is my town. I grew up here. Everybody I know is here. Half of 'em may be right-wing idiots who think it's okay to tell everybody else how to run their lives and kill anybody who disagrees, but the other half are pretty decent folks. Hell, the city council damn near voted to defy the federal ban on hyperdrives. They were only one vote short. If we emigrate, we'll be giving up on that half, too."

For once, Donna didn't have a snappy comeback. She pursed her lips and cocked her head to the side, looking at him thoughtfully. "That's a good point," she said.

"Thank you."

"Not good enough to make me want to stay here, but it's a good point."

He shook his head. "So what do you suggest we do? Move to Alpha Centauri? It'll be just as full of idiots as America within a decade."

"I bet it'll take longer than that. It's a whole planet, after all."

"Maybe. But still, that's where everybody's going."

The waitress finally showed up with their beer. Trent's was considerably darker than he'd hoped, and when he tasted it, the intense bite of hops nearly made him choke. "Damn," he said after she'd gone. "About the only thing this stuff's got going for it is it's strong."

"My, but you're in a cranky mood today, aren't you?"

"Gettin' blown into a launch crater does that to a guy."

"You know what I think? I think sittin' around on your butt all day does that to a guy. You haven't been happy since, hell, I don't know how long. Certainly not since since the Palkos cancelled their house contract."

"Considerin' that was my last paycheck, I imagine you're not too far off."

She looked down at the tabletop.

"Hey, it's okay," he said. "I'm not pissed about that."

She raised her head again, and her eyes were glistening. "How about if I lost my job?"

"Huh?"

"Would you be pissed if I lost my job?"

Donna worked in a jewelry store in the White Mountain Mall; probably the most stable job in America at the moment. People were dropping their money into gold and gems as fast as they could, before the value of the paper dropped all the way to zero. Donna only worked three days a week, but her job was why they were still able to eat out once in a while.

"You didn't lose it, did you?" he asked.

"Not yet. But Cheryl told me to take next week off. Apparently the government has seized our inventory. 'To prevent panic buying,' they say."

Trent would never understand how Donna could sit on news like that for hours, waiting for the right time to deliver it. When Trent lost his job, she'd known about it the moment he got in the house. Hell, before that, probably, by the way he'd slammed the garage door. But she—she hadn't given him a clue until just now.

"Damn it," he said. "Those sons of— Aw, damn it. I'm sorry."

"Me too."

"Not your fault." He reached across the table and took her hand in his. "I know just what you're thinkin' right now, and it's not true."

"What, you mean the U.S. government isn't made up of selfish bastards who couldn't give a shit about what's actually best for the average person?"

He couldn't help a wry grin. "Okay, that's true enough, but I was thinkin' about you. It's not your fault."

"I know that. But we're going to be getting mighty hungry in about a month even so."

"Don't worry," he said, wishing he could feel half as confident as he forced himself to sound. "We'll figure out something."

"I hope."

He gave her hand a squeeze. "Now I know why you're so hot to head off into the wild blue yonder."

She shrugged. "Yeah, well. If nothing else, it'll be a good vacation, and lord knows, we could use one."

"I suppose we could."

The waitress showed up just then with their hamburgers. Trent looked at the half pound of beef in a bun and the pound or so of "freedom fries" surrounding it on the plate. He'd been hungry before, but suddenly he felt ravenous.

"Eat up," he said. "Sounds like we're going to be up half the night packin'."

The moment they got home, Trent plugged in the truck to recharge the batteries. They hadn't used much power just on a trip downtown and back, but he liked to keep them fully charged, and he always started a trip that way. You never knew when your next chance to plug in would be, especially when you were going off-road, and interstellar travel was about as off-road as you could get.

While Donna started packing food and clothing into the camper, he dug out the components for the hyperdrive and mounted them into their places. The field coil went into a cubbyhole between the camper and the cab, where it would be as close as possible to the center of the truck. The actual electronics went behind the seat, where they could get to it in an emergency even if they were in space. Not that they would be able to do much if anything went wrong. Neither he nor Donna were techie enough to troubleshoot more than a burned-out fuse, but they could at least do that much. The computer that controlled everything would sit on Donna's lap during launch and on the dashboard afterward, Velcroed down so it wouldn't drift loose in free fall.

The power to run the hyperdrive came straight from the truck's plasma cells. They were good for about 200 miles on the ground, or maybe fifty hyperspace jumps, depending on how close to a planet you were for each jump. According to Allen Meisner, the more mass you were near, the more energy it took. It had something to do with the way space was bent around planets and suns and stuff. Trent had a hard time seeing how you could bend something like space, but Allen had sworn it was true, and the guy had designed an engine that not only bent it but folded it in two, so he ought to know.

Trent plugged everything in and tested the connections, then went inside to see if Donna had the computer ready. She was still working at it, her face glowing pale blue in the screen's light.

"I had a hell of a time finding a copy of the control program," she said when she noticed him standing beside her. "Homeland Security has been shutting down U.S. websites that post it, and of course most of the foreign sites I checked had the program in their language."

"How about England, or Australia?"

She shook her head. "England can't spit without permission from the U.S. anymore, and Australia's sites are under pretty much constant hack attack from HomeSec. But I finally found an English-language version on a ten-minute mirror site in Denmark."

"Good. Let's plug in the computer and make sure it can talk to the drive."

They went out to the pickup and set the computer in place on the dash, then connected all the various cables and powered it up. Donna loaded the program and ran a diagnostic routine, which reported everything ready to roll.

"Good enough," Trent said. He felt his heartbeat quicken, and he looked out to the street, half expecting to see Tom the cop drive up in his patrol car. There wouldn't be much defense if he did; the pickup was pretty clearly capable of interstellar flight now.

"You got enough food loaded?" he asked.

"There's at least a couple month's worth, if we don't mind ramen noodles for the last week or so."

"That ought to do." He certainly hoped so. You never packed for a day in the mountains, not when a broken axle could strand you there for a week, and you didn't pack for a week on an alien planet, even one with people already living on it. A mishap on landing could put you out of touch for anywhere from a month to forever, depending on the mishap.

Donna went back inside to finish packing their clothes and random other stuff. While she was doing that, Trent powered up the compressor and filled the air tanks. There were two of them, both under the seat, each one good for about three hours of breathing. More than enough time to jump from star to star, find a planet, match velocities, and land, provided everything worked right. If things didn't work right, well, that's why there were two tanks.

While the compressor huffed away on the tanks, he checked the door and window seals to make sure they hadn't gotten scuffed in the five months since he'd installed them. Had it really been that long? He supposed it was. He'd poured all his time and money into fixing up the truck for space, but they hadn't actually gone anywhere since their first trip. He couldn't have said why not; they'd survived the experience well enough, and they'd had tons of fun in the process. There'd been a few harrowing moments, but no more than happened on any four-wheeling trip. Of course the government had done their best to discourage more trips, but that wouldn't have stopped them if they'd really wanted to do it. They just hadn't gone again.

Maybe he'd been afraid of scratching up the truck. Parachute landings didn't give a guy a whole lot of control over where he came down.

It didn't matter. They were going now. He whistled softly while he made his pre-flight check, stopping occasionally to look up at the starry sky.

and left them rolling to the side as well, so he hit both right-side valves for a quick burst to cancel their roll, then just tapped the right rear one. The pickup came to a stop with the Sun just below Donna's window.

Trent watched the last of the rocks tumble away, wondering if any of them would make it back to Earth. NASA had suggested that people should go five hundred thousand kilometers or farther on the first jump so the Moon could sweep up most of the debris, but even that didn't guarantee clear space around the planet. Several communications satellites in geosynchronous orbit had already been hit, and it was just a matter of time before something whacked the space station or another hyperspace traveller. Some people were worried that near-Earth space would become so dangerous in a few years that nobody could use it, but Trent imagined someone would figure out a cleaner way to launch before that happened. Big ski jumps, maybe, that people could drive off just before they hit the "go" button.

That would probably cut down on casual trips even more than the government ban. It was hard enough to jump from solid ground, but Trent didn't particularly want to find out what a mid-air jump would feel like. What if you pushed the wrong button, or the hyperdrive decided not to work that one time? Catching air on a whoop-de-do was one thing, but coming back down hard after a truck-high jump could do nasty things to your suspension.

That was a worry for another time. They were here now, and their dirt cloud was pretty much dissipated. "Okay," he said. "No point hanging around here. Let's make tracks for Alpha Centauri."

Donna nodded. Her hair billowed out all around her face, and she casually swept it aside with her left hand while she set the computer up on the dashboard with her right, shoving it against the windshield where its webcam could see straight out over the hood to get a position check on the stars. After a few seconds of comparing its interna

They left first thing in the morning. Trent drove them out of town a ways, then found a spot way off the road and between a bunch of rocks where their launch crater wouldn't get in anybody's way. They got out and put on their Ziptite suits—human-shaped plastic bags that would theoretically hold air long enough for them to get back to the ground if something went wrong—then climbed back into the cab, keeping their helmets rolled down around their necks so they wouldn't waste the internal air. The suits weren't any more legal in the U.S. than the hyperdrive, but there was a lively black market business in them, along with electronic parts and air tanks and the various other equipment a person needed to build and fly an interstellar vehicle. Trent just hoped there was some quality control on all that stuff. It would have been a whole lot safer if the government regulated it, but of course they didn't care about that. Just like they did with drugs, once the feds outlawed something, they figured it was your own damned fault if you used it and got hurt.

The only thing a person could do was to inspect everything as carefully as he could himself, and have a backup for as many systems as possible. The suits were like that; with any luck, it wouldn't matter if they worked or not, because they were the backup for the truck itself.

So they checked all the door latches and the window seals, then overpressurized the cab to 20 p.s.i. and waited for ten minutes to see if the pressure would hold. Trent checked to make sure the .270 in the gun rack was strapped down, and he looked for anything else that might be loose or get loose, but he'd taken care of all that last night. Donna turned on the radio and they listened to Led Zeppelin and Pink Floyd and Lynard Skynard on KSIT while they waited, singing along to "Have a Cigar" and "Sweet Home Alabama." When the station broke for commercials and the pressure gauge on the dash was still holding steady, Trent switched off the radio and looked over at Donna.

"Ready?" he asked.

She was the computer expert, so she held the laptop that controlled the hyperdrive. She checked its screen, then said, "Ready."

He opened the stopcock by the door handle and lowered the pressure to normal again. Rock Springs was over a mile high, so "normal" was only 12 p.s.i. It felt thin after breathing nearly twice that for a few minutes, but they hadn't been overpressured long enough to worry about the bends. He closed the stopcock, tugged his seatbelt tight so he wouldn't bonk his head on the roof when gravity let go, and took a deep breath. "Okay, let's do it."

She was belted in on the passenger side, not normally where she rode when they were just out for a drive, but this time she needed the shoulder belt as well as a lap belt. She grinned. "Hang onto your hat, cowboy. We could wind up miles from here." And she tapped the "enter" key.

The Earth vanished, except for the hemisphere of dirt and rock that was inside the jump field. That immediately started boiling out from under the truck, drifting away in all directions. A few bits of dirt drifted up inside the cab, but Trent had vacuumed to keep debris from getting into their eyes, so there was only what they had tracked inside just a couple minutes ago.

The seatbelt held him down well enough that he didn't feel like he was falling. Donna loved roller coasters and stuff like that anyway, so she wouldn't care even if she was falling.

She giggled. "That was half a million kilometers."

Trent took a deep breath. Half a million. Kilometers were shorter than miles, but it was still a long damned ways from home. And this was just a pit stop to dump the dirt and make sure everything was working before they took the big jump between stars.

He ran through his mental checklist. The pressure gauge was holding steady. The air tanks were full. The batteries were charged. There was a steady patter of dirt and rocks against the undercarriage, but none of the ominous squeals or groans that would mean something was about to blow.

The Sun drifted diagonally from upper left to lower right across the windshield. It was brighter without the atmosphere in the way, but not too much so. The biggest difference was in the contrast: anything sunlit was bright and colorful as ever, but the shadows were stark and black.

The fact that the Sun was moving meant that the expanding cloud of debris was pushing unevenly against the bottom of the truck, putting it into a slow tumble. Not a big problem at the moment, but they would need to kill that spin before they tried to jump to anywhere in particular. The hyperdrive could send the pickup in any direction, so they didn't need to be pointed at their target, but they did need to be steady when they jumped so the drive could aim properly.

Trent had installed compressed air jets on the corners of the bumpers for just that purpose. Now he watched for a moment until he got a feel for the truck's motion, then reached to the control panel he'd bolted below the radio and pushed the valve for the front left jet. There was a soft hiss from the air tank under his side of the seat, and a cone-shaped patch of fog shot upward in front of the truck.

"That looked almost like hitting a puddle," Donna said.

He laughed softly. "I guess some things don't change n matter where you go four-wheelin'."

The shot of air slowed the truck's tumble just a little, bu not enough, so he pushed the valve again. That overdid i

star map to the view outside, the computer flashed the "locked on" window. She pulled down the "destination" menu and selected Alpha Centauri from the preset choices, and an automatic targeting window popped up with the coordinates and the distance. On their first trip into space they'd had to key in the coordinates by hand for the stars they wanted to visit, but now there were over a thousand choices already programmed, and new ones were added to the online database every day as people reported in from their travels.

The computer displayed the same image that they could see in front of them, and put a red circle around one of the bright stars. "There it is," Donna said. "Alpha Centauri, here we come." She pushed the "enter" key.

There was a moment of disorientation, so brief that it was hard to decide if it was even real or not. The stars may have shifted just a hair, but that was too subtle to be sure of, either. The only real difference was the position of the Sun: it had shifted from the right side of the truck to a little below and behind. Only it wasn't the Sun now. It looked exactly the same to Trent, but unless the hyperdrive had messed up, this was Alpha Centauri A, the brighter of the two stars that made up the Centauri double.

"The computer needs a sky sweep to find planets," Donna said.

"Okay." Trent hit both of the front jets at once, and the nose of the pickup dropped downward. He let it go for a full revolution, then used the rear jets to stop their motion again.

The computer flashed an information box on the screen, and Donna said, "Looks like we're about sixteen million kilometers from Onnescu." That was the name of the first settler on Alpha Centauri's habitable planet, and while he hadn't tried to name it after himself, that's what people had started calling it, and the name stuck.

Sixteen million kilometers wasn't much in space. Trent looked at the computer screen and saw a red arrow pointing to the left and down, so he used the right jets and then the front jets until the arrow became a circle around one of the stars that drifted onto the screen. He looked out the windshield at the same patch of sky and eventually spotted the planet, just big enough to show as an oblong blob instead of a point of light.

"Taking us in closer," Donna said, and hit the "enter" key again.

The planet jumped upward and much, much closer, filling the entire view out the windshield and to both sides with swirly white cloud patterns.

"Woo hoo!" Trent yelled, flinching backward. "That . . . was a good shot."

Donna smiled. "Beats the hunt-and-guess method we used on our first trip, doesn't it?"

"I dunno. I think I just about had a heart attack there. When we were huntin' and guessin', I kind of expected surprises." He watched the clouds for a few seconds to see if they were getting noticeably closer, but instead they seemed to be receding. Good. That meant they had some time to check things out before they jumped again. "Let's see if we can pick up their beacon," he said. He flipped on the citizens' band radio under the dash and punched the channel button down to 1, the agreed-upon frequency that colony planets would use to broadcast who lived there and who was welcome to join them. Trent already knew about Onnescu by word of mouth and the flyer they had picked up at the brew pub, but he wanted to check and see how the beacon system worked. CB radios normally had just a few miles of range, but the beacons were supposed to broadcast with a lot more power than usual, reaching anything within line of sight for thousands of miles. Theoretically, three of them in synchronous orbit could provide coverage to anyone anywhere near the planet. Trent had added a power amp to his transmitter, too, for the same reason. He wanted to be able to talk to the ground while he was still in orbit.

When he tuned to channel 1, a clear, resonant male voice

commenced in mid-sentence: ". . . la costa oeste en el continente más grande del planeta, es uno que se parece a un taco mordido . . ."

"What the heck?" Trent switched to channel 2, but that was broadcasting in Chinese or Japanese or something similar. He switched to channel 3 and finally got English:

". . . everything from desert to rain forest. It's practically a second Earth, with an average temperature just three degrees warmer and gravity ninety percent of normal. The atmosphere is thirty percent oxygen, and the rest nitrogen and carbon dioxide. The plant life is non-allergenic, edible, and pretty, and the animal life is both exotic and plentiful. Our largest settlement is called Bigtown, on the banks of the beautiful Firehose river, which flows out of the Pointy Mountains. We're located at forty-one degrees north latitude, seventy-three degrees east longitude, with the prime meridian running straight down the western coastline of the largest continent on the planet, the one that looks like a taco with a bite taken out of it. Drop in and say 'Hi,' and let us show you what we have to offer."

There was a brief hiss of static, then the voice said, "Welcome to Onnescu. We're the very first extrasolar colony, started by Nicholas Onnescu only two weeks after the release of the hyperdrive plans. We're open to colonization, and we welcome anyone who shares our view that a planet is a place to live, not a place to exploit. We're happy to see people of all races and religion, including no religion at all, but we ask people who practice fundamentalism of any sort to please find another planet. We also ask new arrivals to please leave their political agendas at home. We want our society to be based on compassion and courtesy, not conflict or—"

Trent switched off the radio. "Kinda talky, aren't they?"

Donna laughed. "Well, with all the wackos looking for a place to practice their own breed of craziness, it probably doesn't hurt to be specific."

"I suppose not. I wonder where we fit into this grand scheme of theirs."

"We won't know until we go look."

He took a deep breath, then nodded.

"Can that thing find Bigtown for us?"

"If it can recognize the shapes of the continents, it can."

He looked out at the planet again. He couldn't see much besides clouds at first, but then he spotted a sharp edge that had to be a coastline, and then his eye started to get calibrated to the view and he picked up a big lake and a river valley that emptied into a wide delta. "Is that the Firehose?" he asked hopefully. They had binoculars, but as close as they were, it didn't seem like they needed them.

"I don't think so," Donna said. "According to this, we're over an island called Weaselnose, about a third of the way around the planet from Bigtown." Another window popped onto the screen and she said, "We're moving at about twenty-six thousand kilometers per hour relative to Bigtown. That'll take twelve minutes to cancel."

Another twelve minutes in space. That was actually a fairly short time to match speeds with a target planet, but Trent was already sweating like a pig inside his plastic pressure suit. "Let's get moving, then," he said.

"Here goes." She selected Bigtown from the "city" submenu. Trent saw that the "cancel velocity" option was already selected by default; that was smart. The landing sequence would take them to just outside the atmosphere right over their target, and you didn't want to be moving twenty-six thousand kilometers per hour when you got there. Especially not if you were aimed at the ground.

The landing program would do what Allen Meisner called a "tangential vector translation maneuver," calculating the right spot to take them so the planet's gravity would slow them down and curve their path to match Bigtown's. On their first interstellar trip—to a planet about fifteen light-years away in the constellation of Cetus—they'd had to figure out everything on their own, eyeballing their target and guessing their velocity, then keying that into Allen's first-generation control program and waiting to see how close their guess had been. It had taken them several tries to get it right, leaping around the planet like a dog trying to find the right angle on a badger, and even then they'd gone in too fast for comfort. They'd had the first supersonic pickup in history for a minute there before air friction slowed them down enough to let them pop the chutes and come down the rest of the way easy.

More recent versions of the software would set them at the top of the atmosphere with a thousand-kilometer-an-hour *upward* velocity, do a quick check with landmarks on the ground to make sure their relative velocity was actually what it had calculated, and then drop them ten K at a time until the atmosphere got too thick to punch an instantaneous hole in. By that time—thirty seconds after they arrived—most of of that last thousand would be gone, and their downward velocity would be just about zero.

In theory. Like most Internet freeware, it worked so long as everything else worked, too, but there were always bugs in those programs just waiting to pop out the moment anything unusual happened. Commercial software might have been more reliable, but the U.S. government had put the skids on that right away, and as Donna had discovered last night, they were doing their damnedest to prevent people from getting foreign programs, either. Trent and Donna were lucky to have even a freeware version.

Bigtown was already selected, and the computer said it knew where they were, so Donna hit the "go" button and the program zapped them to the other side of the planet. Trent couldn't see it directly, since it was night on this side, but there was a big dark patch behind them where no stars shone. He gritted his teeth for a second, waiting for the moment when they slammed into the atmosphere at thousands of miles an hour, but the program had worked the way it was supposed to and they merely rose up from the night side of the planet, losing velocity as gravity tried to reel them back in.

He looked over and saw Donna grinning like a thief. She loved this. Flying through space with nothing between her and instant death but a plastic bag and Trent's welding job didn't bother her a bit. He appreciated her faith in his abilities, but right now he could vividly recall every cold joint and curse word that had gone into reinforcing the pickup for space, and he remembered every story he'd heard of the poor bastards who hadn't sealed up well enough or who simply didn't understand how much pressure 14 p.s.i. put on a windshield. People went into space with no way to control a tumble, and no backup parachute in case the first one snarled on the way down. Trent had heard about several people who tried to land on the Moon, not understanding that the Moon had no atmosphere for a parachute to work in. Some of the new craters could apparently be seen from Earth if you knew where to point your telescope.

"You're looking mighty serious for a guy on vacation," Donna said. "What are you thinking about?"

"Nothin'," he replied automatically.

"What kind of nothin'?"

He sighed. She was always asking him that, and he never knew how to answer. But she never gave up, so he said, "I guess I was thinkin' about evolution. Space travel's going to weed a lot of people out of the gene pool."

"Yeah?"

"Yeah."

"Is that a good thing, or a bad thing?"

"Guess it depends on your point of view. It's mostly going to be the dumb ones or the unlucky ones who die, but it's only going to be the dumb or unlucky *adventurous* ones. The ones who are too chicken to even try it will stay home and live to a ripe old age."

"Not us, then." She said it playfully, but Trent looked

out the windshield at the hard, unblinking stars and felt the hair stand up on the back of his neck.

"Not if we do too much of this."

She shrugged. "I'd rather die doing something than just sitting around waiting to grow old."

"Me too, but I sometimes wonder what sort of things are worth dying for."

She looked out the windshield, too. "Sights like this are worth it," she said after a moment. She cocked her head to the side, then pointed. "Look, there in Cassiopeia. That extra star? That's the Sun."

Cassiopeia. The "W" shaped one up near the north star. A year ago, Trent wouldn't have been able to tell it from Orion, but the last few months had made him a reluctant convert to popular astronomy. He followed Donna's outstretched finger and saw the five zigzag stars, plus another zig.

"Which end is the extra one?" he asked.

"The left side."

So that was the Sun. It was a little brighter than the other stars, a fact that Trent found somehow encouraging.

He checked his watch. They still had five minutes to go before landing, but they'd been sealed up in the truck for maybe fifteen minutes already; it was probably time to refresh their air. He opened the stopcock by his door handle and let a couple of pounds of pressure out, swallowing to make his ears pop and watching the moisture in the air flash to fog in the vacuum outside, then he closed the stopcock and replenished what he'd bled off from the compressed-air tank under Donna's side of the seat. When he was designing their pickup starship, he'd spent a long afternoon trying to decide whether or not he wanted to store their breathing air and their maneuvering air in the same tank. It was just plain old compressed air in either case, but it somehow seemed scary to think of watching your breathing air whoosh into space every time you maneuvered, so he had decided to separate them. Then of course he had plumbed them together so he could use either one for either purpose, reasoning that it gave them a backup system in case one tank sprang a leak.

He had positioned the pressure relief jet to push against the truck's center of mass, so it wouldn't start them spinning. They might pick up a few feet per second of sideways velocity, but that was nothing to worry about.

He looked out again at the Sun hanging there ahead of them, then back at the dark planet blocking the stars behind them.

"This is one of those, what-you-call-'em, metaphor moments, ain't it?" he asked.

Donna gave him an odd look. "How do you mean?"

He shrugged. "I don't know. Just . . . here we are, headin' out from the dark past into the bright new future, ready to roll the moment we get wherever we're going. . . ."

He left it hanging, already embarrassed and afraid to say anything more, but Donna reached out and took his hand in hers, their plastic spacesuits crinkling softly, and the look in her eyes told him he'd said something right.

But where were they going, anyway? Trent looked at the Sun hanging there in the distance, surrounded by more stars than he could see from the ground even on a clear dark night in Rock Springs, and wondered. Bigtown today, but where tomorrow? Where the day after that? He didn't have a clue.

When their twelve minutes were up, the navigation program beeped a ten-second warning, then flipped them a third of the way around the planet, directly over Bigtown. The planet was overhead now, which meant that the pickup was about to enter the atmosphere upside down. Trent used the front air jets to shove its nose down until the planet slid around behind them, then beneath them. He hit the back jets to stop their motion, but inertia carried them on for a couple of seconds, and they wound up nose-down with the planet spread out in front of them like a map.

Beneath scattered puffy clouds was a long mountain range, all snow-capped peaks and green forest, running diagonally from upper right to lower left. Rivers cut meandering lines out into the foothills, which gave way to smooth grassland stretching off into the distance. Nicholas Onnescu had picked a good spot to settle.

Suddenly it expanded, then again and again as the navigation program dropped them ten kilometers at a time toward their target, which Trent assumed was not Bigtown itself, but a flat spot a ways out of town. The horizon went from curved to straight, and the view became more and more like the everyday sight from a high-flying airplane. Then the computer beeped at them and the view stopped changing.

"We're as low as it can take us," Donna said, "but we still have some upward velocity, so don't pop the chute yet."

"Right." They were at the wrong angle for that anyway. Trent used the rear jets to push them around until the planet was below them, then hit the front jets to stop that motion, but he'd reacted too late again and they overshot the other way, going in tailfirst now. "This is trickier than it looks," he muttered.

"You're doing fine. We've still got fifteen seconds."

"Heck, let's take a nap," Trent said, hitting the front jets, then immediately hitting the rear jets. That took them about halfway around to where they needed to be, so he did it again. That put them at the right angle front-to-back, but the left-side jets apparently had more push than the right-side ones, because now the ground was drifting upward on Trent's side. He tapped the right-side valves just as the computer apparently decided they had risen high enough for it to make another ten-kilometer jump downward, so it looked for a second as if the air jets had somehow shoved them down hard.

Trent flinched back from the controls, then laughed nervously. "Damn! I'm gettin' a little punchy here."

"You're doing fine," Donna said again. "According to this our velocity is just about zero, so we want to pop the chute in about five seconds anyway. Four . . . three . . . two . . . one . . . now."

There was no sound of air rushing past, but Trent knew that they had just sped up to about three hundred kilometers per hour in those five seconds. That was about two hundred miles an hour, a little fast to be opening a cargo parachute if you were down where the air was thick, but up here in the thin stuff at the edge of space, that was just about right.

He reached up to the switch panel above the rearview mirror and flipped the left-hand toggle, but his plastic glove caught on the right-hand one and flipped it, too. There was a double bang from overhead as the fiberglass cover over both parachutes popped open, then a long couple of seconds while the chutes streamed upward.

"Shit," he said in the silence. "That was our reserve chute, too." Now they didn't have any backup if they had to abort their landing. They could expand the jump field to include the canopies, but that took a lot more power, and it would still leave them with both chutes unfurled in vacuum. They would have to go outside in their Ziptites and fold them up, a job that was anywhere from dangerous to impossible, depending on whose stories you believed. But trying to enter an atmosphere with a chute already deployed was just as dangerous.

He was expecting a hard jolt when they both filled at once, and it didn't disappoint him, but it was nothing like their first time. Then, they had been guessing their speed by eye, and the jolt had left marks on their butts from the seat springs.

That had been on the way out. On the way home they'd guessed better, and their first chute had deployed just fine, only to get zapped by a laser satellite that had apparently thought they were an incoming missile. Their second chute had gone the same way a few minutes later, and they'd had to jump back into space and radio for help—help that wouldn't have come if Allen Meisner and Judy Gallagher hadn't just returned to Earth with the aliens they had met on their own travels.

"Well," Donna said, "With two parachutes, we'll have a soft landing."

"We can hope."

Trent leaned against his side window and looked up. He couldn't see straight overhead, but he could see almost half of each parachute and they both looked fully inflated. A little scrunched on the sides where they touched, but nothing serious. They glowed bright white in the sunlight, brand new and clean with only the exaggerated exclamation point of the company logo breaking the smooth expanse of nylon. Trent couldn't read the Cyrillic words stenciled on the rim of the chutes even when he was standing right next to them, so he had no idea what the company was called, but as long as the chutes worked, he didn't really care.

The view out the side window went on forever. They

were still a long ways up—probably fifty miles or so. It would be a long ride down. A long time to kick himself for his clumsiness. He couldn't believe he'd done that. One little slip, and now they could be in deep shit if anything else went wrong.

He couldn't see straight down, either. He should have angled the side mirrors downward before they left Earth, but of course he'd forgotten to do that. He wondered what else he'd messed up, and how soon they would find out about it.

Donna reached out and put her hand on his leg. "It's all right."

"No, it's not all right. That was a dumb-ass move, and now we could find ourselves in trouble in a real hurry."

"We'll be fine."

He didn't say anything. Experience had taught him that times like this were when he was most likely to stick his foot in his mouth, adding that to the growing list of screw-ups. So he just sat there and watched the ground slowly become more detailed as they dropped.

"At least we've got nice weather for a landing," Donna said.

"There's that," he allowed.

It was hard to tell from high up whether or not there was any wind on the ground. They were undoubtedly drifting sideways with whatever high-altitude winds happened to be blowing, and with two chutes holding them up longer they would drift farther than usual, but that wasn't a problem. It was the ground weather that mattered. It wouldn't take much of a crosswind to tip them over when they landed, if they came in sideways. That was one of the drawbacks of a jacked-up truck. One more worry to add to the list.

The ground looked rougher and rougher the closer they came. What had seemed like smooth prairie now became filled with shadows of rock outcrops and meandering streams. It was either morning or evening down there, which meant the light was coming in low and highlighting the terrain, but it looked like there was plenty of terrain for it to highlight. It would be fun four-wheeling once they were down, but it could make for a hairy landing.

How had he gotten them into this mess, anyway? They could have just taken an afternoon drive out to Flaming Gorge or something and been home for dinner.

The pickup was spinning slowly clockwise, giving them the full panorama every thirty seconds or so. One of the shroud lines must be a little longer than the others, spilling a little more air from one side of the chute and shoving it around.

"Pretty, isn't it?" Donna said.

"Huh?"

"It's a whole different planet out there, stretching off as far as you can see. Look at the way the sun glistens off the river out there. And the mountains. That's a glacier, isn't it?"

Trent looked where she was pointing. Tall gray peaks stuck up through a blanket of snow that looked white as cotton except for a long snakey line of dirt that wound down through a wide canyon from the middle of the range.

"Yep, that's what it looks like," he said.

"I wonder if anybody has skied down it yet?"

"Glaciers are full of crevices. You ski over what looks like smooth snow, and the next thing you know you're a hundred feet down in a crack with a broken neck."

She looked over at him. "What's gotten into you?"

"Maybe some common sense."

"Or maybe a little too much self-criticism. We're going to be okay, Trent. So we're coming down under both parachutes. People do that on purpose all the time."

"They're idiots," Trent said.

"And you think you're an idiot, too?"

"Feels like it," he admitted. The mountains swept away to the left and he found himself looking out at the vast sea of grass. "I mean, just because everybody else is rushin' off into space, does that mean we have to do it, too? So what if we're out of work? We can find other jobs. We've got our own house and our families right there, too. What made us think we had to go zoomin' around the galaxy?"

"Because it's there?"

He snorted. "Yeah, right. So's Australia, and we never tried that."

"We couldn't afford to go to Australia."

"And now we're landing on Alpha Centauri." He shook his head. "I don't know. It made all sorts of sense when I was sealing up the truck and doing all the wiring and stuff, but now I just don't get it."

Donna looked out her side window. "We're coming in." She took the computer off the dashboard and held it in her lap, tapping at the keyboard a few times. Trent recognized the emergency bailout screen when it popped up. Hit the "enter" key now and the hyperdrive would take them a hundred thousand kilometers straight up. Useful if they were about to land in the water or on a steep slope or something, but with the jump field set to fifty meters so it would include the parachutes, it would suck power like a short circuit, and then they would either have to go outside in vacuum and repack the chutes or go back to Earth and holler for help. Not something Trent wanted to do twice in a row.

Bigtown wasn't hard to spot now that they were close to the ground. It was too far away to see houses or streets, but there was a dirty smudge of smoke in the air over one of the valleys up by the foot of the mountains. Trent guessed it was maybe fifteen miles away; an easy drive if they managed to land okay.

He put his head up against his own window, trying to see as close to straight down as he could. It looked like they were going down in some rolling hills, but there were rock outcrops and steep gullies all around, any one of which could be a problem, and he couldn't tell what was directly beneath them.

The pickup swayed gently. They must have crossed

through the boundary between an updraft and a downdraft or something. This close to the ground the air could get turbulent.

Duh! This close to the ground, the air was breathable, too. Trent laughed and popped his top and bottom door latches, then pulled the regular handle and opened the door. There was a little whoof of air as the pressure equalized, and the smell of green growing things came wafting in.

He leaned out and looked straight down. "Shit. Big rocks. Get ready to jump."

"I can't do that if your door's open!"

"I can't see where we're landin' with it closed. We're drifting a little; we might miss 'em." It would be close, but with two parachutes they weren't dropping all that fast, and the closer they got to the ground, the more it looked like they were going sideways.

There were a couple of trees beside the rocks. It looked like the pickup would clear the first one, but it was going to come right down on the second one. Trent tried to gauge how big it was, but from this angle it was just a big puff of green. Then he thought to look at its shadow, and nearly told Donna to jump. The shadow was at least fifty feet long!

And the trunk was only six inches thick. The light was coming in low, that was all.

They were definitely going to hit it. He slammed his door and leaned back in the seat, grabbing the steering wheel and getting his feet ready on the juice pedal and the brake. "This is going to be rough, but don't jump no matter what."

"No?"

"No. Not even if we tip over. Just hang—"

There was a loud *crunch* and they pitched forward, then an equally loud *snap* and they pitched back, wobbling and spinning around under the parachute. They'd just snapped off the top of the tree. Donna yelped, but she kept her hand off the keyboard, even when branches slapped and screeched upward past her window.

The rockpile swung past just a couple feet in front of them, moving around to Trent's side, and then the tires hit the ground and the pickup lurched sideways. It rose up on two tires, but Trent turned the wheels into the roll and juiced the motors, and the truck spun halfway around before coming to a stop with a clang as the front bumper hit another rock. In a stock vehicle, that would have blown the air bags, but Trent had disabled those the first day he'd taken the pickup four-wheeling and had never hooked them up again.

He turned to Donna, and he couldn't help grinning. "Okay," he said. "Now we're havin' fun."

The first thing they did was peel out of their spacesuits and turn them inside-out to dry. Trent flapped his a couple of times to shake the sweat out of it, then draped it over the hood while he and Donna gathered up their parachutes and re-folded them. The air felt cold at first as the sweat evaporated from his clothing, but it didn't take long before he started to warm up again. His right leg hurt a little where he'd bruised it falling into the crater last night, but once he started moving around again it loosened up and he hardly noticed it.

One of the two canopies had wound up draped over the tree they had busted, so he had to climb up and carefully unhook it. The tree looked a little like a pine, but it didn't smell like one. It had more of a vegetable smell, like broccoli or lima beans or something like that. Trent was afraid it would be rubbery like a vegetable, too, but the bark was rough textured and dry, and the branches were stiff enough to hold his weight. The ones that had busted were oozing orange sap. When Trent touched some and held his finger to his nose, he discovered that's where the smell was coming from. It wasn't particularly sticky, but he was willing to bet it would get that way when it dried a little.

"We can't fold up the parachute with this stuff smeared all over it," he said when he'd pulled the canopy free. He climbed back down out of the tree while Donna got a Taco John's napkin from the glove box and dabbed at the gobs of sap.

"It comes off pretty easy," she reported, so they set to

work with napkins and a shop towel and within a few minutes they had it cleaned up. There were still orange stains on the white nylon, but that didn't matter. Battle scars made for good stories back home.

By the time they'd cleaned and folded both chutes, their spacesuits were dry, so they turned them right-side-out again and folded those up, too. Trent wiggled under the truck to see if the tree had damaged anything vital, but aside from a big dent in the underside of the bed and a lot of scrapes between it and the bumper, everything looked fine. While he crawled back out again, Donna opened the camper and went inside to make sure everything had survived in there, and to open the vents in the roof and the walls to let air circulate even when the door was closed.

She came back out with a can of beer. "It's kind of early our time to start drinking," she said, "but I think the day's just about over here. Doesn't the sun look closer to the horizon than it did when we were coming down?"

It was hard to tell for sure, since the horizon was so much nearer now that they were on the ground, but it only took a few more minutes to see that the sun was dropping. "Looks like we've only got another hour or so of daylight," Trent said. "Not enough time to make it to Bigtown before nightfall, and I'm not sure I want to go bushwhackin' on unfamiliar ground in the dark. Looks like we'll be camping out tonight." He smiled as he said that. He hadn't camped out in months.

Donna said, "Let's at least find us a stream. I'll want more than a spit-bath in the morning."

"One stream coming up," Trent said gallantly. From what he had seen on the way down, there were streams coming out of the mountains every few miles all along the front range.

They climbed back into the cab and he switched into reverse to back around the rock they'd clipped with the front bumper, but an amber light came on in the dashboard as soon as he fed the motors power.

"Uh-oh. Looks like that tree did more damage than I thought." It was the right-rear motor light, so he got out and slid under the truck again, and sure enough, there was a six-inch-long piece of branch sticking out of that one's control box. The motor itself looked okay, but the branch had speared the electronics that ran it. He could probably wire around the box and run the motor manually if he had to, but its power level and its regenerative braking system wouldn't be coordinated with the other motors, so it would constantly be making the truck swerve left and right as he accelerated and decelerated. Better to just disconnect it entirely and run on the other three. When he got back home he would have to buy a new control box; another expense he didn't need, but that was one of the risks of four-wheeling. Nature was tough on machinery.

He had to reach way up around the motor to get to the power plug. He'd mounted all the motors that way so he wouldn't snag a wire on a branch or something while he was four-wheeling. It had worked pretty well until now, but he guessed he couldn't expect it to protect them from a whole tree. At least with the truck raised up so high, it was easy to work underneath it. He wrapped the loose power cable around a frame member and tied it in a knot so it wouldn't flop around, then crawled back out and slapped the dirt off his clothes.

Donna had unlatched the airtight side windows and stowed them behind the seat, then rolled down the regular windows so they could breathe Onnescu's air instead of their compressed Earth air. She had also unplugged the computer and stowed it in its slot beneath the dash. Now she was flipping through their music disks. "Twang or bang?" she asked Trent as he slid back into the driver's seat.

"Bang," he answered without hesitation. You don't jump

four light-years, fall fifty miles under a parachute, snap a tree on landing, and then listen to somebody whine about their no-good daddy.

She slotted in a disk she'd burned last summer, before any of this hyperdrive business had happened. It started off with Slow Children's six-minute anthem, "Dumb Enough to Drive," which pretty well matched Trent's mood. He backed the truck away from the rock, ignoring the left-rear motor's warning light, and drove forward through a low patch of bushes. If they made any noise scraping past the undercarriage, he couldn't hear it over the music.

Back home, four-wheeling was pretty much confined to existing roads. The BLM didn't like you driving over their prairie, and ranchers certainly didn't like you driving over their pastures. The forest service blocked off anything that even looked like you could drive a truck on it. There were lots of old logging and mining roads, though, if you knew where to look, and even the official access roads to the high lakes and stuff could get pretty hairy. Even so, road driving was nothing compared to striking out cross-country. The truck's big balloon tires provided some cushion, and the foot-and-a-half of travel in its suspension provided more, but nothing could smooth out the jolt when you found a rock with one wheel and a hole with the other. Trent kept the motors in low range, but he and Donna were still whooping and hollering and hanging on for dear life every few feet.

He had no idea where they were going, and didn't really care. He aimed them in the general direction of Bigtown whenever he had a choice, but mostly he just drove. They weaved between rock outcrops and clumps of trees, dropped into gullies and climbed hills, detoured to look at a field full of blue flowers (Donna's idea) and a lightning-blasted tree trunk (Trent's idea), and sang along with the music when they weren't screaming in terror or laughing with relief at surviving yet another argument with gravity.

Trent tried not to spin the tires or turn sharp enough to

skid. A lifetime of being told that bare ground was fragile had burned the message into his head pretty deep. He didn't necessarily want to leave tracks so long as he could *make* tracks, and do it in style. The balloon tires helped; they distributed the pickup's weight over a much wider patch of ground than regular tires would have. That hadn't been Trent's reason for buying them—he'd got them because they were good in mud and they looked cool—but he was happy enough to think that they were environmentally friendly to boot.

Half a dozen times over the next hour they stopped to watch someone else land. Most of the new arrivals were too far away to see more than their parachutes, but one came right overhead: a bright green and yellow ultralight aircraft piloted by someone in a polar parka. Presumably he had a Ziptite suit on underneath all that insulation, but that looked to be his only concession to vacuum. He waggled his wings as he flew over Trent and Donna, and Trent tooted the horn at him in response.

"Either that guy's nuts," Trent said, "or he's the smartest person I've seen yet." They watched him fly on toward Bigtown, covering the same distance in a couple of minutes that Trent and Donna had driven in an hour. He didn't have to worry about parachutes, either. Or leaving a launch crater. A guy could commute to work that way pretty easy.

"Don't even think about it," Donna said.

"Huh?"

"I know that look, Trent Stinson. Space flight is dangerous enough; I'm not going to worry about you flyin' around in an electric kite, too."

"Yes *ma'am,*" he said. Her tone of voice said she was joking, but he knew her well enough to know that it would remain a joke only as long as he didn't try it. There were limits to her tolerance for his gung-ho attitude, and he could push those limits only so far. He'd been surprised she'd let him build a hyperdrive and outfit the truck for space, but on that she had been curiously quiet, even encouraging. At first he'd thought maybe she was just being polite to their guests—Allen was, after all, the inventor of the hyperdrive, and Judy was an astronaut, so it wouldn't have looked good to badmouth space travel when they were around—but even after they'd left she'd been all for it. Getting shot at on the way home from their first trip hadn't even dampened her spirits for it.

He wondered how Allen and Judy were doing. The Galactic Federation they had started was still expanding, adding new species every couple of days as the secret of the hyperdrive snowballed out into the galaxy, so Judy was almost certainly chin-deep in paperwork dealing with that, but Trent couldn't imagine Allen doing a desk job. He was more likely in a lab somewhere, probably on the enormous spaceship of the alien Tippets, inventing something new to surprise everyone with. Antigravity would be good, Trent figured. That would be the last step that would really make hyperspace travel safe. Maybe he should track Allen down and suggest it.

The sun was getting pretty close to the horizon when they finally came up over a rise and saw a long, sinuous line of trees meandering off into the distance. Silvery water glinted between the trunks in the last rays of sunlight. It didn't look like a big river—maybe ten feet across—but it was plenty big enough to camp by. Trent drove the truck toward it down a long, gentle slope that ended in an impenetrable thicket of six-foot-high bushes, then drove along the side of the hill looking for a break in the thicket.

It was a long time coming. The thicket went on and on, choking off access to the water as effectively as a prison fence. There were no fords, no game trails, not even a bare rockslide they could climb down. Every inch of ground within twenty feet of the water was covered with dense brush. "You know," Trent said after a while, "these bushes are starting to look downright unfriendly."

She nodded. "Yeah. I wonder how the animals get any water."

They hadn't seen any animals yet, but that wasn't surprising. Animals tended to get out of the way of something the size of a pickup, especially if they hadn't seen one before. Now Trent was beginning to wonder if they had been starved out long before he and Donna had gotten here. From the looks of those bushes, a rabbit would have a hard time getting down to the stream.

"Nuts to this," he said at last, when the sun was below the horizon and the sky was starting to turn pink. "I've got a machete; let's just make us a gap."

"That seems kind of destructive just to reach the creek," Donna said, "but it looks like that's going to be our only way."

"It's a wild planet," Trent said, pulling to a stop on a grassy patch of level ground next to a spot that looked like it might be a little thinner than the rest. "Nobody's made any campsites here ahead of us."

He got out and rummaged behind the seat for the machete, dug some more until he found a pair of gloves, and marched down to the brush line. He could hear the stream gurgling softly only a few feet away, but it was completely hidden behind the brush.

He expected to see three-inch thorns studding the branches, but the bushes looked more like chokecherry, complete with clusters of dark brown berries, maybe a quarter inch in diameter, nestled among soft, round leaves. Trent wondered if they were edible. He wasn't about to try it on his own, but somebody had no doubt tried them already, and they—or their survivors—would know. He would have to remember to ask when they got to town.

If they ever made it. Town was on the other side of the stream, and Trent's first whack with the machete felt like he'd struck a clump of steel cables. A couple of branches flopped over, broken but not cut all the way through. So much for the mighty swordsman image. He took a bigger swing and managed to slice them off, plus another one below. This was going to be work.

He hacked away for five minutes or so before he had to take a break. In all that time, he'd only carved a tunnel about four feet into the bushes. He would have told Donna to forget it, that they'd just use water from their storage tank tonight, but he was already sweating so hard and stained with orange sap that he needed a bath before he crawled into his sleeping bag.

As he stepped back from the bushes and swept his sweaty hair out of his eyes, he caught sight of a star way up in the darkening sky. It glowed like Venus at its brightest, but this was almost straight up, and now that he looked at it for a few seconds he could see that it was moving ever so slowly toward the south.

"Check that out," he called to Donna, who was inside the camper fixing lunch or dinner or whatever they were going to call it. She stuck her head out and he pointed. "Somebody coming down in something shiny. They're still high enough to catch the sunlight."

"Neat." She watched for a while longer, then went back inside. Trent went back to work on the bushes, but he kept sneaking glances at the descending "star." It grew redder as it fell deeper into the atmosphere, catching more and more sunset light. As it drew closer he could see that the parachute was the bright part; the payload was just a dark speck under the bright silver canopy. It really sparkled, like it was made of tin foil or something. Trent wouldn't be surprised if somebody had tried that—they tried everything else, it seemed—but he doubted if that's what this was. Whatever they'd used here was actually working.

It was coming down a couple miles to the south. Trent watched until it dropped behind the hill, then went back to work on the bushes. He was getting better at it with practice; he learned to slice upward rather than downward, so the roots would hold the bushes in place while the machete cut through the stalks. That way it only took him another ten minutes or so to cut a path down to the water.

It felt like the middle of the forest primeval down there. It was only thirty feet wide or so, but the bushes gave way to full-size trees along the banks, and the trees leaned over the water from both sides, shading out what little light was left in the day. Trent bet it would be gloomy down there even at noon.

He stuck a hand in the water. At least it was cool. He wondered if it was safe to drink. Then he wondered if it was even safe to stand right next to the bank like he was. Some rivers on Earth had crocodiles in them, just waiting for dummies like Trent to lean over and provide an easy snack.

He needed a flashlight. He backed away and scraped his way through the hole he'd cut in the thicket, went around to the passenger side of the truck, and got the light out of the glove box. It was a plasma-cell Q-beam, basically an aircraft landing light powered by a small version of the same kind of battery that ran the truck's wheel motors. He switched it on and aimed it at the tunnel into the forest.

If it had looked spooky before, it looked doubly so now. Stark shadows splayed out in all directions, all pointing directly away from him and bobbing and weaving with his every motion. He advanced into it anyway, crouching low to squeeze through the gap, then standing up among the trees and shining the light around in a slow circle. The trees were covered in moss, and vines hung down over the water from some of them, but the vines didn't move, and the trees were just trees. He shined the light into the water and saw that it was crystal clear, and not very deep. It was mostly gravel-bottomed riffles connecting shallow pools. If there were crocs in it, they would have a hell of a time swimming very far.

He shined the light straight up. Nothing waiting to jump on him from overhanging branches.

"Trent?" Donna asked from the inner edge of the bushes. "Is it safe? Can I come in there and wash up?"

"I think so," he answered, but when he thought of Donna leaning down over the water, maybe even sticking her face into it, he said, "You know what, we don't have to re-invent the wheel here. We're close enough to Bigtown to reach 'em by radio; why don't we fire it up and just ask someone before we do something stupid."

"That makes sense, I guess," Donna said.

They squeezed out through the bushes again, adding yet more orange stains to their clothes. Donna's white T-shirt looked like someone had tried to put tiger stripes on it. Trent was wearing a brown and blue cotton work shirt, so it wasn't so apparent on him, but he made a mental note not to wear anything he cared about until he knew whether or not the sap would wash out.

He leaned into the cab of the pickup and flipped on the CB, tuning to channel 19, the informally agreed-upon general-contact channel. It was already busy, so he waited for a break where he could interrupt, but then he heard one voice say, ". . . at least twenty miles south of town . . ." and another voice said, ". . . nobody out that way that I know of," and he started listening.

"We can't just leave 'em out there," said the first voice.

"We can if we can't get to 'em," said the second. "They'll have to wait 'til morning. Unless you want to try drivin' twenty miles in the dark. Or *landin'* in the dark."

Trent picked up the microphone and said, "Break one-nine. This is Trent Stinson, and I'm quite a ways south of town at the moment. Is there something I can help you with?" He had a bad feeling he knew what the problem was.

"Hold up, Greg," the second voice said when he released the microphone switch. "There's somebody else on the channel. Who's that again?"

"The name's Trent, and I'm south of Bigtown by at least

fifteen miles with a good cross-country rig. You got an emergency out this way?"

"We don't know for sure," said the first voice, Greg, "but we think there might be. We got a couple garbled transmissions from somebody on their way down about twenty minutes ago, but their signal stopped cold when they hit the ground. Could be nothing, but they could be hurt."

"You sure they didn't just bail out at the last moment?" Trent asked.

"It's possible, but we're pretty sure he went all the way. There was a hell of a crashing sound just before the signal cut off."

Donna said softly, "That's got to be the one we watched come in."

"Yeah," Trent said. The pretty light in the sky. Now he felt somehow guilty for enjoying its descent. He looked up at the patch of hillside it had gone behind and keyed the microphone. "Roger, unless somebody else was in the air about the same time, we saw 'em come down just a couple of miles away. I've got a pretty good direction fix on their landing site. We could probably be there in half an hour if there aren't any of these damned brush-choked streambeds between us and them."

Greg said, "If you're south of the Greenwall, you're clear for quite a ways."

"I don't know if this is *the* greenwall, but we're sure south of *a* greenwall."

"Well then, I imagine the folks out there would appreciate it if you could go check in on 'em. Do you know first aid?"

"The basics," Trent said. "We may need to talk with somebody who knows more once we get there. You got a doctor?"

"We can get one by the time you need him."

"All right, then. We're on our way."

Donna said, "Give me a minute to batten down the hatches in back," and disappeared inside the camper.

Greg said, "Let's shift up to channel 22 for further contact."

"Okay. Shifting to 22." Trent punched the "channel-up" button three times. "Trent Stinson here, transmitting on 22. You read?"

"Loud and clear."

"All right. We'll keep you posted on our progress. Stinson out."

Trent clipped the microphone back on the dashboard and climbed up to stand in the open doorway where he could reach the smiley-face covers over the spotlights mounted on the roll bars and on the top of the camper. There were six lights: three aimed forward, one for each side, and one aimed straight back. He uncovered them all, then sat in the driver's seat and flipped the master switch. The hillside and the brush and the trees flashed into brilliant relief, even brighter than with the handheld light. And all around them, only fifteen or twenty feet away, dozens of creatures the size of big dogs stood blinking in the sudden glare.

around out here at night. They weren't in your chamber of commerce brochure."

Greg sounded surprised. "Holy shit, did you run into a pack of hoodlums?"

"Is that what you call 'em? Big round-headed doggy things?"

"Those are hoodlums. But they've pretty much abandoned the woods around Bigtown. We haven't seen any in a couple of months."

"Well, they haven't abandoned anything around here. Except us when we killed a couple."

"You *killed* a couple? Just like that?"

Trent laughed. "We didn't have a whole lot of choice. There must have been fifty of 'em."

"Damn," said Greg. "Well, I'm glad you made it through that okay. A lot of people haven't been so lucky."

"I bet." Trent hung up the microphone and turned to onna. "Remind me to suggest we just drive up to Jackson ext time we decide to go somewhere."

"They've got wolves up there," she said. "They come down t of Yellowstone."

"Shit."

They ate their sandwiches while they drove. Trent bolted down in about six bites and wished he had more, but he n't about to stop and fix another sandwich while some- was waiting on him for help. He kept the truck in low even so. The spotlights lit up everything bright as day hundred yards around, but the shadows were inky pools that could have hidden anything, and the last verybody needed was for the rescuers to get into an t themselves.

y didn't play any music this time, either. The only as from the truck itself: the soft whine of the mo- the squeaks and rattles as they jounced over the round. It seemed like they were forever detouring

They were dark gray, four-legged, and had big, round heads with large, toothy mouths. He didn't think they'd sneaked up just to see what he and Donna were doing. He yelled, "Close your door!" and slammed the driver's door, then lunged across the seat and grabbed the passenger door just as one of the creatures leaped for him. It clipped the end of the door as he swung it around and fell back to the ground with a loud yelp of surprise.

"Donna, are you all right?" Trent shouted, but the screeching sound from the back of the truck didn't sound good. He flipped open the glove box and grabbed the pistol, aimed it out the passenger window, and fired at the nearest dog-creature. The noise was deafening inside the cab, and he didn't even come close to hitting his target, but the shot did what he'd hoped it would do anyway: all of the creatures on that side of the truck turned tail and ran into the night. Trent spun around on the seat and fired out the driver's window, and the few on that side that hadn't already fled left claw marks in the grass as they skedaddled—except for the one that his wild shot had hit. That one flipped end over end, yelping and contorting its body from side to side as it ran blindly into the thicket, bounced off the net of branches, and fell over, still twitching and howling in pain.

Trent didn't give it a second glance. He threw open the door and raced around to the back of the truck, where he saw a big splash of blood in the spotlight's glare, with another of the round-headed creatures twitching in the middle of it. Donna stood in the camper doorway, a look of total surprise on her face and a bloody butcher knife in her hand.

"Are you all right?" he gasped.

"I was putting it away," she said.

"What?"

"I was making sandwiches while you were cutting brush. I thought I'd better put everything away before we started driving again, and then you shouted to close the door and I turned to do it but the . . . the whatever it was jumped for me and I just instinctively put my hands up and I . . . I got him in the throat."

"Jesus. I guess you did." She was breathing hard, and she held the knife as if it might turn on her next. He looked out into the circle of light around the truck. He didn't see any of the creatures, but he didn't expect they would stay spooked for long. "Come on," he said, "let's get out of here."

She turned away and tossed the knife into an open drawer, slid the drawer shut, and grabbed the two ham sandwiches sitting on the countertop. "All right."

Trent covered her with the gun while she climbed up into the cab, then slammed the camper door and went around to climb up on the driver's side. When he had slammed that door and rolled up the windows, he lowered the gun and leaned back in the seat. "Damn, that was a little too close," he said.

"Yeah," said Donna. Her eyes were wide as saucers, and her hands shook until she set them in her lap, the sandwiches still clutched in either hand.

Trent wasn't doing much better. He slowly eased his finger off the pistol's trigger, popped open the cylinder and ejected the two spent cases, then refilled the cylinder with fresh bullets from the glove box. He left the pistol next to the flashlight on the seat between them.

"You sure you're okay?" he asked.

"Yeah. How about you?"

"My ears are ringin' like crazy, but other than that, I'm all right."

"Okay, then," she said. "Let's get out of here. We got people to rescue."

"The blind leading the blind," Trent said, but he released the brake and accelerated up the hill.

He stopped at the top and pointed out where he'd see
the parachute go down. It was right below Orion, whi
was way low on the horizon here, and tilted on its left si
"We just aim for the belt and we're bound to run ac
'em," he said.

"The belt?" Donna said. "What about that brigh
on the horizon next to Betelgeuse?"

Trent didn't know Betelgeuse from apple juice
saw the light she meant. "That looks like a star to m
sky below it."

"There's not usually two bright stars in O
shoulder." She got the computer out of its slot ur
and woke it up, then stuck it up against the wi
the webcam get a view of the stars. She fed th
navigation program and clicked the pointer
to the horizon, and a label popped up next t

"Sirius?" She asked. "But that's way
Orion." She pulled down a menu and got
formation window. "Oh, okay. It's only 9.
guess it could move quite a ways acro
short jump to Alpha Centauri."

Trent leaned over next to his wir
Cassiopeia, where the Sun added a
short jump, Donna said, but it wa
couple of stars, at least. And aft
wild animals, he suddenly felt a

While Donna folded up the
under the dash, he radioed Gr
their way. "And just for future
might think to warn people a

around some obstacle or another in their path, but Trent kept bringing them back into line with Orion whenever he could, and they slowly worked their way south.

He looked over at Donna and tried to imagine what that must have felt like when the hoodlum jumped her. Killing it with a knife! Trent had never had to fight anything or anyone with a knife and he never wanted to. That was way too personal for comfort.

She noticed him looking at her and said, "What?"

He looked away. "Nothin'," he said automatically, but then he kicked himself for saying that. It wasn't nothing. He cleared his throat and said, "Actually, that was . . . well, that was really something back there, coming around the side of the truck and seeing you with that knife in your hand. I wouldn't have wanted to be one of them hoodlums just then."

She laughed. "Just call me Xena. But don't ask me to do it again."

"Never."

He risked another look at her. She had always been a babe, but right now she could cause a riot in a church. She was fully charged and glowing with the power. If they didn't have to be somewhere in a hurry, he would be parking this truck and tearing her clothes off right here in the front seat, and by the look she was giving him, she felt the same way.

"I'm beginnin' to see why some people like to get into trouble," he said.

"Don't you start thinking—"

"I'm just saying. Some people."

"Okay."

"Still, I bet you'd look mighty good in one of them pointy brass bras and a—"

She whacked him in the side. "About the time you start wearing a loincloth."

"That ought to look good with a cowboy hat."

She giggled. He laughed and reached out and gave her a squeeze on the leg, but the ride was too jouncy to let him keep his hand there for long.

After a couple of miles by the odometer, he saw a flash of light off in the distance. He flicked the truck's lights off and on a couple of times, and the other light did the same. He got on the radio again and said, "Somebody's blinking a light at us. You had any more contact with them?"

"Nothing yet," said Greg. "Let me give 'em another try." He was gone a minute, then came back with, "Nope. Still silent."

"All right. I'm bettin' that's them, though."

Trent concentrated on driving. The terrain rose and fell, taking them out of sight of their target at least half the time, and when they would pop back up over a rise it would invariably be to one side or the other of where they thought it should be, but they drew steadily closer, and eventually they found themselves on a long flat stretch of grass and wildflowers that led straight to the downed ship.

Calling it a "ship" was a courtesy, earned only because it had made the jump between planets. It looked like it had started out life as a water tank, and that life had apparently been long and hard. Long streaks of rust ran down its sides, and several irregular patches of varying age had been welded to it. If it had ever held air, it didn't now; it had come down tilted and the side that had taken the brunt of its weight on impact had crumpled like an accordion, splitting its seams wide open.

Its glittery silver parachute lay limp on the ground, stretching off into the dark beyond it. The silvery foil was such a sharp contrast to the rusty tank that Trent would never have guessed they belonged together if he hadn't seen the tank descending beneath it. Whoever built this rig must have spent all their money on the hyperdrive and the parachute, and made the spaceship out of the only thing they had on hand.

A white blob of fur with irregular black spots ran out to bark at them when they drew close. Trent normally didn't like dogs much, especially the kind that screeched more than barked, like this one did, but with wild animals out there in the dark, he was happy to see this one. Then he noticed how many legs it had: at least six, plus a couple of tentacles that waved back and forth from the top of its head. That was where it kept its eyes.

A bigger creature stood atop the tank, waving a flashlight enthusiastically at the pickup. It was about four feet tall, scaly and glisteny brown rather than hairy and white, with thick, snakelike arms and legs that ended in sharp claws. It stood on four of its six legs, bending upward in the middle like a centaur. Its head was a narrow triangle with the pointy end aimed forward. It looked like it might be smiling, but then again, its mouth could just be a permanently curved slit full of fangs. Trent let off the juice and let the truck coast to a stop a couple dozen feet away.

"Oh, boy," he said softly.

Donna took a deep breath and let it out slowly. "They could be perfectly nice."

"Uh-huh." He drove a little closer to the tank and parked, leaving the lights on. "You stay here until we know for sure."

When he opened his door and stepped out, the alien shouted something like "Baki!" and waved the flashlight's beam in an arc around the curved side of the tank. Did he want Trent to go around to that side? Trent reached up onto the seat for his own flashlight and, keeping an eye out for hoodlums, followed the alien's light around to a ragged hole in the side of the tank. The furry mop on the ground kept pace with him about five feet away, screeching the whole time, while the alien above yelled "Gabat!" from the top of the tank. Trent hoped it was just trying to quiet its dog, because if it was shouting at Trent, he had no idea what it wanted.

It took him a second to realize that the hole in the tank

wasn't part of the accident. Someone had made a doorway with a cutting torch and not bothered to file the edges smooth. It was only about four feet high, but it started two feet off the ground; Trent only had to lean down a little bit to keep from hitting his hat.

The inside of the tank looked like somebody had taken a moving van and shaken it, which was about what had happened, he supposed. Boxes and wooden crates and sacks of stuff were piled hip deep, and more stuff was tied to the walls and hanging from the roof. There were easily identifiable things like shovels and rakes and pitchforks in a pile near the door, with less familiar twisty things and squiggly jiggers mixed in. Some of the crates held animals—though not any animals Trent had ever seen. A three-foot yellow tentacle stuck out between the slats of one crate, weaving around in the air and blinking the eye at its tip, and the hisses, honks, and croaks coming from the other cages didn't sound much more reassuring. The air didn't smell so great, either.

It took a second to see the owners among all their possessions, but Trent waved his flashlight around and finally saw a bigger version of the scaly creature on top of the tank standing over another one who was lying flat on its back on a pile of blankets, and two more small ones hiding behind the standing one. These guys at least had eyes in more or less the right place, even if their limbs were more tentacles than arms. The one on its back had a bad gash on the left side of its head, still wet with dark purple blood. The standing one didn't seem hurt, but one of the kids—if that's what the little ones were—was cradling one of its tentacles protectively with its other one. An even smaller child hid between the standing parent's legs, and at the sight of Trent it began to cry out in long, ear-piercing wails.

"It's all right," Trent said, raising his voice to be heard over the din. "I'm here to help."

The standing parent—Trent guessed it was the mother—said something in a rapid-fire voice full of t's and k's. Trent missed about half of it because of the screeching mop-thing outside and the crying baby inside, but it wouldn't have mattered if he hadn't. "Sorry," he said. "I don't speak whatever it is you're talkin'."

He felt something at his side and whirled around, banging his head against the ragged edge of the doorway, but it was just Donna. The alien mother snorted, but whether it was laughter at Trent or alarm at Donna, he couldn't tell.

He caught his hat before it could hit the ground and wedged it back on his head. "Damn it, I thought I told you to stay put."

Donna said, "Until we knew they were friendly. They didn't blow your head off when you stuck it through the door, so I figured it was okay." She edged past him. "Do they need as much help as it looks like from outside?"

He moved aside to let her have a look, keeping his flashlight pointed in through the door. She leaned in and said loudly, "Are you okay in here?" Then, softer, she said, "Oh. No, it doesn't look like it, does it?"

The mother said something else fast, waving one of her snakey arms at the hatch that had plugged the hole and was now lying on the only bare patch of floor. It was just a big slab of metal with rubber door molding around the edge and a broken gate hinge welded to one side. The mother pointed at the hatch and then at the gash in her mate's head.

"Got it," Trent said. "The door broke loose and clocked him one."

The father—if that's what he was—had left a big puddle of purplish blood on the floor, and the side of his head was colored with it, too, but it looked like he had quit bleeding. Trent watched the alien's chest to see if he was still breathing, and was happy to see it rise and fall in slow, even rhythm. Of course that might not be normal for one of his kind—the mother was breathing about four times as fast—but then again she had reason to be excited.

Donna squeezed in through the hatch and crawled over a pile of farm tools to the father's side. "How's his pulse?" she asked. "Heartbeat? Thumpa-thumpa?" She whacked her chest just left of center, then held up her left arm and put her fingers across the wrist. "Do you guys normally have a pulse?"

More rapid alien speech, barely audible over the baby and the mop. The mother picked up the baby and tried to shush it with little clicking sounds, but it kept crying.

"We're gonna need a translator," Trent said. He went around the tank, sweeping his flashlight out into the night to make sure no hoodlums were waiting to ambush him, but there was only one pair of eyes out there, and they belonged to the mop-creature that continued to screech at him from about five feet away. He looked up at the top of the tank, where the first alien—an adolescent son, Trent guessed—still stood with its flashlight, and said, "We're calling for help. He'll be okay." The alien didn't reply.

The truck's lights were still blazing. Trent left them on and drove around to where they would do some good, and where he could stand beside it with the microphone in his hand and still see through the hatch. He keyed the microphone and said, "Trent Stinson calling Bigtown. Do you copy?"

He had to turn up the volume to hear anything over the barking mop and the crying baby, but he could make out Greg's voice saying, "Bigtown here."

"We're at the landing site," Trent said. "Turns out they're aliens. Kinda lizardy guys, brown and slimy with four legs and two tentacles for arms. Pointy heads. You know what kind they are?"

"Can't say as I do from that description," Greg said.

"Well, we need somebody who can translate for 'em, because we can't understand a word they're sayin', and one of 'em's got a big gash in the side of his head."

Greg took a second to respond. "Is he conscious?" he asked.

"Nope," Trent replied. "But he's breathing, and he's not bleeding anymore."

Donna, from inside the tank, called out, "He's got a heartbeat, but it's real fast. Faster than the one who isn't hurt."

Trent relayed that information to Greg, and Greg replied, "The doctor says you should probably try to wake him up. That's what he'd do with a human patient, anyway. Pinch him or slap his cheeks or do whatever it takes, but get him awake."

"Got it." Trent leaned toward the doorway. "He says wake him up."

If noise could have done it, it already would have. Donna didn't even try that. She just turned back to Trent and said, "Get me some cold water."

He went around back to the camper and grabbed a bottle of water from the fridge. He never drank bottled water at home, but it was a lot more convenient on the road to just buy a case of the stuff prepackaged than to fill a bunch of jugs and canteens. He took the hand towel from the rack beside the sink, then went back and handed the water and towel through the hatch to Donna.

She wet the towel and showed it to the mother. The mother sniffed it, then touched it gingerly, then stuck the end of her tentacle in her mouth. "Bakbak," she said, and wiggled her head.

"Is that 'yes' or 'no'?" Donna asked. She lowered the towel toward the father's head and asked, "Yes?"

"Bakbak," the mother said again.

"Well, she isn't trying to stop me," Donna said, and she laid the towel on his sloping forehead. She gave that a few seconds, but when it didn't wake him she dribbled a little water directly onto his face. The mother bent down next to him and said loudly, "Magalak! Kanado!" She patted him under his toothy jaw, then when that didn't work she took a deep breath and gave him a good slap on the end of his nose.

That did the trick. The father snorted and turned his head aside, then he opened his eyes and tried to raise up. "Ti, ti!" the mother said, holding him down.

He groaned and raised his left tentacle to his temple. He tried to wet his lips with his tongue, then croaked, "Gatsa."

Donna handed him the water bottle. He looked at it for a moment, and at her, then he took a tiny sip and said more heartily, "Gatsa."

He drank a little, then tried to sit up again, and this time the mother let him. He winced at the pain in his head, but he managed it, then he looked out the door into the intense light from the pickup. "Onnescu," he said softly, and there was wonder in his voice.

"Bakbak," the mother said. She said something more to him that Trent couldn't catch, and he replied with more incomprehensible words, and they twisted their tentacles together.

Donna said, "That's right, this is Onnescu. You made it. It looks like you came here to stay."

They damned near came here to die, Trent thought, but he didn't say anything. They had survived the landing, and it certainly looked like they had brought enough stuff to start a new life with. That's probably why they had landed so hard; there had to be a couple tons of tools and animals and who knew what else in their makeshift spaceship. Trent saw the corner of a chest of drawers peeking out from behind a crate of animals, and a black metal box that looked for all the world like a steamer trunk beside that.

The father swung his legs around to the only patch of bare floor left and slowly stood, leaning hard on his mate. He was wobbly, but he made it, standing there with the side of his head all covered with dried blood. Then he saw the little one holding its right tentacle protectively with its left, and he bent down and spoke softly to it.

The mother answered for it, and the little one held out its tentacle. There was a big purple spot about halfway up, and when the father gently touched it, the little one cried out in pain.

"Can you break one of those?" Trent asked.

"I wouldn't think so," Donna said, "but something's sure wrong with it."

What to do about it was even less obvious. Trent got on the radio with the doctor again, and the doctor advised bringing the father and the young one into town for him to look at.

It took a while to get that across to the alien family, but they pantomimed the father and the child climbing into the pickup and driving off several times until the aliens finally got it. The father clearly didn't like that idea, and Trent couldn't blame him. He didn't know Trent and Donna from Adam, and he wasn't about to abandon all his animals and possessions, nor leave his wife and the other two kids with them while he ran off to town—though the doctor said with a head wound like his, that's exactly what he should do. The father pantomimed that he was okay, that he would take it easy for a few days and he would be fine. But he couldn't very well say that about his child.

At last they settled on a solution: Katata, the mother, would take the injured child and the baby to town with Trent and Donna, while the father and his oldest son would stay with the animals and start their farm right where they landed. That had probably been his intent in coming down where he did: to be close enough to town that he could take things in to market, but far enough away that the land wouldn't already be claimed yet. He'd succeeded in that. In fact, if it hadn't been for the hard landing, he'd have succeeded at everything he'd set out to do. Trent had to give the guy his grudging respect. It was one thing to seal up a truck and head into the great unknown for a job hunt, but to do it in a rusty water tank, with all your family and all your possessions, one way—that took guts. And desperation. Trent couldn't imagine what conditions on this alien's home planet must be like if this looked like a good idea to him.

He got a bit of an idea on the drive. He had originally thought that Katata and the children could ride in the camper, but Katata took one look at the tiny table and bench seats and all the cabinets overhead and shook her head "Ti." Even when Trent tried to explain that the cabinets were latched tight and nothing would fly open, she just pointed to the front seat and said, "Katata bok gaba." He couldn't very well insist that they ride in back when she obviously wanted to ride in front, so Donna squeezed in a little closer to him than usual, the child with the injured tentacle, Talana, sat next to Donna, and Katata held the baby, Dixit, on her lap.

And while they drove, Katata told them what life was like on her home planet, Bekat. They started out with no words in common besides "ti" and "bakbak" and "gatsa," but it was amazing what she could convey through pantomime, and with each concept Trent and Donna understood, she taught them a word to go with it so she wouldn't have to pantomime it again.

Apparently a spaceship had fallen out of the sky on Bekat about a hundred days ago. The astronauts—humans, if Trent understood the pointing at him and at the starry sky—had given the secret of the hyperdrive to the aliens, who had immediately begun blinking out on interstellar jumps of their own. Those who could build a spaceship without getting it stolen first, anyway. There was either a war going on, or the place was nothing but bandits and guerrillas fighting over the last dregs of civilization, Trent couldn't figure out for sure which, but if he understood Katata right, everybody who could get out was doing so. Problem was, the army—or the bandits—knew that, and were actively hunting down and killing anybody who tried to leave.

"That's nuts," Trent said when he finally understood the situation. "If people want to move out, let 'em go."

"So says the guy from the United States," Donna said.

"Yeah, well, at least our government only shoots at us on the way *back*."

Donna got a thoughtful look on her face.

"What?" he asked her.

"I wonder if it's a racial thing? Or religious. Maybe the people in power don't want the other guys to get a leg up somewhere else."

That was possible. Humans certainly acted that way if you gave them the chance. Right after Allen dropped the hyperdrive plans on Earth, people had been afraid that the first nation to get a colony started would nuke the rest of the world to prevent anyone else from getting away. Those fears had been well grounded, too. Several countries had actually started throwing bombs before the Galactic Federation put a stop to it. There was no reason to assume that aliens would be any more civilized.

Were Katata and her family refugees? The stuff they had brought with them certainly didn't look like the sort of belongings a rich family would take with them to the stars. They were obviously farmers, and not terrifically well-off ones at that. Just the sort of folks who, among humans, anyway, always wound up doing the grunt work while the fat cats skimmed off any profit they might make.

Trent wondered how they would fare on Onnescu. There wasn't much government here to speak of, certainly no immigration police or any of that, but things would change. They would have to. Onnescu was probably one of the fastest growing population centers in the galaxy at the moment. It was the closest planet to Earth, one of the most Earthlike yet discovered, it didn't have any intelligent natives living on it, and the people who had already moved here actually wanted more people to join them. Their goal, or so they said in their flyer, was to start a new society using all the best ideas from Earth's history, and build a second Earth without all the environmental problems and social problems of the first one. An admirable goal, Trent thought, and probably much more difficult to realize than the colonists expected, but even if they fell short of the entire picture, they could still wind up with something a hell of a lot better than back home.

He wondered if they had counted on immigration from beyond Earth. Not that it should matter, but he bet it would to some people. Even so, Katata and her family probably stood a better chance here than on a planet where people tried to kill you for getting out. By the time the notion of racial purity raised its ugly head here, they would already be locals.

Their biggest problem was going to be the slime. The whole right side of Trent's pickup cab was dripping with the stuff. Every time he hit a bump, the aliens would lurch against the door or the dashboard—or against Donna—and every time they did, they left a fresh smudge of goo. Donna was starting to look like a Jell-O wrestler on her right side, and Trent was beginning to wonder if they would ever get the stuff out of the seat. Katata and her kids didn't even seem to notice that they were doing it, which meant it was probably a normal thing for them and not just a reaction to stress, and if that was the case, then they were going to have a hard time dealing with humans. Trent didn't mind getting his pickup slimed for a good cause, but he doubted if people would put up with it on a regular basis.

Maybe they could keep a tarp handy. If Trent had been thinking quicker, he could have done that here. But even that was probably more than most people would be willing to do. Just went to show, there were always complications no matter where you went.

Trent kept all the lights on while he drove. They rolled through a hundred-yard circle of near-daylight, making good time when they found a smooth stretch and slowing to get through the rocky parts. Trent radioed ahead and asked if there was a road already cut through the Greenwall, and Greg talked them toward the closest of three that he knew of. It was a couple of miles out of their way, but it was worth the detour; once they found the notch in the trees and forded the stream, they picked up a track they could follow all the way to Bigtown. It wasn't much at first, but it was better than nothing, and the closer they got to town, the more well defined it became. It had even been smoothed out in places.

Even so, it was well after midnight local time when they saw their first house lights. The outlying homesteads were spread quite a ways apart, but they drew closer together as Trent kept driving, until eventually the pickup was rolling down a wide city street with houses on either side. The street wasn't paved, but it was straight and relatively smooth, except for the mudholes, which grew more and more common closer to the center of town. Trent grinned as he powered through them, throwing big sheets of mud out to the sides and up over the hood. Katata and her children squealed in alarm the first time it happened, but Talana's squeal changed its pitch the second time, and Katata's echoed her child's the time after. Pretty soon everyone was doing it, and then Donna taught them how to shout "Woo-hoo!"

The center of town was all shops, bars, restaurants, and hotels. Some of them were wooden frame buildings like any others back home, but others were made of rough-hewn logs like old homestead cabins, and one was made of round river rock cemented together like an old Scottish castle. There was a log bridge over the river itself, and more businesses beyond. A few trees stood here and there, especially near the river, but Trent saw more stumps than live ones.

It was hard to believe that this was all less than five months old. Trent had heard how frontier towns had grown up practically overnight in the American West, but he had never really understood the magnitude of what people could do when they put some serious effort into it. These people clearly didn't want to live in a rural backwater; they wanted a *town*. They just didn't want it to be on Earth.

Some of the inhabitants were out and about. People waved and called out to them from the doorways of bars as they rolled past, and Trent slowed down so he wouldn't splash mud all over them. The streets downtown were churned to a froth by all the traffic, to the point where Trent wondered if he was going to get through the muck with only three drive wheels, but the pickup wallowed through it in fine form, and a few blocks past the river they rose up onto drier ground again.

Greg talked them in to the hospital—a squat log building on a side street about six blocks north of the center of town. The exterior looked like a dude ranch bunkhouse, but lights blazed from its windows, and big blue signs pointed to the emergency entrance. Trent parked close to the doors and set the brake.

"The ambulance arrives," he said, opening his door and stepping down to the ground. He went around to the other side and helped Katata and her children down, wiping his hands on his pantlegs when he was done, then he reached up for Donna, but she took one look at the slimy seat and scooted out the driver's side. It was hardly worth the effort. Her entire right side was already wet with the aliens' slime, her white T-shirt practically transparent from her shoulder to the middle of her chest except where streaks of orange sap from the bushes Trent had cut by the stream had stained it. It was clear that she wasn't wearing a bra.

A tall, gangly Asian guy met them at the door. "I'm Doctor

Chen," he said in heavily accented English. He wasn't dressed like a doctor—his blue jeans, red flannel shirt, and hiking boots made him look more like a logger or a construction worker—but he had a stethoscope draped around his neck and a little fanny pack with a red cross on it.

Trent made the introductions. "I'm Trent. This is Donna, Katata, Talana, and Dixit. Talana's the one with the hurt . . . whatever."

Dr. Chen looked apprehensively at the aliens. It was hard to tell what the aliens thought of him. If they were scared, they didn't show it, but they didn't say anything, either. They just stood there, Katata holding the baby in one tentacle and draping the other over Talana's shoulder.

"Come inside, and we have see," Chen said.

The building might have had a log exterior, but the inside was clean and bright, with smooth white walls and a tile floor. The emergency room took up at least a third of its space, and there was a hallway leading to several smaller rooms beyond it. The emergency room had two exam tables with crinkly paper sheets covering the cushions, and curtains on rails that could be pulled around them for privacy, just like in any other hospital.

An Asian woman dressed in drab green scrubs ran some kind of high-tech instrument on the far end of the room. She looked up when she saw people entering, did a theatrical double-take, then waved "hello" and went back to her work.

"Please sit patient on table," Dr. Chen said. When Katata didn't respond, he motioned setting Talana down, and she did. He reached out and gingerly touched the alien child's slimy right tentacle at the bruised spot just above where it was cradling it with its left. Talana shivered under his touch, but whether it was from pain or from the idea of being prodded by a curious alien was hard to say.

"Where does it hurt?" Chen asked.

Katata spoke to the child, and the child responded by

pointing with the tip of its uninjured tentacle. Both tentacles were maybe three inches thick at the shoulder and tapered to about the size of a person's little finger at the tip. The injury was about two-thirds of the way down the right one, where it was maybe an inch thick.

Chen brushed his fingers gently along Talana's skin. Talana quivered again, then winced when he got to the injury. Trent wondered what the doctor could do for what was essentially a snake with a broken back, how he could even tell what was wrong, but Dr. Chen acted like he knew what he was doing. He reached for Talana's other tentacle and felt the same spot there, squeezing fairly hard to feel the underlying structure. "There are bones," he said. "Like vertebrae." He flexed the uninjured tentacle in an arc, then tightened it into a loop about eight inches in diameter, getting a feel for how it normally moved. Then he put his hand inside the loop and said, "Squeeze." He clenched the fingers of his other hand to show what he wanted.

Talana tightened the tentacle around his hand, the slimy skin sliding noiselessly, like a velvet rope being drawn into a knot. The knot slid down the length of the tentacle a few inches until it was narrow enough for a good grip, then Talana squeezed.

Chen nodded appreciatively. "Very good. Strong. Harder, please." He flexed his free fingers again, and Talana obliged.

"Ah! Okay, stop now. Stop!" He tugged his hand free and shook it, and Talana jerked the tentacle back as if it had touched something hot.

"Toca," the child said.

"You okay," Chen replied. "You do just what I ask." He took the other tentacle and draped the end of it over the same hand. "Now do again."

Talana tried to wrap the tentacle around his hand, but the end of it slid less than halfway around before Talana cried out in pain and stopped.

"Okay," Chen said, lowering his hand. "No need to try

again." He turned toward the woman across the room and said something to her in what sounded like Chinese, of which the only word Trent could understand was "X-ray."

She looked up from her equipment and replied in Chinese, then came around her workbench and wheeled the mobile x-ray unit away from its parking spot against the wall. It looked like the bottom half of a refrigerator with a computer keyboard and monitor set at an angle on top, with a hinged arm holding an oblong plastic emitter overhead. Trent looked at the arm, then at the arms of the woman pushing the unit toward the alien child. Both were built on pretty much the same principle, which made him wonder if an alien x-ray machine would have a flexible arm.

Dr. Chen took a wide black film tray from the machine's cabinet and set it on a cart beside the exam table, then draped Talana's injured tentacle across the flat surface near one end of the tray. He covered the rest of the tray with a heavy metal plate, apparently to keep the entire piece of film beneath it from being exposed at once, then positioned the business end of the x-ray machine over the tentacle while the technician worked at the keyboard to set up the shot.

"Okay, everyone but patient go into other room," he said when they were ready.

Trent and Donna moved away, but Katata didn't.

"You too," Chen said, waving her after Trent and Donna, but she said "Ti" and stayed put.

"That means 'No,'" Donna told him.

"I assume." He thought it over, obviously wondering how he was going to get the idea of minimizing exposure across to a worried alien mother, then he said, "Okay. Take baby. Let mother stay." He gently lifted Dixit from Katata's tentacles and handed the baby to Donna, who made a face, but she took it from him and held it against her already-slimy side. Dixit wrapped its tentacle around her waist and rested its head against her right breast. Katata looked at Donna and her baby, then at Talana, then at the x-ray machine.

"It's all right," Donna said. "We'll be just over there." She pointed down the hallway toward the patient rooms.

Katata clearly didn't understand what was going on, but she stayed by her injured child while Trent and Donna moved away with the baby. They paused at the door and watched as the doctor handed her a lead apron and showed her how to put it around herself, then did the same for Talana and himself. The technician put on her own apron, then turned to make sure Trent and Donna were clear.

She said something in Chinese, waving them on out of the room.

"Nothin' like a language barrier to add to the excitement," Trent said as they dutifully walked down the hallway. He peered into the dark rooms as they passed. The two on the left were typical patient rooms, with beds and curtains and even televisions bolted to the walls at the end of the beds. "They've got TV here?" he asked incredulously.

"Probably just for showing videos," Donna said.

"Oh. Yeah, that makes sense."

The rooms on the other side of the hallway were offices. The one in back was lit, so they went in and sat in the chairs there, careful not to slime anything. The alien baby looked around at the desk and the shelves of books and the piles of papers on the desk, then reached out for one of the papers. Its tentacle was fast; it had the paper before Donna could stop it.

"No, no," she said. "Ti." She tried to wrestle the paper free, but the baby cinched its tentacle tight, crumpling the paper into a fan and holding it high out of her reach.

Trent got up to help her pry it out of the baby's grasp, but the baby whipped its tentacle around and squealed in protest.

"Jeez, I hope that's not somebody's insurance form or something," Donna said.

"I wonder if insurance would pay out here?" Trent got a grip on the baby's shoulder, then worked his way up to the paper. Slime dripped off his fingers, but he didn't let go until he'd rescued the paper. He wiped it dry as best he could against his shirt, then looked to see what it was, but the writing was in Chinese.

"I somehow expected things to be done in English out here," he said. "The place was founded by an American, after all."

Donna nodded. "You'd think. But the way the U.S. is clamping down on people leaving, I guess we're just outnumbered."

"So because they want everybody everywhere to think and act like Americans, they wind up with a colony that doesn't even speak English as a first language. That's really bright."

Dixit kept squealing and reaching for the paper. Trent looked for a blank piece, finally pulling one out of the inkjet printer on the corner of the desk, but Dixit wasn't interested in that paper. Only the original one would do.

"How about this one?" Trent asked, holding up a preprinted form that was at least empty of handwriting.

Dixit started to howl. Trent tried crumpling up the blank paper and tossing it from hand to hand in front of the baby's face, and that distracted it for a moment, but not long.

Donna tried singing to it, but Trent could barely hear her over the baby's squeals.

"Okay," she said, standing up again. "Time to go back to Momma."

Dixit quieted down as soon as she started moving, so they took their time walking back down the hallway. When they got to the exam room, Dr. Chen looked up and said, "Okay you come back now. Just take a minute to develop." His assistant wheeled the x-ray machine back into its spot, then took the film plate into a back room.

Donna handed Dixit back to Katata. It was hard to tell who was the most relieved.

Everyone waited impatiently for the x-rays to be

developed, Dr. Chen fussing with a tray full of equipment and with the light table while the rest of them just shifted from side to side and fidgeted. Trent's eyes kept straying back to Donna, whose wet shirt was clinging to every curve. She might be a mess, but she looked so alive and so . . . so *real,* that he could have swept her off her feet and made love to her right there on one of the exam tables if he wasn't afraid it would scare the aliens. She caught him looking at her and blushed, which only made him ache for her all the more.

At last the doctor's assistant came back with a two-foot by foot-and-a-half negative and stuck it on the light table. There were four shots of Talana's tentacle, presumably at different orientations, but they all looked pretty much the same to Trent. He had seen pictures of dinosaur skeletons with their long tails made up of short little segments of vertebrae or whatever; these x-rays looked a lot like that.

"So they do have bones," he said softly.

"Oh yes," Dr. Chen said. "And this one has fracture right here." He pointed to one of the segments, maybe two inches long and half an inch wide, that had the faintest of shadows running diagonally across it. "See from side? Very clear." Chen said, pointing to another image where Trent couldn't spot anything unusual at all. "Not broken completely, but definitely fractured. We will need cast."

It took some explaining to make Katata and Talana understand what he intended to do, but they must have had casts or something similar on their homeworld, because they didn't protest when he got out the gauze and the plaster and started building one on Talana's tentacle. He positioned it so the tentacle rested against Talana's body more or less like an arm, and the injured bone plus two or three more on either side were immobilized. He worked fast, because the plaster set quickly. By the time he fashioned a sling and wrapped it around Talana's neck, the cast was hard enough to give off a solid *thunk* when he rapped it.

"Very good," Chen said. "Now we wait overnight and see

how tentacle feels in morning. Make sure no complications before we send home. You have place to stay?"

"Yeah," Trent said. "I mean, yeah, Donna and I do, but the camper would be pretty tight for all five of us."

"No problem. Family can stay here tonight."

They managed to get that across to Katata, pantomiming her and her children going into a patient room, then the sun going across the sky once, then Trent and Donna coming back in through the front doors.

"Bakbak," Katata said when she figured out what they were talking about. Then she snaked out the tentacle that she wasn't using to hold Dixit and grasped Trent's hand with it, curling around his fingers and palm a couple of times and giving him a light squeeze. "Batakit," she said.

She did the same to Donna, and Donna replied, "You're welcome."

"We'll be back in the morning," Trent said, and he and Donna let themselves out into the night while Dr. Chen showed his patients to their room.

Trent waited until he was outside to wipe his hands on his pants. Donna laughed and did the same, then they stood beside their pickup, smelling the wood smoke in the air and listening to the night sounds. Most of them were of human origin: music and laughter from the bars, and off in the distance a vehicle crunching along a street, but behind it all was the constant rush of the river and the whisper of air moving through the trees.

"Well, here we are," Trent said.

"Not quite how we expected our first night to be, is it?" said Donna.

"Nope. But you know, it feels good. I haven't felt this useful in ages."

"Me neither." Donna slid her arm around his waist and leaned her head against his chest. "Kind of puts things in perspective when you find someone in worse shape than you are, doesn't it?"

"I guess." Trent had never really understood why another person's problems made your own seem less important, but they did.

"Now what?" Donna asked.

"Good question. You tired yet?"

"Not really. I'm still kind of wound up."

"Me too. And it sounds like we're not the only ones stayin' up late. Want to check out the night life in Bigtown?"

"Sure. Let me get out of these messy clothes, and let's go."

Trent put his arms around her and gave her a long, slow kiss. "You want a hand with that?"

There was barely room for both of them in the camper, but Trent pulled the door closed behind them and made sure it latched. It was pitch dark for a second before he found the light switch and flipped it on. When he turned around, Donna was already wriggling out of her shirt. She had her arms in the air and her shirt over her head, so he reached out and cupped her breasts in his hands and said, "Guess who."

She giggled. "Oh, Bob, how did you get in here?"

"Try again," he said, giving her a squeeze.

"Jeff? Dennis? Gosh, there's so many people it could be."

"Is that so?" he said, surprised at how much some other man's name could jolt him even when he knew she was just playing with him. He reached up and grabbed a handful of her shirt, intending to whisk it off her in a single tug, but he misjudged the angle when he pulled, and he heard it rip as it came over her head. "Oh, jeez, I'm sorry!" he said, but then he saw the look of wanton lust on her face and he whispered, "Whoa, maybe I'm not."

She flung the shirt aside, grabbed the front of his shirt in both hands, and pulled it open. It had a snap-down front, and the first couple of snaps popped loose the way they were supposed to, but the rest of them didn't have a chance. The sides of the shirt tore instead, leaving Donna with two handfuls of cloth and a look of total astonishment.

Her nostrils flared out, and a slow grin spread across her face. "Hang onto your hat, cowboy," she said in a voice that was breathy and deep. "We could wind up miles from here."

"Hang onto it, hell," Trent said, sweeping his Stetson off his head and tossing it onto the counter beside the sink. "I'm gettin' it out of your way. You look like you mean business."

"Damn right I mean business." She took another couple fistfuls of his shirt and yanked them apart, ripping it all the way up his back.

Clothes went flying. Trent had never seen Donna like this, had never felt quite so out of control himself, but he wasn't about to stop and question it. They stripped each other bare, shredding every piece of clothing they could in the process, and had their way with each other right there on the floor of the camper. If anybody was watching the pickup, they would know for sure what was going on inside, but Trent didn't care. Let the envious bastards watch all they wanted.

"Yee-haw," he said in the moment of calm afterward. "That was worth coming all the way to Alpha Centauri for."

She was snuggled up against him with her head on his chest. "You think so, do you?" she asked softly.

"I don't know. Maybe we ought to do it again just to make sure."

"You think we'd survive it?"

"If we didn't, I'd die happy."

She laughed and snuggled in closer. "I just want to hold you for a while."

"Good enough by me." He ran his hands lightly over her back, amazed as always how warm and soft she was. Who would have believed that somebody as gentle and feminine as her could literally rip the shirt right off his body? For that matter, he'd never been quite so fired up before, either. He wondered what had triggered it. Was it just the release of so much tension built up over the last few months, or was it something about the planet? Or maybe something about Katata and her kids? If it was some kind of alien hormone, then her kind weren't going to have any trouble fitting in around humans at all.

They were still wide awake half an hour later. Wide awake and hungry. It was about dinnertime by their clock, and the only thing they'd had for lunch had been a sandwich. So they put on fresh clothes, intending to pile into the front of the pickup and drive back downtown to find a likely place to get a burger and a beer, but when Trent opened the passenger door for Donna, he saw all the alien slime still waiting for them.

"Oh, yuck," Donna said, which pretty much summed up how he felt about it, too. He got a shop towel from under the seat and wiped off what he could until it was soaked, then got two more out of the back and he and Donna both wiped off the rest of the goop as best they could. Trent laid out a tarp anyway, so Donna wouldn't get any on her clothes from the stitching in the seat.

"Okay, let's try this again," he said, helping her up into the cab again. Then he went around to his side and climbed in himself, flipped on the lights, and headed back down the dirt street toward downtown.

There was less activity now than when they had driven through on the way to the hospital, but a couple of bars were still open. They were right across the street from one another, so Trent parked in front of the one on the right since it had an open spot handy. There were maybe half a dozen vehicles on each side of the street, and he noted with satisfaction that all of them were electric. That made a certain amount of sense when he thought about it: you couldn't very well take a gas rig into space. Every liquid from the fuel to the crankcase oil to the transmission fluid would boil off into vacuum within a few minutes of exposure, and even if you did manage to seal everything up somehow, there wouldn't be any gas stations where you were going. There weren't necessarily electric generating stations on every planet, either, but any place with a settlement would have at least a wind turbine or a bank of solar cells. Onnescu obviously had more than that; there were street lights at every corner, and the bars had neon signs in the windows.

Most of the buildings were built of peeled logs, the cracks between them sealed with quarter-rounds of smaller logs nailed into place. They hadn't been painted, but they looked almost white in the streetlight; evidently the local trees had pretty pale wood. There was a boardwalk alongside the buildings so pedestrians didn't have to step in the mud. Trent had parked in front of a land office, and there was a hardware store next to that, and then the bar. By the laughter and music coming from inside, someone inside was having quite a party. Trent took Donna's hand in his and said, "It looks safe enough, but if there's trouble, we're gettin' out fast, okay?"

"Okay."

Trent pushed open the swinging doors—just like an Old West saloon—and they stepped in. He had half expected the whole place to go quiet, but only a couple of people even noticed them, and they just smiled and waved.

All of the activity seemed to be centered around three or four tables that had been pushed together in the middle of the room, where everyone watched a gray-haired guy with a thin face and a big nose stretch a wide rubber band back toward his chest as if he were about to shoot it at someone. He let fly, but the rubber band didn't go anywhere. Something about the size of a BB did, though: it bounced off a beer mug across the table from the shooter and ricocheted straight at Trent's head. Trent ducked just in time, and heard it whack the top of his hat before it rattled off toward the bar.

Now everybody went quiet.

Trent didn't really like being the center of attention of a bunch of strangers, but he figured since he was already there, he might as well make the most of it. He reeled back a step and said, "I been shot!"

"Lord, call the medic," said the gray-haired guy.

"He's busy with a family of aliens," Trent said. He took off his hat and inspected it for damage, but he couldn't even find a dent. "Guess I'll live."

"Good. I'd hate to have my last night on the planet marred by a murder. Pull up a stump, and have a beer on me."

Trent glanced at Donna, who shrugged and said, "Sure, why not?" so they snagged a couple of chairs from a vacant table and the gray-haired guy's friends scooted around so there was room at his table for them. There were seven or eight other men, mostly Trent's age or younger, five or six women about the same age, and two aliens. They were about a foot taller than the humans, with dark red skin mottled with black, and thin as rails. They had two arms each, though, build pretty much like a person's, and their heads were close enough to normal that they could probably pass for human on a dark night. They had beer mugs in front of them like everyone else, and nobody seemed to be paying them any special attention, so Trent just nodded to them along with everyone else and sat down. After an evening with Katata and her brood, these guys seemed perfectly normal.

The gray-haired guy hollered something in what sounded like Spanish to the bartender, then held out his hand to Trent and said, "Name's Nick."

"Trent Stinson," Trent said. "This here's Donna."

"Pleased to meet you both. This is Glory." He gave the woman to his left a squeeze. She was maybe half his age, blonde, buxom, and smiling like a lottery winner. Trent guessed she'd had three or four pints of beer besides the half-empty one in front of her.

One of the guys across the table from Trent said, "You're the Trent and Donna that brought the aliens in to the hospital?"

"That's right." His voice sounded familiar. "You're Greg, aren't you?"

"Yeah. Hey, that was a stand-up thing you did."

Trent shrugged. "Actually, it was mostly sittin' down and drivin'. Thanks for talkin' us in."

Greg laughed. "Hah! If sittin' and talkin' can help people out, I guess we're in good shape around here! So how's the kid?"

"Broken bone about halfway down one tentacle," Trent said. "Doctor Chen put a cast on it, but he wants to keep her overnight to make sure it'll be okay."

"Good man," Nick said. "I'll miss him."

"That's an understatement," Greg said. "First time *you* get a broken bone, you're gonna do more than miss him."

Donna said, "You're moving?"

"Yep. Glory and I are going to find a planet of our very own. One that's not likely to be found by anyone else for a long, long, time. Then we're going to settle down and do the Adam and Eve thing."

"The Adam and Eve thing?" Trent asked.

"Live by ourselves," Nick said. "Raise a family. Start our own civilization from scratch, with our own legends and our own beliefs."

Donna frowned. "You mean just the two of you?"

"Yep."

"But . . . your kids would have to . . . have kids with each other."

"Yep," Nick said. "That ought to give evolution a good kick-start. I bet they'll adapt to the planet inside a couple dozen generations."

Trent figured that was just about the stupidest thing he

had heard all day, and was trying to figure out a diplomatic way to say so when the bartender came over and set a couple pints of beer in front of him and Donna, plus a big bowl of popcorn.

"Any chance of gettin' something serious to eat this time of night?" Trent asked.

"Sorry, no hablo inglés," the bartender said.

"Kitchen's closed anyway," said Nick. "But there's plenty of popcorn."

"Oh. Well, thanks." Trent shrugged. They could get some real food when they got back to the camper.

When the bartender left, the woman next to Greg said, "We've been trying to talk Nick and Glory out of it all night, but they're committed."

"Ought to *be* committed," Greg said.

Nick laughed. "You aren't the first person to say that! My neighbors back on Earth thought so, too, when I told 'em I was coming out here, but now look at this place. I might as well have moved to Los Angeles."

Trent tried his beer. It was considerably thicker than Bud, but it actually tasted pretty good. He took a handful of popcorn and settled back in his chair, trying not to look too much like he was starving.

"How do you plan to keep from being discovered?" he asked. "From what I hear, about a third of the planets a person can live on are already inhabited. And humans aren't the only ones lookin' for new real estate." He nodded toward the two aliens at their table.

"There are four hundred billion stars in the Milky Way alone," Nick said. "Even if every third one is already spoken for, that's still a lot of places to go. And the Milky Way isn't the only galaxy, either."

"You're going to a completely different *galaxy*?"

"We might."

Glory shook her head. "I don't think so. The velocity difference on that scale is huge. We'd be days just matching speed with the local stars. For that matter there's the rotation of the galaxy to consider even if we stay right here in the Milky Way. The farther we go, the more the relative difference in velocity."

"Oh," Nick said.

Oh indeed, Trent thought. He could almost hear the rush of air as his first impression of Glory flew out the window. "You, uh, know orbital mechanics?" he asked.

"No, we're just acquaintances," she said. She winked at Trent, and he felt himself blushing.

Donna said, "How does that work, about things moving faster the farther you go?"

Glory thought about the question for a second, then stuck her finger in her beer and swirled it. "The galaxy spins kind of like that," she said. "We're about two-thirds of the way out from the middle, moving along with everything else. If we're here—" she pointed to a spot near the handle of the mug "—then our vector is aimed toward Greg. But if we jump over here—" she pointed to a spot halfway around the mug "—everything else is moving *away* from Greg at the same velocity. So we have to kill twice our galactic orbital velocity to match speed with the stars in that region of space. That's a worst-case scenario, but even if we just jump halfway around, everything's going sideways. We'd have to change 1.4 times our orbital velocity to match the stars in this region of space."

"How much velocity are we talking about?" Donna asked.

"Quite a bit. The galaxy rotates about once every quarter of a billion years, and we're about thirty thousand light-years out from the center, so we're moving about half a million miles per hour. That's about thirty times the velocity of a satellite in low orbit around a planet."

Trent hoped she hadn't just calculated those numbers in her head. He was feeling dumb enough as it was; if she could do math like that on the fly, he didn't want to know.

Donna seemed to be following her, though. "Holy cow," Donna said. "No wonder you don't hear of colonies more than a couple of hundred light-years away."

"Actually," said Glory, "It takes a few thousand for the difference to really become a problem. The biggest reason people don't go farther is because our star maps aren't that good. Until we got the hyperdrive, we couldn't measure interstellar distances all that accurately beyond a hundred light-years or so."

Trent wondered what she did for a living. Astronomer, maybe? Whatever it was, he bet she wouldn't be doing much of it playing Adam and Eve with Nick.

"How far back to basics do you plan to go when you settle on your hideway planet?" he asked.

"That'll be part of the experiment," Nick said. "We'll take what we can carry in one load—mostly tools and books and stuff—and we'll teach our kids everything we know, but the tools won't last forever, or the books, either. It'll pretty much depend on memory after the first couple of generations."

"And condoms," Greg said, and everybody laughed.

Trent looked over at Donna to see if she understood what was so funny, but she shrugged and shook her head. "We're missing the joke," Trent said.

"Nick was showing us how to make a slingshot with a wedding ring and a condom when you walked in."

Nick held up what Trent had thought was a rubber band. Now he could see that it was indeed a condom.

Nick said, "Unlubricated ones work best. What you do is, you poke the open end of the condom through the ring, then fold it back over the ring so you've got a stretchy pocket that's held open in front. Drop a piece of gravel, or in this case a popcorn granny, down inside . . ." He did that. "Hold the ring tight between your fingers, stretch the end with the granny back to your nose, aim, and fire." He let go and the condom flapped forward just like a regular slingshot. The granny pinged off the same beer mug as before, and zinged off toward the back of the bar.

"Use a thumb ring and a rock, and you can kill a chicken with it," Nick said.

"You're going to teach your kids to hunt chickens with a condom and a ring?" Trent asked.

"I'm going to teach them to hunt chickens with their brains," Nick replied. "We'll eventually run out of condoms and rings, but brains will be the one resource that'll grow exponentially."

"If you don't freeze to death the first winter."

Nick pocketed the condom and slipped the ring on his finger. "We'll settle in the tropics. We've got just as good a chance of making it as anybody. Probably better."

One of the aliens said something in a soft voice that sounded like it was coming from the other end of a long concrete culvert. A second behind him, a louder synthetic voice spoke from the pendant hanging by a silver chain around his neck. "Nick makes very much sense. He and Glory will provide backup for all of you when other colonies fail."

It took Trent a second to puzzle out what he meant. "Doesn't look like this place is in a whole lot of trouble," he said.

"Not today," the alien replied. "But war comes soon. Earth likes not uncontrolled colonies. What it can't control, it will kill."

"It's too late for that," Trent said. "There's already too many colonies for anybody to stop 'em all."

"Tell that to the United States," said Nick. "They've been threatening us since day one, and they're threatening everybody else they can find, too. Any colony that tries to recruit enough people to make a go of it the civilized way winds up on their watch list, and if you let a Frenchman or an Arab or a Korean move in, or if you try a form of government other than a dictatorship under one of *their* chosen puppets, boom, you're on their shit list. Economic sanctions, embargoes, shows of force. You haven't lived until you've been buzzed by an F-16. They haven't started bombing yet, but how long do you suppose that'll last?"

Trent took another swig of his beer. "The Galactic Federation won't let them bomb—"

"The Galactic Federation won't do a damned thing. It's no more able to stop them than the UN could stop them from walking all over the Middle East twenty years ago. There's at least seventy members in the Federation, and half of them would love to see humanity blow itself up. They're not going to stop it; hell, they'd probably egg 'em on if they thought they needed to." He looked at Trent and Donna for a long moment, then said, "Sorry if I've offended you, but I was an American, too, until five months ago, and it was the government's belligerent foreign policy that made me leave. That and the way they lied to us about damn near everything they did."

Trent felt like he should defend his country, but if what Nick was describing was true, it didn't sound like there was much defense. And sad as he was to hear it, it fit with what he'd seen back home.

Donna said, "If you left five months ago, then you must have been one of the first ones here."

Everyone at the table laughed. "The very first," Nick said. "My full name is Nicholas Onnescu."

"Oh," said Donna. "And you're going to leave the planet that's named after you?"

Nick nodded solemnly. "Believe me, it's not a decision I made lightly. I would love to stay here and watch it grow into something wonderful, but I don't see that happening. Eventually the U.S. is going to decide we're a threat, and that'll be the end of it. I don't want to stay just to watch it all go up in flames when the war starts."

"What about you guys?" Donna asked the others. "You're not all bailing out, are you?"

Greg said, "Not me. At least not yet. I haven't been convinced that it's hopeless. For one thing, we're inviting as many aliens to move in as we can, so it's not just a human conflict. That might move the Federation to intervene if the U.S. tries anything, and with any luck the U.S. won't risk it in the first place once they realize they'll be starting a war with more than just other humans."

Trent looked over at the two aliens. "How do you guys feel about that?"

The same one who had spoken before said, "Exchanges of hostage may work, but even if not, we must do this to repay for damage we did long ago."

"Damage to who?"

"Humanity."

Trent laughed. "Can't have been too long ago. We just got into space a few months back."

The alien said, "We were in space long before. We traveled the slow way, spending many years between stars. We came to Earth when your species was still young. Very amusing was your science. Anything not understood was work of God. So we became God. Worked miracles, took offerings, then went away. Never thought people would continue to worship us after we left. Now we find you again, and we see how belief grew, how it fights with science, how it makes you fight with each other. We never intended such things. Never understood danger until now, but damage already is."

These guys were on Earth thousands of years ago? Trent said, "You're trying to tell me you're responsible for religion?"

"Belief was already there," the alien answered. "But we made it stronger."

Trent took a long pull on his beer. What was he supposed to say to that?

Donna saved him the trouble. "How many other species have religion?" she asked.

The alien shook his head. "No others we meet."

"None?"

"Zero."

Nick laughed softly. "None of the hundred or so intelligent races that we've discovered so far have religion. Kinda makes you wonder, don't it? Are we special, or are we just, well, special?"

Trent knew which way he felt at the moment. These aliens' ancestors must have had quite a laugh when they stumbled across humanity. A whole race that believed in imaginary beings, who fought wars over whose imaginary beings were stronger. The temptation to take advantage of that must have been too strong to resist. He looked at the two aliens sitting at the table with him, with their red skin and gaunt features. Was it just coincidence that they looked like comic-book devils, or had some of the people who passed along the legend to their children known what was going on?

There was a long silence at the table, then Nick snorted and said, "Well, we've sure been a ray of sunshine for you two, haven't we? I never even asked what brings you here. The boundless opportunity of a frontier planet, I assume?"

Trent shrugged. "It's about half job hunt, half vacation. We were thinkin' about relocating if we found the right place, but after that little pep talk of yours, I don't know if that's such a smart idea."

"Earth's no safer than anywhere else," Nick said. "Maybe less. The U.S. is used to keeping its wars at arm's length, but this time one's going to wind up right in their laps. Anybody with a hyperdrive can drop a fast rock on a city, and they'll do it if the U.S. pushes 'em too far."

"Yeah." Trent wondered how many of the terrorist attacks in the last few months had been from colonies trying to shake off the iron fist. The government had blamed them all on the French and the Arabs, who had been fighting U.S. domination for decades, but that wasn't necessarily the whole story.

"Your best bet is to look for something farther out, even if you do have to spend a day or two changing velocity," said Nick. "There's a limit to how thin the U.S. can stretch itself."

There was a limit to how thin *humanity* could stretch itself, too. Trent wasn't a city boy, but he didn't want to be a hermit, either. Or a farmer. He wanted to buy his groceries in a store, and when he lost a wheel motor in his truck, he wanted to be able to buy a new one without going halfway across the galaxy to do it. And when it came right down to it, he wanted his neighbors to be human beings.

He didn't say any of that, not with Nick and Glory headed off to play Adam and Eve, and with two aliens at the table. He just dug another handful of popcorn out of the bowl, washed it down with the last of his beer, and said to Donna, "It's gettin' kinda late. You 'bout ready to hit the sack?"

It wasn't all that late, Rock Springs time, but she got the hint. "Yeah, that sounds pretty good," she said. She finished up her own beer, and the two of them stood up.

"Well," Trent said, "It's been a pleasure meetin' all of you. Nick, Glory, good luck to you wherever you wind up. And Greg, thanks again for talkin' us in."

"Any time," Greg said. "You going to stick around for a while?"

"Don't know yet. If the alien kid's doing okay in the morning, we'll probably have to take the family back home tomorrow. That's a long ways into the sticks, and a long ways back if we decide to drive it. We may just take off for another planet once we get out there. We wanted to see as many different places as we could before we have to go home."

Greg nodded. "I understand. Drop by the dispatch office before you leave. I might have a courier job for you if you're interested."

"Carryin' what?"

"We can talk tomorrow."

"Right." He obviously didn't want to say anything more in a bar full of people. "Where's the dispatch office?"

"Two blocks down and a block to your left." He pointed. "It's the building with the radar dish on top."

"That ought to be easy enough to spot."

"It is."

"See you later, then." Trent took Donna's hand in his and they went out into the night.

The air was cooling off. Trent looked up at the starry sky before he got into the pickup. Except for Orion and Cassiopeia, the constellations looked just the same here as they did back home. The Big Dipper wasn't in the north, though. At least Trent didn't think it was. Without the sun to help him, he suddenly realized he had no sense of direction here. In more ways than one.

"What next?" he asked.

Donna said, "You know, I actually could just climb into bed and read for a while."

Reading was a sure-fire way to put Trent to sleep, but he supposed that might not be such a bad idea. Morning would be along in just a few hours, and Katata and her kids would probably be eager to get back to the rest of their family as soon as they could.

"Sounds good to me," he said. They walked down the boardwalk to their pickup, but when they climbed inside and closed the doors, he laughed and said, "I just realized we don't have a good place to park for the night."

"We could just drive out of town a ways."

"We could, but we'd probably wind up in somebody's driveway or something."

Donna thought for a moment, then said, "Actually, the best place is probably right back at the hospital. That way if Katata gets a little jumpy being in a strange place all by herself, she can at least look out the window and see that we haven't abandoned her."

"Now that's smart." Trent backed out onto the street and headed back the way they had come. Spending the night in a hospital parking lot wasn't exactly how he'd imagined their first night on Onnescu, but he supposed it could be worse. Given their landing today, they could easily be the ones inside the hospital.

He parked close to the building. While Donna went into the camper to make the bed, he went around to the emergency entrance to see how Talana was doing and find out if he could plug in and recharge the pickup's batteries, but the lights were out and the door was locked. There was a big red button beside the door with a sign beside it that said "Ring for service" in about a dozen languages, but Trent didn't think Dr. Chen would like to be dragged out of bed just to say "Sure, you can plug in."

Trent decided he could pay the hospital a few dollars for the charge if it wasn't okay, so he went back around the side of the building and searched along the wall until he found a power socket, but it wasn't shaped right.

"Damn," he muttered. This was getting ridiculous. Half the people on the planet didn't speak English, and they didn't even use standard power plugs. Was this what all the colonies were going to be like?

As Trent had expected, Katata was up and ready to go at the crack of dawn. Dr. Chen had given Talana one more checkup and decided she—he had apparently decided his patient was female and her younger sibling was male—was probably going to heal, so there was no reason to hold her any longer, and every reason to get back to make sure Katata's mate, Magalak, was okay.

They stopped at the dispatch office on their way through town. Greg was right: it was easy to spot. The radar dish was only a few feet across, and it looked like it was made out of rabbit wire bent into a bowl, but it was the only parabolic reflector in town, and it called even more attention to itself with its constant circling. It squeaked as it turned, too.

Donna and the aliens stayed in the truck while Trent went in to talk to Greg. They had spread a tarp over the seat this time, and Donna had worn some old clothes, so she didn't mind too much, and Trent was glad to have her there to keep Dixit from messing with things he shouldn't. Trent had taken the pistol out of the glove box and put it in the camper last night, and he'd tucked the rifle behind the seat, but who knew what other mischief a baby could get into, even with its mother right there.

Greg met him at the door. "So you're taking off today?"

Trent nodded. "Yep. Provided we can get a recharge somewhere. We used up a lot of juice doing all that driving yesterday."

"Of course," Greg said. "You can plug in while we're

talking." He showed Trent the outlet closest to where he had parked, but it was the same as the hospital's.

"You got an adapter?" Trent asked.

"Adapter? Oh, that's right, you're using American, and all our stuff's from Australia. Just a sec." He went inside, and a moment later came out with the right plug.

"Is it one-ten, or two-twenty?" Trent asked.

"Two-forty, actually. Will your charger work with that?"

"I don't know. Let's see." He opened the hood and looked at the label on the power distribution unit, which wasn't very helpful, but there was a slider switch in the back that had "115" showing through the window. Trent got a thumbnail on it and shoved it the other way, and sure enough, it said "230." "That ought to be close enough," he said. He pulled the cord out of its reel above the bumper and plugged it in.

"We got juice?" he asked Donna.

She looked at the dash light. "Says we're charging."

"All right. Don't let me forget to set that back to normal when we get home."

"Right."

"And we might as well top off the air tanks while we're plugged in," he said.

"Good idea." She flipped the switch, and the compressor started up.

Trent turned back to Greg. "So what kind of stuff do you want hauled, and where's it going?"

"Mail," Greg said. "And the destination, well, that's the tricky part. It's a French colony." He led the way inside, while Trent tried to decide whether or not he was joking.

"I'm an American," Trent said at last. "They'll shoot us on sight."

"Not if you have the right password."

The inside of the building was divided into four rooms. Greg led him into the one in back on the left. It looked like a control room at NASA or something; there was a big desk with at least a dozen computer monitors surrounding the command chair, and there was a stack of short-wave radio transceivers off to the side. There were half a dozen conversations going on at once, turned down low, but still audible. One of the monitors showed the steady circling of the radar dish, and several specks of light flared as the refresh line swept over them.

Trent whistled softly. "I had no idea you were this high-tech."

Greg laughed. "The computers and radios were bought used in Korea, and the radar is made from a microwave oven."

"An oven?"

"A magnetron's a magnetron. As long as it broadcasts microwaves, that's all you need. And a dish to pick up the reflections." He sat in the chair and pointed at the screen. "We've got nine incoming commuters this morning. There's usually ten, but Sergei's out with the flu."

"That's pretty good radar if it can tell you that."

Greg grinned. "We subversives have our ways. So would you take a bag of mail to a French colony?"

There was an extra chair beside the desk. Trent spun it around and sat on it backwards. "What happened to your regular courier?"

"He's out with the flu."

"Ah. And what makes you so sure you can trust me? I am an American, after all."

"So was I, until I moved here. We're not all a bunch of warmongering imperialists. You went to a lot of trouble to help somebody yesterday, and you're going to a lot more trouble to help them again today. Plus you're out here looking for work, despite your government trying to keep you locked away at home. Not your typical party-line American."

"I could be a spy, settin' you up to trust me."

"You could. In which case, you'll get to read a lot of

letters to friends and family. Just make sure you put them back in the right envelopes before you deliver them."

Trent took a deep breath. A French colony. All his life, he'd been told that the French were stuck-up, hateful, anti-American bastards who opposed anything the U.S. did just out of spite. He didn't believe that any more than he believed that all Arabs were terrorists, but a lifetime of indoctrination hadn't exactly left him a Frog-lover, either. And he suspected the feeling was mutual.

"So we just pop into orbit, give them the password, and they welcome us with open arms?" he asked.

"Your contact does. You probably won't see anyone else."

"And if we do?"

"Say 'bonjour.'"

"Yeah, right." He could imagine how that would play out. "Are we supposed to bring a mail sack back here?"

"Normally, yes, but I doubt if they'll trust you that far."

Trent ran his fingers through his beard. "But you think they'll let us go once we know where the colony is?"

"The U.S. already knows where it is. Unfortunately. They've got no secrets anymore."

"Hmm." So they said. Trent watched the little blips descend through the radar screen for a minute, imagining him and Donna as a blip on a French radar screen. What else besides an old microwave oven would be pointed at them?

"How much does this pay?" he asked.

"A hundred bucks Australian. That's about two-forty American. Paid up front, because I trust you."

Two hundred and forty bucks. A day's pay at a decent job. It would be good money for a simple jump and drop, but not nearly enough if anything went wrong. And Trent couldn't legally bring Australian money into the U.S., not since the Australians wound up on the uncooperative nation list. On the other hand, it might be good to have some non-U.S. money while he and Donna were in space. By the sounds of things, being a U.S. citizen outside the U.S. was even less of a good idea than he'd originally thought. And if they still had any cash left when they decided to go home, he supposed they could exchange it in Canada before they crossed the border.

"We just drop off the mail sack and we're free to go," he said. "No questions asked, no shots fired."

Greg nodded. "That's right."

Trent drummed his fingers on the back of the chair. He should go ask Donna what she thought, but he already knew what she would say. A couple of hundred bucks *and* a chance to see a French colony and live to tell about it; of course she would want to go.

"All right," he said. "We'll do it. Where is it, and what's the password?"

Greg wrote down a name and a set of coordinates on a piece of note paper. "The planet is called Mirabelle, and it's probably already in your preset destination list if you've got a recent update of your navigation software, but here's the coordinates in case it's not. Those are relative to here, so don't forget you're already 4.2 light-years from Sol if you use the coordinate system to go anywhere else from there."

Trent made a mental note to tell Donna, even though she would probably already know that.

"When you get there, you'll see a continent shaped like this." Greg drew an elongated bird shape, and made a little circle on the upper back. "Right about here is a big crater, easy to spot from orbit. It's flooded, so it'll look like a perfectly circular lake. You want to land about ninety kilometers to the south of it, at the junction of two major rivers. Land on the east bank. It's a big, grassy plain, so you've got lots of room for error." He drew the rivers, and a squiggly circle for the plain.

"When does the password come in?" asked Trent.

"You'll use two of them, actually. The first one, on channel 8, just before you enter the atmosphere, you say 'Le facteur va attérir,' which means 'the mailman is landing,' and they'll say, 'Quel est le mot de passe,' and you say—"

"Hold on, hold on. You've got to write all that down."

"Sure." Greg jotted the words below the drawing of the continent. They didn't look much like they sounded. "Okay," he said. "Today's password for entry is 'poisson.'"

Trent laughed nervously. "Poison? This is getting more cloak-and-daggerish by the second."

"Actually, poisson means fish."

"As in 'something's fishy here.'"

Greg looked hurt. "It's just a mail drop, I swear. But if you don't want to do it . . ."

"I said we'd do it." Trent took the note and read aloud, "Lee factor va a terrier."

"Spoken like a native."

"Yeah, right." He folded the note and went to stick it in his pocket, but then he remembered that Greg said he'd need two passwords. "I assume the other password is for when we turn over the mailbag to whoever's on the ground?"

"That's right. But this time it's you asking them for the word, so you know you're giving the mail to the right person."

"Makes sense." Trent supposed there were just as many French thieves who would steal a mail shipment as there were any other nationality. "So we say . . ." He opened the note. "We say 'Quel est le mot de passe,' and after they're done laughin' their asses off at our pronunciation, they say what?"

"Chapeau."

"Which means . . . ?"

"Hat."

"So we say 'fish,' and they say 'hat.' Got it. What else do we need to know?"

Greg glanced at his radio rack. "Don't be too talky on the radio. You'll be safe enough while you're still in space, but it'll put them on the spot. They don't like transmitting too much from one point on the ground."

"Why not?"

"It gives the bombs a signal to home in on."

They looked at one another for a few long seconds before Trent said, "Bombs."

"Actually, just rocks coming in at high velocity, but they have about the same effect. The U.S. hits anything that looks like a military installation."

Trent looked around the dispatch office, and felt the hair standing up on the back of his neck. "Like a radar base?"

Greg nodded. "Yeah, like that. This'll be one of the first targets if Nick's right about the future of Alpha Centauri."

"But you don't think he is."

"Not for a while yet. Maybe never, if public opinion back home changes fast enough. But there's a reason the guy with the American voice is running the radios."

Trent supposed there was some sense in that. It was probably a lot easier to bomb somebody who didn't speak your language.

He looked at the map again. "That crater to the north, there. How new is it?"

"About two months."

"And you can see it from orbit?"

Greg nodded. "They were setting up a smelter. Big no-no."

"I guess." Trent stuck the paper in his wallet, and the five orange $20 bills that Greg gave him, wondering what he'd just gotten himself and Donna into. It looked like they'd find out soon enough.

The mailbag was just a big canvas sack about the size of an army duffel, and weighed maybe fifty pounds. Trent laid it on the floor of the camper where it couldn't roll around too much, then he went to the front and unplugged the charger. Donna had already shut off the compressor when the air tanks were full, so they were ready to roll.

The drive back to the aliens' landing site was much more fun in daylight. It was a lot easier to see where they were going, for one thing, and this time they had a chance to look at the scenery, too. The sun was coming in low to their left, lighting up the mountains full on and making them seem like they were towering over the town, even following the pickup out onto the plain. Trees to their right glowed silver in the morning light, and the ones to their left made dark silhouettes with silver halos around their edges. Houses peeked out between them, and little white columns of smoke rose from chimneys as people got up and started their day.

Nobody seemed inclined to try a pantomime conversation with so much to look at, so Donna slotted a disk into the player and everyone bopped and sang along to the music while Trent drove. They angled away from the Firehose, but the river was easy to spot even from a couple miles away. It was a solid wall of vegetation meandering from Bigtown all the way to the horizon. Off in the distance, where the trees blended into a single color, it looked like a piece of Christmas ribbon standing on edge. Every now and then another piece of ribbon would join it, and the Firehose would get wider and taller.

The ground between streams was much more open. People had plowed and planted crops for miles around town, which made Trent glad they had found the road on their way in last night. He could have ripped a long swath through a couple of dozen farms if he had just driven in cross-country.

The only open water was in the irrigation ditches that led from the Firehose to the fields. Trent wondered if the ditches would soon be choked with vegetation, too. It looked like plants here really huddled around water, which meant it must get good and dry in the summertime.

It already felt like summertime, but Trent had no idea what season it really was. Donna could probably figure it out from space just by looking at the way the sunlight hit the planet, and Nick's sweetie, Glory, could probably calculate it from the angle of the Milky Way in the night sky or something, but Trent didn't have a clue. He wondered if Nick had known when he'd landed here.

It was hard to believe those two were really going to play Adam and Eve somewhere. Trent didn't even like camping out for more than a week or so; he couldn't imagine someone living off the land for the rest of their lives. If he were Nick—hell, if he were Glory—he would make damn sure their hyperdrive still worked and their ship still held air for years to come, but they didn't seem concerned about that at all.

Different strokes for different folks, he guessed. A lot of people thought he and Donna were nuts for sticking around Rock Springs, for mostly the same reasons he thought Nick and Glory were nuts. Too rural, nothing to do, no shopping, no culture, no whatever else people who didn't like the place thought was important. They didn't see what it *did* have, the rugged beauty of the rock outcrops, the wide open feel of the high desert, the sense of community you felt when you knew not only the people on both sides of your house but the people on both sides of you in the phone book.

It got pretty dry there in the summer, too. Rock Springs didn't even have as much vegetation in its riverbeds as they had around here on the flats. Of course the rivers were dry most of the year, and it was pretty generous to call Bitter Creek or Killpecker Creek rivers in the first place. And the altitude was enough to make the air seem twice as dry as it actually was, and make your blood as thick as soup to boot. When he thought about it in those terms, nobody in their right mind would pick Rock Springs to settle in, not with so many more hospitable places right there on Earth, but somebody had started a town there a hundred years or so ago, and a lot more somebodies had moved in.

He looked at Onnescu rolling past under his wheels. Little bulb-shaped blue flowers dotted the ground where it hadn't been plowed, and bushes with red branches and purplish-green leaves covered the hillsides. There were even rock outcrops. It was pretty enough, and there were certainly enough wide open spaces to suit just about anybody, but it didn't call to him the way the countryside back home did. It wasn't just the threat of war with the U.S., either, though that certainly put a damper on his enthusiasm. He just wasn't sure if anything would measure up to the place he'd spent his entire life.

He owed it to Donna to give it a shot. She had always wanted to get out of that two-bit mining town and see the world. He laughed quietly to himself when he thought of the next world she would see. A French colony. Who'd have thought?

They found the Greenwall easily enough, and by daylight they could see that it was just the next drainage coming down out of the mountains south of the Firehose. The road led them directly to the ford, but from there they were on their own. Tire tracks led off in several directions, but none of them were clearly from Trent's pickup, and the tracks petered out in just a few hundred yards anyway.

Trent drove up to the top of a hill and pulled to a stop. From up there they could see for miles in every direction, but they couldn't see Katata's landing site, not even when Trent got out the binoculars and scanned the terrain ahead of them.

"Well," he said, "I guess we'll have to do this by dead reckoning. We were camped closer to the mountains by a mile or two, and we headed pretty much south from there, so I think we need to angle that way." He pointed at about a thirty-degree angle toward the mountain from south. "Does that seem right to you?"

"As right as anything," Donna said. "Katata, what do you think?" She pointed out toward the south.

Katata looked out over the rolling hills and writhed her tentacles left and right over the dashboard, like a pair of snakes thinking about striking the windshield. At last she settled on roughly the same direction that Trent had pointed, and said, "Baktataka."

Talana said, "Ti, ti!" and pointed farther to the left. Then of course Dixit spoke up with a squeal and pointed to the right, waving both of his tentacles out the passenger window.

Trent laughed. "Well, if we average everybody out, we're in pretty good agreement." He picked out as much of a route as he could see from the hilltop, then drove down onto flatter ground and tried to follow it from memory.

He climbed another hill every quarter mile or so to keep his bearings. From the fourth one, they could see something glinting in the sun quite a ways to the left of where he thought the landing site should be, but when he checked with the binoculars he could see the silvery parachute hanging from a tree, flapping softly in the morning breeze.

"That's it," he said.

Katata spoke excitedly with her kids, and they squealed in delight.

"Next stop, your new home," Trent said.

That turned out to be overly optimistic. It took a couple more hilltop reconnoiters to correct their path, because Trent kept steering too far to the left. It was all the hills and gulleys in the way; he had to pick a direction around them, and he was always a little off in his guess when he tried to head the same direction on the other side. It had actually been easier navigating by Orion last night.

Katata and her family were a long ways out of town. Twenty miles didn't seem like much on a civilized planet, but out here, without a vehicle, they might as well be doing the Adam and Eve thing. He hoped they could grow and hunt all the food they needed, because there wasn't going to be much grocery shopping in town for them.

At last they topped a rise and saw the parachute and the water-tank spaceship in the grassy meadow below. And now that they had daylight, they could see the stream that ran along the edge of the meadow just a couple hundred yards away.

"You know," Trent said, "You guys picked a decent spot. You just might do okay here."

When they drew closer, they could see that the father and the child who had stayed behind had been busy. A bright yellow tent stood beside the water tank, and the animals had been released from their cages and tethered outside. A corral made of branches from the brush along the stream was about half finished.

The youngster ran out to greet them as they drove up, the yappy mop pet right at his heels. Big, ungainly birds flew up into the air ahead of them, squawking indignantly as they flapped off to the sides and landed again. The father, Magalak, came out from around the side of the tank to see what all the commotion was about, and when he realized who it was he dropped his axe and ran after his son, scaring the birds all over again.

Katata and the kids bounded out of the truck the moment it came to a stop, and everyone leaped together in a big family hug. Tentacles snaked over and around their bodies like ropes, and Katata and Magalak nuzzled their noses into each other's necks like vampires going for the jugular. Magalak lifted Dixit into the air and swung him around, and Talana proudly showed off her cast for all to see. Katata made Magalak hold still while she inspected his head wound, but it must have looked all right to her, because she didn't linger on it. Instead she gave him another squeeze and went for his neck again.

"Well," Trent said, a little embarrassed at watching them smooch it up, "it certainly looks like they're happy to see one another."

He and Donna got out of the truck, and Katata rushed over to them and babbled something full of k's and t's and a's, gripping their hands in her tentacles and tugging them from side to side.

"You're welcome," Trent said, and Donna said, "You'd have done the same for us, I'm sure." Magalak came over and spoke more solemnly, but just as unintelligibly, and Trent and Donna said "You're welcome," half a dozen more times; then Katata said something to Talana and Talana came over and they repeated the whole exchange.

It was rapidly becoming an "Aw, shucks" moment. Trent looked over at Donna and said, "We ought to get going. We've got mail to deliver."

"Yeah, we probably should." To Katata, she said, "We're going to take off now. It was a pleasure to meet you, and I'm glad you're all okay. Next time we're out this way, we'll look you up and see how you're doing."

"Good luck to you," Trent said, reaching out to shake Magalak's tentacle.

Magalak suddenly held up his tentacles and said "Bata-bata!" then rushed back to the tent and emerged with a bottle of green liquid about the size and shape of a two-liter pop bottle. He thrust it into Trent's hands and said, "Tarit! Bogota tarit, boo." He mimed drinking it, then staggered from side to side.

"It's gotta be hootch," Trent said to Donna.

She laughed. "The universal thank-you."

"Must be pretty good stuff, the way he's acting." Trent said to Magalak, "We appreciate the thought. Thank you. We'll, uh, save it for a special occasion."

He and Donna went back to the pickup and folded up the tarp that Katata and the kids had been sitting on, then got their Ziptite suits out of the camper and pulled them over their clothes. Magalak watched for a moment, then suddenly burst into a long speech, pointing over toward the creek as he spoke. He mimed driving over there, then made a "pop" noise and threw his tentacles into the air.

"You want us to take off from over there?" Trent asked. "It'll leave a big crater right beside the creek." Then he realized what Magalak wanted. "A pond! Sure, we can dig you a pond." He repeated Magalak's gestures, then held his hands out in a circle. "How big you want it?" He widened the circle, then made it smaller.

"Taga!" Magalak said, making a big loop with his tentacles. "Bataga!"

Trent laughed. "Okay, one big honkin' reservoir comin' up."

Katata and Magalak and the kids all gave them one more round of squeezes, then they climbed into the pickup's cab and sealed it up. Trent checked the air gauges—full—and the power gauge—down to three-quarters again after the morning's drive—and Donna got the computer out and hooked it up. Trent overpressurized the cab and watched the gauge for a couple of minutes to make sure they didn't have any leaks. When they were sure they were in good shape for space, they waved goodbye to everyone and drove across the meadow toward the spot where Magalak wanted the reservoir.

"How wide should I set the jump field?" Donna asked.

The wider they set it, the more power it would take, especially right on the surface of a planet. And from the sounds of it, they wouldn't have a chance to recharge at their next stop. On the other hand, a puddle wasn't likely to do anybody much good, especially if the summers were dry here the way Trent suspected. "How about thirty feet or so?" he said. "That'll hold quite a bit of water, and it'll still leave us with quite a bit of juice to get around on."

"Thirty feet it is." Donna tapped at the keyboard.

Trent pulled the pickup about twenty feet from the creek. Magalak would have to dig a short ditch to fill his reservoir, but this way it wouldn't wash out or silt up.

The whole family was standing next to their water-tank home, Magalak and Katata with their tentacles wrapped around each other's waists, and the children in stairstep progression beside them. "Onnescu Gothic," Trent said. He waved. The aliens waved back, and Dixit jumped up and down, trying to break free of Talana's grasp and run toward the pickup.

"We better go before he gets loose," Trent said.

"I'm ready any time."

"Then let's do it."

Donna punched the "enter" key, and the planet vanished.

Gravity vanished with it, but a second later the pickup surged upward, pressing them into the seat again. Rocks and dirt flew past the windows, chased by billowing clouds of steam.

"Whoa!" Trent said. "I didn't expect that."

"There must have been a lot of water in the ground right next to the stream," said Donna. "It's all boiling at once."

They watched their soggy dirt bowl break up and blow away, the upward pressure slowly easing as it did. The fog glowed bright white in the sunlight, and the rocks cast long shadows through it.

"This must be what it looks like inside a comet," Donna said.

"Yeah? I thought they were mostly ice."

"Nope. They're full of rocks, too."

The sun was coming in from the right, creating a bright halo on that side of the pickup and an equally bright rainbow on the other. They were going to have to wait a while for it to dissipate before they could get a position fix on the stars.

"I wonder if this'll be visible from the ground tonight?" Trent asked.

"Hmm." Donna squinted her eyes, thinking hard. "We're five hundred thousand K out, which is like three hundred thousand miles, so it would be about . . . I'm guessin' at least a couple thousand miles per degree looking up from the ground, and this might spread to twenty miles or so before it's too thin to reflect much, so that would make it . . . what, a hundredth of a degree wide? I think that's too small to see. What are you smiling at?"

"You're so sexy when you do math."

She blushed. "No wonder you couldn't keep your eyes off Glory last night. And I thought it was just her boobs."

Trent laughed. "I thought I was gonna drop my teeth when she started in with that velocity stuff. Blonde, boobs, and brains. Who knew?"

"Just goes to show you shouldn't judge a book by its cover."

"Yeah," Trent said. "I definitely prefer judging by what goes on under the covers."

Donna gave him a playful whack on the shoulder. "Men," she said.

An empty .45 shell floated up from the floor. Trent snagged it and tried to stick it in his pocket, then remembered he was wearing his Ziptite suit and stuck it in one of the seat cover's pockets instead.

Then he remembered that the pistol was still in the camper. Here they were, a couple of Americans about to land on a French colony, and their pistol was in the back. It might as well be on Earth, unless he wanted to seal up his Ziptite, pop open the door, and go back and get it. He had considered putting a hatch between the cab and the camper, but he'd figured it would be too likely to break the seal when they landed, so he'd left the two compartments separate.

At least the rifle was still behind the seat. That would have to do. Trent unbuckled his seatbelt and twisted around until he could reach it, then stuck it in the gun rack and pulled the bungee straps over it so it wouldn't drift loose.

"Expecting trouble?" Donna asked.

"Just makin' sure I'm ready in case there is any. You ready to make the jump?"

She set the computer in place on the dashboard and brought up the destination menu. "Mirabelle's on the list, so we don't have to use the coordinates, but the computer can't get a lock on the starfield yet."

Trent could just barely see a few of the brightest stars through all the fog and dirt outside. "We may have to jump again just to get out of this," he said.

"You want to?"

"Might as well. Won't cost us much now that we're off the surface. Assuming you've got the jump field tightened up."

"I do."

"Then let's give it a try."

"Okay, another five hundred K." She pushed the "enter" button, and most of the fog vanished.

Now the stars were much clearer, but so was Onnescu. It was a flat ceiling of clouds and ocean just overhead.

"Jesus!" Trent said. "What did you do, hit reverse?"

"We must have tumbled halfway around," she said. "We're still in launch mode, so the drive takes us straight up."

And "up" was right back to Onnescu. That was a little too close for comfort. "Jump us again," Trent said.

She did, and Onnescu blinked out. Now the stars were bright, and only a few rocks had followed them through both jumps.

The pickup was nosing upward, so Trent gave the front air nozzles a burst. The air tank under the seat hissed, two jets of fog shot upward from the front bumper, and the stars steadied out.

"We've got a fix now," Donna said.

"All right, then, let's do it."

"Okay. Loading Mirabelle. Hmm. It's 56.4 light-years away. That's a pretty good jump."

It would be the farthest they'd ever gone, that's for sure. Distance wasn't supposed to matter much to the hyperdrive, but it did to Trent. For a moment he wished they could just go back to Rock Springs and drop the mailbag off at the post office there, but he'd gotten them into this, and the only good way out was to go through with it.

The computer put an arrow in the upper left corner of the screen. Technically you didn't need to be pointing at your destination when you jumped, so long as the computer knew your orientation, but Trent used the jets until it was on the screen anyway.

"Fire when ready," he said.

Donna put her finger over the "enter" key, then looked out the windshield before she pressed it.

There was a definite moment of disorientation, much stronger than before, and the stars changed this time. Trent looked for familiar patterns and didn't see any at first, but then he noticed the belt and sword and left leg of Orion shining just the same as always. The shoulders and the right leg were shifted upward and to the right a bit, but not too bad. Sirius wasn't near the left shoulder anymore.

He looked up to find the dippers, but they weren't there. He saw a string of seven or eight fairly bright stars that might have been the big one, but it was scrunched pretty bad. The Little Dipper was unrecognizable, and so was Cassiopeia, assuming he was even looking in the right patch of sky.

He took a deep breath and said, "That definitely took us somewhere."

Donna nodded. "Yeah. Now we just have to find Mirabelle." She set to work with the computer, and in a few seconds it had crunched its star map until it matched the view outside. "Says we're still a light-year away. I guess that's not too bad for a fifty-light-year jump. Ready to go closer?"

"Do it," Trent said.

They jumped again, and this time a bright star shone in from Donna's side. The computer compared the starfield to its map, and they did the full sky sweep for it, but they had to jump again and let it do another check before it could tell which points of light were stars and which ones were planets.

"According to this, Mirabelle is that one," Donna said,

pointing high to the left. It was just a blob of white like any other star, but when Trent squinted at it he could convince himself that it showed a disk.

One more jump and it was definitely a planet. It was half in shadow and half in light, and none of the continents they could see were shaped like a long bird, so they jumped to the other side and there it was. They didn't see the crater until they jumped to within a few hundred miles, but then it was pretty clear. With binoculars, it was sharp as a tack.

"What's our ground speed?" Trent asked.

"Only eleven thousand kilometers per hour," Donna said. "Heck, that's nothing. Five minutes of correction and we're there. Here goes." She called up the tangential vector translation menu, clicked the crosshairs just a nudge inland from the crater, and hit "go," and they popped partway around the planet to let its gravity cancel their velocity.

They had only been in space for ten minutes or so. At this rate they could probably make it all the way to the ground without needing to refresh their air, but Trent wanted to make sure they were thinking as clearly as possible on their way in, so while they waited for the program to take them back over their landing site, he bled off half their air and refilled it from the tank.

"Might as well see what their beacon says," he said, switching on the CB radio and turning it to channel 1.

The broadcast was in French, of course. They couldn't make out any words at all. Trent switched to channel 2, and they could tell that one was in Spanish, but they couldn't understand it, either. Channel 3 sounded like Russian. There was nothing in English all the way up the dial.

The vector translation program beeped at them, and a few seconds later zapped them back over the crater.

"Okay, we need to get close enough to find where the two rivers join," Donna muttered, tapping at the keys.

"Hold up a sec." Trent used the jets to point the nose of the truck straight down so they could see better.

"Taking us in closer," Donna said, and the view expanded in three distinct jumps. There were clouds over maybe a third of the continent, but they could see a big river running out of a range of mountains into the crater, and another big river joining it a little ways inland, maybe ten times the crater's diameter away.

"There it is."

"Okay." Donna clicked the crosshairs on the computer image of the junction, and the landing program shifted them sideways until they were directly over it. Then it took them down two jumps.

Donna zoomed the computer's view in on the junction between the two rivers. "There's the plain we're supposed to land on," Trent said, tapping the screen. It was more golden than green, but it looked flat where it peeked through the clouds.

"Got it." Donna clicked on that, and the hyperdrive shifted them sideways again. "We're good," she said. "Twenty seconds to zero velocity."

"Oh shit, I need to give 'em the password!" Trent yanked the microphone off its clip and punched channel 8 on the radio, then he realized the paper with the French phrase on it was still in his wallet. And the wallet was inside his Zip-tite suit.

"Damn, damn, damn," he muttered as he peeled the suit down off his shoulders and jammed his hand between the plastic and his pants. He fumbled his wallet out of his hind pocket, tore it open, and grabbed the paper out of it, letting the wallet drift free. Donna caught it on the rebound from the windshield, and Trent turned the paper right-side-up to read, "Lee factor va a terrier. Lee factor va a terrier, over."

The radio hissed for a second, then a heavily accented male voice said, "Who is this?"

"Poisson," Trent read off the note before he realized that that wasn't the response he was supposed to get. Why had they spoken English? "Poisson," he said again, and then just to be sure he said, "Fish."

There was a long silence before the voice said, "Very well, you may land."

“Five seconds to zero velocity,” Donna said. “Three, two, one, zero. Okay, now we’re falling.” Trent frantically worked the air jets to orient the pickup for the drop while she said, “Picking up speed. Fifty, a hundred, two hundred, three.”

The second the pickup was level with the ground, he flipped the parachute release switch, careful to hit just the first one this time. There was a bang from overhead, then a couple more seconds of free fall as the canopy billowed upward, then a hard lurch as it filled out.

Trent waited for the sickening moment of free fall that would mean they’d been fired upon, but it didn’t come. “Get ready on the bugout button,” he said anyway. His heart was beating faster than when they’d landed on the tree.

He wanted to call on the radio to this mysterious person on the ground and find out who they were and why they spoke English, but Greg had cautioned him against too much chatter. He was just going to have to wait until they landed and could talk face-to-face. Assuming the guy who spoke English was the same one they were supposed to hand over the mailbag to.

He stuck his arms inside the Ziptite suit and pulled it up over his shoulders again, then looked out at the planet. There was a big arc of clouds out in front of them; part of a weather front by the looks of it. He leaned up next to the window to see how thick they were directly beneath them, but he couldn’t see straight down.

“Damn it, I forgot to turn the mirrors down again.”

“That’s all right,” Donna said. “When we get down where

the air's breathable, you can do the same trick you did on Onnescu."

"I guess. It just irritates me to be so dumb twice in a row. Makes me wonder what else I've forgot."

"Nothing important, I'm sure." She grinned at him and said, "Don't sweat the small stuff."

"Yeah. There's plenty of big stuff to worry about." He could think of a dozen things right off the top of his head, and most of them didn't even have anything to do with landing in enemy territory. But they were committed now, and everything he could do to ensure their safety had either already been done or it was too late to make any difference, so he tried to relax and admire the view on the way down.

There was no sign of civilization. No town at the river junction, no plumes of smoke from factories or power plants or even from houses as far as they could see, and no tilled fields, either. If there hadn't been radio beacons announcing who lived here, the place would look like an uninhabited planet.

"I wonder if there was anybody here before the French," Trent said.

"I don't know," Donna said. "I never saw any samizdat for Mirabelle."

"Big surprise there."

There was a hell of a mountain range off in the distance. The peaks went on and on, and were mostly covered with snow. Clouds hid some of them from view, while others stuck up clear through the clouds to glisten bright white in the sun. There was forest on the flanks of the front range, but that was the only vegetation above the plains; everything else was ice and rock.

"Looks cold down there," Donna said.

"It does."

As they drew closer to the ground, they began to realize that a lot of what they had originally thought was clouds was actually snow-covered ground. There were still plenty of clouds, though, and it looked like they were going to fall right into a big one. Its billowy top rose up to meet them, looking almost solid in the bright sunlight.

"If there's lightning inside that, we're out of here," Trent said.

"Got it," Donna said, resting her hand on the dashboard near the computer.

When they hit, the change was instantaneous. The world suddenly went totally white, then rapidly darkened to gray. Streaks of moisture beaded up on the windshield, and the truck jounced up and down as the cloud's internal winds buffeted the parachute. Trent craned his neck to see if the canopy was staying open in the turbulence, but all he could see were the shroud lines disappearing into the fog.

"Hope this doesn't go all the way to the ground," he said.

"It won't."

He wished he had Donna's confidence. He could easily imagine them coming down on one of those cloud-covered mountain peaks and tumbling all the way to the bottom. It had looked like level ground beneath them when they had picked their landing site, but who could say what was hidden inside the clouds? You could find single mountains off by themselves in various places on Earth; why not here?

He had just about convinced himself they should jump back into space when they fell out the bottom of the cloud and saw the ground laid out below them, still a mile or two away. Trent took a deep breath and let it out slowly.

They were spinning around about once every fifteen seconds or so, which gave them a good view of the countryside, but there wasn't much to see. The ground was mottled yellow-white and flat as a pancake for miles around. When they got closer, they could see big puffs of yellow grass waving in the breeze, sticking up between snowdrifts that ran in parallel lines like frozen ocean waves.

"It's definitely cold down there," Donna said.

"The wind's blowing, too." The grass clumps were all

bent to the side and bobbing up and down, and snow swirled off the tops of the drifts. It was hard to tell how fast it was blowing, but if the parachute didn't collapse when they hit the ground, it could drag them sideways halfway across the continent. If they didn't have a sack of mail to deliver, Trent would have bailed out of this landing, but he had to at least give it a try.

There was no sense opening the door to look down. They could see what they were going to hit way out in front of them. Trent just made sure he and Donna were belted in tight and grabbed the steering wheel to brace himself.

The final hundred feet or so seemed to take forever, but when they hit, it felt like they had come in without a chute at all. The truck lurched up and sideways, and a huge cloud of snow billowed up around them, completely blinding them for a second before it swirled away. Trent felt the pickup tipping to the right, so he goosed the motors and cranked the wheels into the tilt and brought it upright again, but when he let off the juice the pickup kept rolling. It bounded up over a snowdrift, caught air for a second, then plowed nose-first into the next drift, throwing up another big cloud of snow.

"The chute's draggin' us!" Trent growled. He concentrated on steering, hoping that the fabric would catch in a clump of grass, but when they plowed through four more snowbanks without slowing, he decided to change tactics. The shroud lines stretched out straight ahead of them, but they slacked up for a second when the pickup crested a snowbank, which meant the wind wasn't blowing much faster than they were moving.

"Hang on!" he said, and he tromped the juice pedal. The wheels spun for a second, and the uneven power to three wheels made the truck slew around sideways, but he turned into the slide and brought it back straight before they went over. And now the shroud lines were on the ground. He aimed for them, driving right over the top of them and running up their length until he drove right onto the parachute canopy. He braked to a stop while he was still on top of it, and cloth billowed up around them, flapping like mad now that it was pinned down, but it couldn't inflate with the pickup sitting astride it.

"Can I breathe now?" Donna asked.

"I think so." Trent set the brake and waited to see if it would hold. The pickup lurched back and forth as the parachute tugged on it, but there wasn't enough cloth free to drag it anymore.

The radio crackled to life. "Mon dieu! Etes vous—are you all right?"

Trent picked up the microphone. "I think so. I don't dare move until we get the chute folded up, though, or it'll drag us to hell and gone again."

"Stay right there. I will be there in several minutes to help."

"Roger. Thanks." Trent popped the latches on his door and cautiously opened it, expecting the wind to snatch it out of his hands, but it wasn't blowing all that hard. Maybe fifteen or twenty miles an hour was all. There was just a hell of a lot of surface area on the parachute.

There was a lot of surface area on his hat, too. He felt it lift up, but he grabbed it before it could go anywhere and set it on the back of the seat.

He stepped outside. The air swirled down the open neck of his Ziptite and bit right through his shirt. "Jesus," he said, "It's colder'n a witch's tit out here. Let me get our coats."

Donna laughed. "How cold?"

"Very fucking cold!" Trent yelled as he closed his door and fought his way through the billowing parachute to the camper. He had to watch his footing in the snow; the Ziptite suit's plastic feet were slick as skis. The chute had wrapped itself around the whole back end of the pickup, so he had to pull it away from the camper and cram it under the truck so he could get to the door, but that actually helped cut down on the amount of it catching the wind. He popped open the door and leaned in just far enough to open the storage compartment with their sleeping bags and other cold-weather gear in it, dragged out his own coat and put it on right over his Ziptite, then grabbed Donna's coat and went back around to the cab and handed it in to her.

While she was putting it on, he went back to look at the parachute and see how they could fold it up without it getting away from them, but he would have to drive off it to even begin to fold it properly, and there was just too much wind for that.

He looked at the situation for a few seconds, his ears growing steadily colder until he pulled his stocking cap out of his pocket and tugged it down over his head. "Welcome to the Riviera," he muttered.

The cloth at his feet was wedged up against the tires. Trent grabbed a handful of it and wadded it up in his arms, tugging more and more of what wasn't actually under the wheels from beneath the pickup until he had all the free cloth he could get in his hands. Maybe he could tie it up with a rope or something, and then drive off of the rest of it and do the same to that? Or . . . yeah. He got one arm around the ball of parachute cloth, opened the camper door with his other hand, and shoved the cloth in through the door.

"Drive forward a few feet!" he yelled.

Donna popped open her door. "What?"

"Drive forward a few feet. I'm gonna pull the parachute loose a little at a time and shove it inside the camper."

"Oh . . . okay." She closed her door, then a few seconds later the pickup rolled forward.

"That's good!" Trent slapped the side of the truck and she stopped while he gathered up more parachute, then he had her drive forward again and gathered some more until he finally got it all inside the camper. The shroud lines were a tangled mess, and there was no way he or Donna were going to fit in the camper themselves until they got the chute folded up and stowed in its proper place, but at least they wouldn't get dragged downwind anymore.

He climbed up on top of the pickup and unbuckled the shroud lines so he could shove the whole works inside the camper. While he was up there, he spotted motion far out across the plain. A big cloud of snow was approaching from the side.

"Company's coming," he shouted down to Donna.

"I see them."

Trent tossed the shroud lines to the ground and closed the empty parachute cover, then shoved the last of the lines in the camper along with everything else and slammed the door on the whole works. He hurried around to the cab again and climbed in, grateful for the warmth and still air inside.

Donna took his hands in hers. "Man, your fingers are like icicles."

"They'll be all right." He released the brake and goosed the truck forward, turning toward the oncoming cloud of snow. Whoever was out there, he wanted it clear that he had taken care of his own parachute.

Donna had left the computer on the dashboard, and Trent could see that the emergency bugout screen was still active. One keystroke would take them out of a bad situation, but unless they were about to die it would send them into an even worse one, because the door latches weren't tight. He and Donna could probably seal up their Ziptites before they passed out from lack of oxygen, but he didn't want to try it.

They could at least improve their odds. "Snug up your door," he told her. He reached over his left arm with his right and did his own latches while he drove. Then he reached behind his head and undid the bungees holding the rifle down. Donna gave him a funny look, but she did her door, too.

They looked ridiculous with their winter coats over their spacesuits, but Trent didn't care. It was a hell of a lot warmer that way than with either coat or suit alone, and with any luck they wouldn't have to stay bundled up for long. He did make one concession to appearances, swapping his stocking cap for his cowboy hat. Nothing said "Don't mess with me" quite as well as a black Stetson.

The oncoming vehicle was painted white. They were almost on it before they saw it at the head of its plume of snow. Trent veered to the right, intending to pull up alongside it and talk with the driver window-to-window, but the other driver veered the same way.

"Look out, idiot!" Trent muttered, swerving the other way, but the other driver did the same thing and they wound up aimed head-on again. They both hit the brakes and skidded to a stop with just feet to spare. Trent was working up a good rant about lunatic Frogs, but then he realized that the other driver was facing him from the same side of his vehicle and he burst out laughing instead.

"The French drive on the left!" he said. They hadn't always, but the anti-American sentiment in Europe had changed many things.

He wasn't about to make Donna do the talking, not when he'd been the one to get them into this situation, so he shifted into reverse and cranked the wheels hard left, spinning the pickup around practically in its own length, then he backed up until he was even with the other truck.

The other driver was laughing, too. He was bundled up in a white coat and white stocking hat, and he had a big beard to rival Trent's, except that was mostly white, too. He waited for Trent to unlatch his inner window and remove it, then roll down his outer window; then he rolled down his own and called out across the three-foot gap between their vehicles, "Bonjour! Welcome to Mirabelle."

If Trent had ever doubted the need to jack up his pickup's suspension as high as he had, the last shred of doubt vanished in that moment. The Frenchman's vehicle looked like a military troop transport or something, with big tractor tires and a blunt, boxy body with an articulated frame, but Trent was able to look the driver straight in the eye and say, "Thanks. We've got your mail sack in back."

The other man nodded, then simply looked at Trent, clearly expecting him to say something more. Trent couldn't think what it might be, but Donna whispered, "The password," just as the Frenchman said, his accent making the words almost comical, "That's a verra nice chapeau you have there."

"Right," Trent said, slapping himself on the forehead below the hat's brim. "Man, I'd forget my head today if it wasn't attached. Sorry about that."

The Frenchman laughed again. "De rien. You no doubt have many things on your mind at the moment. This is most unusual for us both, eh? How is it that an American brings our mail?"

"Sergei has the flu, and we were headed out this morning, so Greg asked us if we would make a side-trip long enough to drop it off."

"I see. Eh bien, he must have his reasons to trust you, and here you are with the mail after all, so that trust was not injustifié. Do you wish to transfer the mail here, or would you like to go somewhere a bit less exposed?"

Trent wondered if he meant that in terms of weather or strategically, but either way the answer was the same. "Let's get out of this wind. I've got my parachute balled up in the camper, and it'd be a damned sight easier to fold up if it wasn't flappin' all over the place."

The Frenchman nodded. "Yes, no doubt it would. Come, then, I will lead you to my sanctuary. It's only a few kilometers from here. Perhaps you would have time to take déjeuner—the lunch—with me? I seldom have the chance to practice my English with a native speaker."

"Well . . ." Trent said, but Donna leaned over before he could say anything more and said, "We'd love to."

The Frenchman smiled wide. "Ah chère madame, you will not have the regrets! Follow me!" He rolled up his window and pulled forward, swinging around to the left and heading back the way he had come. Trent hit the juice to follow, discovered the embarrassing way that he was still in reverse, then shifted into forward and took off after him.

"Lunch?" he asked Donna as they bounded through the snowdrifts after the Frenchman.

"It sounds like fun. Who else do you know who can say they've had lunch with a French person?"

"Nobody," Trent said, "And that includes us if we want to stay out of jail. It may be just lunch out here, but back home it's fraternizing with the enemy."

"Fraternizing," she said, and she laughed. "A French word. I'd love to see them charge us with that."

"No you wouldn't," Trent said, but he couldn't help smiling. If anybody could make the court look ridiculous over a single word, it would be Donna.

Big clouds of snow billowed up behind the other vehicle. Trent had to hang back to keep from getting blinded by it. "I wonder why they settled here?" he said. "They have the whole planet to choose from. You'd think they would pick someplace warmer."

"It probably was warmer when they chose it," Donna said. "Seasons change. And some people like winter."

That was true enough. Trent didn't mind it himself, but he appreciated easing into it a little more gradually, preferably after a long, hot summer. He'd just endured a long winter back home, and their day on Onnescu wasn't nearly enough warmth to make him happy to see snow again.

On the other hand, it made for some excellent four-wheeling. The snow was just deep enough to be fun, and the drifts and the clumps of grass kept things interesting.

After they'd driven for ten or fifteen minutes, the terrain

began to change. The ground started rising up into shallow hills, and taller plants dotted the low spots between them. They weren't quite bushes and they weren't quite trees; they looked more like big barrels with maybe a dozen branches sticking out like angled spokes from the top edge. A single triangular leaf flapped like a pennant from the tip of each branch.

"I'll bet those trunks are full of water," Trent said. "Like cactus."

"It'd be ice this time of year," Donna pointed out.

"Maybe. Unless they've got some kind of antifreeze."

"We'll have to ask our guide when we get wherever we're going."

That didn't take much longer. The barrel trees became more common over the next couple of miles, growing taller and thicker as well, until the vehicles were driving through a forest of them, winding between trunks maybe twenty feet thick and thirty feet tall. After another mile or so of that, the Frenchman pulled to a stop beside one and stepped out of his truck.

The snow wasn't drifted nearly as much here. When Trent opened the door, he couldn't feel any wind on his face, either. He stepped to the ground, and the smooth plastic soles of his Ziptite suit immediately slipped out from under him, landing him on his butt in the snow.

"Trent, are you all right?" Donna hollered from her side of the cab, just as the Frenchman said, "Did you hurt yourself?"

"I'm okay," he said, and he used the edge of the door for support while he pulled himself up to his feet again.

"Perhaps you would be more . . . grippy? No . . . more stable without the pressure suit," the Frenchman suggested.

"That's for sure." Trent didn't really want to remove a layer of protection, but if they were going to have lunch with this guy, he couldn't very well stay suited up the whole time. So he took off his coat, peeled out of the suit and tossed it in the cab, then put on his coat—and promptly fell on his butt again.

"Mon dieu! You are having the bad luck today."

Trent could either laugh or get mad, so he laughed. "I'm havin' the cowboy boots instead of the work boots, is what it is." He pulled himself upright again and tried a few cautious steps. If he dug in his heels it was just possible to walk. "Watch yourself," he said to Donna. "It's slick as snot out here."

"Come into my home," the Frenchman said, waving an arm behind him. "It's warm and dry."

"Let's get you the mail sack first," Trent said. "My job's not done until it's delivered." He went around to the back of the pickup, opened the camper, and began pulling out the parachute.

"Would you like help to fold that?"

Trent wasn't really sure he wanted a Frenchman handling something his life depended on, but he could use the help, and he supposed he could keep an eye on the guy. "Yeah, thanks," he said.

Donna had peeled out of her Ziptite inside the cab. She climbed down and helped them stretch out the parachute along the length of the tire tracks they had just left, then she and Trent folded it up while the Frenchman shook the snow off the stretch just ahead of them. Trent climbed up onto the cab and packed it away in its fiberglass pod, making sure it was buckled properly to the roll bars and that the pod's release mechanism was armed.

He climbed back down, careful not to slip this time, and hauled the mail sack out of the camper. "Here you go," he said, handing it over.

"Merci." The Frenchman threw the sack over his shoulder like Santa Claus. "Now, please, let us go inside where it's warm!" He walked around his vehicle and marched straight up to the tree just beyond it.

Trent figured his house must be behind the tree, but the

Frenchman reached for a stub of branch and pulled on it, and a round-topped door swung open, revealing a hollow interior filled with furniture and glowing with light from above.

"You live in a tree!" Donna said, delighted.

"I do," said their host. "It's . . . how do you say . . . it's cozy, but it's home." He stepped aside to let Donna enter first, and Trent followed her in.

The walls were about a foot thick, and irregular, just like the outside of the tree. They were pale yellow, and they had been polished until they shone. They enclosed a space about the size of a fair-sized living room, but that space was used much more efficiently than most. There were storage cabinets to the left of the door, a kitchen beside that with more cabinets overhead and a round window over the sink, a bathroom next to the kitchen, a dining table with two chairs set in the middle of the room, and two soft chairs and several storage cabinets taking up the space to the right. Trent looked up to see where the light was coming from, and saw that the tree was hollow all the way up, with a translucent white cover over the opening at the base of the branches. A ladder ran up the wall to a circular balcony about five feet wide that ringed the tree about halfway up, and through the hole in the middle he could see a bed and a desk. The air didn't smell musty or stuffy like the inside of a log; it smelled more like a forest on a still day, with just a hint of fresh-cut wood to it.

"This is quite the place you got here," Trent said.

"Thank you!" their host said, closing the door behind him. He hung the mail sack from a peg next to the door and hung his coat over the sack. "But I forget my manners. I have not introduced myself. I am André Condorcet."

"I'm Trent Stinson, and this is my wife, Donna."

"Enchanté," said André, making a little bow to Donna. "Let me make you something warm to drink." He went to the kitchen and filled a pan with water, which he put on a hotplate. "Do you prefer tea, or coffee?"

"Coffee would be great," Donna said. She slipped off her coat and draped it over the back of one of the chairs.

"Same for me," said Trent. It was plenty warm in the tree house; he took off his own coat and laid it over Donna's. "So does everybody here live in trees?" he asked.

"Not all," André said. "But most of us do. It's much more convenient than building a house, and prettier, yes?"

"And much harder to see from orbit," Trent said.

André looked at him askance. "Yes, there is that advantage as well."

He didn't elaborate, and from the look on his face Trent figured he probably shouldn't have brought up the subject, but Donna said, "Is our pickup going to cause problems? It's bright red."

André shook his head. "I think not. So far, only large groups are targeted. And industrial sites. We have learned not to gather in one place or to build anything that might be mistaken."

"Or to use the radio too much," Donna said.

"Or that, yes." André busied himself putting a pan of milk on the hotplate, getting big bowl-shaped mugs from one of the cabinets, and preparing a chrome coffeemaker that looked like it might double as lab equipment.

There were modern appliances all through the house. Electric lights, a computer, a video screen, stereo equipment. If the walls had been square, it would be easy to forget that this was a tree house.

"How do you generate power?" Trent asked.

"Solar panels," André said. "The dome atop the tree is painted with the flexible cells. It provides enough electricity during the day to keep me through the night, if I am careful."

It didn't sound like he had enough extra to let Trent top off his batteries before they jumped again. In fact, André couldn't run that big truck of his very often if he had to charge it with solar cells. "How do you deliver the mail, then?" Trent asked. "Put it in barrels around the necks of Saint Bernards?"

André smiled. "It would be a long walk for many dogs. Our houses are kilometers apart, so we use the relay. I ski to several of my neighbors' trees, and they ski to their neighbors' trees, and so on until everything is passed along."

"Sounds like it could take days to get your mail if you're on the far end of the line."

"Yes, it does. But life moves more slowly for us. We are in no hurry to go anywhere, for we are already here, no? Humanity's long struggle to leave the nest is over, and Mirabelle proves very . . . hospital? Hospitable. We can relax and enjoy life as it was meant to be lived." André took the pan off the hotplate, poured the water into the coffeemaker, and closed the lid, sealing it with a half-turn twist. Then he lifted a lever from the side of the canister and pressed it back down slowly, apparently squeezing the water down through the grounds.

"Doesn't it get lonely out here?" Donna asked.

André nodded. "That is the, how do you say, the downside. But you are here today, and who knows what tomorrow may bring."

"I'm surprised you're so happy to see a couple of Americans," Trent said.

André worked the lever on the side of his coffeemaker again. "I had assumed that you were ex-Americans, living now on Onnescu. Are you actually from the United States?"

"Rock Springs, Wyoming," Trent said. "That's just a little to the left of center."

He tensed up, expecting André to tell them to leave, or worse. The Frenchman did seem to be considering it, but then he just shrugged and said, "Eh, bien, I think maybe you two are not the ones who send bombs. Maybe you are not your government." He pushed the plunger on the coffeemaker again. "It's a theory of mine that not all

Americans are the . . . how do you say . . . the jingoistic conquer-monkeys."

Donna laughed. Trent managed an embarrassed smile. "We'd like to think that, too," he said, "but it sometimes looks like we're the only ones who aren't."

André said, "Perhaps there are more than you think who feel as you. It's always the vocal minority who have their way, while the others silently chew their beards and plot rebellion." He poured coffee into the mugs, then before Trent or Donna could stop him, he poured an equal amount of warm milk into all three. "Ah, this should warm you up!" he said, handing them each a mug.

Trent had to admit it smelled pretty good. It looked like chocolate milk, and the mug was so low and wide that it felt more like he was drinking out of a cereal bowl, but he tilted it to his lips and took a sip. It was definitely creamy. Almost sweet. And as strong as the coffee tasted, he was glad he wasn't drinking it straight.

"How do you get milk clear out here?" Donna asked.

"How else? We brought cows." He waved an arm toward the table. "Sit! Relax. I will fix the lunch. Do you eat lapin?"

"I don't know," Trent said. "What's lapin?"

"Rabbit. And before you get your hopes up, I have none, but the dandinant is very similar, and I do have that."

"What's a dandinant?" The name sounded suspiciously bug-like. Trent hadn't heard that the French were into insects, but he knew they ate snails, which was just as bad.

André wrinkled his brow. "It's . . . how to describe it? A little creature native to Mirabelle, like a skunk without the smell, but yellow and green to blend in with the grass. It's round, and it walks like this." He bent down and shuffled a few steps, waddling from side to side like a bear. "They are very common, and very tasty as well."

Trent looked over at Donna to see what she thought. They had eaten some alien fish on their first trip off Earth and lived to tell about it, and André had apparently eaten these dandinants before, so it sounded safe enough. Donna nodded her agreement, and said, "Sure, it sounds great."

"Excellent," André said. "Sit!" he said again.

There were only two chairs at the table. Trent pulled one out for Donna, then went around to the other side of the table and sat in the other. The floor wasn't perfectly flat—it looked like André had smoothed it with an adze or something—but Trent was able to wiggle his chair around until it rested on all four legs. André busied himself in the kitchen, taking a pan of shredded meat and several unknown vegetables from a small refrigerator and setting to work on the vegetables with a knife.

"So how come you speak English?" Trent asked.

André said over his shoulder, "When I was young, the United States was not the way it is now. Then, your country was the shining hope of the world, the strongest force for peace anywhere. You were admired. Most of my generation learned to speak English, for it seemed the entire world would soon become American."

"That's hard to imagine," Trent said. "Seems like the whole world's been pissed at us for as long as I can remember."

André looked at Trent for a moment, giving him a once-over that had Trent wondering what the Frenchman was looking for until André said, "The change happened about the time you were born, I would guess." He turned back to his vegetable cutting. "Terrorists attacked you on your own soil for the first time, and in response your country went insane. Instead of trying to stop the cause for terrorism, America instead began conquering other countries it considered threats to its own security. This of course worried other countries, who prepared to resist an American invasion, but that buildup of weapons made them threats in turn, and so it progressed until America went from the most admired nation to the most feared, and terrorism became the only way to fight back."

That wasn't quite the way Trent had learned it in school. He'd learned that terrorists were all religious fanatics, and that the United States had acted to stop them when the United Nations wouldn't. But he didn't want to get into an argument with André over it, so he just said, "There's no justification for terrorism, no matter what the provocation."

André nodded. "There, you see! All Americans are not the same."

"I don't think anybody supports terrorism," Trent said.

"Someone must," André said, "or we would not have such a nice big lake to the north of here."

"Touché," said Trent.

"Aha! You speak French." André laughed.

"About two words of it."

"What would be the other?"

"Garage."

"Ah, of course. We have the joke in France, that when America renamed French fries 'freedom fries,' you also tried to rename the garage, but for some reason 'car hole' did not catch on."

Trent was just about to take another sip of coffee, but his sudden laughter blew it into his eyebrows instead. Donna was already laughing at André's joke, but she laughed even harder when she saw Trent dripping onto the table. André handed him a dishtowel and said, "My apologies! I did not mean to—"

"It's all right," Trent said. "You told me there was a joke comin'." He wiped away the coffee and handed the towel back. "I'll have to remember that one when we get back home."

"So you are going back to America, then? I assumed that once you left, you would not go back."

"We're just sort of scouting around for possibilities at the moment," Trent said. "We might move, and we might not, depending on what we find. But even if we decide to move, we've got to go back for our stuff."

"Ah, yes, your stuff. 'Etoffe,' we say, and it's perhaps no coincidence that our word 'etouffer' means to suffocate. I thought I might despair when I moved here, because I could not bear to give up all my 'stuff,' but in the end, I learned what was important to me and what was not. It was a valuable lesson. I sometimes think a person should move every year, and only take with them what they can carry."

Donna said, "We met a couple on Onnescu who plan to find their own planet and play Adam and Eve, all with just one load of belongings."

André whistled softly. "That is dedication. Maybe a bit extreme, but one must admire their ability to renounce worldly things."

"We'll see how long they stick to it," Trent said. "I'd be surprised if they lasted a year before they moved back to civilization."

André chuckled softly. "That is what my sister said to me when I moved to Mirabelle. I have eight months to go, and much can happen in that time, but I think I will prove her wrong."

He set the chopping board full of vegetables aside and picked up the pan he had used to heat the milk. The light grew suddenly brighter in the house, and Trent assumed that the sun had just come out from behind a cloud, but it seemed awfully bright. André paused with the saucepan in his hand and looked out the kitchen window, then he whispered, "Merde."

The light grew brighter.

"Baissez-vous!" André yelled, dropping to the floor. "Go down!"

Trent dived for the floor, his chair clattering over backwards, and threw his arm around Donna as she dropped down beside him. Coffee poured off the table onto their legs from their overturned mugs, but they didn't have time to move. The ground heaved underneath them, throwing them and everything else in the house into the air for a second, then just as they landed again, there was a deafening explosion and they were thrown sideways into the kitchen cabinets.

Wood and rocks and dirt rained down over them. Trent pulled Donna close and covered her head with his arms, realizing in a moment of wry clarity that she was doing the same for him. A chunk of branch the size of his leg smashed down beside them and tumbled away. The table had overturned; Trent grabbed it by a leg and pulled it over the top of their bodies, and they felt the jolts as more debris bounced off it.

After what seemed like half an hour, but was probably only ten seconds or so, the patter of falling rubble stopped. Trent stuck his head out from under the table and looked up. The top half of the tree had vanished as if a giant's fist had just swatted it away, and clouds roiled overhead like smoke over a wildfire.

"Are you okay?" he asked Donna.

"I . . . I think so." Her voice sounded thin and distant through the ringing in his ears.

"André?" He turned to the Frenchman, who was sitting up and shaking the dirt out of his hair.

"Je vis," he croaked. Blood ran down his left arm from a gash in his shoulder.

Trent staggered to his feet and helped Donna up, then turned to André and extended his hand. André looked at Trent's hand, then looked up into his face, and for a moment Trent thought André was going to come up swinging, but he took a deep breath and grasped Trent's hand and pulled himself to his feet.

"My apologies," he said. "I évidemment miscalculate the risk."

"You've got no reason to apologize to us," Trent said. "We're the ones that owe you the apology, and a whole lot more than that." He looked up at the gaping hole where the top of the tree had been. "Son of a bitch. I can't believe those bastards would drop a bomb on us just for . . . for what? Parking two trucks side-by-side?"

"One of which just arrived from off-planet," André said. "It must have looked like a rendezvous militaire." He kicked aside an overturned chair and staggered to the door. "And since they did not kill us with their first attempt, we should expect another. We must go."

He tried to open the door, but it was wedged tight. He kicked at it, and it moved a little, but not far enough. Trent stepped up beside him and the two of them kicked together, knocking it another few inches before it stuck again. Donna slipped in between them and said, "All three at once. One, two, *three*!" They kicked in unison, putting everything they had into it, and the door cleared the jamb. Two more good kicks shoved it wide enough to squeeze out through.

André grabbed his coat and the mail bag on his way out. Trent and Donna scooped up their coats from the floor where they had fallen and followed him outside, to look in stunned amazement at the destruction all around them. None of the trees had their branches anymore, and most of them were missing the top part of their trunks as well. Several had been uprooted and toppled, making instant hollow-log habitat for brontosaurs. And all around, the ground was strewn with chunks of wood, huge boulders, rocks, and dirt.

Trent's pickup was on its side. He ran over to it and looked for damage, but it didn't look like it had been hit with anything bigger than his fist. There were dents all over, and when he climbed up onto the passenger side, which now pointed straight up, he found a bull's-eye crack in the window, but it looked like ground movement had tipped the pickup, rather than something knocking it over. It actually looked like they had been lucky: a boulder the size of a refrigerator lay right where they had parked. If the pickup hadn't already been on its side, the boulder would have smashed it flat.

André's truck was still on its wheels. There was an eight-foot-long log sticking out of the roof just behind the articulated joint in the middle, but when André climbed into the cab and fed power to the motors, it rolled forward without hesitation.

Through the blasted trunks of the trees beyond him, Trent could see the rim of the crater the meteor had made. It was at least twenty feet high, and there didn't seem to be much curve to it. It looked more like a dam than a crater, with steam or smoke or vaporized rock rising up in a big white plume behind it. How big a rock had the U.S. dropped on them, anyway?

André circled around and called out from his window, "I will winch your vehicle upright."

"I don't think that'll work," Trent said. "We'd have to drag it forward first to clear this boulder, and that could do more damage than tippin' over did."

"You have no choice," André said. "You must move within ten or fifteen minutes, or risk the next shot is being more accurate."

That's how long it would take to do a tangential vector

translation with another big rock. Instead of matching velocity with the ground, the bomber would be maximizing the difference, sending a piece of asteroid straight down at orbital velocity or more, but it was the same basic idea. Let the planet's gravity do the work, and incidentally create a near-infinite supply of bombs. They wouldn't even have to sacrifice a hyperdrive engine. They could program that to detach itself and jump to safety once the rock was on the right trajectory.

Trent looked up into the sky. The clouds were too patchy to offer much cover. Whoever was watching them could jump wherever they wanted to in order to see the ground. Trent felt the hair prickling on the back of his neck at the thought that someone was looking at him right now, bringing another meteor to bear on him.

He raised his right hand and gave them the one-finger salute. Donna laughed, and he looked over at her with a sheepish grin. "The last great act of defiance, eh babe?"

"I think we've got a lot more defiance in us yet," she said, and there was fire in her voice. She was hefting a rock in her hand as if she was thinking about pitching it all the way into orbit to knock down whoever had bombed them.

"You have to survive to fight another day," André said. "Damage or no, you must move now."

"We can jump straight into space without havin' to drag the truck anywhere," Trent said. Provided they hadn't sprung any leaks. The cracked window wouldn't matter; that was just the regular glass. The Lexan inner window was still stout as ever. Trent had no idea how the door seals had fared, but he didn't see that he had much choice. If they righted the pickup and tried driving anywhere, they would just be inviting another strike the next place they stopped. They had to get off the planet for the colonists' safety as well as their own, and they had a better chance of staying sealed up if they didn't drag the pickup on its side first.

"You are right," André said. "Go quickly, then. And when

you get home, well, perhaps it is time for revolution, yes?"

"No perhaps about it," Trent said. "Heads are gonna roll when word of this gets out."

André smiled grimly. "The metaphor amuses me. France will gladly provide the guillotine. Now go!"

Trent bent down to give Donna a hand up, but she passed him the rock she was carrying first. It was about the size of a baseball, almost black, deeply pitted, and way heavier than it looked. "I think this is part of the meteor that hit us," she said.

"Sure looks like it." Trent had seen pictures of meteorites before, but he had never held one in his hand. It weighed at least three or four pounds, and was cold as ice. Whether that was from the snowy ground, or if it was still cold from being part of an asteroid that had been way the hell and gone away from the sun just a few minutes ago, he couldn't tell, but it felt like he was holding a little bit of space in his hand. He opened the passenger door and dropped the meteorite carefully into the pickup's cab, making sure it hit the side of the driver's door and not the window.

Donna climbed up the truck's undercarriage to the passenger side, then swiveled around and slid feet-first down inside the cab to stand on the driver's door. She immediately started scrambling into her spacesuit, and Trent leaned down to check the parachute pods while she did that. Both fiberglass housings looked solid, and the wiring that led to the latch releases looked good, too. He would have liked to test them, but there was no time for that.

"Hand me up my suit," he said, stripping off his coat and exchanging it for the plastic Ziptite. His footing was no better on the truck's waxed paint than on snow; he had to grip the open door with one hand to keep his balance while he slid his legs into the suit and tugged the top half up over his shoulders.

He finally got it on and started to climb in after Donna, but he paused with his feet in the doorway and called out to

André, who still waited beside them in his own truck, "I'm sorry about . . . well, about all of this. I'll do what I can to put a stop to it."

"May you succeed in that!" André said. "And may we meet again in better circonstances."

"Damn straight. Keep your powder dry, dude."

André got a puzzled expression on his face, but then he just shrugged and said, "Always."

Trent dropped down beside Donna and let the door slam closed above him. It was a tight fit, like trying to squeeze into a one-person shower stall. The cab was a couple of inches too short for Trent to stand upright in, and he almost clonked Donna on the head with his elbows when he reached up to latch her door's vacuum seals. Donna bent down to latch the driver's door and put the inner window in place, then she pulled the computer out of its slot and plugged in the data line.

"It sees the hyperdrive," she said.

"That's a good sign." Trent cracked the valve on the air tank and watched the air pressure gauge in the dashboard rise a few pounds. He worked his jaws until they popped, then he shut off the air flow and watched the gauge. It stayed steady. Normally they waited ten minutes or so to be sure, but they didn't have that kind of time.

"Let's seal our Ziptites all the way just in case," he said, putting his hat on the gun rack. He pulled his hood over his head and squeezed the seam tight, then folded it over and sealed the interlock down as well. The suits had an emergency air tank that was good for about fifteen minutes of breathing, but he could last for a couple of minutes on the air trapped in the suit, so he left the tank's valve closed. With any luck, they would be in space and know if they needed the suits or not before they ran out of air.

"Ready?" Donna called, her voice muffled from inside her own suit.

Trent looked out the windshield. André was driving

away, his articulated truck twisting oddly as first the front tires, and then the rear, jounced over rocks in their path. The log sticking out of the top flopped back and forth like a toggle switch, no doubt grinding the hell out of whatever was inside, but André didn't stop. He was fleeing two dangers: Trent and Donna's hyperdrive field as well as another meteor strike.

Trent grabbed the Jesus bar at the top of the passenger window with his right hand and braced himself against the dashboard with his left. "Do it," he said.

Donna hit the "enter" key, and Mirabelle vanished.

The pickup's cab didn't seem much bigger without gravity. Trent pushed himself away from the passenger door and tucked his legs into the driver's footwell, curling around Donna as she pushed herself the other way and slid into her normal position. Their coats were flying loose inside the cab, so Trent grabbed them and stuffed them behind the seat, then he grabbed the rifle that was also floating free and bungeed it back into the gun rack, wedging his hat between the rifle and the back window. The meteorite went in the glove box, then they buckled their seatbelts and let the spring-loaded inertial reels pull them down against the seats. Trent checked the air gauge while Donna put the computer up on the dash so it could get a fix on the stars.

Dirt and snow boiled away from the passenger side of the truck, quite a bit of it banging into the windshield this time since it had a straight shot. Fortunately, not much of it stuck. It was already frozen by the time it hit, and it just glanced off and tumbled away into space. The driver's side window was completely covered with icy dirt, but that was boiling away like mad, too, and shoving the pickup outward with a pattering noise like hail on the roof. Then they felt a hard bump from beneath and the pickup started tumbling, too. The big boulder came into view just a few feet from the passenger window, but it was moving slowly away, and on the next swing around it was a couple car-lengths off, rotating on its long axis and spewing dirt outward in a ragged spiral.

The air gauge was holding steady at eighteen pounds.

That was a bit much, so Trent opened the stopcock in his door to vent a little out, but nothing happened. The nozzle was apparently plugged with dirt. That could be a real problem in a few minutes. If they couldn't vent their old air, they couldn't add any fresh. If they tried it, they would overpressurize the cab and eventually blow out a window or a door.

"Problems?" Donna asked, barely audible inside her pressure suit.

"Maybe." Trent opened the valve all the way, but the pressure gauge stayed rock steady. At least the cab wasn't leaking.

His suit was starting to fog up from his breath. He reached up and unsealed it, then rolled the hood down around his neck. "Let's see if there's anything in the glove box I can shove through there and unblock that valve," he said, leaning across Donna's lap to open it and look.

There were a bunch of fast-food napkins, the flashlight, a bottle opener, a Wyoming map, and a screwdriver. He tried poking the screwdriver in the stopcock's opening, but the spout was too curved to accept more than an inch or so. The church key was too wide, and a rolled-up napkin wasn't stiff enough to shove through whatever was blocking the valve.

Donna unsealed her bubble helmet, too, and started digging in the seat cover's storage pockets. She came up with a couple pens, a handful of CDs, and a little spiral notebook.

"How about the wire from this?" she asked.

"That might do it."

Donna tried to unravel it, but the fingers of her pressure suit were too thick, so she took the screwdriver and pried a loop of wire free with that.

"Careful," Trent said. "You don't want to poke a hole in your glove."

"Right." She slid the screwdriver into the spiral and pried out another couple of loops until several inches of wire extended out from the top of the notebook, then she handed it over to Trent.

He shoved the wire in the stopcock and wiggled it around, bending it so it could slide around the curve of the spigot, but it hit something hard just a couple inches in and wouldn't go any farther. No amount of wiggling helped.

"We're wasting time," he said, handing the notebook back to her. "Has the computer got a fix on our position yet?"

Donna looked at the screen. "No. I think we're spinning too fast."

Orion's squashed body slid past their windshield at a pretty good clip, going right to left. That meant the pickup was rotating sideways, as if it were spinning on an icy patch of road. Trent thought it over for a second, trying to get a clear mental picture of their motion, then he reached up to the top door latch on his side and said, "Get ready to zip up if this doesn't work."

"What are you going to do?"

"Kill two birds with one stone." He popped open the latch, and air immediately began to whistle out of the cab, blowing a wide cone of fog outward just beyond his window and shoving them away from the ragged hemisphere of dirt they had brought into orbit. Since the air jet was at the top of the cab, it also shoved them over sideways, adding another axis of rotation to their spin. It didn't actually work that way—Trent still wasn't sure why it didn't, but Allen Meisner had told him that you couldn't rotate two different ways at once. What happened was that the two different motions combined to tip the nose down and flip the pickup end-for-end.

It didn't matter. He would correct for that later. He kept his eyes on the air gauge, working his jaws to let his ears pop while it dropped, and when the needle hit twelve pounds, he snapped the latch closed again. The whistling jet of air stopped, and the pickup continued to nose over forward as if nothing had changed, but now they were a couple dozen feet away from the main mass of dirt and rock they had brought with them. Trent pressed the valves for the rear bumper jets, afraid they would be plugged, too, but he heard the rush of air through the lines, and their downward motion stopped. He had overcorrected, so he had to hit the front jets for a short burst, and two clouds of fog shot upward in front of them.

"Those work, at least," he said happily. "And you'll note that we're steady as a rock now. I'm definitely gettin' better at this." He retrieved his hat from behind the rifle and stuck it on his head. He always felt better driving with his hat on.

The stars were hard little diamonds, unwinking and unmoving save for the chunks of ice and rock that still tumbled away from them.

"You're so good," Donna said. She looked at the computer screen and said, "It's locked on. Where do we want to go?"

That was a good question. The only people with the power to stop the United States were the Galactic Federation, but the Federation had to know what was going on already, and they were apparently unwilling to start bombarding one nation to stop it from bombarding its rivals' colonies. Besides, Federation headquarters was in a space station about fifty light-years from Earth in Cetus, and docking with a space station took a lot of time and maneuvering air. Trent didn't know how much of either they had before their luck ran out. They could go back to Alpha Centauri, but the people there already knew what was going on, too, and were powerless to stop it.

Trent and Donna couldn't even do anything to stop the person who had dropped the bomb on them. He might be in high orbit around Mirabelle, but it would be nearly impossible to find him without radar, and it would be even harder to hit him with anything if they found him. It was tough enough to target a landing site within a few miles; pinpointing the intersection of two pickup-sized objects moving at different velocities and different angles was way beyond the capability of a homemade hyperdrive system with a shareware navigation program.

Besides, the guy who dropped the bomb was probably just a soldier. Pissed as Trent was at him, he wasn't ready to murder someone who was just following orders.

There was only one real choice: go back home and confront the people responsible on their own turf. Trent had no idea how to go about that yet, but he knew something like this had to be stopped at the source.

"We've got to go back to Earth," he said.

"Right." Donna pulled up the menu and selected "Sol" from the list of stars. The computer drew its red circle around one of the stars on the right side of the screen, and closer to the middle it drew a squashed squiggle that it claimed was Cassiopeia. Trent looked out the windshield to see if he could spot it in the real view, but it was hard to recognize anything out there. The computer might be able to correct for the distorted shapes of the constellations at this distance, but Trent couldn't recognize anything other than Orion, and that was way off to their left.

It didn't matter. If the computer knew where the Sun was, that was good enough. "Let's go," he said.

Donna pushed the "enter" key, and there was a moment of disorientation, much more intense than Trent remembered it from the last time. The stars didn't so much shift as blink out and get replaced with new ones.

"That shouldn't have happened," he said.

"What?" asked Donna. She had been watching the computer screen, not the view out the windshield.

"The stars completely changed. They shouldn't have done that just jumping back to Earth."

"You must have just blinked or something," she said, but then she took a good look herself and frowned. "Where's Cassiopeia? It should be straight ahead now."

"I don't know. It's all different." There was still a wide band of Milky Way stretching diagonally across their field of view, and hundreds of individual stars scattered at random, but none of them connected up in familiar patterns. Even Orion was gone.

"I must have picked the wrong star on the menu," Donna said. She tapped at the computer's keyboard, and a couple seconds later it made the Homer Simpson "D'oh!" noise.

"That's not the happy sound," Trent said. He looked over at the screen and saw the words "Unable to orient" in a little message box.

Donna tapped at the keys and got the "D'oh!" again. "No, it's not. It doesn't recognize anything."

"What do you mean, it doesn't recognize anything? It took us here; it must know where 'here' is."

"You'd think." Donna tried again, but still got the Homer "D'oh." "Okay," she said, "let's see what's on the menu next to 'Earth.' Hmm. Earl's Place and Edens I, II, and III. How far away are these guys?" She used the touchpad to stretch the window out a little and said, "Nothing over fifty light-years. It shouldn't have any trouble finding landmark stars at those distances."

"We went a lot farther than that," Trent said. "I felt it, and everything changed."

Donna tapped a few more keys and another window popped up on the screen. "Says here we went 60.4 light-years."

"I don't think that's right." The hair was starting to stand up on the back of his neck. If the computer was messed up, they were screwed.

Donna bit her lip in concentration. "Yeah. Let's hit 'undo' and go back to Mirabelle and try this again."

"Sounds good to me."

Donna popped up the "edit" menu and picked "undo." Trent felt the momentary disorientation of a hyperspace jump, but the stars only shifted a little this time. He looked over at Donna.

She said, "According to this, we just jumped 60.4 light-years back to Mirabelle."

Trent tried to see any familiar patterns in the stars. "I'll believe we went 60.4 light-years, but we didn't go back to Mirabelle."

"That's for sure." Donna called up the locator window again anyway, but it just went "D'oh" like before.

"How 'bout if you actually pick Mirabelle off the destination menu?" asked Trent.

She tried that, but another window popped up on the screen with the message, "Unable to fix starting location."

"I don't want you to fix it," Trent said. "I want you to *find* it."

"That's what it means," Donna said. "It doesn't know where we—"

"I know what it means. I was just givin' it shit."

"Oh. Well, it apparently won't take us anywhere if it doesn't know where we are."

"It took us 60.4 light-years just now."

"That was 'undo.'"

"So are we gonna have to 'undo' a hundred times or so to get back home?"

"No, that would just jump us back and forth between here and where we were a minute ago. I think."

"You think. You're supposed to be the navigator."

She didn't reply to that, and he immediately realized how it had sounded. "Sorry. I didn't mean it like that. You're doing everything you can; I know that."

She didn't reply to that, either. She just took the computer down off the dashboard and held it on her lap with her left hand while she typed with her right. She was clumsy in her Ziptite suit, but she took it slow and careful, pulling the plastic glove tight over her index finger so she would only hit one key at a time. Trent waited as patiently as he could, but he had never been much good at letting somebody else do the work. He knew Donna was better with computers than he was, though. If anybody was going to figure out what had happened, it would be her.

He looked at the stars while he waited. There were a lot of them. It seemed like there were fewer of them than usual, but that might have just been because his eyes hadn't adjusted to the darkness yet. There were still quite a few. There was a constellation that looked a little like a duck, and one that looked like a fountain, or maybe a tree. No dippers, though, or Cassiopeia, or Orion, or any of the other familiar ones.

At least not out the front. He craned his neck around and looked out the side and as far back as he could, but nothing looked familiar there, either. His mirror was crushed flat against the body of the pickup, but he couldn't see anything familiar in Donna's mirror, either, even when he leaned forward to see around the big bull's-eye crack in her window.

He reached forward and pushed the buttons for the front air jets. The air tank under the seat hissed, two jets of fog shot upward from the front bumper, and the truck nosed down.

"What are you doing?" Donna asked.

"Havin' a look behind us. Maybe something will look familiar there."

"Not likely, but it's worth a try."

He let the pickup nose over until he figured half the sky had slid past, then hit the rear jets until they came to a stop. It stopped cold this time, too. Twice in a row. He peered out at the stars in that direction, but he didn't have any better luck seeing anything he recognized. Donna wedged the laptop between the dashboard and the windshield again and let it get a good look with its webcam, but after a few seconds it said "D'oh" again.

"I'm gettin' mighty tired of that noise," Trent said.

"I could change it."

"I didn't mean that. I'm just getting tired of it not knowin' where we are."

"Me too." She sat back in her seat and said, "I can't find what's wrong. It thinks it sent us to Sol on that first jump, but now that it can't figure out where we are, the only thing it will let us do besides 'undo' is 'explorer mode,' where we give it a direction and a distance."

"That'd be fine if we knew what direction and distance to give it."

"Yeah."

Trent was starting to sweat inside his Ziptite suit, but he ignored it and tried to think things through. "Okay, we were pointed a little to the side of the Sun when we jumped. We obviously went too far, right? 'Cause if it was just the wrong direction, we'd still be able to see familiar stars."

"Right," Donna said.

"So if we just head back the way we came and keep jumping until we see something familiar, that ought to work, shouldn't it?"

Donna considered that for a minute. "It would work if we knew for sure what direction we went, but that could have been off, too."

"What are the odds of both numbers bein' wrong?"

She shrugged. "I have no idea, 'cause I don't know what happened."

"Well, we've got to do something," Trent said, "because we've only got about five hours of air. We didn't refill the tank before we left. And we didn't recharge the batteries, either." He pointed at the gauge, currently reading only half a charge. "Drivin' all over hell and gone today ate up a lot of juice."

There was a long moment of silence in the cab of the pickup. Donna looked out the windshield, then over at Trent. "For the computer to not recognize anything, we had to jump at least a couple of hundred light-years. It's supposedly good that far before the constellation patterns change too much. So if we jump back a hundred light-years at a time, we should eventually hit something it recognizes."

He could hear the tension in her voice. She started talking faster when she got tense, which made it harder for him to understand her, which made him tense, as if he wasn't tense enough already.

He took off his hat and scratched his head. "That would work as long as it actually jumps a hundred light-years when we tell it to. It didn't go to Earth when we told it to do that."

"Yeah."

"And we can jump two hundred at a time, can't we? If it's good for two hundred light-years out, that's a bubble four hundred across, right? So if we go two hundred at a time—"

"You're right. Provided we go straight back the way we came. But if we're off a little bit, we could cross through the edge of familiar space in one jump and keep on going."

"We could, couldn't we. Damn. Okay, then a hundred."

She nodded. "Okay. So which direction is back the way we came?"

That was a good question. They hadn't been pointed straight at the Sun when they jumped. The computer could correct for angle, so they had just let it lock on and do its thing. But Trent remembered seeing Orion out his side window just before they jumped. And afterward . . . what was out there then? He didn't remember.

"Can you call up the webcam's picture from right after we got here?" he asked.

"I think so." Donna ran through the menus for a minute, then a starfield popped up in a separate window.

"Okay, if that's what we were lookin' at after our first jump," Trent said, "then we were headin' for this patch of sky right about here." He tapped the screen over on the right side, where he remembered the blinking star that the computer had said was the Sun.

"You're sure?" Donna asked.

"Pretty close. Back up to the image from before we jumped."

She did, and he was relieved to see Sol shining right where he expected it to be. "There. We were sittin' steady, so the same spot on the next screen has to be the direction the hyperdrive supposedly took us, right?"

"That sounds logical."

She switched to the image from right after they had arrived, and Trent put his finger where the Sun had been a second ago. "There. So a hundred and eighty degrees away from that should take us back the direction we came, right?"

"I . . . think so. Yeah, that sounds right.

"So can that thing tell us what's exactly a hundred and eighty?"

She shook her head. "It's just a webcam image. Maybe if we spun the truck around and took continuous video we could time it or something, but the computer needs more data than just a picture to compute something like that."

"Never mind," Trent said. "We can figure that easy enough on our own." He looked on the screen image for an easily recognizable landmark, found it in a triangle of three bright stars just a little to the left of the direction they had come, then looked outside to see if he could find it out there. He couldn't, so he hit the front jets again, and watched the stars stream past.

He almost missed it. The three he was looking for were off to the left, hidden by the post between the windshield and his side window until he moved his head. That was definitely them, though. "There," he said, pointing.

He hit the rear jets to stop their motion. Of course it was too much to ask that he could bring them to a perfect stop three times in a row. He undershot at first, then overshot correcting it, then undershot again before he finally got them stopped. "That's this bit right here," he said, pointing at the same stars on the screen. "And the direction we came is between those two stars there." He looked outside again and found them directly out his side window, nearly obscured by the mud smeared across the outer glass.

Donna realized what he was doing. "So if that's the direction we came, then *that*—" she turned and pointed out her window "—is the direction we want to go. We need a transit or something so we can get an exact angle."

"Sorry, we're fresh out of transits. But we do have this map." Trent got their Wyoming road map out of the glove box and stuck it in the air between them, nudging it gently until one folded edge pointed at the stars that had replaced the Sun after they jumped. "Sight down that and make sure it's aimed right," he told Donna.

She bent her head down and peered along the edge while he leaned back out of her way. She adjusted the map's position with her fingertips until it was just right, then said, "Okay, now."

"Lean back," Trent told her. She ducked aside and he sighted the other way along the same edge. He had to look through the cracks in her window, but he could see a few distinctive stars there. "Got it," he said. "That little fishhook business under that bright one there."

She looked out her window. "Let's do it again to make sure."

"Okay."

She leaned in, but instead of leaning back, he leaned in, too, snatched the map out of the air between them, and gave her a big kiss.

"You silly, this is serious," she said, but she was smiling.

He smiled right back. "Kissin' you's serious, too."

"We'll have time enough for that when we get home."

"That sounds like a promise," he said.

She looked him in the eye from two inches away. "You get us home safe, cowboy, and you can consider it anything you want."

"Deal." He kissed her again, then set the map back in the air between them.

She lined it up on the two stars next to the triangle again, then he sighted down the edge to the same fishhook constellation. "That's definitely it," he said.

"Okay." She stuck the computer on the dash, shoving it hard against the junction between dashboard and windshield so the webcam was aimed straight ahead. "We need to turn so it's onscreen," she said.

That meant blowing more breathing air into space, but Trent supposed there was no way around it. The computer expected to be lined up front-to-back, so they couldn't just aim it out the side window. He used the jets as sparingly as possible, tipping the pickup to the right with the side nozzles, then stopping that motion and dropping the nose again until they were pointed pretty close to their target. There weren't a whole lot of stars out there, only a couple dozen bright ones and maybe twice that many more dim ones. He wondered if any of them was the Sun. From a hundred light-years away, could you even see the Sun? He didn't know.

Donna used the computer's touchpad to scoot the mouse pointer to the little fishhook constellation on the screen. The touchpad wasn't very responsive with her hand encased in a plastic bag, but she kept at it until she got it. "Right there?" she asked.

"A little to the right. Yeah, about there."

She tapped a function key. "Okay. That's now zero, zero. Now I enter the distance . . ." She hit another function key and typed in 100. "Check that to make sure," she said.

"I trust you," Trent told her, but she just looked at him until he leaned forward and looked at the number she'd typed in the "distance" box. "Says one zero zero."

"All right." She tapped another function key, and a little window popped up with the message, "Press Enter to jump."

"Ready?" she asked.

He took a deep breath. "Ready."

"I sure hope this damned thing works this time."

"Me too."

She pressed the "enter" key. There was the usual moment of disorientation, and most of the stars jumped a little, but not enough to lose track of. About half of them hardly budged. Those were the big bright ones a long ways off. Trent tried to make them resolve into any kind of familiar pattern, but had no luck.

Neither did the computer.

"Well," he said, "I guess we couldn't expect it to work the first time. Try it again."

Donna did, but they had no more luck.

"Once more."

Still no luck.

After the third jump they sat there side-by-side, looking out the windshield without saying anything. They had just gone three hundred light-years. Far enough to get lost if they weren't already. Trent was pretty sure they were aimed at the right patch of sky, but if they were off even by a little bit, that error would get greater and greater the farther they jumped. How far could they go before even a couple of degrees of error became two hundred light-years wide? He wished he'd paid more attention to story problems in math class.

He looked at the battery gauge: already a nudge lower than it had been just a few minutes ago. They couldn't just jump around at random until they hit a familiar section of the galaxy; at a hundred light-years to the leap, they couldn't even cover a thousandth of it. They would run out of battery power if they kept jumping, but every breath took them a couple of seconds closer to the time when they would run out of air.

The Milky Way seemed thicker here. The whole windshield looked foggy with it. He was about to mention it to Donna when he realized that it *was* fog. The truck was losing heat to space, and their breath was condensing on the glass. He could run the heater, but that sucked juice out of the same batteries that the hyperdrive did. They were just going to have to towel off the windshield. And shiver, probably, before long. At least they had their coats.

"Well, what do you think?" he asked.

Donna shook her head. "We could search for weeks and not find anything familiar."

"We don't have weeks," he said.

"Not in space. But if we can find a planet and land, we can take our time figuring out what happened. I could maybe find the bug in the program."

"And if you can't?"

She took a deep breath. "Well, we'd at least be on the ground somewhere."

"Playing Adam and Eve like Nick Onnescu and his sweetie?"

She made a face. "No offense, but let's try a couple more jumps."

"Deal." While she typed in another hundred light-years and checked to make sure that the computer was still locked onto the same point in space, Trent got the shop towel from under the seat to wipe the fog off the windshield, but when he shook it out, it fell to pieces.

"What the hell?" he said, and then he remembered. He'd

used it to wipe the alien slime off the seat after they'd dropped them off at the doctor's office. And then he remembered their romp in the camper that night. "Oho," he said. "That explains it."

"What?" Donna asked.

"Our clothes. When we ripped 'em off each other." He could feel himself blushing. "I thought we were just hot, but it looks like we had a little help from Katata and her kids." He showed her the shop towel. "That slime of theirs must be like battery acid."

She laughed, but he could hear the disappointment in her voice when she said, "I thought that was a little strange. I felt like Supergirl or something, but I just figured it was that super strength you read about people gettin' sometimes in accidents and stuff."

"You were still super," he said, and he kissed her again.

She was blushing, too, and batting her eyelashes in that "aw shucks" way she did when she was embarrassed, and she looked so beautiful he suddenly figured it wouldn't be so bad finding an uninhabited planet somewhere and doing the Adam and Eve thing with her. But they were going to give it a couple more jumps first.

He stuck the towel back under the seat and got a paper napkin out of the glove box to wipe the window with. He had to stretch to reach Donna's side, and his seatbelt kept trying to pull him back, but he managed it without knocking the computer off the dash. When he was done, the napkin looked a lot like the shop towel, but that was just moisture.

He checked the seat, but that seemed all right. Either alien slime didn't eat vinyl, or he'd gotten it off quick enough. "Okay," he said. "Let's give it another try."

The computer was ready. Donna hit "go," and the stars shifted, but they were no more familiar afterward than before.

"One more?" she asked.

Trent shrugged. "Fifth time's a charm." He didn't think

it would do any good, but he didn't particularly like the idea of landing on a strange planet and trying to debug a computer program, either, even if Donna did all the debugging.

Donna triggered the jump. More stars leaped past, but none of the ones that appeared in front of them were familiar.

"Well," she said, "We're building up a pretty good map of this section of space, wherever it is. We can triangulate on practically any star we can see from here."

Trent wished he could decide. Jumping for a planet seemed like a step backward, especially when they were running low on power, but jumping around in the dark didn't make any more sense. Nothing really made sense at the moment. He felt dumb, like he was missing something obvious. What was it? It was right there on the edge of his brain, but he couldn't get a handle on it. What was he forgetting? He tried to think what it could be. Little alarm bells were going off in his head. They'd been going off since they'd gotten lost—what, fifteen or twenty minutes now—but this was different. This was . . . fifteen or twenty minutes.

"Shit, we're runnin' out of oxygen!" He cracked open his door seal and listened to the rush of air venting to space until the pressure gauge on the dash dropped to 5 p.s.i., then he sealed the latch and opened the air tank's valve, watching the pressure rise again. When it hit 10 he stopped the flow and took a couple of deep breaths. He didn't feel any smarter.

"We should have spent the extra money for carbon dioxide scrubbers," he said. "This is about the least efficient system you can get."

"Don't go blaming yourself," Donna said. "It was fine for what we intended to do."

"Famous last words." The air release had set them rolling again, so he had to vent more air through the bumper jets to bring them to a stop. He took another deep breath, trying to clear his mind. His heart was beating faster now, but he couldn't tell if it was from oxygen deprivation or just plain old fear of dying. "Maybe we should find us a planet," he said. "We need some thinkin' time. Can you tell which of these stars are like the Sun?"

She nodded. "The computer can calculate their magnitude now that it knows their distance. We just have to look for one that's the same magnitude as the Sun."

That didn't sound so hard. "Okay, then, let's do it."

Donna put the computer in her lap again so she could work easier, and after a couple of minutes she said, "There's not that many stars around here. We've got only four good candidates within twenty light-years."

"We only need one if it's the right one. Do any of 'em stand out?"

"Nope."

"Pick one, then, and let's go."

Their first jump took them close enough to spot planets. Donna let the computer get a good look, and Trent used more air to spin the pickup in a slow roll so the computer could see the whole sky, then they jumped again so it could triangulate on the planets.

It spotted seven of them, but the two closest to the star were gas giants, and there was nothing at all in the right orbit to support life. They picked another star and tried it again, finding a better spread of planets, but when they jumped close to the most likely candidate for landing, they could see that its atmosphere was thick and white from pole to pole, like Venus.

"Runaway greenhouse," Donna said.

"Runaway planet, too," Trent said. "Look at that bugger go." It was receding visibly, like a home run going over the back fence.

"Wow." Donna called up the landing program and had it calculate their velocity, and frowned when she read the number. "Five hundred and thirty-seven thousand kilometers an hour? That can't be right."

Trent watched the planet shrink from golf-ball size to the size of a grape. "I think it could be. That thing's bookin' it."

"Well, we're not going to land on it anyway, so I guess it doesn't matter." She made the landing program go away and popped the interstellar jump window back on the screen. "Let's try another star."

Trent eyed the power gauge. Down to a quarter now. But what else could they do? "Okay," he said.

The next star had one gas giant close in, but there was a more Earth-like planet in the right spot for life. They jumped close to it and had a look. It was a brief look because that planet was moving just as fast as the other one, but they had long enough to see cloud patterns and blue oceans and brown continents that looked pretty much like home.

"That might do," Trent said, "but damn, that speed. We'd be a week tryin' to catch up."

"Maybe not," Donna said. "There's that gas giant right there. If we used its gravity, we'd change velocity pretty quick."

"How quick?"

She called up the landing program again and let it crunch on the information from their triangulation jumps. "Hard to say for sure until we make our first pass and figure out how massive it is, but if it's Jupiter's size, it would take us about three hours."

Trent checked the pressure gauges on the air tanks. A nudge over two-thirds full on the left tank, and three quarters on the right. He hadn't calibrated the gauges for time, but if each tank held about three hours' worth, then . . . "We've only got about four and a half hours of air. That'd be cuttin' it pretty close."

"Yeah." They watched the dwindling planet for a bit. Trent couldn't help thinking that their hope for survival was dwindling just as fast. They had fifteen or twenty more jumps before they ran out of juice, and not enough air to take the time to use them right. "How many jumps does it figure we'd have to take to slow down usin' the gas giant?" he asked. The only way to make this big a velocity change was to jump close to a planet and fall away from it, then when you got so far out that its gravity started to weaken, you jumped back closer and fell outward again, but the closer you jumped, the more energy it took.

She clicked the pointer on the "details" box and said, "Six jumps. We could cut it to five by drifting farther before we go back for another pass, but it would take longer."

"Shit." Landing would take three or four more, depending on how particular they were over their landing site. That wouldn't leave them very many jumps to get home on.

He tried to think. "They can't all be movin' this fast, can they?"

She shrugged. "I don't know. All the planets in this solar system are."

"We'd save a lot of power if we didn't have to change so much velocity," he said.

"You want to try another star?"

They would have to make two more jumps at the least—one to get there and one more so the computer could triangulate on the planets—and one more to get close enough to see if any of the the planets were any good . . .

"No," he said. "Air's top priority at this point. Power we can do without if we have to, but not air."

"So you want to match velocity with this planet and land?"

"I don't see much choice."

"Me either."

"Let's do it, then."

Donna called up the landing program and told it to catch up with the fleeing planet. She couldn't pick an actual landing spot, since it was already so far away that it was just a blob on the computer's screen, but they could do that later. The gas giant was already selected as the gravity source, so she just hit "go."

The starfield on their left became a solid wall of yellow and orange haze. It looked like they were about six inches from it, but it began to recede the moment they arrived.

"Damn," Trent said. "How can that program be so accurate jumpin' from planet to planet, and so far off goin' from Mirabelle to Earth?"

"I wish I knew," said Donna.

They watched the gas giant recede, going from a flat wall

to a three-quarter disk with a big nightside shadow on its lower-left side, then dwindling further until it was just a big parade-float balloon and finally about the size of a basketball, all within the space of a few minutes. Then the landing program jumped them back and they did it again, only slower.

The long minutes of waiting were tough on the nerves. Donna couldn't do anything with the computer while it was in the middle of the landing sequence, so they couldn't even keep trying to figure out what had gone wrong with it, and Trent kept wondering when it would suddenly decide to do it again. One more bad jump and they'd be out of luck.

His throat felt dry. There was plenty of beer left in the camper, but he and Donna would have to seal up their suits and open the cab to go get it. That would waste at least fifteen minutes of air even if they waited until it was at its worst before they vented it.

"I should have put a hatch between the cab and the camper," he said.

Donna looked over at him. "I thought you decided it would be too likely to break the seal when we landed."

"Yeah, but I could sure use a beer about now."

"Me too." She shivered. "And a blanket. I'm cold."

"We can at least do something about that." He twisted around and pulled their coats from behind the seat.

Instead of putting hers on, Donna unbuckled her seatbelt and scooted closer to him, pushing herself down to the seat until he put his arm around her and pulled her tight against his side, then she tucked her coat around their legs like a lap blanket. He draped his over their upper bodies and tucked the arms in behind them to hold it in place.

"Just like old times," he said. She had always used to ride in the middle when they went four-wheeling outside of Rock Springs. You couldn't do that very well in space, because you needed the shoulder harness to hold you against the seat when you landed, but they wouldn't be doing that for a while yet. She rested her head on his shoulder and he rested his head on hers. Her hair smelled nice. Strawberry shampoo, and her own Donna scent that he always figured he could pick out blindfolded.

The gas giant was pretty. The clouds weren't as thickly banded as Jupiter's; they were more like Saturn's, just wide, even bands encircling the entire globe. He wondered what made one planet do one thing and another planet do another. Rotation rate? Chemistry in the clouds? He didn't have a clue. There was so much stuff he didn't know about space. It made him feel like a total idiot. Donna was always reading books about it, or had been since the whole business had landed in their laps five months ago, but he couldn't make himself sit down and read about orbital mechanics and planetary formation and stuff like that. It was too much like school, and he'd never liked that, either. He'd always been an outdoor guy. Give him a fishing pole and a mountain stream over a book any day.

He wondered if he'd ever see a stream again.

"What you thinking about?" Donna asked softly.

"Nothin'."

"What sort of nothin'?"

He smiled. "Okay, I was thinking about going fishing."

"Where would you go? If we were home, I mean."

"I don't know. Little Sandy, maybe. I've always liked it up there."

"Me too." She laughed. "Remember when I fell in the beaver pond?"

"Face first in the mud. Man, you were a sight. You looked like some horror-show monster. Gave me nightmares for weeks."

"Me too." They were silent for a few minutes, then she said, "We're going to be okay."

He nodded. "We don't have much other choice."

The gas giant wasn't quite as big as Jupiter, so it took almost four hours to kill their velocity. Every time they refreshed their air, Trent winced at the sound of the old air rushing out and the new rushing in, but they had to do it or asphyxiate on their own carbon dioxide. They traded back and forth between Donna's door and his so they wouldn't have to use the maneuvering jets to kill their spin every time, so that saved a few extra breaths. He just hoped it would be enough.

When the main tank ran out, they started using air out of the maneuvering tank. It was tempting to consider all of that to be breathing air, but Trent knew they needed to keep some for adjusting their position when they fell into the atmosphere. It would do no good to make it to safety only to go in upside-down and wrap the parachute around the pickup.

They napped fitfully between recharges, partly trying to conserve air and mostly because they hadn't slept in a day and a half, but Trent kept waking out of daydreams of good times on Earth only to find himself about to die in the ass end of nowhere, and he decided he'd rather just stay awake. He was glad he wasn't alone out here, but he would have given anything, even the last of his air, to have Donna home safe instead. It was her idea to come on this particular trip, but he'd been the one who turned their pickup into a spaceship in the first place. Who had he been kidding? He wasn't an astronaut. If he'd just accepted who he was and left it at that, he wouldn't have gotten either of them into this mess.

He was glad when the computer dinged at them to warn them that the velocity change was about complete. It gave him something else to think about. Something to keep his hands busy, too. At least when they were landing, he could *do* something. If he didn't screw that up, they could be on the ground in another half hour, which was a good thing because that's about all the air they had left. He didn't want to think about what would happen if the atmosphere wasn't breathable.

Donna slid over to her side of the cab and buckled in while the computer took them back to where it thought the Earth-like planet ought to be. It was off by about half the planet's width, which wasn't that bad considering all the jumps they'd made and the velocity change they'd gone through, but it took another jump to put them into position just outside the atmosphere, and once they picked their landing site it would take another two at the minimum to fine-tune their position and velocity so they would come in slow enough to deploy the parachute. That was cutting it awfully close. If they ever got home, it would be on the last couple of electrons in the plasma cells.

There weren't many continents here. What land there was was mostly islands; circular bull's-eyes with tall peaks in the middle. "Volcanoes," Trent said when he realized what he was seeing. And now that he had the right image, he realized that a lot of the clouds down there were actually active eruptions.

"Let's pick one that's dormant," Donna said.

"Good idea."

They didn't have a whole lot of time to decide. Every minute they spent looking meant another minute cancelling the downward velocity they picked up from the planet's gravity. So Trent just pointed at the first island he saw that looked big enough to provide a good target and didn't have a big thunder cloud over its peak. "There."

"Done," said Donna. She clicked the pointer on the widest stretch of flat land on the computer's image of the island, then hit the "go" button. The computer zapped them over to the night side of the planet for a minute or so to kill their velocity, then popped them back into place and dropped them into the atmosphere. They made one big jump, then two more small ones, feeling out the point where the hyperdrive couldn't go any farther, then began to drop from there. Trent used a couple more bursts of air from their dwindling supply to orient the truck so they were coming in with the parachutes on top.

"Airspeed is fifty, seventy-five, a hundred," Donna called out. At a hundred, Trent flipped the parachute release switch, using the one they hadn't used last time. Might as well put equal wear on them both. He'd considered using them together, since there would be no second chance if this landing didn't go well, but then he remembered that it would just take them longer to land if he popped both chutes. They could do it down lower, just before they landed, if they wanted to, but there was really no need. One chute was enough for a normal landing.

There was the usual two seconds of free fall after the release as the parachute billowed upward, then the hard lurch as it filled out.

Then they were falling again.

"What the hell?" Trent craned his neck and stuck his head against the window so he could look up. The parachute was a shredded mop of flapping rags, and there was a big cloud of white confetti above that. It looked like the thing had exploded.

Could somebody have shot at them with a laser satellite? They hadn't tried to call anyone on the radio, because they had been too far away when they were at the gas giant, and they hadn't had time before they lined up for landing. There hadn't seemed much point anyway; out here, the odds of finding humans, or even aliens who used the same radio frequencies as humans, were ridiculously small.

Something had happened to their chute, though. Should they jump back into space and try the radio? Maybe they could negotiate a rescue, or at least permission to land. But they only had one or two more refreshes of air; hardly time enough for any of that. And the more he looked at the shredded parachute overhead, the less it looked like laser damage. Nothing was melted; it just looked shredded.

They were picking up speed fast. The remains of the parachute were ripping free like party streamers. "Hang on," Trent said. He jammed his fingers going for the other chute switch, and he and Donna braced themselves for the jolt. When it came, it shoved them deep into the seat, hard enough that Trent felt the air tank under his butt. He prayed that this chute would hold, please hold, just get us to the ground goddammit hold, and he held his breath for the moment of free fall that would tell him he and Donna were dead, but it never came. He looked up and saw the canopy filled out firm and round above them, and he remembered to breathe.

"What happened to the first one?" Donna asked.

"I have no idea," Trent said. "It doesn't look like it was shot. It's more like our clothes and that shop towel, but the alien slime didn't even get close to that parachute."

She frowned. "No, but the tree sap did."

"The tree sap?" He slapped his forehead. "The tree sap! Of course. This is the chute that got hung up in the tree. And we got sap all over our clothes, too. And I wiped it off the parachute with the shop towel."

She looked up at the good chute. "I'm glad they didn't both come down in that tree."

"Me too." He looked up again and saw the old chute hanging in the shroud lines of the good one. What was left of it flapped a little in the breeze, but it wasn't fouling the lines or anything.

He looked down as much as he could. As near as he could tell, they were right over the island. He didn't have the mirrors aimed downward this time, either, but he could see big puffy clouds floating serenely over the central volcano, casting shadows on its flanks. They didn't seem to be moving very fast, which was a good thing. It wouldn't take much wind to blow the pickup out over the ocean.

Donna reached across the seat and took his hand. Her fingers were like ice, even through the Ziptite suit. He rubbed them in his palms, not sure if that would warm them up or not, but he did it anyway.

He had to refresh their air one more time on the way

down. That left just a few pounds in the tank, enough for maybe one more cabful, but if things went right, they wouldn't need it for a while.

And it looked like things were finally going right. There were trees on the island, and several streams running down off the volcano. As they grew closer, they could see wide, flat beaches and grassy meadows. Some kind of herd animals were grazing in the meadows.

"I think we could have done lots worse," Trent said. "'Specially if those are palm trees."

Donna said, "More people are killed by falling coconuts than airplane crashes."

"That's a risk I'm willing to take," Trent replied. He smiled and added, "I'll make us coconut helmets. And a coconut bikini for you."

"How come I have to wear clothes?"

He thought about that for a second. "'Cause otherwise we won't get anything done?"

"Depends on your definition of 'anything.'" She was giving him that look again.

He just shook his head and looked at the ground. They were only a few hundred feet up now, aimed for a big patch of green grass or something. As long as the same stuff was directly beneath them, too, they couldn't ask for better. "Hang on," he said, and he leaned back in the seat.

It was a perfect touchdown. The pickup bounced once and came to rest on level ground, and the parachute slid to the side and collapsed right beside them. It would be a piece of cake to fold it up and stow it again.

Trent looked over at Donna. She was grinning like a goof, and he realized he was, too. They'd made it. The sun was shining bright, and a little breeze was rippling the grass in front of them.

Normally if they were exploring new planets they would have a mouse in a cage who would get the dubious honor of taking the first breath while they waited in their Ziptite suits, but this trip they hadn't expected to go anywhere that didn't already have people on it. Trent considered having Donna seal up while he tried it, but there seemed little point. Either they could breathe it or they were dead. So he just unlatched the top and bottom of his door and popped it open, and Donna did the same on her side. They looked at one another, then each took a breath.

It smelled fresh and grassy. And a little spicy. "Smells like cinnamon," he said. "Not bad. Kind of sweet."

Donna had a funny look on her face. "What are all those stars doing down here?" she asked.

He was about to ask what she meant when he saw them himself: bright swirls of light looping around a central dark spot, a dark spot that grew wider and wider as he watched. He heard a ringing in his ears, and he felt like he was back in space again, floating weightless.

"Shit!" he yelled. "Seal up! There's something wrong with the air." He knocked off his cowboy hat and flipped his hood over his head in one motion, squeezed the seam closed, then reached down to his side and cranked the suit's tiny air tank's valve open. He heard the hiss of air filling the suit just before the darkness expanded all the way, and he fell forward into the steering wheel.

Somebody was honking at him. Trent jerked awake, certain he'd fallen asleep at the wheel, and the honking stopped. Sure enough, he was in the pickup, and he'd apparently run off the road, because there was grass all around.

His head hurt. And he was wearing a Ziptite pressure suit. He looked over to Donna's side of the seat and saw her slumped half out of the truck, hanging by her shoulder strap. She was wearing a Ziptite, too. How the heck had they wound up here? Had they wrecked? Something wasn't clicking. He felt like he'd been asleep for weeks, and needed another week to bring his mind up to speed.

He pulled Donna upright. She was limp as a sack and her head lolled to the side, but she was breathing. Her suit was sealed tight. Why? He couldn't remember.

The sun was shining bright and warm through the windshield. Trent shaded his eyes and looked out at the volcano straight ahead. It looked impossibly high and steep-sided, like a cartoon drawing. Snow covered the top third or so.

Volcano. They'd been about to land on a planet full of volcanoes. No, they'd landed, and opened up their suits, but the air was bad. Sulfur dioxide, maybe, like you sometimes got in the mines. Did volcanoes put out sulfur dioxide? He seemed to remember that they did, but he wouldn't bet on his memory of anything at the moment.

His suit was making little popping sounds: the pressure relief valve at the back of the bubble helmet letting out excess air. It was stiff, too, from being pressurized. Moving his arms took effort; they wanted to stick straight out from his sides. He forced them down to his waist and shut off the air tank's valve, then thought to check Donna's. She had never opened hers. He did that for her, letting her suit inflate and start popping for a minute or so and praying that the fresh air would bring her around. If it didn't, he wasn't sure what to do. He could seal up the cab and fill it from the tank under the seat, but that would take up just about all the air they had left, and there would still be sulfur dioxide or whatever the bad stuff was mixed in with it. If they were going to fill the cab, their best bet would be to jump into space first, let all the bad air out, and then refill it.

Which meant he needed to repack the parachute. He turned off Donna's air tank so it wouldn't bleed dry, then he climbed down to the grassy ground, pulled the good chute out to its full length, and folded it up. It hardly took any time; he couldn't have asked for a better surface to work on.

The truck looked like it had been in a wreck. Both sides were dented and scraped up, and the driver's-side mirror was smashed flat to the door. The fenders hadn't been shoved into the tires, though, which was at least some comfort. They could still drive it if they had to.

His memory was starting to come back now. He almost wished it hadn't when he realized how hopeless their situation was, but he supposed he would rather meet his end with his wits about him than confused and wondering what was going on.

He gave himself a fresh shot of air, did the same for Donna, who was still breathing evenly, then climbed up to the top of the cab and repacked the good parachute into its pod. The shredded one he just unbuckled and tossed its lines to the ground, then wadded it up and threw it in the camper.

Donna was coming around when he climbed back into the cab.

"How you feelin'?" he asked.

She tried to put her hand to her forehead, but bumped

into the bubble helmet instead. "My head hurts." Her voice was muffled by her suit.

"Mine too. It's something in the air here. We can't breathe it."

"Where are we?" she asked.

"The ass end of nowhere with practically no air left," he said. "We've got to move fast."

"Where are we going?"

"Another planet." He looked at the power gauge, turning his head to see past the condensation on the inside of his helmet. "We've got enough juice for half a dozen more jumps, and air enough to fill the cab one more time. Plus what's in our suit tanks. If we go now, maybe it'll be enough to get us somewhere that's got air we can breathe."

"With no refreshes?" She shook her head. "That's not enough air."

"I'd rather die trying something than just sit here and suffocate," Trent said.

"Yeah." She didn't sound quite sure of that.

He noticed his hat lying on the floor between them, picked it up and automatically went to stick it on his head, but it wouldn't fit over the bubble helmet so he laid it on the back of the seat instead. His brain still wasn't up to full charge.

"Can you run the computer?" he asked.

She looked at the screen, then out the windshield. "I think so. It's starting to come back."

"Good. We're going to need to find us another planet in just a couple of jumps."

"I don't know if I can do that," she said.

"Let's at least try."

"Okay." She took the computer off the dashboard and set it in her lap. "We'll have to try another star. This was the only planet in this system that was even close to habitable." She started tapping at the keyboard, bringing up previous screens from when they were jumping around looking for good stars. "There's only one other Sun-like star in this whole region that we haven't already been to."

"We've only got one shot anyway," Trent said, thinking that they didn't actually have even that. They needed enough air to let them find a planet, match velocities, and land on it, which would take at least half an hour, and probably longer. It was ridiculous to even try, except that there was no alternative.

There was no room for any more mistakes, either. He went over the steps in his mind: jump into space, let out the bad air, refill with good air . . .

Let out the bad air. The valve was stuck. They could just crack the door seals again, like they had done before, but it was harder to keep the pickup from going into a spin when they did it that way, and if it did, they would have to waste more air through the maneuvering jets to bring it to a stop. It would be safer if he could fix the release valve in his door first.

That was easier said than done. The nozzle stuck out only half an inch, but that was far enough for the weight of the truck to bend it sideways when it had tipped over. He would need a pair of Vise-Grips to bend that back into shape, and if dirt had gotten inside before it was bent, it would probably stay blocked even if he straightened it.

It could take ten or fifteen minutes to fix, way more time than they could gain by not using the maneuvering jets. Okay, forget that. Just go. But if they ever got out of this, he vowed to put a rubber hose on there for a nozzle instead of a chrome pipe. Hell, a valve stem off a tire would work perfect.

"Ready to go?" Donna asked.

"Yeah . . . no! Wait a minute." He was missing something. Something obvious.

"What's the matter?"

Valve stems. The truck had four valve stems, five if you counted the spare. It would take way too long to yank one off a tire and replace the nozzle on his door with it, but he had just gotten a sudden image of what would happen if he tried it. Twenty-five pounds of air pressure would come roaring out of the tire. At least a cabful at one atmosphere, maybe more.

"We've got five extra air tanks!" he shouted.

"What? Where?"

"The tires!"

He leaped out of the cab, slipped on the grass, picked himself up off his butt, and rushed around to the camper, where he grabbed the lug wrench out of the tool box and began spinning the nuts off the wheels, leaving only one attached—but loosely—to each hub. That way he wouldn't have to bust them loose in space with nothing to push against. The truck wobbled when he leaned into the wrench to loosen the last nut, but the single bolt on each wheel held well enough to keep it from going anywhere.

He had to refresh the air in his suit twice more while he worked, and he was panting again when he was done. He could see pretty well through the helmet now because the condensation had collected into droplets and was running down the plastic bubble, dripping onto his neck and running down his chest under his shirt.

Donna slid down to the ground and went into the camper, emerging with the rope, which she tied to the roll bar as high up as she could reach on her side. After she'd secured one end, she laid the coil alongside the roll bar and used the loose end to tie the coil down so it wouldn't go anywhere, but she used a slip knot on that end so it would be easy to release, leaving one end tied tight to the roll bar and the rest of the coil free.

"What's that for?" Trent asked. He had shifted over to the spare, and was removing it completely from its bracket on the side of the camper. He would start with that one, even though it was a smaller tire. With any luck, that would be all they needed.

Donna said, "You're not going to have time to remount those in space, but we're probably going to need 'em again. You can tie them to the rope, and we can remount them after we land."

She was absolutely right. "That's thinking ahead. Good." He picked up the lug nuts and threw them into the camper, almost threw the lug wrench in after them, then thought better of it and took that with him into the cab. He might need that in space if he couldn't get the last lug nuts off with just his fingers.

They had just about used up the air in their suits. Donna helped him roll the spare tire up onto the seat, then the two of them squeezed into the cab with it and slammed their doors. The spare fit lengthwise between the back of the seat and the dashboard, so there was actually still a fair amount of room.

"Okay!" Trent said. He latched his door tight and made sure his window was sealed. "Let's do it."

Donna latched her door and checked her window, then picked up the computer and set it on her lap again. Trent peered around the front of the tire to see what she was doing. She was just calling up the launch window when he noticed something moving out her window, and he looked past her to see an alien creature about seven or eight feet tall walking toward them, leaning on a long stick that it held in two of its four hands.

"Wait!" he said.

Donna paused with her finger over the button. "What now?"

"Behind you. We've got company."

She turned to look, and they both watched the alien take a few more cautious steps toward them. It stood upright on two legs, but it looked more insectile than human with its narrow waist, four arms, and a long, oval head on a slender stalk of a neck. It was more than just a big bug, though: it was wearing a red-and-white striped blanket draped over one shoulder and wrapped between its two sets of arms, then tied around its waist. Its stick was sharpened on the top, pretty obviously a spear. It stopped maybe twenty feet away and bobbed its head up and down.

"Somebody lives here," Donna said. "Do you think they'd be able to help us?"

"I don't know," Trent said. He wanted it to be so, because the odds of their finding another planet with air they could breathe in the short time they had left was pretty minuscule, but they would have to communicate the concept of oxygen to the natives, and actually *get* some from them, in the same amount of time. All from a guy carrying a spear that didn't even have a metal point. "It doesn't look good," he said. "I don't think this guy is techie enough to even understand what we need, much less provide us with it."

"What if he's a sheepherder or something, and there's a regular city just over the hill?"

"We'd have to get there, and I've already unbolted the wheels."

"We can't just leave!" Donna protested. "Not without at least trying to talk to him."

"I don't think we have a choice," Trent said. "We've got one chance to find another planet, but only if we go now."

"But—"

"Look out!"

The native had cocked back its spear. It took three running steps toward them and threw it straight at Donna.

"Shit!" she yelled, and she jabbed at the keyboard.

18

The hyperdrive tossed them into space. The front couple feet of the spear clattered against Donna's window, adding another set of cracks to the ones already there, then tumbled away to join the dirt and rocks and grass that came boiling up from below. The spare tire between them tried to tumble, too, but Trent held it steady with his right hand.

"Good reflexes," he said.

She looked over at him with wide eyes. "He tried to kill us!"

"Yeah, he did. And now he's probably at the bottom of a crater, tryin' to claw his way out while the edges collapse in on him. Maybe it'll make him think a little next time."

"Why am I not convinced?" She took a deep breath. "Damn it, that's twice in one day. I'm starting to get a little paranoid."

"Me too," Trent admitted. "But they haven't got us yet, and they aren't going to if I have anything to say about it." He reached up to the upper latch on his door. "Okay," he said. "Open yours the same time I do mine, and we'll let all the air out. As soon as it's gone, latch your door tight again and I'll refill the cab with air from the tire."

"Got it."

"Go."

He popped the latch open, and air whooshed out. When he'd used the door seal to let air out before, he had just cracked it open a little so he could control it, but this time he opened the latch all the way and let everything roar out as fast as it could. Donna did the same with hers, so the pickup didn't pick up much spin, but it did start to tumble forward a little. They would have to use the jets to correct for that when they were done, but it couldn't be helped.

Trent watched the fog blow out into space, dissipating into nothing a few dozen feet away. The stream of air grew fainter as the air in the cab got thinner and thinner, and at the same time his pressure suit grew stiffer. The little valve in the back of his helmet popped like a bag of microwave popcorn as it tried to keep the same pressure differential between inside and outside. At last Trent could see no more fog rushing away from the pickup, and the gauge on the dashboard read zero.

"Okay," he said. "Button 'er up again."

He looked around the tire at Donna. She was saying something—he could see her lips moving—but without any air in the cab, he couldn't hear her at all. He watched her secure her door again, and he made sure his own was latched down tight, then he unscrewed the valve cap from the spare tire and realized his mistake. With his Ziptite suit on, he couldn't get a fingernail into the valve to let any air out.

"Shit!" he muttered. He needed something pointy. A pen, or a knife point, or—or the wire he was using earlier to try to unplug the air release valve in his door.

He reached around the tire for the seat pocket where Donna had stowed it, fighting the inflated suit's tendency to push his arms straight out, but she had seen his problem and was already ahead of him. She popped open the glove box and grabbed the can opener, handing it over with the round side toward him so he wouldn't stab his suit.

That would do. He poked the tip into the end of the valve stem and sighed in relief when a cloud of fog billowed up into the cab. It took a few seconds for the air pressure to register on the dashboard gauge, but it slowly started to rise, and his Ziptite suit started to loosen up. Trent kept the valve button down until the gauge read ten pounds, then let off. He tucked the church key into the seat pocket on his side, then reached up and unsealed his Ziptite helmet.

The air stank like rubber, but his vision stayed steady after half a dozen breaths. There was oxygen in it.

"I think it's safe," he said.

Donna unsealed her suit and wrinkled her nose, then scratched furiously at her head. "Damn, these things itch." Trent was so used to hearing her voice muffled from inside her suit, it sounded like she was shouting.

He couldn't help laughing. "It saved your life, and you're complaining because it itches?"

"I'm not complaining. I'm just making an observation."

The tire kept trying to get away. There wasn't anyplace for it to go, but in free fall it wouldn't stay in the seat, and it kept banging into Trent or Donna or the dashboard or the roof. Finally Trent shoved the center seatbelt through the slotted wheel and had Donna latch it down on her side. It still tilted from side to side when either of them bumped it, but at least it wasn't flying loose anymore.

Trent's ears popped, adapting to the lower pressure in the cab. He worked his jaws until they settled down, then used the bumper jets to stop the pickup's slow tumble. The jets were more sluggish now than when they had a full tank of air behind them, but that actually made them easier to use. Maybe he should put a pressure regulator on that line when they got home.

Donna put the computer into its spot on the dashboard and let it get a good look at the stars, and when it locked on, she picked the last Sunlike star from the list of nearby candidates. They had to drop the nose a little to get it onscreen, but not by much. "Here we go," she said when the computer got a lock on it, and she hit the "enter" key.

It was a good jump. They could see their target as a much brighter-than-average star off to the left. Donna let the computer get a look at the stars from this vantage, then jumped closer, allowing it to triangulate the position of any planets it could see.

There were three; two bright ones that looked to be gas giants in close to the star, and a smaller one in the habitable zone. "So far, so good," Donna said. "I'm taking us in for a closer look."

"All right." Trent's ears popped, but he kept his eyes on the power gauge. It was already nudging the top of the "E," but it dropped a needle's width more when they jumped.

The planet was much closer, though. It was about as big as the Moon from Earth, and although it was mostly in shadow, they could see big swirls of cloud and blue ocean in the quarter that was lit by the star.

"Looks promising," Trent said. "How fast is it moving?"

"Let's see." Donna called up the landing program and let it crunch on the image for a minute, but it didn't return a value.

"We have to get closer," she said, reaching for the computer again.

"Hold up there," Trent said. "At this point we've got more air than power. Let's think this through so we can do it in as few jumps as we can get away with." He leaned forward to look at her around the front of the tire, and his ears popped again. He glanced at the air gauge, then took a cold, hard look at it.

Seven pounds of pressure, and dropping.

"Forget I said that. We've got a leak somewhere."

He listened for the telltale hiss of air into vacuum, looked for fog drifting away outside, but he couldn't hear or see anything.

"Check your door latches," he said, doing just that on his own side, but they were tight. So was the window. He didn't have a seatbelt caught in the door, either.

"I'm tight over here," Donna reported.

"It's going somewhere." He bent down as far as he could to listen close to the floor, but he couldn't hear anything there, either. Apparently it was a slow enough leak that it didn't make much noise.

If they stayed at seven pounds for long, they would be

courting the bends. Trent didn't like it much, but he got the can opener out of the seat pocket and let more air out of the tire until the gauge read ten pounds again. When he shoved his thumb into the tire's side, the rubber bent quite a bit; there wasn't much air left in it.

"Okay," he said, "we still need to make as few jumps as we can, but it looks like we've got to be quick about it after all. How few can we get away with?"

Donna looked out at the planet. He followed her gaze; it looked no different now than before.

"It's not moving very fast," she said. "We shouldn't have to make more than one jump to correct our speed for landing. So one jump to get close, and if we can pick our landing site without jumping again, then one jump to match velocity, one more to put us back over the landing site, and two or three more to drop us to the top of the atmosphere. That's, what, four or five jumps."

"That may be more than we've got juice for," Trent said. "I'd only bet on three for sure, especially close to a planet."

She pulled the computer into her lap again. "Let me see what I can set in the preferences." She tapped at the keyboard for a minute or so while Trent watched the air pressure drop a pound. With the tire between them, he couldn't even see what she was doing, but by the sounds she was making he got the idea that there wasn't just a "minimum jumps" option she could set. At last she said, "I can tell it to take us straight to the top of the atmosphere over our landing site after the tangential vector translation and not to give us any upward velocity when we get there. That should cut the number of jumps we need down to three, but if we guess wrong about where the top of the atmosphere is, we could fall a long ways before we get there, and burn up our parachute when we do."

Trent said, "And if we try to jump too deep, we use up the last of the charge on our batteries without goin' anywhere."

"Right."

He thought about that for a few seconds. "And it'll only work if we can find a good landing site on our very next jump, right? So this one's got to be just as accurate as the others."

"Right," Donna said. "We've got to make sure we wind up over the sunlit side of the planet, close enough to pick out a landing site."

"Can we do that?"

"I think so. We've got a good fix on its distance now, and the only reason the computer can't get a velocity reading is because it's not moving fast enough to show any sign of motion from here, so if I click on a spot just a little ways out from the sunlit part that we can see, we should wind up within half its diameter or so of the surface, and not moving all that fast."

"All right," Trent said. "That sounds doable. Now let's think about the air situation." He looked at the gauge, down to eight pounds again. "We've got maybe five more minutes on this tire before it's completely flat. It'll take me at least five more to get another tire loose and wedged in here. Do you think we should do that before we jump, or is there going to be enough time on the other end?"

"There'll be time during the vector translation," Donna said. "That should take at least five minutes. But we've probably got enough air in our pressure suits and in the regular air tank to get us down, don't we?"

Trent looked at the gauge. Seven pounds again. "It'd be really tight," he said. "And we'll need maneuvering air just as much as breathing air. I'd feel a lot safer saving what's in the tank for that."

"I'd feel a lot safer without you going outside in deep space," Donna said.

"Me too," Trent admitted, "but I don't think we've got any choice." He used the can opener to let the last of the air out of the spare, which brought the pressure in the cab up to nine pounds. "Let's go pick us a landing site, and then I'll switch tires while we're changing our velocity to match it."

"All right." Donna put the computer on the dash again, waited for it to make sure it knew where they were and what direction they were aimed, then put the pointer just over the day side of the planet and pressed "enter."

The planet blossomed into existence outside her window. Trent could barely see it around the tire, but its light reflected brightly in the cab. "How's it look?" he asked.

"Good. There are continents, at least."

He reached forward and used the jets to tip the pickup sideways, then swung it around so they could both see the planet through the windshield. It looked like they were maybe a couple thousand miles up, far enough to see quite a bit of it. The right-hand third or so was in shadow, but there was plenty to see in the sunlit part. Now that they were close, their relative motion was easy to see. They were falling toward it at a fairly steep angle, and going in pretty fast. They had a few minutes before they hit, though. Time enough to find a place to land, if their air held out that long.

There were indeed continents: two long skinny ones on either side of the equator that looked like they had been one big one not too long ago, the edge of another big one just sticking out of the shadow, and a big triangular one that reached nearly from the equator to the pole out in the sunlit side.

"There," Trent said, pointing at it. "That one covers the widest range of climate. If we wind up stuck here, we'll want as many options as we can get."

"That . . . makes sense, I guess. I wasn't thinking that far ahead." Donna didn't sound very excited at the prospect, and he didn't blame her. But without power to run the hyperdrive, they were about as stuck as stuck could be, even if they could plug their leak and refill the air tanks.

Unless someone else was already here. Trent turned on

the radio and tuned it to channel 1, but got only static. Same on 2 and 3. He picked up the microphone and called out on channel 9, and again on 19, "Hello, is anybody home? This is Trent Stinson calling for anybody who can hear me. Hello?"

Static.

"No such luck," he said. "All right, let's assume we're going to be living here a while."

Donna said, "Do you see anyplace that looks especially good?"

He didn't, not right away, but he could tell where *not* to go. "That looks like desert," he said, pointing to a wide brown patch with no clouds over it that ran along one side of the triangle and extended deep into the interior. There was a long line of mottled white and green along another side, the side that ran diagonally from equator to pole, and there was a big arc of cloud just off the coast that looked like a storm front sweeping in. Compared to a desert, that looked ideal. "That looks like mountains," he said. "If we could land close to those, we'd have better odds of findin' water. And probably game and fish and trees, too."

"Do we want the ocean side, or the inland side?" Donna asked.

That was a good question. Oceans, in theory anyway, were good for fishing, and they made the climate more steady. But there wasn't a whole lot of flat ground between the mountains and the sea. If they missed just a little bit on either side, they could wind up in deep trouble. On the other hand, if they came down too far from the mountains on the other side, it looked like things got mighty dry mighty fast. And without power, they couldn't drive to the mountains once they were down, either.

"Ocean side," he said at last. "As far from the coast as we can get without actually landing in the mountains." He fished the binoculars out of their case and started scanning for likely sites, but his ears popped again and a glance at the pressure gauge told him their time on this cabful of air was just about up.

So close! Another fifteen or twenty minutes and they could probably make it to the ground without having to use a second tire, but they only had another few minutes' worth in their Ziptites and another few minutes in the air tank under the seat. That might get them to the top of the atmosphere, but they still had quite a while under the parachute before they fell deep enough to breathe it.

Provided they *could* breathe it. But there was no point in worrying about that. Unlike the last time, there really wasn't going to be another chance if this didn't work out.

They only had five minutes or so before they hit the planet. Not enough time to exchange tires, but they had to do it. "Tell you what," he said, handing the binoculars over to Donna. "Zip up, and you keep searching for a good landing site while I'm swapping out the tire. If you find one, give a yank on my rope so I'll know to tuck in close to the pickup, and you go ahead and make the jump to match velocity with it."

"Your rope?"

"I'm not going out there without tying myself down." He reached behind the seat and pulled out the tow rope he always kept there, tied one end to the steering wheel and the other end around his waist. He left six feet or so of loose end and tied the lug wrench to that so it couldn't get away from him.

"That's smart. Come here a second." She leaned out and around the tire and puckered her lips.

He leaned forward and kissed her. She was sweaty and just as scared as he was, but she was still the most beautiful woman in the world as far as he was concerned. Hell, the most beautiful woman in the whole damned galaxy.

"You be careful," she said.

"I will." He pulled his hood over his head and sealed it,

and she did the same for hers. He wouldn't use the air out of his suit tank for a minute or two; that would give him that much more time before he ran out.

"Ready?"

"Ready." Her voice was muffled again.

"Okay, let's blow the door seals. One, two, three, go."

They popped open the latches on their upper door seals, and what little air was left in the cab roared out into space. The pickup tilted downward in front, so Trent hit the maneuvering jets to bring it back up. He had to do it a second time before all the air was vented out of the cab, but Donna needed the pickup steady when she jumped.

He opened the door. His suit had stiffened up again, but he managed to stick his legs outside and grab the tire with one hand while he steadied himself against the door with his other.

The tire wouldn't budge. Of course not; it was seat-belted down. And the buckle was on Donna's side.

"Unbuckle it!" he said, knowing full well she couldn't hear him. He reached around the tire as far as he could and pointed, and she understood. She pushed the release button and the tire suddenly came free, and he backed out into space with it in his arms. Then he noticed everything else coming out behind it: their coats, the binoculars, the lug wrench, his hat. Donna grabbed the coats and binoculars, and the lug wrench was tied to him, but his hat kept coming, wobbling like a black flying saucer as it made its getaway out the door.

His reaction was pure cowboy instinct: he let go of the tire and grabbed his hat. The tire instantly started drifting upward, so he flipped the hat into the cab like a Frisbee and made a grab for the tire, but he misjudged his motion in the stiff pressure suit and hit the sidewall with his hand. The tire flipped over and clipped the top of the cab, rebounded and hit him on the head, then bounced away as if it were rocket propelled. He made another lunge for it, but it was already out of reach, and there was no way he was going to leap into space after it, not even with a rope tied around his waist.

"Screw it," he muttered. He could do without a spare, especially since the truck was probably never going to move again once they landed, but he had damn well better not lose the next tire.

Which one should he take? He decided on the left rear; that would be the easiest one to get into the cab, because he wouldn't have to swing it around the door or over the whole pickup from the other side.

He looked in at Donna for a second. She was gripping his hat hard enough to crush the brim, but it didn't look like she even knew she was holding it. Her mouth was wide open, and so were her eyes.

"It's okay," he said, knowing she couldn't hear that, either. He gave her a thumbs-up with his right hand, and mouthed, *I love you* in exaggerated words.

I love you, too, she mouthed back. *Be careful!*

"I will," he said, nodding. "Find a landing site!" He pointed at the planet, now a bright wall of clouds and continents and oceans directly in front of them, then he reached for the side of the pickup's bed and pulled himself hand over hand back to the rear tire. He didn't need the lug wrench, which was a good thing, because it was all he could do to hold himself in place with one hand while he spun the already-loosened lug nut off with his other. The fingers of his suit wanted to splay out like a Mickey Mouse glove, and he had to fight hard to grip the tiny nut. Plus the pickup itself kept moving around; not much, but every time he pushed himself one way, it moved a little bit the other, so he was constantly misjudging distances.

The tire immediately tried to get away when the lug nut came loose, so he flipped the nut toward the door, hoping it would bounce inside and Donna would catch it, but it ricocheted off the armrest and flew away like a tiny chrome star. To hell with it. If he ever mounted this tire again, he would make do with four nuts. He grabbed the tire by one of the slots in the rim and steadied himself against the side of the truck, which set it bobbing around until they both settled down, then he pulled himself and the tire back toward the door.

He was panting like crazy. He probably needed a shot of fresh air, but he would need another hand to do that. He had to get the tire inside first.

He grabbed the open door like a shipwrecked sailor grabs the side of a lifeboat. There was a bad moment when he thought the tire wouldn't fit inside, but Donna grabbed it and pulled while he pushed one-handed, and it slipped in, compressing the seat and scraping along the roof as it went.

Trent was seeing stars now, the loopy kind inside his helmet. He cracked open his air tank and let it refill his suit with fresh oxygen, then shut it off again and tried to climb into the cab, but the tire was right where he needed to go. He gave it a little shove, and Donna scooted out of the way as best she could, but the tire was so fat that she couldn't fit between it and the windshield, and there wasn't room for both her and Trent and the tire to sit side-by-side on the seat. This one couldn't be turned around to fit the narrow way like the spare had, either.

"Jesus Christ, now what?" Trent growled. There was plenty of air in the tire, but no way to put that air in the cab without leaving the tire there, too. He grabbed the door frame and tried climbing in overhead, but there wasn't room for that, either. The pickup bobbed around while he pulled and pushed, trying everything he could think of, but there wasn't room in the footwell, nor between the steering wheel and the windshield. He was screwed.

His rope trailed away toward the planet, writhing like a snake on a hot road. So close. The pickup had fallen considerably farther in the last minute or two. It looked like he could just reach out and touch the surface now. Donna might get that chance, but unless Trent could hang on outside through the entire vector translation and the parachute descent, breathing his own carbon dioxide the whole way, it looked like he would only wind up touching the inside of a grave.

The rope slid back toward him, looping around his body. He felt it tugging on him, then realized it wasn't the rope. Something was pushing on him.

Air. They were hitting the top of the atmosphere. It wasn't thick enough for friction to melt anything yet, but at the speed they were moving they were about five seconds away from becoming a big meteor.

He looked in at Donna and pointed frantically at the planet, mouthing the word *jump!* over and over.

She could barely reach the computer. The tire was leaning forward against it now that the pickup was being pushed backward by the onrushing air. She had to shoulder it aside, then it took her another couple of seconds to lock in her landing site and hit the button. Trent felt himself slip around until he was hanging by the door frame, and the door banged him on the knuckles, but he held on, and a second later the planet vanished.

The wind ceased in the same instant. He rebounded into the edge of the door, bounced off it like the balloon he was, then finally wedged himself between door and frame. The pickup wobbled in reaction, but he hung on until it steadied out. Below his feet he saw a big black hole in space with a crescent of sunlit planet capping it at a jaunty angle.

He looked inside. Donna held up her hands, all five fingers splayed out on her right, and three fingers extended on her left. Eight minutes. Plus some more under the parachute. Might as well be forever. He didn't have that much air left in his Ziptite.

Now she was pointing frantically toward the back of the pickup. What else was the matter? He looked over his shoulder, but the camper looked the same as always, its aluminum sides reflecting the starlight and the little bit of sunlit planet.

The camper. He whacked himself on the forehead, his gloved hand bouncing off with a hollow *boing*. He could throw another tire in the camper and wait out the landing in there. Donna would have to do the whole thing herself, but she knew how.

He nodded and said "Okay!" with exaggerated lip motion, then grabbed the roll bar and pulled himself over to the other rear tire. If they were going to land with two tires missing, they should be on opposite sides, and on the same end. Then he realized that he had better open the camper door first, because he couldn't very well do that with a tire in his hands.

He crawled over the top of the camper, never letting go with one hand until he was sure the other was gripping something solid, until he was upside-down next to the door handle. He'd designed the door to open inward, so air pressure would seal it tight when they were in space and none of their food or anything would be exposed to vacuum. He had never figured on having to open it in space, but he had wondered what he would do if they landed somewhere where the air pressure was lower than where they started. Even half a pound per square inch added up to a lot of force on something the size of a door; he would need a crowbar to pry it open.

Fortunately, he had thought of that, and had put a valve on it just like the one in the driver's door. With the spigot on the outside, of course. He cracked it open and was relieved to see fog shoot out of it. The camper's seals were still tight, anyway.

It was a regular water faucet, with the spigot aimed downward. That wouldn't have been a problem on the ground, but in space it worked just as well as the maneuvering jets in the bumper. The pickup started to nose over under the thrust. Trent tried to twist the spigot around, but it was screwed in tight, so he did the only other thing he could think of: he cupped his hand underneath it and let the air blow against his hand.

That seemed to work. He felt the pressure pushing against him, and he had to hang on tight with his other hand, but the reaction pulled the back of the pickup down again.

Trouble was, the air was cold! It felt like he was sticking his hand in the blast from a fire extinguisher. He held it there as long as he could stand it, then shut off the valve for a second and shook his hand to get some warm blood flowing into it. He took the opportunity to give himself a fresh shot of air in his pressure suit, then went back to venting the camper, first shooting air straight out of the spigot, then cupping his hand underneath it and reversing the thrust.

It took four times, alternating hands, before the air was all gone and he could open the door. He left it just slightly ajar so nothing could get out, then pulled himself around to the right rear tire, careful to make sure he had a good grip with his nearly numb hands, and started spinning off the lug nut. It was tough to do with stiff fingers and stiff gloves. He got it partway off, but the last few turns were being a bugger. He couldn't get a good enough grip on the nut, and every time he did, his whole body wanted to twist clockwise when he tried to unscrew it.

He finally realized it wasn't just his clumsiness. The nut was stuck. He reeled in the lug wrench and fitted it to the nut, then managed to spin the nut off with one good flip of the wrench. The pickup started to spin the other way, but much more slowly. He hung on tight, and when he stopped the wrench, the pickup stopped, too. He didn't even try to save the nut; just let it float away. Four nuts would have to do on this wheel, too, if he ever remounted it.

The tire came free on its own, and he made a grab for the slot in the wheel before it could get away, then he pulled himself around by the bumper until he could shove the tire into the camper. He closed the door on it so it couldn't get away, then worked his way back around to the cab to untie his rope.

Donna was wrestling with her tire, tugging it around a few inches at a time as if she could roll it farther into the cab and make room for him. "It's not going to go, babe," he said softly, and a moment later he was glad she couldn't hear him, because he figured out what she was doing. She was trying to bring the valve stem around to a point where she could reach it.

He grabbed the steering wheel with one hand and helped her rotate the tire until the stem was on top, then he got the can opener out of the seat pocket—careful not to let it slip out of his hand—and passed it over to her.

"How much time left?" he asked, tapping his wrist in case she couldn't read his lips.

She checked the computer, then held up three fingers. He had to move.

"I'll see you on the ground. I love you, baby." He reached forward with his free hand. She reached around the tire and grasped his hand in hers, and they just looked at one another for a moment through their foggy, condensation-streaked bubble helmets. He never wanted to let go, but he had to, and they both knew it. Without a word, they gave each other one final squeeze, then he backed up and untied the rope from the steering wheel.

He kept a death grip on the door frame until he looped the rope around the roll bar, then he wrapped the end around his hand a couple of times. If he slipped, at least he could reel himself back to the roll bar.

He grabbed the door in his left hand and the roll bar in his right and slammed the door, nearly knocking himself loose in the process. The pickup wobbled like crazy, but he held on and watched Donna reach over and snap the latches from inside.

He felt a moment of unreasoning panic at the sight. Locked out of his pickup in deep space! He knew this was their only hope of survival, but still.

He probably had less than two minutes before the computer took them back to the other side of the planet. With a final wave to Donna, he pulled himself hand over hand around the side of the pickup to the camper, opened the door, and pulled himself inside. The tire took up most of the space, but he had room enough to slide in below it. Wedging his feet against the sides of the cabinets so he couldn't slip back outside, he let go of the free end of the rope and pulled on the end tied to his waist, pulling it free of the roll bar and piling it all up in a writhing wad behind him.

He swung the door closed before anything could fly back out. It was pitch black inside now. He almost turned on the light, but stopped himself when he remembered that the camper drew its power from the same batteries that the hyperdrive did. Lights didn't draw much juice, but the batteries were down to so little that he was afraid even a minute's worth of light would put them below the critical level for their last jump. He felt around the door frame to make sure it was closed tight and the rope wasn't in the way of the seals, then turned to the tire and felt for the valve stem, took the cap off, and realized he didn't have anything ready to hold the valve open with.

There were a million pointy objects in the camper. Forks, toothpicks, paring knives, even can openers if he could just find them in the dark. He felt for the sink, finally found it up by his shoulders and realized he was upside down, then he patted his way along the cabinets until he found the silverware drawer, unlatched it, and reached in for a fork. Everything was jumbled up, and he couldn't tell a fork from a spoon in his pressure suit.

He had to have some light. The drawer below the silverware had a flashlight in it, if he could recognize that by feel.

Actually, he was already seeing light, and not the good

kind. He reached to his waist and opened the air tank, and it hissed for another few seconds before falling silent. Empty. Okay, he had about two minutes left now.

Flashlight first. He opened the drawer, felt for anything cylindrical, found it next to something soft, and slid his hand up the side until he hit the switch. Light!

Three pot holders, a roll of duct tape, and a pair of scissors tumbled into the air, bouncing off the counters and ricocheting across the camper. There were already half a dozen forks and spoons and butter knives floating free, too, from the other drawer. Plus the lug nuts he had tossed in on the ground, and the parachute, drifting like a jellyfish behind the tire. The flashlight cast stark shadows as he waved it around. It was eerie; everything looked alive the way it moved so smoothly, yet none of it made a sound in the vacuum.

To hell with a fork. He let the flashlight go and grabbed the scissors, then turned to the tire, found the valve, and jabbed the pointed end of the blades against the tiny button, smiling at the jet of fog that rushed out around his hand.

There was no pressure gauge in the camper. He wondered how he would know when there was enough air to breathe, but then he slowly became aware of a faint hissing noise, and the soft *tink* of silverware and lug nuts bouncing off the cabinets. Yeah. The thicker the air was, the more sound it transmitted. There was more than one way to skin a cat.

He kept letting air out of the tire, occasionally slapping his hand against the sidewall and listening to the *whack*. When it sounded about as loud as he remembered similar sounds before with his suit sealed, he reached up to the top of his helmet and opened it.

There was a little puff of air out of the suit. He took a cautious breath. The air in the camper stank just as bad as the air from the spare, maybe even worse, but he could breathe it.

Or could he? He felt a moment of disorientation, almost as if he were going to pass out, but it was gone just as quickly. He took another couple of breaths, waiting for the swirling vision that would mean he was out of oxygen, but it didn't come. What had happened?

Then he realized what it was: the hyperdrive jump back over their landing site. He had maybe thirty seconds before Donna opened the parachute, and the air was full of utensils.

He could never gather it all up in time. The only thing he could do was grab the tire and hold it to the floor so he wouldn't wind up under it when the jolt came, and try to hold himself down against the floor as well.

The seconds seemed to take forever. A hundred heartbeats, anyway, but that probably didn't mean much. He was probably thumping away at two hundred or so a minute. He couldn't remember it ever beating this hard. It'd be just his luck to have a heart attack now that he'd saved his ass again for, what, the third or fourth time today.

He heard the faint hiss of the air jets in the bumper, transmitted through the frame of the pickup. That would be Donna leveling out their approach into the atmosphere. Then he heard the bang of the parachute pod opening. He risked a glance upward. No knives overhead, but the flashlight was right there, ready to klonk him. No time to grab it; he just tucked his head down and made sure his butt was tight against the floor.

The jolt felt like a giant kicking the pickup upward, hard. Silverware rained down all around him, the lug wrench hit beside him with a loud *clang,* and the flashlight bounced off his head to skitter across to the door, throwing wild shadows everywhere as it spun. The camper floor had no give to it at all, but the tire did: it bounced up and smashed into the ceiling, broke off a couple of drawer handles on the way back down, and would have crushed Trent's knees if it hadn't flipped sideways off the drawers and smashed the table instead.

Then the camper was silent. Gravity kept everything on the floor. The parachute was holding.

There was more than enough air in the tire to keep him breathing all the way to the ground. Donna would have enough in front even with the leak. Now all they had to do was survive the landing. And hope that this planet's air was better than the last one's.

Hell, that was the distant future, Trent thought. He didn't have to worry about dying for at least fifteen minutes or so. He leaned back against the cabinet and took a deep breath.

Something was clicking, like hot metal cooling off. Tick-ticka-tic-tic . . . tic-tic. He listened to see if he could figure out what it was, but of course it stopped just as he gave it his attention. He leaned back against the cabinet and heard it again: tick-ticka-tic-tic . . . tic-tic. There was a pause, then it came again.

Donna! She was tapping "shave and a haircut" to let him know she was okay. He snatched up the lug wrench and whacked it against the metal floor, *bang-banga-bang-bang . . . bang-bang*.

He heard more tapping, just a steady rhythm of it, then silence, so he banged out a dozen more himself. He wished he knew Morse code, but all he knew was SOS, and he didn't want to send that message.

"Hey, can you hear me?" he shouted.

If she could, he couldn't hear her response. It didn't matter; just knowing she was okay was all he needed.

He picked up the flashlight and shined it around the interior of the camper. The tire rested precariously on the remains of the table, the shredded parachute and his tow rope draped over it. Knives and forks and pot holders and lug nuts lay all around the floor. He supposed he could make himself useful and put those away before they landed. If they wound up rolling over, it might be nice not to have to worry about getting stabbed or beaten to death in the process.

He untied the rope from the lug wrench and from his waist, put the lug wrench and nuts in the tool box in the cabinet by the door, and started fielding silverware and shoving it back into its drawer. It felt strange to be riding in back, essentially doing the housecleaning, while Donna drove, but he had just as much confidence in her as he had in himself at the moment. She had always been better than him at running the computer, and she was the one who had thought of using the camper while he was still trying to wedge himself into the cab. If they were ever going to find their way home, it would be because she figured out where they were.

There was something sticky dribbling out of the refrigerator. He opened the door and saw the problem: the orange juice had boiled during the couple minutes in vacuum and the pressure had burst the seam on the carton. A tube of instant rolls had blown open, too, gooing up the top shelf. Trent thought about trying to clean it up, but Donna had wedged everything in tight so it wouldn't shift around during weightlessness or when they drove, and he didn't imagine he could get it repacked right in the few minutes left before they landed. He wiped up the worst of the mess from the floor with the ruined parachute, then folded the parachute so the goop was in the middle and laid it on the floor where he could sit on it and use it for padding.

Without its rear wheels, the pickup would tilt backwards pretty steep when it hit. Trent scooted past the tire and pulled it down to the floor, then shoved it up against the door, figuring he would rather wind up on top of it than under it if he had a choice. It wouldn't lie sideways, so he left it upright, but he wrapped the rope through the wheel a couple of times and tied it to the door handle so it couldn't bounce around in a crash. Then he sat down on the folded parachute, put his feet up against the tire, and waited.

He heard more tapping from up front. No pattern, but after a few seconds he realized it was getting steadily faster. A countdown? He braced himself against the cabinets and against the tire, took a deep breath—and had it knocked right back out of him.

The jolt was way harder than the parachute opening. It would have broken his butt if he hadn't been sitting on something soft. As it was, it rocked him backward and yanked his legs to the floor, then pitched him forward into the tire. He reached out with his arms to keep from hitting his head on it, but the pickup spun sideways and he clonked his head on the cabinet instead. There was another hard jolt, another spin, then three more sharp shocks before they came to rest. This was definitely not their best landing.

On the other hand, they didn't tip over. The pickup was listing to the left as well as to the rear, but that seemed to be the last of the banging around.

Trent untied the tire from the door and hauled it up the sloping floor out of the way, wedging it into the bench seat next to the table. Then he grabbed the door handle and pulled, but the door wouldn't budge. Was the camper stuck against something? That shouldn't keep the door from opening inward. The only thing that could do that would be air pressure, which meant that the atmosphere was thinner than normal. Or that Trent had overdone it when he had filled the camper with air from the tire. Relying on sound wasn't exactly the most accurate way to judge pressure.

He tugged again at the handle, but there was no way he could open it against even a few pounds of pressure, and the relief valve was on the outside. There was a vent in the ceiling and two in the side walls, though, put there so he and Donna could close the door at night and not suffocate, and the covers on those had a lot less surface area than the door. They wouldn't open with just a tug on their handles, either, but Trent dug a butter knife out of the silverware drawer and pried the edge of the ceiling vent away from its seal, and that did the trick. He heard a whoosh of air, and when he tried the door it opened easily. Light streamed in, and with it a big swirl of cool mountain air. He held his breath for a second, then forced himself to let it out and take another breath. They were going to have to breathe the stuff no matter what.

It smelled of green growing things. Recently crushed growing things. He took another breath and climbed down out of the camper, ducking his head to clear the top of the door. The pickup had come to rest at an angle on a fairly steep hillside, but the back end was facing mostly uphill, putting the ground outside almost as high as the camper's floor. By the looks of the gouges in the dirt, the front wheels had rolled and the back end had dragged along behind it, slewing from side to side until the pickup had skidded to a stop. They had narrowly missed several big arrow-shaped trees, and had plowed up a couple of rocks the size of watermelons, but they hadn't rolled over. Trent couldn't figure why not; the pickup was listing so far to the driver's side that the rear bumper wasn't even touching the ground on the right.

The parachute should have been snagged in a tree, given the truck's zigzag path around so many of them, but it lay flat on the ground over to the right, draped over some knee-high bushes and rippling just a little in the soft breeze that blew up the hillside. Evidently the trees were just far enough apart, or the tufts of branches at their tops were flexible enough, to let it slip past.

It didn't matter. They were down, and safe for the moment. Provided the pickup didn't tip over and roll on down the hill before Donna could get free. He rushed around to the passenger side to make sure she was okay. She had unlatched her door, but was having trouble holding it open against the pickup's sideways tilt, so he grabbed it and held it out for her, pulling down on it to make sure the pickup didn't roll over before she got free.

"We made it!" she shouted. "My god, I thought we were dead when I saw where we were coming down."

"I'm glad I *couldn't* see, or I'd have probably died of fright." He helped her get her feet on the step, then wrapped his arm around her and lifted her down to the ground. "Man, you're a sight for sore eyes." He held her close, resting his head on hers and breathing in the scent of her hair. Breathing. He was still breathing.

Metal creaked, and the pickup shifted. Trent grabbed the open door and pulled down on it again, and he was just about to ask Donna to grab the rope from the camper when he spotted the other one already tied to the roll bar right above her head. Donna had put it there so he could tie down the tires once they'd used their air, but he hadn't needed it.

They needed it now. "Grab that rope and run it up to that tree," he said. "I don't want this thing going over again if we can help it."

"Damn right." She pulled the loose end of the slipknot and backed up the hill with the coil, ran it around the closest tree and pulled it tight, then wrapped it around the trunk again and started a bowline knot. The tree looked stout enough; a foot thick at the base, and at least thirty feet tall. There were just a few branches up high, all pointing up at the same angle, which gave the whole tree the look of a huge arrow that had buried itself point-first in the ground. The branches looked a little like the trees themselves, bare and straight except for a tuft of needles at the outer end of each one.

Beyond the tops of the trees, a bird circled high above the top of the ridge. The sky was dark blue, darker than Earth's sky even in Rock Springs, where the elevation made it bluer than most places. The air was definitely thinner here. There were still clouds, though; a couple of puffy ones out in the distance and some high wisps of horsetail overhead.

"Try that," Donna said when she finished her knot.

Trent let up on the door. The rope tightened, and the pickup shifted, but it didn't go over, even when he let the door swing closed.

"Whee-oo," he said, standing back and looking again at the hillside they had come down. "That was some pretty damned good driving, little girl."

"I didn't do half of it," she said, picking her way carefully back down toward him. The hillside was dotted with round-topped rocks that looked good and slick, so she had to watch her footing. "We were jouncing around so bad, I only got my hands on the wheel a couple of times."

"Well, that was a couple of trees we didn't hit. You did great." The pickup had come to rest in a pretty good pile of rocks, too, but it seemed to have shoved most of them aside rather than bouncing over them. That was good; without the rear tires, it wouldn't take much to smash the wheel motors.

Trent was sweating like a pig inside his Ziptite suit, even though the air temperature was probably only sixty degrees or so. He peeled the suit down around his waist, then sat down on the ground and pulled it off his legs. He helped Donna out of hers, rolled them up together, and took them inside the camper. While he was there, he popped open the fridge, which was a total mess inside now, and rummaged through it until he found a couple cans of beer. He wiped off the orange juice against his pants and carried them back outside.

"Now there's a good idea," Donna said, taking one of the cans from him.

"Careful when you open that," he said. "It got shook up pretty good."

"No shit."

Trent let the pressure out slowly, then opened the can and took a long swallow. This was what beer was supposed to taste like, and this was just about the best occasion for a beer he had ever had.

"Here's to landings you can walk away from," he said, tapping his can against Donna's.

"Walk is the word," she said. "I think our four-wheelin' days are probably over in this truck."

"Oh, I wouldn't be so sure of that," he said. "This is a tough old beast. We may not have a lot of battery juice left, but once I get the wheels back on 'er, we can coast a hell of a long ways."

He peered around the side of the camper to see just how far that might be, and wasn't surprised to discover that they were maybe a thousand feet up a mountainside. It was peppered with more arrow-shaped trees and rocks and bushes, and the slope led down toward a valley that led out to an open plain.

Now that he was on the driver's side, he could see why the pickup was listing so far over. It wasn't just the slope of the hill; the left front wheel was missing, too. With only one lug nut holding it on, and loosely at that, it was no wonder. The first sideways impact had probably stripped the nut right off the bolt, and the tire had bounded down the hill on its own.

He looked for signs of it below. There were marks on the trunks of some of the trees where stuff had tumbled down the slope and smacked into them, but it was hard to tell what was done by rocks and what might have been from the tire. Wherever it had gone, though, it was a long ways downhill.

Donna came up beside him. "I was trying for that flat stuff out there," she said, pointing, "but we were so close to the atmosphere and so far inland that it was almost on the horizon by the time I could get the crosshairs lined up on it. The computer must have thought I was pointing at the mountains."

Trent shivered at the memory of hanging onto the door frame while the top of the atmosphere tried to blow him loose. He said, "Given how fast you had to pick a place, I'd say you did pretty damned good."

"Well, thanks for saying so." She turned once around, taking in their surroundings. "So now what?"

"Parachute first," he said, setting his beer on a rock. The rock shifted a little, and he thought better of using it for a table, digging the can into the dirt beside it instead. He and Donna lifted the nylon parachute free of the bushes and stretched it out along the hill beside the pickup, then folded it up. The pickup was leaning over so far that Trent was able to pack the chute into its pod without climbing up onto the cab, which was a good thing because he wouldn't have trusted the rope to hold it with his weight on there as well. As it was, he got the job done as fast as he could and backed away again. Last thing he needed was to get crushed by his own pickup after all the other things that had happened today.

He looked for his beer, found it a foot or so farther away from the rock than he'd remembered setting it, but didn't give it a second thought. His mind was on the pickup.

"We need to lift this thing up and get it level again," he said. He set his beer back down next to the rock, went around to the back and got the jack out of the camper, then pulled the tire out and laid it flat on the ground, too. If he put that on the left front side, the pickup would be nearly level.

He had to go around front to find a spot where he could fit the jack in under the shock mount, thanking his lucky stars that he had a screw jack. There was just room to slide it in between the dirt and the flange. He fit the crank into the slot, then backed out as far as he could and spun it a couple of times until it started to lift, but just as he expected, the pickup began to slide forward. He would need to chock the tires—well, the one remaining tire—to keep it from taking off downhill.

The rock he'd set his beer next to would be perfect. He went around to the back and picked it up, surprised at how light it was. Was the gravity lower here than on Earth? He hadn't noticed much difference in his own weight, but then he was so pumped on adrenaline at the moment that he wasn't sure he could tell.

Light or not, the rock had a good flat bottom. It was shaped a little like an army helmet, only half again that size. It was smooth as a river rock, which made Trent wonder what it was doing on a mountainside, but that didn't matter as long as it would serve as a wheel chock. He carried it around to the passenger side, where he wedged it in front of the tire, then he went back to the camper for a handful of lug nuts and the wrench. Might as well snug down the tire that was already mounted before he put any more weight on it and snapped off its stud, too.

The rock had shifted an inch or so. Probably came loose when he went into the camper. He nudged it up snug again, then spun lug nuts on the four open studs and cinched them down with the wrench, along with the one that had been holding the wheel on by itself. That one was pretty badly stripped, but he managed to get it snug again.

The rock was loose again when he finished. He shoved it tight against the tire, then went around and started jacking up the pickup, which crept forward until the right front tire was tight against the rock, but then it stayed put.

It took quite a bit of cranking to get the hub up high enough to fit the wheel on it, but the jack had just enough reach. Trent bolted the wheel in place as quickly as he could, then found another rock and wedged that in front of the tire before he lowered the jack. This rock was practically identical to the other one: helmet shaped and flat bottomed. A perfect wheel chock. He lowered the tire onto it, and was glad to see it sink into the dirt an inch or so under the pickup's weight. With both front wheels blocked like that, the truck shouldn't go anywhere now.

Just in case, he climbed up to the cab and set the emergency brake, grabbed his hat from the dashboard, and jumped back to the ground. He was going to need to get that other tire out of there before long, but he didn't want to mount it until he had the mate for it. Now he regretted letting that spare go.

At least the truck was sitting level now. The tire he had just mounted was kind of low, but not flat, which was actually about perfect to match the slope. The rear bumper was touching ground all the way across now, and the rope that

Donna had tied to the tree was slack. Trent hiked up and untied it, then coiled it up and tossed it into the camper.

Donna had been sipping her beer and watching the whole proceedings with amusement.

"What?" he asked.

She grinned. "You're never happier than when you're messing around with mechanical stuff."

"True," he said. He walked over and put his arms around her. "Except maybe when I'm messing around with you."

He heard a *swish* and a *thunk* just behind him, and Donna's eyes widened like camera irises. He turned around to see a four-foot arrow quivering in the ground right where he'd been standing.

21

"Into the camper!" he hollered, giving her a swat on the butt. "The pistol's in the clothing drawer."

He jumped up to the cab and pulled open the door, unhooked the bungees holding the rifle in the gun rack, then leaped back down, jacked a round into the chamber, and fired uphill. He didn't bother to aim; he just wanted to make whoever was shooting at them duck until Donna was safely under cover.

The gunshot echoed away to silence. Trent ran a couple of steps to spoil the aim of anybody who might be thinking of taking a second shot, then glanced back at the arrow in the ground to see if he could tell from the angle it hit where the archer was, but it was pointing almost straight up. He looked into the treetops, thinking maybe they had a sniper up in one of the tufts of branches at the top, but there didn't seem to be much room for anybody in those trees. A gray bird about the size of a turkey vulture was flapping down to land on one, but there was no sign of anybody with a bow.

"Trent, get in here!" Donna called out from the camper.

He took a couple fast steps to the side, swirling around to look in as many directions as he could, but he couldn't spot any movement. Just the bird, which was too heavy for the branch it was trying to land on. The branch snapped off at the base, and the bird flapped away with it clutched in its claws.

Had someone been shooting at the bird? That arrow had come almost straight down; not likely if Trent had been the target. But who would be shooting at birds when a pickup truck with two aliens in it had just dropped out of the sky?

He didn't hear any battle cries, or even any animal noises that might be natives communicating with fake bird calls. The only noise on the hillside was the pounding of his own heart. He jumped to the left another two steps, putting himself just one leap away from the camper door, but he didn't really want to reduce his field of vision to a two-foot-wide rectangle, especially one that faced into a hillside. A whole army could sneak up on them and they'd never know it from in there.

He looked up at the bird, just in time to see it drop the branch. It had carried it quite a ways before letting go, circling halfway around and rising another thirty or forty feet above the treetop. Trent watched the branch arch downward, not tumbling the way he would expect. The tufts of needles at the end stabilized it so it came straight down—straight at Trent.

He leaped backward, tripped over a rock, and sprawled on his back, firing a wild shot into the air when he hit. The branch thunked into the ground right where he'd been standing, just like the first one.

"Trent!" Donna yelled, rushing out of the camper. She grabbed him by the arm with her left hand and tugged him toward the doorway, the pistol waving wildly in her right hand, but she stopped when he began laughing.

"It's not funny!"

"Look," he said, pointing upward.

The bird circled around and flapped in for a landing atop another tree, picking one of the dry branches at the base of the tuft. The branch broke off under its weight and it flapped away with it, spiraling upward until it was about twice as high as the treetop before straightening out and dropping it.

"Stand back!" Trent warned, rolling to his feet and backing away another few feet. Donna backed away with him, keeping her eyes trained upward, until the arrow *shwonked* into the dirt right where she had been standing.

"That . . . that bird just tried to kill us!" she said, her voice rising in indignation.

"It does seem pretty deliberate," Trent said. He raised his rifle and followed its flight as it swept toward another tree, but he didn't fire. "You think it's intelligent?" he asked. "We're pretty much stuck here; I don't want to go pissin' off the locals if I can help it."

"It's already trying to kill us," Donna said. "I don't know how much worse it can get."

"A hundred of 'em at once," Trent said, but she had a good point. They were already under attack. They had to show these birds, intelligent or not, that you couldn't try killing a human without consequences.

"Sorry, buddy," Trent whispered, bringing the rifle up to his shoulder and sighting through the scope, keeping his left eye open to track the bird as it flapped in to land on another arrow branch. There was a half-second of stillness while the branch bore its weight; Trent brought the scope to bear directly in the middle of its body and squeezed off a shot.

The bird's chest exploded in a shower of silver disks, as if it had been stuffed with quarters. The branch broke at the same moment, and bird and branch both fell straight to the ground, the disks fluttering down like leaves after them.

The tree was maybe fifty feet upslope. "Keep your eye out for more," Trent said to Donna, and he started climbing up toward it, kicking his boots sideways into the hill for better footing and looking upward every few steps.

The branch had arrowed into the ground like the others. The bird lay on its back just a few feet away, dead. The bullet had punched right through its body, not doing a whole lot of external damage, but thick, dark blood—almost black it was so dark—oozed like molasses out of the bullet hole, and there was a big bare patch of gray-blue skin where a bunch of quarter-sized translucent scales had been knocked loose.

The remaining ones overlapped like fish scales, giving the bird an aerodynamic, almost metallic look. The scales were smaller on the wings and head, and curved to match the contours of its body. Its head was about the size of a hawk's, with the same kind of beak. Good for tearing flesh. It didn't look like there was room for much brainpower in there, but Trent wasn't going to jump to conclusions just yet.

He picked the body up by a clawed foot and carried it back to the pickup. Donna was turning slowly around, like a radar dish, her eyes never leaving the sky.

"You're going to make yourself dizzy doing that," he said.

"Better dizzy than dead."

"Have a look at this," he said, laying the bird at her feet. "I'll keep watch."

While she examined their would-be killer, he pulled one of the arrows out of the ground. It was much harder to free than he expected, and when he looked at the tip he saw why: it was barbed. The whole shaft was that way. It was probably just the leftover flanges from needles that had sloughed off as the branch grew, but it made an effective arrow. Most likely an effective seed, too. Trent bet that the barbs at the tip would develop into roots if he'd left the arrow in the ground. And the pointed end would probably grow into a taproot, though there might not be any need for it, as sharp as it was. This one had buried itself six inches deep, anyway.

He looked into the sky. No more birds. Plenty of arrows, though. Fifty or sixty per tree, at least.

"Which came first," he said, "the arrow or the archer?"

"Hmm?" Donna was stretching out one of the bird's wings. It had about a three-foot span just on that one side. Up close, its scales made a soft rustling sound.

"I'd bet anything these arrows are how the trees reproduce," Trent said. "Because they make good arrows, birds carry them farther than seeds would go on their own, and if they don't hit a target, they plant themselves instantly, ready to grow."

"Could be," Donna said. "They certainly work as arrows, anyway." She looked up, then around at the hillside, then back at the bird. "I think it's just a bird," she said at last. "There's nothing artificial here, no clothing or paint or jewelry or anything like that. And with hunting weapons growing wild, they wouldn't have to develop intelligence."

"How do you figure that?" Trent hefted the arrow like a spear, then gave it a high lob downhill. It arched over beautifully, perfectly balanced, and stuck when it hit.

She shrugged. "Just a theory, but I was thinking that if you hand a species everything they need, there's no incentive to work for it."

Trent snorted. "Seems to be that way in humans, anyway." He looked for his beer, found it in the dirt where he'd picked up the rock to chock the tires with, and took a long swig. "Weird to think that evolution could *keep* something from developing intelligence, but I can see how it might." He scanned the sky again. "I imagine we'll find out for sure soon enough, but in the meantime, we're going to need some protection."

He tried to think what might work. A hardhat would be a good start, but they hadn't brought any, and a hardhat wouldn't protect the shoulders or chest or back anyway. They needed chain mail, or maybe even full plate armor, if they planned to spend much time outdoors.

Or they needed to get out of the woods. Those arrows were fairly heavy; he was willing to bet a bird this size couldn't carry one more than a mile or so. He looked out into the flatland beyond the mountains. It might be possible to drive that far. The pickup could probably make it down the slope they were on with just three tires, and the regenerative brakes in the wheel motors would generate power on the way, which would give them a little extra battery juice to make a few miles on flat ground. They would need the fourth tire once they got there, but he was willing to bet they would find it down at the bottom of the slope.

He looked upward. Still no birds. Even so, the back of his neck itched with anxiety. What else would turn out to be dangerous around here? The mountainside had taken on a more sinister cast in the last few minutes.

He loosened the rifle's strap and slung it over his shoulder, then went into the camper and got the holster for the pistol. "Here you go," he said, handing it to Donna. "Until we're sure what's safe and what's not, we should both stay armed."

She didn't protest. Trent kept an eye out while she belted the holster around her waist and slid the pistol into it.

When he had first looked out of the camper after their landing, he had thought they had come to rest in a pretty good pile of rocks, but now that he had a minute, he could see that they were actually pretty lucky. There were plenty of rocks around, but the pickup seemed to be sitting in the middle of a clear spot maybe thirty feet across. It looked almost as if they had been blasted away by the impact of the pickup's landing, except that the real impact zone was uphill a ways.

One of the rocks shifted a little. Settling, apparently, from being dislodged in the crash, except it was at least ten feet away from the pickup. Why would it have been dislodged way over there?

Another rock shifted. Trent heard a soft click just behind him and whirled around, unslinging his rifle in the same motion, but he saw nothing that might have made the noise. The rock he'd tripped over during the arrow attack was the only thing even close.

But hadn't it been right in front of the camper door? Now it was a couple feet beyond it. He couldn't have kicked it that far when he'd fallen or he'd have landed on it.

"What's the matter?" Donna asked.

"I'm not sure," he said, unwilling to voice his suspicion without more evidence.

He kept his eye on the rock, glancing up into the sky every few seconds to watch for more birds, too. He nearly missed it when the motion came, but he caught it out of the corner of his eye: the rock lifted up about an inch and fell forward with a soft *thump*.

"Son of a bitch," Trent whispered. "They're alive."

"What are?" Donna hadn't seen it.

"The rocks. Watch." He pointed at the one in front of him.

"The *rocks*?" Her tone of voice made it clear how little she believed that.

"Just watch." Trent waited, not quite aiming his rifle at the rock. He heard a soft thump off to the side, and then another quite a ways behind him, but he didn't take his eyes off the one in front of him, except to glance overhead and make sure there weren't any more birds with arrows up there. Now that he was listening for them, he heard a steady patter of little thumps from all around.

After maybe twenty seconds, the rock he and Donna were watching lifted up and scooted forward again.

"My god, you're right!" Donna said. "They *are* alive."

Trent looked out at the others, most of them at least ten feet from the pickup and receding an inch at a time, and he couldn't help laughing. "Not only that, but they're running like hell. We probably scared the shit out of them when we crashed down here in the middle of 'em."

He pulled loose the second arrow that the bird had tried to spear him with, stuck the tip under the edge of the rock at his feet, and flipped it over, but it rolled right on around and flopped back onto its flat bottom. Now Trent knew why they were round on top, but he wanted to see how they moved. He flipped it over again, this time stopping it with the arrow before it could roll all the way. The underside was smooth and bony, like the underside of a turtle, with three little ovals spaced evenly around it about an inch in from the rim. As he watched, the ovals flipped up in front and down in back, pivoted through a 180-degree turn, and closed up smooth with the rest of the shell again. The rock did that a couple more times, then it started wobbling from side to side. Trent let it go, and the wobble intensified until the rock rolled back upright.

He felt a little wobbly himself. He had picked up two of them and carried them around without even knowing they were alive. If they'd been snapping turtles, they could have bitten his nuts off.

There didn't seem to be any openings for a mouth or a tail. Trent wondered if the leg holes doubled as mouths, or if the shells opened up somehow when they were grazing. Assuming they grazed. The rock camouflage and the slow crawl could be for sneaking up on other animals—and then what?

He looked at the arrow in his hand, and then at the mobile rock. Not camouflage; protection. These guys had sacrificed mobility for armor against aerial attack.

He glanced skyward again. No more birds yet, but if these guys had evolved armor to protect themselves, then the birds had to be fairly common.

"Oh no," Donna said suddenly, putting a hand to her mouth.

"What?"

"You trapped two of them under the tires!"

He had. He went around to the front of the pickup, half expecting to see that they were making a break for it like their buddies, but the tires had scrunched them into the dirt hard enough to keep them put.

"You've got to let them go," Donna said.

"Yeah, I guess I should." He could find real rocks to block the truck with. But when he tried to nudge the live ones out from under the tires, they were wedged too tight to move.

"I'll have to back it off of 'em," he said, going around to the driver's side. He opened the door, but the other tire was still in the seat, so he pulled that out and laid it on the ground, then climbed up into the cab, put the pickup in reverse, released the brake, and fed power to the motors. The gauge read empty, but there was still a little juice. The left rear wheel spun freely until he switched in the anti-slip traction control, and that fed all the power to the front wheels instead. The pickup didn't even budge, so he fed it a little more power, and suddenly the front wheels spun, spitting both rocks out to tumble down the slope like loose bowling balls.

He let off the power and put on the emergency brake again, then climbed back down to the ground. "Damn," he said to Donna. "I don't know if I did 'em any favor."

"They would have died if you'd kept them trapped under the tires." She looked over at the other rocks, still flopping softly away from them. "They must overbalance once in a while on their own. I'll bet they're designed to take a roll down a hill without hurting themselves."

"Hope so." Trent looked at the tire on the ground, then at the empty hub it had come off of. "I'd kind of like to go after the other tire before something tries to poke holes in it or eat it or something, but I'm not too thrilled about the idea of hauling it back up here. What do you say I mount this one and we just coast downhill until we find the other one?"

"Can we drive with just three tires?"

"Downhill, we can. All the weight will be on the front."

"Okay, I guess. There's no particular reason to stay here."

Trent looked up into the sky. There was another bird, still a long ways off, but gliding toward them. "You can say that again," he said.

With the rear tire in place, the pickup leaned forward at an alarming angle. Trent buckled himself in and made sure Donna was belted tight, too. At this slant it would be easy to slip forward and whack their heads on the dashboard, and if Trent lost control and the pickup rolled, he wanted to make damned sure they both stayed inside.

"Ready?" he asked.

She grinned at him. "Go for it, cowboy."

He shook his head. Why she trusted him so much, he would never know. *He* sure didn't trust himself to get them down in one piece, not off a slope this dizzying, with one tire missing and precious little power to get them out of a jam. He had to raise up in his seat to see the ground in front of them. They'd driven down hills this steep before, but only for a couple hundred feet before they leveled off. This one looked like it went on forever.

It wasn't going to get any easier by waiting. He released the emergency brake and eased off the foot brake, and the pickup rolled forward. There was a moment of free acceleration, then the motors' regenerative braking system kicked in and the pickup slowed as if it had hit a patch of glue. The cab rocked forward and slewed to the left. The tires on that side were both about half flat, which made the ride even mushier than usual, but it actually helped their traction, for which Trent was grateful. The motors and the foot brake could keep the tires from turning, but only traction could keep them from skidding. He eased his foot off the brake until the pickup was creeping downhill at just a couple of miles an hour, and concentrated on not running over any of the armored rock-creatures.

"We need a name for those rock guys," he said, swerving a little to the left to miss one. The pickup tipped backward and to the right, the bare hub briefly kissing the ground before he pressed harder on the brake, bringing the front down again. They bounced on the low tire and skidded a few feet before the anti-lock brakes took over and brought the pickup to a shuddering stop.

"Yow!" Donna said, gripping the Jesus bar, then she giggled and said, "Thrill a minute. How about creepers?"

"Hmm. Maybe. That sounds more like a bug to me, though." Trent let off the brake and steered gently to the right to avoid a tree about thirty feet downslope.

"Or floppers," Donna said. "That's more how they move."

"That doesn't sound slow enough. How about bunkers, because they're armored. Or tanks because they're both armored and mobile."

She made a face. "Too military. How about snailstones?"

"Too . . . I don't know." He had almost said "Too plain," but that wasn't it. Besides, snails definitely called up the right image.

"What do the French call those snails they eat?" he asked.

"Escargot," she said.

"Right. So these could be escar-don't-go. Or don't-go-very-fast."

"Oh, sure. I can just imagine you about to trip over one, and me shouting 'Hey, watch out for that escar-don't-go-very—never mind."

As they approached the tree, Trent saw that there were dozens of arrows in the ground all around it. He glanced up to see if there was a bird up there, but didn't see any. He didn't see any dead animals with arrows through them, either. It looked more as if the tree had just dropped a bunch of branches.

"Oh, right," Trent said. "The rocks. Or the tire. When they hit the trunk, it shook the tree, and the arrows that were loosest fell out."

Donna looked out at the thicket of newly planted seedlings around the tree's base and said, "That makes sense. I hope the tire isn't full of arrows when we find it."

"Me too."

Trent tried a gentler turn to the left to aim them straight downhill again, and this time the pickup stayed on its front and left-rear wheels.

"Snail rocks," he said, thinking aloud. "Slow rocks. Slow granite. Slow . . . what?"

"Slow motion?"

"Or just slo-mos."

"Yeah! Slo-mos. I like that. So what do you call a group of 'em?"

He dodged one, cutting it close so the pickup wouldn't tip, imagining the surprised creature running away at top speed for minutes after they passed, and making it about five feet in all that time. "A delay?" he said.

"A delay of slo-mos," Donna said. "Yeah, that works."

"So what about the birds? What do we call them?"

"Cupids, of course."

"Of course."

He slowed to examine some black marks about ten feet up the trunk of another tree. Tire marks? Maybe. There were certainly enough arrows on the ground at its base. The tuft atop the tree looked about half bare.

Donna said, "And a group of them could be a cherubim."

"Hmm," Trent said.

"Don't like that?"

"It's kind of clumsy."

She thought about it for a few seconds while Trent

eased them around a fallen log. "How about a valentine?"

"Perfect." Just then he saw a glint of something silver downslope to the right. "Hey, is that it?"

Donna looked to see where he was pointing, then squinted. "I don't know. Could be." She got the binoculars out of their case and focused on the shiny object, and said, "Yeah, that's it!"

"Hot damn." Trent aimed for it, letting off the brake a little in his eagerness to make his four-wheeler truly a four-wheeler again. They jounced over a rock—a real one, judging by its jagged shape—and teetered a moment on the right-front and left-rear tires, but Trent hit the brake again and brought the pickup back under control. He wanted to roll down on his wheels, not on the roll bar.

The runaway had come to rest in a thicket of brush reminiscent of the stuff that clogged the streams on Onnescu. It didn't have orange sap, though, or thorns. Trent parked the truck a few feet away, checked cautiously for anything moving in the sky or on the ground, then climbed out while Donna covered him with the pistol. He picked up a fist-sized rock and pitched it into the thicket next to the tire, and was happy to see that the branches didn't writhe like tentacles or anything, so he tried a cautious step up on the trunk that had been bent over by the tire's impact. It held his weight, so he leaned forward and grabbed the tire and pulled it out of the branches. The sidewalls were scraped up from hitting rocks and trees on the way down, but it didn't look like anything had actually punctured it. Either the arrows weren't sharp enough to penetrate rubber, or the tire had bounced out of their way before they had time to fall to the ground.

It only took a couple of minutes to mount it to the hub. He had to borrow a nut from one of the other wheels, which left only one wheel with all five nuts left, but that wouldn't matter for off-roading. Trent put the jack and lug wrench away, piled back into the cab, and rubbed his hands together in satisfaction. He had his pickup back. It was beat to hell and almost out of juice, but it was whole again.

"All right," he said happily, "let's find us a place to call home for a while."

23

They didn't make it all the way out of the mountains. Down toward the bottom they had to use too much battery power to drive around brush and downed logs. They wound up in a gently sloping valley with a stream running through it, with a flat meadow up on a bench above the water channel and trees and bushes all around. About half the trees were arrow trees, but the others were more like cottonwoods, with big branches holding up wide canopies that provided lots of shade—and cover from aerial attack. It was as good a camping site as they were likely to find, so Trent coasted the pickup to a stop beneath one of the broad-canopy trees and set the brake.

"Well, Eve," he said to Donna, "it looks like this is what Eden's going to look like for you and me. What do you think?"

"I think we could have done a lot worse," she said.

Trent took the rifle off the gun rack and stepped down to the ground, looking all around for anything that might be dangerous, but except for a few mobile rocks out in the open meadow it looked like they had the place to themselves.

The tree they had parked beneath looked like a regular Earth tree, with lots of wide branches and regular spade-shaped leaves at the ends. Nothing lived in it that Trent could see. The ground under it was covered with tiny little round-leafed plants, like those waxy little weeds that Donna kept pulling out of the garden. It looked like that was what this place used for grass. They hadn't seen any flowers on the way down here, and there weren't any in the meadow, either. Maybe plants on this planet hadn't evolved flowers.

The stream was wide enough that a person couldn't quite jump across it, but there were plenty of stepping stones. It made a happy gurgling sound as it cascaded from pool to pool. It would be a good fishing stream, if there were fish in it. Several arrows standing in the pools made Trent guess that something lived in there, something that the birds could eat. He hoped he and Donna could eat it, too. And there were the slo-mos. If those guys proved edible, the two of them wouldn't have to worry about food for a long, long time.

They needed helmets, though. They hadn't managed to drive out of cupid range, and they couldn't spend their whole lives under the canopies of these big leafy trees. They could probably dodge anything that they saw coming, but there was bound to come a time when they didn't look up quick enough, and as much as he would hate giving up his Stetson, generations of cavalry had proved that felt hats weren't much good at stopping arrows.

He understood how people on Mirabelle must have felt all the time, wondering when death would rain down out of the sky on them. Except no amount of armor could protect them. Nothing could stop an asteroid moving thousands of miles an hour. The only way to stop that kind of attack was to stop the attacker.

He wondered if that would be possible here. Or even desirable. Arrows dropping out of the sky weren't exactly a good thing, but the only way he could think of to stop it was to kill the cupids, and wiping out an entire species would probably cause a lot of damage up and down the food chain. Not to mention killing a lot of cupids, who might not be such bad guys once you got to know them. People thought wolves and bears had to be killed until they learned how to live with them instead.

With any luck, the question would remain academic. He and Donna needed protection now, not years from now; he wouldn't even begin to consider eradicating the cupids unless they wound up stuck here for life.

That was a real possibility. They didn't have enough battery power to drive out of the valley, much less jump from star to star, and even if they could charge the batteries somehow, they had no idea where they were. Way the hell and gone away from Earth, that much was sure, but that didn't help them figure out how to get home.

Donna came around the back of the pickup and put her arm around his waist. "What you thinking about?"

"Nothin'," he said automatically.

"What kind of nothin'?"

He smiled and gave her a squeeze. "The way too serious kind. We've survived a meteor strike and almost runnin' out of air and a mountainside landing and hostile natives; that's probably enough serious shit for one day."

"My thoughts exactly. How about we have us a picnic lunch? We never did get that meal André fixing for us, and that was hours ago. My stomach's trying to digest itself."

Trent had been too scared and too busy to even think about food, but the moment Donna mentioned it, his mouth began to water and his stomach growled like a lion. "Oh, yeah, I could eat a horse," he said.

"How about a ham sandwich?" she asked.

"Make it two."

"Coming right up." She went into the camper and started making domestic noises.

Trent followed her long enough to get their picnic blanket from under the dining table's bench seat, then took it outside and laid it out on the ground beside the truck. He looked up into the tree and stepped out to the edge of its canopy to check the sky, but he still didn't see anything moving. All the same, he couldn't make himself relax. He kept waiting for the other shoe to drop.

Donna came out of the camper a couple minutes later with three sandwiches and a bottle of water. Trent wasn't a big water fan, but he supposed they ought to ration the beer a little. No telling when they'd get more. Probably when he brewed some. He hoped his own stuff would taste better than the beer he got in brew pubs.

The sandwiches were wonderful. Trent wolfed his first one in about six bites, then forced himself to make the second one last until Donna was done with hers. She wasn't wasting any time, either, so it wasn't a great hardship. Neither of them spoke more than "Mmmff, good!" until the sandwiches were gone.

There were no ants. Trent kept waiting for little creatures to crawl up onto the blanket and go for the bread crumbs, but he only saw a couple of brown stick-like things about an inch long, and those just crossed the blanket on their long, spindly legs and kept going. There were no flies or mosquitoes, either. The air was just the right temperature, and the ground was soft under the blanket; perfect conditions for a nap, except Trent couldn't bring himself to let down his guard yet.

There was plenty of work to do anyway. They were definitely sleeping inside the camper until they were sure it was safe outside, which meant he had to repair the table that the tire had smashed, because that folded down level with the seats to make their bed. And there was the helmet question. What could he use to make helmets? He supposed he could cut up a tool box or something for the sheet metal and hammer it into some kind of hat, but he didn't really want to ruin a perfectly good tool box unless he had to. He wished he'd thought to bring some extra diamond plate along, but when you're coming down under a parachute, you don't want a whole lot of unnecessary weight. He hadn't brought welding equipment for the same reason.

He had a saw. Maybe he could cut down a tree and hollow out a chunk of log for a helmet. And he could split a log and hollow the halves for shoulder-guards. Maybe saw one into boards for chest and back protection, like those advertising sandwich boards that people wore on street corners.

He laughed out loud at the image. The thing would weigh a ton.

"What's funny?" Donna asked.

He told her what he'd been thinking, and she laughed, too, but not at that. "There's helmets lying around all over the place," she said. "Most of 'em are full of slo-mos, but I'll bet we could find a couple of empty shells without too much searching."

He tilted his head back and gazed up into the branches of the tree. "Good grief, what else am I missin'?"

She leaned forward and kissed him. "Nothing you can't solve the hard way, I'm sure."

"I guess that's a compliment."

"That's how I meant it."

"Well, then, that's okay."

He stood up and looked out at the meadow. There were several slo-mos out there, but he couldn't tell a dead one from a live one without going out and tipping them over. So he shouldered his rifle and walked out into the open, keeping a weather eye out for cupids while he walked up to each slo-mo in turn, tipped it over, and waited to see if it tried to right itself.

One of them flipped much more easily than the others, and when it did, a lizard-like creature about the size of a hamster scuttled out of it and made a beeline for Trent's boot. He jumped back and kicked at it, and it changed course for a clump of bushes a few dozen yards away, zigzagging like a soldier storming a gun emplacement all the way.

The slo-mo shell was empty. The bottom was half chewed away, and the inside was just a hollow cavity. The walls were about a quarter of an inch thick, and hard as bone. Definitely hard enough to stop an arrow, and probably bullets, too. Trent tried to bust out the rest of the underside, but it just flexed in his hands. He would have to take a hammer to it, and probably a file to smooth off the rough edges. The domed part was too big to fit comfortably on a human head, but with a little padding he supposed it would work okay.

He tried to find a second one, but everything else in the meadow was still alive, except for several rocks that turned out to actually just be rocks. He went over to the bank and looked down into the creekbed, but that was so full of round rocks that he would have to go down and turn them all over just to see which ones were real and which weren't.

He carried the empty one back to the camper. Might as well see if he could make one work before he hunted up another.

"It's funny," he said. "It's just about the perfect shape for a helmet already. You've got to wonder how come."

"Form follows function," said Donna, holstering her pistol. She had been keeping watch on the sky while he was out in the open. "It's basically the same shape as a turtle shell, too."

"No it's not. Turtle shells are a lot flatter."

"Tortoise shells, then. Land turtles. They're tall and round like this."

"That's true." He got his tool box out of the camper and started chipping away what was left of the bottom, using a hammer at first, then busting off pieces with pliers when he got closer to the rim. The inside was smooth and dry, with little grooves crisscrossing it where muscles had been attached. There was still no indication of a mouth hole or an anus, and the shell definitely didn't open up to let the inhabitant stick its head out, which made Trent wonder if these things even *had* heads. Maybe they were just mobile stomachs, like starfish.

Once he chipped away the last of the flat bottom, he stuffed a towel inside and tried it on. It came down over his eyes until he adjusted the towel, and then it bumped into his back at the base of his neck. That might not be such a bad thing, actually. Firemen's hats did that.

"What do you think?" he asked Donna.

"You look like a little kid with his dad's army helmet," she said, laughing. "But it looks like it should work."

"Good. A little shoulder protection, and I think we'll be in business. Let's see if we can find another one."

Keeping an eye out for cupids, he scrambled down the creek bank and started poking around among the rocks there. Most of them were just rocks, but there was a gravel bar at the tail of a bend in the stream where a bunch of driftwood had collected, and there were a couple of helmet-shaped rocks in among the branches. One was definitely a slo-mo; it was upside down and he could see the flat underside.

It had a hole chewed in the bottom, too. He nudged it with the barrel of his rifle, but nothing leaped out of it, so he tipped it over and a bunch of brown water poured out the hole.

"Eeew," Donna said. "You're wearing that one."

"Okay." He swished it around in the pool, filling and emptying it until the water came out clean. The stream was cold; evidently it was runoff from snowmelt higher up in the mountains. That was too bad for bathing, but encouraging in terms of predators and parasites. On Earth, at least, cold-water streams had a lot fewer nasties in them than warm ones. It would also make a good place to chill his beer, once he made sure nothing would run off with it.

He carried the shell back up the bank and set to work on it with the hammer and pliers until he'd chipped away all but the curved upper half. There were still some stringy ends of tendons attached to it, so he scraped those away with his pocket knife, then went back to the stream to wash it out again. While he was down there he hauled out a six-inch log from the driftwood pile that looked like it would make good shoulder guards and dragged it up to their campsite.

While he set to work on the log with a saw, Donna went into the camper and started cleaning up the mess in there. She came out with the ripped-up parachute and asked, "What do you want to do with this, anyway?"

"Keep it," he said automatically. He didn't want to throw

anything out, not with civilization a million light-years away, and maybe forever. The sections that had been weakened by sap were probably useless, but there were still big pieces of cloth that weren't. It would never make a parachute again, but if he and Donna were truly stuck here, they might wind up wearing it before they learned to skin and tan hides.

"We should wash it," she said, "so the acid doesn't spread and eat the whole thing."

"Good thought. Here." He took it from her, unwound the shroud lines from the bundle of cloth, and threw the bundle down into the biggest pool in the stream. He tied the shroud lines to the tree so it wouldn't float off downstream. "It's not exactly washing, but that ought to give it a good soak, anyway." He didn't know if the sap was water soluble or not, but it was worth a try.

He went back to work on the log, cutting off an eight-inch section and splitting it in half, then hollowing it out with the claw of a hammer until he had two inch-thick shells of wood that would fit over his shoulders. They stuck out like epaulets on a military dress uniform, but they would do the job. The wood was harder than pine, and fibrous enough to hang together under impact.

He used a ratchet screwdriver to drill holes in the shoulder pieces and in the helmet, then strung them together with cord from the parachute shroud lines. He made a chin strap for the helmet, put the whole works on, and went to the camper door. "What do you think?" he asked.

It was darker inside the camper than out in the open. He couldn't see Donna's expression, but her laughter told him plenty. "You look like a samurai!" she said.

"Better than a kid in his dad's helmet."

"Well, that, too, but the shoulder dealies are priceless. Hold on a second." She rummaged in a drawer, then came out with their camera. "Hold up your gun and look fierce," she said.

He tried, but she kept snickering, and he couldn't hold a

stern expression while she was doing that. "Take the damned picture, woman!" he said, but he was grinning when he said it, and sure enough, that's when she snapped the shot. He almost deleted it when she showed it to him, but she said, "No way! Take your own if you don't like this one, but that's mine. When we get home I'm going to print it out full-sized and frame it for the living room, and we can hang the helmet and armor underneath it and tell stories about it."

"Oh boy," he said, but he handed back the camera without deleting the picture. In a weird way, it gave him something to look forward to. He hoped he would make it back home to be embarrassed by it, but if he didn't, then at least there would be one good thing about staying stranded the rest of their lives.

He made another set of armor just like the first for Donna, then set to work on the table in the camper. The table itself wasn't broken, so it was a simple matter of finding a sturdy stick and cutting it to the right size to replace the legs that had busted. That was the work of a half hour, then he took the Vise-Grips to the air valve in his door, bending it out straight again. He fished around in the pipe with the wire from the spiral notebook, pulling out a little plug of dirt, then blew through the spigot from the inner side. Free.

The driver's mirror took another half hour to bend back into shape. There was a big crack in it, and the image in the two pieces didn't quite line up, but it would work well enough until he could get a replacement.

He got out the foot pump and refilled the tires. He thought about filling the air tanks, too, but that would be a lot of work, and they weren't going into space again unless he could recharge the batteries, and if he could figure out a way to do that, then he could use the compressor.

He cut up the rest of the log for firewood, and hauled up some smaller stuff from the driftwood pile for kindling. He wasn't sure about sitting outside around a campfire in the dark until they learned what kind of nocturnal animals lived around there, but it never hurt to have a supply of firewood on hand, and it gave him something useful to do. It was starting to dawn on him how long a day could be when you didn't have a plan to fill it.

They didn't need to wear their helmets under the tree.

Trent went out to the edge of its canopy and scanned the sky from time to time, and he saw the occasional cupid riding thermals high overhead, but none of them even came down to investigate. It looked like maybe they weren't going to be as much of a threat as he had thought, but he was glad he'd made the armor just in case.

After Donna cleaned up the camper—which took all of half an hour—she settled down on the picnic blanket with the computer and started poring through the hyperdrive control program, trying to figure out what had gone wrong and where it had taken them. It wouldn't do much good if they couldn't recharge the truck's batteries, but recharging the batteries wouldn't get them home until they knew where they were.

Trent went through everything they had brought with them, counting up how many separate batteries he could find, but there weren't many. Two flashlights, the computer, their phone, a calculator (solar powered, but it had a button battery for low-light use), and a couple spare flashlight cells. Granted, a flashlight battery would run the light for a couple of weeks of steady use, but it wouldn't power a hyperdrive. The camper's stove took its power from the truck's main battery . . . as did the refrigerator, come to think of it. They were going to have to eat the perishable food first, which was probably why Donna had suggested ham sandwiches again for lunch. She was way ahead of him.

He thought briefly about using the calculator's solar cell to recharge the truck's battery, but a few minutes of number crunching with that same calculator convinced him that he and Donna would probably die of old age before a tiny solar cell could recharge a plasma battery.

There was still enough juice in the mains for the radio. He listened on all the channels, and he tried calling on the emergency frequency and the general talk frequency, but there was nobody out there. Ground-to-ground, the radio probably had only a fifty-mile range or so anyway; it would only be useful if someone popped into orbit directly overhead.

He switched it off and sat down beside Donna. "Any luck?" he asked.

"Not yet," she replied. She was reading a help screen for the navigation program's targeting module. "Well, actually, I've learned a couple things. The program stores everything it does in a log file, but the log file says we only went sixty light-years on the jump from Mirabelle, so that probably means the bug in the program is between the part that sets the target and the part that actually sends the command to the hyperdrive."

He wasn't sure he followed all that, but he understood enough to ask, "Do you think you can fix the bug if you find it?"

"I doubt it," she said. "I'm not a programmer, and I don't have the right software for it even if I was." She ran a hand through her hair and sighed. "I'm afraid you'd be better off with Nick and Glory at this point. Glory could probably just calculate how far we went by how much power we used, or by the density of the stars or something."

"The velocity," Trent said. "She was talking about how they move faster the farther away you go. She could probably just look at how fast that first planet we had to catch up with was movin' and figure out right where we had to be."

Donna cocked her head to the side and looked at him out the corner of one eye. "I hadn't thought of that. Of course that's why it was moving so fast. And why we didn't have to do it again for the next one. Once we caught up to the first one, we were moving at the same pace as everything else around here. We just had to make up the difference in speed between the two planets going around their stars."

Trent nodded. "Makes sense. So can you use that to figure out how far we went?"

She shook her head. "I'm not Glory. I don't know how

fast the galaxy rotates, or how fast we were moving back home, or—"

"Once every quarter of a billion years, and the stars around Earth are moving about half a million miles per hour."

She couldn't have looked more surprised if he'd started quoting Shakespeare at her. "You—how did you—"

"You thought I was just staring at her boobs, didn't you?" he said smugly. Truth was, he had been so shocked when Glory had started to talk astrophysics that her words had been burned into his brain like the image of an accident. He thought for a moment and said, "Earth is thirty thousand light-years out from the center of the galaxy, and that half million miles an hour is about thirty times the orbital velocity of a satellite around an average sized planet. I thought it was funny that both numbers came out thirty."

She tapped him gently on the side of his head. "You got anything else tucked away in there?"

"I remember she said it would take days to match speed with another galaxy, so unless she was exaggerating, I'm guessin' we're still in the Milky Way."

Donna laughed. "Now that's a comfort." She turned back to the computer and opened up a drawing window, where she quickly sketched a rough spiral galaxy with an "x" about halfway out from the middle, which she labeled "Sun." She typed "30,000 ly" next to it, and "500,000 mph" next to that. Then she called up the navigation program again and dug through its log file until she found how much velocity change they had had to make—537,000 kilometers/hour—and typed that in.

"Better convert that to miles," Trent said, "or you'll forget to later."

"Actually, I'll be better off converting Earth's speed to kilometers," she said. "All the other numbers in here are metric, too." She did that, then stared at the diagram for a minute. "Okay, let's say we jumped straight out toward the edge of the galaxy. We'd be moving slower than the stars out there. So how far would we have to go to be moving five hundred and thirty-seven thousand miles an hour too slow?"

She might as well have asked how many leaves were on the tree overhead. Trent's schooling had topped out at general math, and he'd gotten a "B" at that. He snorted and said, "I have absolutely no idea."

"Me neither," Donna said, "but if we can figure that out, I think that'll tell us where we are."

For a moment, Trent felt the weight of their situation drop off his shoulders. Donna was a hell of a lot better at math than he was. Maybe she could do it. But a moment later he realized the flaw in her logic. "How do you know we went straight out?"

"I don't," she admitted. "But I have the coordinates of both Mirabelle and Earth, so I can figure out what direction we did go. Assuming we were right about the only bug being our distance."

"And then you can calculate how far we went, just knowing how much faster everything was?"

"Maybe. I've got to account for the Earth's motion around the Sun, and this planet's motion around *this* sun, too, 'cause that's not part of the galaxy's rotation, but if I can do all that, then . . ." She stared at the screen again, then started drawing little circles and connecting them with lines.

"What's all that?"

"That's me thinkin'. Go find something else to do for a while."

"Yes, ma'am."

He got up and put on his helmet and armor, picked up his rifle, and walked out into the open, figuring he probably ought to check out a little more of their surroundings. No cupids upstairs at the moment. Five or six slo-mos out in the meadow. No lizards, but there were little noises coming from the bushes that could be them, or could be something else. He looked for big piles of dung that a big animal would leave, piles of bones or skulls that might show tooth marks of big predators, holes in the ground that might be the dens of nocturnal animals—anything that would help him figure out what kind of place they had landed in. He kept an eye out for berries and nuts and fruit trees, too, finding several promising candidates, and he scuffed up the ground around a few plants that looked like they might have edible roots, but all the while his mind was on the big question: how could he recharge the truck's batteries? He recognized that look on Donna's face. She wouldn't stop working on the math until she had figured out where they were. She might have to learn orbital mechanics first, but she would do it—hell, she would re-invent it if she had to—if that's what it took to come up with an answer.

It made him proud as hell to see the way she dived into stuff like that, but he had to admit that it also made him feel dumb as a post. Before they had left on their first hyperdrive trip, he had tried to learn how to run the computer, figuring that the driving had always been his job when they went four-wheeling, and it would stay his job in space, too, but a couple of days spent reading about vector translations and gravity wells and how to calculate an orbit had shown him just how different flying a spaceship was from driving a truck. Donna had taken to it like a duck to water, though. Within an afternoon, she had run a series of simulated jumps out to Alpha Centauri and back, and she had only crashed their simulated spaceship a couple of times on re-entry before she got the hang of that, too. He had told himself that it didn't bother him, and he built the camper and sealed both it and the pickup's cab to hold against vacuum, and he had figured out the center of mass of the whole works and had hooked up the parachutes directly over that spot so the pickup would land on its wheels, and he had designed and built the maneuvering jets himself.

He had done all that stuff, but all that time he had known that he couldn't fly the thing himself. And now here was Donna number-crunching velocity figures in the hope of saving their asses from a long, slow descent into savagery, while he walked around looking for wild animals and wondering how he could recharge a dead battery without a power supply.

He came upon a small arrow tree only eight feet high or so, with a scattering of yellow bones at its base. A cupid had apparently gotten lucky here a year or so ago. It looked like whatever it had killed hadn't been much bigger than a dog, and the few teeth that Trent could find were flat-topped like a sheep's rather than pointy like a wolf's. That was good news.

The arrow had done well for itself, too. The tuft of branches at its top looked thick and healthy, bristling with mini-arrows a couple of feet long. He bent close to look at the tufts at the end of those and saw that the needles were actually smaller versions of the same thing, and if he squinted, the needles looked like they had little fuzzy barbs sticking out of their outer ends, too. Fractals. He remembered Donna telling him about fractals, how you could build something big out of millions of tiny parts that looked just the same as the big one. That had been something else she had learned on the computer, from a program that made cool-looking drawings on the screen just for fun.

He checked the sky. No cupids. No airplanes, either. He hadn't seen or heard any sign of civilization since he and Donna had arrived. He tried to piece together the bones of the dead animal to see what it might have looked like alive, but they were scattered too much for him to even begin to guess what went where.

Chalk up another thing he wasn't any good at.

He walked on and came to the stream, where he stood on the bank looking down into the water. It bubbled happily over rocks and shimmered in the pools, reflections obscuring what might swim beneath the surface. He supposed he could get out his fishing pole and see if anything in there would take a fly, but he wasn't in the mood for fishing. Not while Donna was reinventing calculus over there under the tree.

He looked down the length of the meadow to where she sat, a little girl alone in the great outdoors. Isaac Newton under the apple tree. The pickup looked ridiculously out of place parked there beside her, a crude, barbaric relic of a world that prized adventure over learning. He blinked and for a second saw it with its tires flat and paint dull, rusting away after years of rain and snow. Would he and Donna still be living in the camper, hoarding their last precious relics of civilization, or would they have built a cabin by then out of arrow trees? Would there be half a dozen kids running around, wearing samurai armor and playing kick-the-slo-mo?

A soft breeze blew through the meadow, rustling leaves and bringing up a spicy odor from somewhere. There weren't any flowers, but it still smelled nice. A little like sagebrush, only not so in-your-face. He could get used to a place that smelled like this.

He crossed the stream at a narrow spot at the head of a little waterfall that fell maybe four feet into a wide pool. A nice bathing pool, if the water wasn't so cold. Maybe they could divert most of the flow around it so it could warm up in the sunlight.

When he climbed to the top of the other bank, he heard more rustling in the bushes, and when he took a couple steps closer, a little brown leathery ball about the size of a porcupine burst out from cover and bolted across twenty feet of open space to another bush. Trent thought briefly about trying to bag it for dinner, but he didn't want to try eating any of the native life just yet. It was one thing to experiment with alien food when you could rush back to Earth and a hospital within a couple of hours, but when you were stuck in the middle of nowhere and your entire stock of medical supplies consisted of a traveller's first-aid kit, it made sense to move a little more slowly.

He completed his circuit of their immediate surroundings without finding any bear dens or dinosaur footprints. The biggest animal he had seen any evidence of was whatever had left the pile of bones with the arrow through it. He felt himself relax a little as he walked back toward the pickup. Even if they did figure out where they were and charge the batteries, they didn't necessarily have to leave here, at least not permanently. They had been looking for a new home when they left Earth; they could do a lot worse than this.

He wondered how André was doing, whether he had gone back to his ruined house to salvage any of his possessions, or if there was too much danger of another strike from orbit. He wondered if anybody else had lived within the blast zone of the first one. André had said that the French colonists lived apart from one another, but he'd been talking to an American. That wasn't necessarily the truth.

Trent didn't think André had been lying to him. He seemed to be just what he said he was; a regular guy trying to make a new home away from the craziness that had swept over Earth in the last couple of decades. But he hadn't been able to escape. Nobody could, unless they were willing to cut themselves off completely. Hide out from America and its attempts to control every other human outpost in the galaxy.

He wondered why the Galactic Federation hadn't done something about it yet. Could they already be as ineffective as the United Nations had been at reining in their out-of-control members? Or were they just reluctant to step into what was, after all, mostly a human problem? The alien races who made up the bulk of the Federation probably had growing pains of their own.

Trent remembered his promise to André when they

parted. Not much of a promise, really; just that he would do what he could to stop his country from behaving so abominably, but a promise was a promise, and he intended to keep it. But how was he going to do that from way out here?

He joined Donna on the picnic blanket and took off his armor, using the towel to wipe the sweat off his neck.

"Any luck?" he asked.

She shook her head. "I'm really wishing I'd paid more attention in math class."

"You'll get it," he told her.

"Yeah, but when? If I was smarter, I'd have figured it out when we still had power and air, and we'd be home by now."

Trent reached out and put his arm around her. "Hey," he said softly, "don't you go beatin' yourself up for not pullin' a rabbit out of a hat. You got us down alive while I was sittin' in back bein' about as useful as tits on a boar."

She took a deep breath and let it out. "It's just . . . I'm sure the answer's there, if I only knew how to find it."

"You will."

"I wish I had your confidence."

He gave her a squeeze. "I've got the confidence because you've got the brains. And you've got all the time in the world to use 'em. Take a break and come back to it later."

She shook her head. "I'm right in the middle of something."

He considered insisting, but he knew how well that usually worked. "All right," he said.

He got up and put on his armor again, checked the sky, and went down to the creek to see how the parachute was doing. To his surprise, the orange stains were just about gone, so he pulled it onto the rocks beside the pool, wringing it out as he brought each armful up, until he had the whole works out of the water. It was all he could do to carry it up to the meadow, but he slung it over his shoulder like a sack of cement and staggered up the bank with it, then he dropped it to the ground, untied the shroud lines from the tree, and pulled it out into a ragged circle so it could dry.

The sun had moved enough in the last few hours to give him a sense of which direction it was going, but by the arc of its track across the sky, it looked like it was setting in the east. That meant they were in the southern hemisphere, then. He wondered how long it would take him to get used to that.

There was still quite a bit of daylight left, so he started checking the pickup's door and window seals, trying to find the place where they were leaking. It was pointless busywork if he couldn't figure out a way to recharge the batteries, but it would be vitally important if he could. No way did he want to breathe air from the tires again.

He couldn't find anything wrong. The window seals were tight; he could see the rubber compressed all the way around them. He inspected the seals on both doors for anything that might have gotten wedged in the way, and he looked for nicks or cuts, but the rubber was as smooth and clean as the day he'd installed it. So was the mating surface on the doors themselves. He checked the doors for alignment, thinking maybe they had been tweaked when the pickup tipped over, but they looked straight. He checked the seal around the wiring conduit from the cab to the rest of the truck, but that looked good, too. Finally, in desperation, he used the foot pump to put forty pounds or so in the air tank, climbed into the cab, sealed it up, and let enough out again to raise the cab's pressure a few pounds above the outside air. He listened for the hiss of a leak, but he was no more successful on the ground than in orbit. After ten minutes he realized why: the gauge hadn't dropped a bit.

That didn't make sense. Why would it leak in space, but not on the ground? He raised the pressure some more, but it held steady. He tried the air valve in his door and it hissed just fine when he opened it, but it sealed tight again when he closed it.

But he hadn't been able to use the air valve when they were in space, because it had been plugged with dirt and bent over. He had had to crack the door seal instead. He did that, popping open the top latch and letting a couple pounds of pressure blow out through the top of his door, then he snugged it down again and watched the pressure gauge.

After a minute, it dropped another pound.

"Son of a bitch," he said. It had to be the way the rubber got pushed outward by the air rushing past it. It probably folded over, and didn't seal right when he latched down the door again.

He used the valve in his door to let all the extra pressure out, then opened the other door, climbed out, and went around to look at the driver's door. Sure enough, the rubber at the top had pooched out through the crack between door and frame. He went back around and popped all the inner latches, then went around to the outside again and opened the door. The rubber seal snapped right back into place.

"Son of a bitch," he said again.

"What's the matter?" Donna asked from her spot on the picnic blanket.

"We didn't have to do all that dumb shit with the tires. We had one more cabful of air in the tank; if we'd just opened the doors all the way, then closed them again and refilled the cab, we'd have been fine." He bonked his head against the door frame a couple of times. "Stupid, stupid, stupid."

"Hey," Donna said. "Don't beat *your*self up for not pulling rabbits out of hats, either. How could you have known?"

"I don't know. I should have, though."

She looked at the door, then at him. "We used the same trick all the way from Mirabelle, and it didn't start leaking until after we landed on the planet with bad air. Why would you suspect it to suddenly start then?"

That was a good question, he had to admit. Why *had* it started leaking then, and not before? Because he'd been more cautious at first, just cracking the seal a little bit and letting the air out slowly? He and Donna had completely vented the cab to space to get the bad air out before they'd refilled it and discovered the leak; maybe it took a lot of air to roll the rubber seal over. But if that was the case, then why had it done that just now? He'd only let out a couple pounds. Maybe because he had popped the latch all the way open, knowing that the reaction wouldn't pitch the pickup over while it was on the ground.

It took a little experimentation to prove his theory, but that turned out to be it. If he let air out gently, it wouldn't turn the seal inside out, but if he let it out in a big blast, even for just a few seconds, it would.

Okay, so now he knew. One more thing to cross off the list of things to do before they could fly again. That left only the two biggies: navigation and power.

Donna had gone back to the computer while he tracked down the leak. From what he could tell looking over her shoulder, she was indeed trying to teach herself orbital mechanics. She stopped long enough to help him fold up the parachute when it was dry, but she went right back to it afterward, and she was still at it when the sun hit the horizon.

"Hey, come on," he said, kneeling down beside her. "You've been at that all day. Time to relax a little. Look at the sunset." It was going down in the mouth of the valley, dropping through layers of clouds as it neared the horizon and giving them silver outlines while coloring them red at the same time.

Donna reluctantly closed the computer and put it in the camper, and the two of them stood beside the pickup and watched the sun go down over the plain beyond the end of the valley. If the ocean was out that way, it was lost in the haze of distance or completely over the horizon.

"I think the days are longer here," Donna said.

Trent laughed. "We've had one hell of a long day, that's for sure. I'm ready for a long night in the sack."

After the sun went down, they fixed another sandwich for supper and ate it on the picnic blanket while they watched the sky grow dark and the unfamiliar stars come out, then they retreated into the camper for the night. Their surprise visit by Onnescu's native "hoodlums" had made Trent reluctant to spend much time outside in the dark until he'd learned a little more about what kind of nocturnal animals might live around here. He made sure the air vents were open so they would have fresh air, and latched the door tight.

They folded the table down and made the bed, using the seat backs and bottoms for their mattress, but not long after they crawled in, Donna sat up and said, "I can't sleep. I'm too close to figuring out how to do the math." She reached for the computer, but Trent pulled her back down.

"Give it up for today. The problem will still be there in the morning. You'll be fresher at it tomorrow anyway."

"But I can't sleep. I've got all these numbers running around in my head."

"Like what? Seventeen? Forty-two?"

"Five hundred and thirty-seven thousand."

"That's a lot of number to be runnin' loose. Why don't you round down to half a million and then forget the zeroes? Doesn't seem like near as much then."

She poked him in the side. "All right, smarty pants. But if the answer comes to me in a dream, it's going to be off by thirty-seven thousand kilometers an hour. Who knows how many light-years away from home that'll leave us."

"Close enough for the navigation program to recognize the stars," Trent said. "Go to sleep."

"I'll try."

She laid her head on his chest and he put his arms

around her, but after a few minutes he realized he was just as wide awake as she was. He had numbers running around in his head, too. His were kilowatts instead of kilometers, but they were just as insistent. How was he going to generate enough power to recharge the batteries?

There were no windows in the camper. The three round moons of the air vents provided the only path for daylight to shine in, and with the mountain blocking their view to the east and the tree overhead, there wasn't any morning light to speak of, either. Just a pale glow from the sides and overhead. Trent had no idea how long he'd slept, but it felt like a week, and he could have done another if his bladder hadn't insisted he rise.

He stepped outside to find the sky gray and rain misting down silently in the meadow. The air was chilly, but not cold enough that he could see his breath. The ground was still dry under the tree. He went around to the other side to pee, but he hadn't brought his armor, so he didn't venture beyond the edge of its canopy. There was no evidence of birds overhead today, but those blue-gray scales of theirs would blend in perfectly with clouds, and he wasn't willing to find out the hard way that they hunted in the rain.

The air smelled wonderful. Either the tree or the ground cover out in the meadow was giving off a new aroma now that it was wet; a crisp, minty scent that made up for the gray light and the rain.

Trent was about to go back to the camper and fix breakfast when he noticed a dark gray shape moving across the upper end of the meadow. It was hard to make out detail through the mist, but it looked like it was about the size of an elk, and it moved on four legs. Its head was big compared to its body, like a buffalo, and its back seemed segmented rather than furry. Was it armor plated? Trent backed away slow and easy, went around to the far side of the pickup to open the door and get out the binoculars, and left the door open while he leaned on the hood and focused on the new animal.

It was definitely armored. Big overlapping plates of bone or horn or some such covered its head and back. Its legs were thick and stumpy to support all that weight. That nixed the first idea that had come to mind: shoot it for the meat and for the full-body suit of armor. It might provide more complete protection from cupids than the stuff he had made yesterday, but not if he couldn't carry it.

Trent watched the animal stump along, bending down every few steps to eat a mouthful of the low, leafy plants that covered the ground. It came to a bush and stripped half the leaves off that, too, by closing its mouth around one branch at a time and sliding it upward.

He heard soft footsteps behind him, and Donna whispered, "What do you see?"

"Looks a little like a buffaloceros," Trent whispered back. He handed her the binoculars and pointed.

He would have sworn their voices couldn't be heard more than a few feet away, but the animal raised its head and looked straight at them for a few seconds before turning back to denude another bush.

"It's huge," Donna whispered.

"Yeah. Glad it's a plant-eater."

It was getting harder to see. Part of that was because it blended in with the bushes, but the rain was starting to come down harder, too. It had been just a soft mist before, but now they could hear it pattering on the leaves overhead. A few drops were making it through now. Trent looked at his woodpile, then out at the sky. It didn't look like it was going to stop raining anytime soon. He didn't really want a fire at the moment, but by nightfall they might, so he went into the camper and got their blue plastic tarp and threw it over the wood, weighing the corners down with logs so it wouldn't blow away. The buffaloceros paid him no attention; just wandered off into the mist.

They had breakfast, finishing what was left of the orange juice and eating cereal with powdered milk reconstituted with bottled water. If they started a fire tonight, Trent figured they could boil some stream water to make some hot chocolate or something. That would be a good first test of the local food supply.

After breakfast, they turned the bed into a table again. Donna got out the computer and went back to work on figuring out where they were. Trent sat beside her and read with her for a while, but he quickly became snowed by all the talk of square roots and inverse squares and gravitational constants. He tried to ignore the formulas and just follow the basic logic of the text, but when it came to figuring out the area swept out in a partial arc around a circle, it was nothing but formulas. "Hell," he said at last, "they say here that pi are square, but any fool knows that pies are round. Cornbread are square."

Donna gave him a sideways grin. "Go find something to do," she said, "before I have to hurt you."

"Yes, ma'am." He put on his raincoat and his helmet and shoulder guards over that, then strapped on the pistol under his raincoat since he didn't want to carry the rifle in the rain, and went outside.

It was raining harder now, a steady downpour that hissed against the leaves overhead and puddled up in the low spots out in the meadow. The stream had risen, and was churning loudly over the rocks. One would occasionally shift in the current, making a deep *clunk* that he felt as much as heard. He was glad he hadn't put his beer in there; it would be halfway to the ocean by now if he had. He stood on the bank and watched the water rush past for a few minutes, trying to decide whether or not it would overflow the banks. If it did, the truck could wind up halfway to the ocean, too. There was probably enough juice in the batteries to drive across the meadow, but the minute Trent tried to climb a slope, that would be the end of their charge. There was no direction but down for the pickup anymore, and there wasn't much downhill left. Maybe a couple hundred feet, total, before they left the mountains behind for good, but there was a lot of uphill and a lot of bushes to go around even on the downhill stretches between here and there.

Too bad. Coasting downhill was the one time when the pickup's wheel motors generated electricity rather than burned it. Trent got an image of one way he could recharge the batteries: He could dismantle the pickup, carry it to the top of the mountain piece by piece, put it together again, and coast to the bottom. If he cleared a road straight down, he wouldn't even use up any battery power going around obstacles. He would gain a kilowatt-hour or so with every trip. That meant he would only have to do it . . . what, a couple of hundred times? Piece of cake. He could probably have it done by the time the kids were ready for college.

That set him thinking, though. Coasting downhill wasn't the only way to rotate a wheel. He could take off a tire and put a crank on the hub and save himself a lot of climbing. He wondered how much power he could generate by hand?

He had no idea, but the computer might. He went back to the camper and leaned in the door. "Hey, does the encyclopedia in that thing have conversion tables for calories to kilowatts?"

"What?" Donna looked up, puzzled, her face lit by the blue glow of the computer screen.

"I want to know how many kilowatts I can generate turning a crank."

"Turning a crank?"

"Or pedals. That might work better."

"For what?"

"Generating power using one of the wheel motors in brake mode."

"Oh. All right. Let me see what I can find." She set to work with a smile, happy to be doing something else for a while, and within just a few minutes she had an answer. "A thousand calories converts to just over a kilowatt-hour. And it says here that the human body burns two to five thousand calories a day, depending on how hard you're working. So if you're putting out five, minus the two it takes just to keep you alive, that gives you about three thousand calories going into the crank, so you can do three kilowatt-hours a day."

And that was assuming a hundred percent efficiency, in both him and in the generator. "I think I'd do better hauling the truck uphill in pieces," he said.

"Huh?"

"Long story. Never mind." He went back outside and watched the rain come down.

He was on the right track, though. The wheel motors were already designed to generate electricity as well as use it. The trick was to find something else to spin them. Harness one of those buffaloceros guys? They could probably put out at least a horsepower. But Trent doubted they would break to harness very well, and even if they did, the motor needed to spin fairly fast to have any efficiency at all.

A windmill? That could work, except that down here in the valley there hadn't been much wind yet. The storm had blown in without stirring much more than a breeze.

Another rock tumbled along the stream bed. Trent felt the hollow thuds as it banged its way to a stable spot. There was plenty of energy there, if he could just harness it.

He looked upstream to where he'd found the little waterfall above the bathing pool. A four-foot drop could turn a waterwheel. It probably wouldn't have a whole lot more power behind it than him turning a crank, but it would be non-stop.

He tried to visualize how it could work. The simplest way would be to set the motor right out over the pool next to the waterfall, so the water could flow past the edge of the tire. He could tie tin cans or something to the tire to catch the water so its weight would turn the wheel. But how could he suspend the motor over the pool? It weighed at least a hundred pounds, a hundred and fifty with the tire.

Run a couple of logs across from bank to bank? The far bank was about the right height, but the one on this side was too high. He would have to dig down three feet to reach the right level. And besides, how could he get the wheel to rotate with the logs in the way? He would have to separate them wider than the tire and build a platform to set the motor on so the tire could spin between the two logs. That meant one of the logs would have to go in behind the waterfall, and there wasn't room for that, so he would have to dig out a space for it, and that was rock rather than dirt back there.

Or he could build a flume, but that would probably be just as difficult. It was starting to look like more work than turning a crank. Okay, try again. Imagine holding the motor out over the pool in his hands. He wouldn't need to stick his fingers out past the tire; why couldn't he do that with the logs? Just stick them out from the far bank and tie the motor to their ends. The tire would be free to spin, and he wouldn't have to build a platform or dig out behind the waterfall or anything.

He could feel his heart starting to speed up. This could work! Arrow trees were tall and straight, and if they were as stiff as the arrows themselves, then two of them would easily hold the motor's weight without bending. He could pile rocks on the other ends to keep them from tipping into the pool. He would have to dismount the pickup's batteries and set them close enough to the motor's control box to hook them up to its leads, but he could do that easy enough.

He could do it. He went back into the camper and said, "I've figured it out. I'm building a waterwheel."

Donna looked up from the computer. "A waterwheel?"

He told her his plan, talking too fast and tripping over

his tongue in his excitement, and he forced himself to slow down and take it step by step. She started nodding as she realized how it could work. "That's great," she said, but she wasn't smiling.

Trent could read her moods like a billboard. "What's wrong?" he asked.

"Nothing."

"Yeah, right. Out with it."

She looked at the computer screen for a second, then back at him. "You've figured out how to fix our spaceship, but I still haven't figured out where we are."

He shook off the rain from his jacket and went inside to sit across from her. "Hey, you'll get it. And if you don't, we'll find Earth by trial and error. We can charge the batteries and go hunting for it, and if we don't find it the first time we can come right back here and try again."

"Oh, sure," she said. "Do you have any idea how big the galaxy is? It's a hundred thousand light-years across. The volume of space that the computer will recognize is about four *hundred* light-years across. We could search at random forever and never hit it."

"We don't have to search at random. We know Earth is about thirty thousand light-years from the center of the galaxy, so we can go to the core, then jump outward thirty thousand light-years and work our way around the galaxy until we hit something we recognize."

"That's still a huge amount of space to search. And thirty thousand is an awfully even number. Glory probably rounded it off so she didn't sound like Spock. If the actual distance is thirty thousand and a half, we'd never find what we were looking for."

"Yeah, all right, but still. We can narrow it down a lot."

"And I could pinpoint it if I was just smarter!"

He took her hands in his. "You're the smartest person on the planet, babe. If anybody can pinpoint it, you can."

"But I can't! That's what I'm trying to tell you. I've been

staring at this damned orbital mechanics textbook for hours now, and it's not making any sense. If we went straight out from the center of the galaxy, and if the galaxy was rotating like a solid disk instead of a fluid, then maybe I could figure out how far we went, but the galaxy isn't solid, and if we went at an angle across it I couldn't figure out where we went even if it was."

"We know what direction we went, don't we?" he asked.

"What?"

"We have the webcam's images of the stars after every jump, and we know what direction we intended to go every time, right? So like we figured before, unless there was an aiming error as well as a distance error, we know what direction we went, and we know what direction to aim to undo it all. All we're missing is the distance of the one big jump."

Even with the door open, not much daylight made it into the camper. Donna's face was lit mostly by the computer screen, and its blue glow made her look icy cold. She pulled her hands away. "That's all we're missing? Hey, that makes everything better. That's what I'm trying to figure out, dumb shit!"

"And you'll get it! Don't worry."

"Don't worry. That's easy for you to say. You've solved your problem."

"Well, excuse me! I'm sorry I'm so goddamned smart." He got up and stomped the two steps to the door, but when he stopped and turned around for one last retort and saw her sitting there in the dim light, he took the two steps back and sat down across from her again.

"I'm sorry," he said. "I didn't mean that."

"Sure you didn't," she said sullenly.

"Look, if I was smart, I wouldn't have pissed you off, now, would I? I mean, it stands to reason. You're my honey bunny ducky downy sweetie chicken pie li'l everlovin' jelly bean. I piss you off, and it's no sex for me."

"Oh, that's flattering."

"But it's flawless reasoning."

"You're trying to use a logical argument to convince me you're not smart?"

"How'm I doing?"

"Well, it is about the dumbest thing I've heard you say all day."

"I could start praising President Stevenson."

"That's not necessary," she said quickly. "You do that, and I'd just have to put you out of your misery." She was trying not to smile, but it looked like she might lose that battle pretty soon.

"How 'bout if I quote him? 'Space travel is bad for business. It'll just encourage people to skip out on their debts, like the government does.'"

"He didn't say that."

"Sure he did. He just didn't use those words."

She pursed her lips, and finally cracked a smile, but it vanished as fast as it came. "Nice try, but I still can't figure out where we are."

He shrugged. "We don't have to do it today. It'll be a couple of weeks before the batteries are charged. Maybe I'll have another brainstorm before then. Or maybe you will."

"Fat chance."

"You never know. In the meantime, come help me cut down a couple of trees."

Arrow trees were tough. The wood was fibrous, and the saw kept binding. Worse, every time they jarred it, it dropped arrows. Donna kept an eye trained upward and called out a warning when one cut loose, but Trent was getting tired of jumping back every time he bound the saw blade. Plus he was starting to sweat under his raincoat.

"There's got to be a better way," he said, pausing for breath.

"We could throw rocks at the branches and knock down all the ones that are ready to come loose," said Donna.

He looked up at the tuft of greenery at the top of the tree. It was forty feet up, at least. He could pitch a few rocks that far, but not many, and not accurately. He could shoot any individual branch he wanted with the rifle, but the bullet would go right through it. Donna was on the right track, though. What they needed to do was jar the whole tree with a good, solid jolt, and shake down all the loose branches at once.

There were a couple of big logs in the stream bed. They were from the leafy kind of tree, all twisty and not much use for suspending a motor over the stream, but one of them might work as a crude battering ram. Trent had to slosh out into the water to reach them, but it didn't matter; his boots were already soaked from walking around in the rain and from fording the stream anyway. He cut off the small end of the closest log, leaving about eight feet of log about the size of his thigh, which he and Donna dragged up the bank to the arrow tree.

"Okay," Trent said when they had gotten into position about ten feet from the tree. "We run toward it, hit it with the log, let go, and keep running. I'm going to go straight through, but I think you should swing wide and go to the side. You'll get out from under the tree faster that way. And watch you don't drop the log on your feet."

"Right," said Donna.

Trent took the front end, and Donna lifted the back. "Hit, drop, and run," Trent said. "Ready?"

"Yeah."

"On the count of three. One . . . two . . . three." He started toward the tree, wobbling a little under the weight, then caught his stride and rammed the log hard into the trunk. It rebounded and he let it go, continuing on past and shouting "Run! Run!"

He heard a patter of arrows hitting the ground behind him, and one clanked off his helmet, but then he was out of range. He turned to make sure Donna was okay, too, and saw her still running.

"You're clear!" he shouted. She slowed to a stop and turned around.

It looked like a miniature forest under the tree. At least two dozen arrows had come down, all but two or three sticking point-first in the ground. Trent pulled them up and tossed them in a pile off to the side, then picked up Donna's end of the big branch and dragged it out into the open again. "One more time?" he asked.

Donna said, "Sure," and picked up her end. He lifted his, and on the count of three they did it again.

Three more arrows came down. Trent tossed them aside with the others and was trying to decide whether or not to give it one more whack when he heard a snort off to the side and looked up to see the buffaloceros lumbering straight toward him.

"Jesus, get in the camper!" he yelled to Donna. She turned and ran, but she had to cross the stream to get there, and it was too wide to leap. The buffaloceros saw her movement and started toward her while she was picking her way across the slick stones, but Trent stepped out in front of it and waved his arms, shouting "Hey! Hey you! Over here."

The buffaloceros turned toward him, lowered its head, and charged. He backpedaled as fast as he could, putting the trunk of the arrow tree between it and him, but the creature didn't seem to see the tree. It crashed headlong into the trunk, shaking it way harder than Trent and Donna had with their log. It staggered back a step just as a hail of arrows glanced off its armored back. A couple whacked into Trent's helmet and shoulder guards, too, and one tore a hot streak down the side of his left leg.

"Ow!" he yelled, dancing back out of the way, but the buffaloceros came after him, sidestepping the tree this time. Trent knew he would never make it across the stream before it caught him, and he didn't want this thing ramming the camper anyway, so he picked another arrow tree and sprinted for it, his helmet tilting askew and his shoulder guards flapping up and down as he ran. He heard Donna screaming from the other side of the stream and heard hoofbeats thundering just behind him, and he poured everything he had into the last few steps between him and the tree. He didn't even slow down; just dodged past and prayed that the buffaloceros wouldn't see this one, either.

It didn't. Apparently it only saw things when they moved. It smacked this tree at full-tilt, too, bringing down another rain of arrows. Trent was already out from under it and halfway to the next tree beyond; he ran to it and skidded to a stop behind the trunk while the beast was still shaking its head from the impact.

It looked around, stupefied, obviously wondering where Trent had gone. It didn't seem any worse for wear. That armored forehead was apparently good for more than just arrows.

Trent held perfectly still while it turned its head from

side to side. Donna was across the stream now and running for the pickup, and her footsteps drew its attention, but the moment it looked away from Trent he picked up two rocks and tossed one at the thing's side.

It bellowed loudly and whirled around, just as Trent tossed his other rock into the bushes to his left. Either the motion or the sound of the rock hitting branches was enough to set it off, and it charged into the brush, scattering twigs and leaves everywhere. Trent picked up another couple of rocks and tossed them out ahead of it, beyond the bushes, and it continued onward, chasing the sound.

It kept running even after it passed the last rock. Trent listened to its hoofbeats receding into the forest, and when he was sure the creature could no longer see or hear him, he walked back to the tree he and Donna had been working on.

She came back from the pickup carrying the rifle. "Are you okay?" she asked.

"Yeah. It didn't get me."

"Something did."

"Where?"

"Your leg."

Oh yeah. He hadn't even felt it after the initial sting, but he looked down at his left calf and saw a rip a couple inches long in his pants, and blood welling up from a cut beneath that. *Now* it hurt.

He sopped up the blood with his pantleg and had a look at the cut. Not very deep. It was more of a scratch than a cut, probably from the rough sides of the arrow. "It'll be all right," he said. He looked back toward where the buffaloceros had gone. "I guess now we know how to call one of those guys if we ever want to. They must like to butt heads like bighorn sheep."

"It's probably mating season," Donna said.

Trent nodded. "I hope one of 'em doesn't mistake the pickup for a female."

He reached for his camp saw, then swore when he

noticed what had happened to it. He'd laid it next to the pile of arrows while he and Donna had been using the log for a battering ram, but the buffaloceros had run right across it in its charge, and the last three inches of it were bent. It was the bow, not the blade, that had taken the brunt of the weight, so at least the blade hadn't snapped, but Trent had to go back to the pickup and pound the bow into shape again. He did it inside the camper with the door closed, setting the flashlight on the counter so he could see and hammering against a chunk of firewood with a towel between it and the floor so he wouldn't attract another buffaloceros.

When he got back to the tree, Donna had cleaned up all the arrows that had fallen around its base. They made quite a stack. Trent would have to build a longbow and see how they worked for hunting.

That was a project for later. He had a waterwheel to build today. He bent down to the cut he'd started and took a few light strokes with the saw, testing his repairs before he put his weight into it. It seemed strong enough, so he started sawing in earnest, and Donna didn't call out a warning even when the blade bound a few strokes later.

"I think every branch that's loose enough to come down this *year* probably did it already," he said as he continued to saw. "That thing really smacked this tree."

"It must have a head like a rock," Donna said.

"Well, that's about how smart it seemed."

Trent finished the wedge, then went around to the other side and started in on the back-cut. He planned to drop the tree uphill parallel to the stream so he could cut off the top and pull it downhill when he swung it out over the waterfall. He kept his eye on both sides of his cut, making sure he was leaving an even amount of wood to act as a hinge when it started to fall. He had to cut to within a half inch or so before it teetered, then he removed the saw and gave the tree a good push. It held for a second, then let go with a groan and a pop, tipping right toward where he'd intended it to land.

The top made a loud *swoosh* as it fanned down through the air, then the trunk thumped to the ground with a deep, bass *boom*. Arrows flew every which way when the tuft at the top slapped down, rattling down like pick-up sticks.

"Let's get under cover for a few minutes in case that guy comes back to investigate," Trent said, leading the way to one of the leafy trees, where they could climb up in its branches if they had to get out of the way. They leaned up against its trunk in the relative dryness beneath its canopy and watched the rain come down.

"Thanks," Donna said after a minute or so.

"For what?"

"For gettin' me away from that damned computer for a while."

He nodded. "It was definitely eatin' on you." He put his arm around her and pulled her up against him. "Tell you the truth, right now I don't care if we ever do get home. We've got food and water and shelter, and in a week or two we'll have power enough to drive around if we need to, and the fridge will work again and we can cook on the stove if we want. A person can't really ask for much more than that."

"Not for the moment, anyway," Donna admitted.

"Not ever," Trent said. "Anything more is just luxury. Hell, the pickup and the stove and the refrigerator are luxury. We could probably get by with a tent and a pocket knife if we really had to."

"And a condom and a wedding ring," Donna said playfully.

"Don't need that with all these arrows layin' around." He tilted his head back and looked up into the leaves overhead. They made a kaleidoscope of green and gray against the sky. "Life is real here. It's all so . . . immediate. Rain and rocks and trees and streams. We go home and we're going to be right back in the middle of all the crap we were tryin' to get away from, only worse because we can't just go on livin' the way we were now that we know what our government is really doing to people."

Donna shifted uncomfortably. "What can we do, though? We'd make pathetic revolutionaries. You could probably assassinate the president if you put your mind to it, but that wouldn't stop anything. You'd have to knock off everyone down to the White House janitor before you got a replacement president who wouldn't just keep the same system in place."

"Killing people ain't the way to make the world a better place," Trent said. "That's the kind of thinkin' that got the country in the mess it's in."

"What, then?"

"I don't know. That's why I'm kind of happy just to hang out here for a while."

Neither one of them had much to say after that. They waited a few more minutes, and when the buffaloceros still hadn't returned they went back out to the downed tree and lopped its top off. They moved over to the second tree that the buffaloceros had head-butted, dropped that one uphill, too, and cut it to the same length as the first one. Then they shoved them both out over the pool below the waterfall, making sure they stuck out just far enough to mount the motor on. There was enough length left on the bank to hold them in place while they hauled rocks up from the stream bed to weigh them down.

That was an all-day job right there. It took a lot of rocks to hold the logs down under the kind of weight the motor and a tire would put on the free ends. Trent tested their progress from time to time by walking out on the span over the water, edging out a few inches at a time until the logs started to overbalance.

"Don't you go falling in," Donna told him. "It's too damned cold today to get wet."

Trent was already pretty well soaked from rain and sweat, but he didn't want to fall into the pool either. Fortunately the logs were as non-skid as sandpaper from the little pockets where arrow-branches had broken free. He couldn't have slipped if he'd wanted to.

They broke for lunch, hauling an armload of arrows down to the camper on their way, then after they'd eaten the last of the ham sandwiches and chased them with a beer, Donna sat down at the table with the computer again while Trent went outside and piled more rocks on the logs. He didn't give her any trouble about it this time. She did have to spend some time at it if she was going to make any progress.

It took another couple hours of rock-hauling to make the counterweight heavy enough to support the motor. It would have been easier if the stream wasn't running high, but Trent had to scrounge his rocks from the upper bank, and his supply grew steadily farther away as he worked. At last he called it good, and went back to the pickup to remove the motor.

The ground was soaking wet, even beneath the tree. He considered waiting for the rainstorm to blow over, but this felt like the kind of rain that could go on for days, and he knew he would go nuts with anticipation if he couldn't test his idea before the day was out. So he took the tarp off the woodpile and laid it on the ground in front of the left rear wheel and slid under the pickup with his tools to begin removing the wheel, motor and all.

It wasn't all that difficult. The motor was mounted to a couple of swing arms that kept it horizontal throughout the suspension's range of travel, and the disk brake and the tire were both mounted to the same hub at the end of the axle that stuck out of the motor. He jacked up the truck to take the weight off it, supporting the jack on a flat rock scrounged from an outcrop at the head of the meadow and backing it up with a length of firewood wedged in next to it, then he simply loosened the bolts on the swing arms until the motor came free.

He left the tire mounted so it would support part of the

motor's weight. That way he could move it by just lifting the other end of the motor and rolling the whole works along, but he didn't put it out on the logs yet. He still needed to figure out what to do for paddles, so the water would actually turn the wheel.

He had plenty of arrows. He supposed he could tie a bunch of them to the sides of the tire so the ends stuck out past the tread, and then tie beer cans with the tops cut off to the ends of the arrows. They wouldn't hold much water, though, and when the motor was in braking mode, it would resist turning pretty hard. He would probably need something that held more water, like hollowed-out chunks of log. That would probably provide enough resistance, but it would be a lot of work to hollow them out. He needed something that was hollow already, and would hold some serious water.

A dozen slo-mo shells would do it, but the rising water had washed all the debris off the gravel bar where he'd gotten his helmet, and there weren't any more dead ones in the meadow. There weren't any live ones there today, either. They must not like flopping through mud. He would have to go out hunting for them to find any at all, live or dead.

The idea of killing a dozen animals just to provide scoops for his waterwheel wasn't all that appealing, either. He decided he would rather walk down the valley a ways, following the stream and checking out any open ground he found along the way. It might even be easier to find what he needed today than on a dry day. Any slo-mos he found out in the open today were most likely going to be dead already, so at least he wouldn't have to keep flipping them over like he had done yesterday.

He had taken off his armor while he was under the truck. Now he put it on again and stuck his head inside the camper. "I'm going for a walk downstream to look for empty slo-mo shells. Back in an hour or two."

Donna had wrapped herself up in a blanket, but with

the blue light from the screen on her face, she looked cold even so. She looked up and said, "Okay. Take the rifle."

"It's too rainy to be carryin' that around. I've got the pistol; that'll do."

"All right. Be careful."

He needed something to carry the empty shells in, assuming he found any. He tried to think what would work, but the only big container they had in the camper was a five-gallon water bucket, and that would only carry three or four slo-mo shells. They had some plastic garbage bags, but those probably wouldn't hold up to the weight. They didn't have a duffel bag or a laundry bag or anything like that. It was starting to sink in just how little equipment they did have, way out here in the ass end of nowhere.

They had a tarp. He could throw whatever he found in the middle of that and gather the ends to make a sack. That would have to do. He pulled it out from under the pickup, folded it as small as it would go, and set off to see what he could find downstream.

The days were definitely longer here. He had hauled rocks for a couple of hours after lunch, and spent at least two more hours taking the wheel motor off the pickup, but the sky was still as bright as ever. That wasn't all too bright today, but the gray didn't have that soon-to-be-dark cast to it that it got at the end of a day. Trent told himself he would turn around at the first sign of darkness, or at the end of an hour, whichever came first. He didn't think he'd forget; he was already growing hungry. They might have to start eating four meals a day if they stayed here for long.

The stream was nearly twice as big now as it had been yesterday. He could hear rocks banging along in the current nearly continuously. Chunks of wood sailed past, bobbing over rapids and swirling around in the pools. He kept his eye out for passing helmets, but none came along while he was looking.

He did find one at the edge of the bank just a hundred yards or so downstream from camp. He picked it up and looked at the bottom, saw that it was still intact, and set it back down, telling himself he would pick it up on his way back if it hadn't moved by then.

His boots squelched with every step. He stopped long enough to pour the water out and wring his socks dry, but within twenty minutes he was squelching again. The ground was so wet, he might as well have been walking in the creek.

The forest wasn't as dense as a mountain forest on Earth. There were wide swaths of open ground between trees, giving Trent a good view of the whole valley as he walked. He zigzagged between helmet-shaped rocks, finding a couple of empty shells and quite a few actual stones, plus a couple of still-living slo-mos that were just weathering out the storm on patches of relatively dry ground. That gave him the idea of looking up on the slopes, where he found a lot more live ones, but none dead. Apparently sick ones or old ones flopped downhill rather than uphill with their last effort.

He went back to the stream and started scanning the bends for logjams. That's where the shell he was using for a helmet had come from; it stood to reason that there would be more of them in similar places, if he could just find one that hadn't washed out.

He kept checking the sky for cupids, too, but he hadn't seen any all day. If they didn't hunt in the rain, they were going to be hungry when the weather broke; he would have to remember to keep an even closer watch then.

He didn't spot any more buffaloceros, either. Everything seemed to be hunkering down, waiting for better weather. After a while, just for the sake of science, Trent crept up to a big clump of bushes and started poking around under it with an arrow, and he scared out half a dozen different kinds of lizards and rodents and even a bird. This one was a lot smaller than a cupid, with bright yellow scales under its wings that flashed like strobe lights as it fluttered off through the rain toward another bush.

There seemed to be plenty of small game around, and if the buffaloceros they'd seen wasn't the only one of its kind, then there was big game, too, but he wasn't finding any predators other than cupids. That wasn't necessarily a bad thing from his point of view, but ecologically it didn't make a whole lot of sense. Where there was a food supply, you would expect something to evolve to eat it. Unless the armor to keep them safe from cupids cut too heavily into their ability to hunt. That would make cupids the top predator in the food chain, but there didn't seem to be enough of them for that.

The more he thought about it, the more the back of his neck began to tingle. Were there wolves out there in the mist, slinking along from tree to tree just out of sight, pacing him until they were ready to attack? Or was there some kind of Jekyll/Hyde thing going on with the slo-mos, and they would suddenly sprout teeth and legs and swarm down upon him by the thousands? It seemed unlikely, but people were finding crazy ecologies all over the galaxy, and not always returning home to tell the tale.

He told himself he was just being paranoid, but all the same he began flinching at every sound, and making 360-degree sweeps of his surroundings every few hundred feet. The two slo-mo shells that he had collected so far seemed awfully light booty to be risking his life for, except that he needed them if he and Donna were ever going to get back home.

At last he came upon a logjam that hadn't been swept away by the rising water, and there in its lee were eight slo-mo shells. Two of them were pretty badly decomposed, but Trent fished them out and tossed them in his tarp anyway. Maybe he could seal them up with duct tape well enough to make them work.

That one windfall brought his total up to ten shells, which made him feel a lot better about his expedition. He considered going on to look for another logjam, but the back of his neck was still tingling, and he was starting to wonder just how many shells he needed, anyway. Twelve would be easiest to mount, because they would be straight across from one another at the points of two hexagons, but he could make do with ten if he had to. It wasn't like the waterwheel had to be perfectly balanced.

He slung the tarp full of shells over his shoulder like Santa Claus with his sack and started upstream again. At least he didn't have to worry about getting lost. There weren't any forks in the stream; if he just followed it uphill, he would eventually run into the pickup.

He heard a rustle of leaves behind him and turned, expecting to see nothing like the last hundred times, but there was a flash of motion in a tree maybe thirty feet away, and a big cat dropped off one of the low-hanging branches. At least it looked like a cat in the body; long and slender on four supple legs, with a sinuous tail at least three feet long lashing back and forth behind it. Its head was more like a huge rat's, with a long snout full of teeth and two beady little eyes set close together above it. Its ears were big for its size, and rounded, like Mickey Mouse ears, but there was nothing funny about the way it moved. It wasn't attacking, but it was definitely advancing on him, completely unconcerned that he could see it.

Why now? he wondered. If this thing had been stalking him, as he suspected it had, why had it chosen now to reveal itself? Maybe because it thought he had already spotted it? He had just reversed direction.

He dropped the tarp and pulled the pistol from beneath his rain jacket. His hands were cold and wet, but he made sure he had a good grip and held the gun steady with his left under his right while he cocked the hammer.

"Stop," he said, but there was no volume in his voice. He cleared his throat and said again, "Stop right there."

The creature did, but only for a second. It tilted its head to the side in obvious puzzlement, then growled a deep, almost subsonic rumble and took another step closer.

"Stop!" Trent hollered, but this time it ignored him.

This creature was at least as heavy as him, and all muscle and teeth. If he let it get close enough to pounce, he was dead. He had no idea whether or not it was intelligent, or whether he could kill it with a .45 pistol, but he was rapidly running out of options.

The tarp had spilled its contents when he dropped it. One of the slo-mo shells had rolled right next to his feet, balancing upside down on its rounded top. Without stopping to think about it, Trent got a toe under the shell and lofted it at the advancing cat, then kicked another to tumble along the ground toward it while the first was still in the air. He bent down and grabbed another in his left hand, hurling it awkwardly after the first two, but it wasn't necessary. The creature had already turned and fled back to its tree, leaping up the trunk and disappearing into its canopy as if it had never been there.

Trent's hands were shaking so bad he didn't trust himself to lower the hammer on the .45 without slipping and firing it by mistake. He just slid it into the holster, then retrieved the slo-mo shells, keeping a wary eye on the tree as he did. The shells all had the same chewed-out hole in the bottom that the ones he had turned into helmets did, and now he thought he knew where those holes had come from. Those rodent teeth would be great for gnawing through a shell.

If that's all the rat-cat ate, then it wouldn't have to be so sleek and fast. Trent bet it ate its share of lizards and rodents and whatever else there was around here, too. It might even go for buffaloceros if it hunted in packs. Trent didn't know if it had been seriously considering him as food or if it was just curious, but he didn't want to find out the hard way.

He steered wide around the leafy trees on his way back to camp, imagining cats in every one and hearing them with every noise. The stream suddenly became a liability as well as a guide, because the closer he walked to it, the more its rush of water masked any sounds that might warn him of another attack.

It was a long walk back, and much steeper than he had remembered it. He found the slo-mo he had left by the bank still in the same spot, so he picked it up and added it to his collection, but this one was still full even if it was dead, and it made the bag a lot heavier. By the time he finally saw the camper he was out of breath and sweating like a horse, but he called out to Donna as soon as he got within shouting range, "Hey, are you okay in there?"

She didn't answer. Fearing the worst, he dropped the tarp full of shells and sprinted the last few hundred feet to the pickup, his shoulder-guards slipping around and flailing at his chest and back as he ran. He stuck his head inside the door, but it was too dark inside for him to see anything. "Donna?" he said. "Donna!"

"Mmmm?" she said sleepily.

"Are you okay?"

"Hmm?" He heard her move, then she said, "Holy shit, what happened to you!"

"Nothing. I just . . . I was just running. You're all right?"

"Yeah. I guess I must have fallen asleep." She tapped the computer's keyboard and the screen lit up. It had gone to sleep, too. "Did you find what you were looking for?"

"More than that. I found this planet's equivalent of a mountain lion. They hang out in trees." He backed out of the camper and looked up into the canopy of the one overhead, but he didn't see anything but leaves and branches up there.

Donna didn't like his news. "A mountain lion! Jesus. That's all we need."

Trent said, "It ran off when I threw stuff at it, so I don't think it was all that intent on gettin' me, but we've got to keep our eyes out." And of course they now had to worry about attack from above even when they were under the trees. The shine was definitely coming off this particular apple.

He went back to the tarp and retrieved his slo-mo shells, dropping them next to the wheel he'd removed. He thought about setting to work cleaning them out and tying them onto the tire, but he was still too jittery to work, and besides, his stomach was growling worse than the cat.

Donna was standing in the doorway with the blanket around her, shivering from the cold. And now that he thought about it, it hadn't been just the lack of the computer screen to light up the camper that had made it so dark in there; it was starting to get darker outside, too.

"To hell with this," Trent said. "We've got to get some hot food in us. I'll start a fire and we can roast hot dogs or something."

"Sounds good to me," Donna said.

Trent picked a spot a little ways away from the truck, but still protected from the rain by the tree's canopy, and stacked some kindling there. He would normally get some rocks and make a fire ring, but the ground was so soaked that there was no real need, and he had thrown all the easy rocks on the counterweight anyway. He got a couple of bigger logs ready to put on the kindling, then got some matches from the camper and tried to light it.

The sticks wouldn't catch. They were soaked through, because he'd used the tarp for a ground cloth and a carrying sack all afternoon. They sizzled and popped and even blackened a little after the fourth or fifth match, but he couldn't get a flame out of even the tiniest twig.

He tried putting some paper underneath, and that burned merrily for a few seconds, but it didn't light the kindling any better than the match had.

"Dammit," he said when the paper burned out. "That should have started at least the little stuff."

"Maybe the wood's green," Donna said.

"It's driftwood."

"Maybe this kind of wood doesn't burn, then."

"Huh?" He looked up at her.

"It's alien wood on an alien planet. Maybe it doesn't burn."

"It's wood," he said. "It's got to burn." He crumpled up another piece of paper and stuck it underneath the kindling, but it did no more good than the first one.

"All right," he said. "Maybe this stuff won't light, but there's two kinds of tree. Let's see how arrows burn." He picked up one from the pile they'd brought over from the trees they'd cut down, digging to the bottom to get the driest one he could find, then breaking it over his knee to expose the even drier wood inside. It took a pretty good bend to make it snap, and when it did, it splintered into long fibers. Perfect.

Except it wouldn't light any better than the other stuff. Trent used up three more sheets of paper just trying to get the toothpick-sized splinters at the ends to go, but no luck. They turned black like the other twigs, but when Trent rubbed them with his fingers he saw that the black was just soot from the paper. The twigs hadn't even charred.

"Okay, time for a little chemical persuasion," he said, standing up, but he stopped before he had even taken a step toward the camper. He hadn't packed any charcoal or lighter fluid, because he hadn't packed a barbecue. Too much weight. Neither he nor Donna smoked, so they didn't have a butane lighter. He tried to think what else they might have that was flammable, but he came up blank. They didn't even have a camp stove, because they had an entire camper with an electric stove in it. About the only thing they had that was flammable was their clothing and bedding. There was the cabinetry, Trent supposed, but they would have to be a lot more desperate than they were now to start burning that.

"For the first time," he said, "I wish I had a gas-powered rig. At least gasoline is good for startin' fires."

Donna said, "How about booze? Alcohol burns, doesn't it?"

That was a thought, but all he'd brought was a case of Budweiser. "We'd have to figure out some way to distill it out of beer," he said.

"Which requires heat."

"Not to mention wasting good beer."

Donna squinted her eyes, obviously chasing down an elusive thought, but if she ever caught it, she didn't let on.

"What?" Trent asked.

"Nothing. I was thinking about the sap that we got on our parachute, but we washed most of that out."

They had, but since it was water soluble, he doubted if

it had been very flammable anyway. On the other hand . . . "We didn't wash out the shop towel. Let's try that." He opened the driver's door and was momentarily blinded by the dome light. He hadn't realized how dark the day was getting. He squinted so he wouldn't blow his night vision any worse than it already was and fished around under the seat until he found the shredded remains of the towel, then he closed the door and half felt his way back to the campfire. He nestled the towel under the little pile of kindling, then put a match to it and leaned back.

The towel smoldered a little, but didn't catch. Trent moved the match right under an orange spot, but that didn't even smolder.

"Shit," he said. "Doesn't anything alien burn?"

"Wait a minute!" Donna said. "What about that stuff Katata's husband gave us?"

They had never even opened the bottle. Trent wouldn't drink the stuff on a bet, not without finding out what was in it first, but he certainly didn't mind trying it as fire-starter.

"What the heck; let's give it a whirl," he said, rising to go get it, but Donna was already ahead of him. She went into the camper and came back out a moment later with the bottle of green whatever-it-was and one of their flashlights. She handed the light to Trent and struggled to open the bottle.

"Dang, the cap's on tight," she said, handing it to Trent and taking the flashlight.

He gripped the cap hard and gave it a good twist, but it didn't budge. It *was* a twist-off, wasn't it? "Here, give me a light on this," he said, holding it out so Donna could shine the flashlight on it. The flashlight was even brighter than the light in the cab, but he squinted and looked at the cap. It was just a black cylinder over the narrow neck of the bottle, but he was able to tilt it so he could see up inside through the glass, and there were threads. Something didn't look right about them, though, and after a moment's thought he realized what it was.

"It's left-hand thread!" he said, twisting the other way, and the cap came off with a loud hiss.

"It's pressurized, too," Donna said.

Bubbles immediately began forming inside, and foam started running over the top. Trent held the bottle over the would-be fire and let it drip onto the kindling and the rag beneath it, then capped the bottle again when he had enough to test whether or not it would burn. No sense wasting it if it didn't. Or if it did, for that matter. Especially if it did.

The odor was enough to tell him for sure he wouldn't be drinking the stuff, even if it proved safe. Distilled garlic would have been sweet compared to the stench that came off the green foam. But that was an encouraging sign, since anything that stinky had to have at least one volatile component to it, and volatile gasses were generally flammable.

He set the bottle on the ground behind him and rubbed his hands clean on the wet weeds underfoot, then dried them off as best he could on his pant legs before striking another match. Donna held the flashlight on the sticks while he stuck the match in toward them.

The stuff caught with a *whoosh* like rocket fuel. Trent snatched his hand back, but not before the hair on his wrist was singed. Flames roared upward at least three feet, burning bright blue all the way. The kindling sizzled and hissed, turned black, then burst into flame on its own, adding a yellow tint to the overall fire. Trent felt the heat, way hotter than a normal campfire, against his face and hands.

"Woo hoo!" he said. "That did it."

Donna clicked off the flashlight and held out her hands toward the fire. "Don't let it go out."

The kindling was disappearing like ice on a stove. It didn't so much burn as melt, dripping down to the wet ground in little rivers of fire that bubbled and hissed as they continued to bathe the wood above them in flame. Trent shoved a couple of inch-thick sticks onto the top of the pile, then set an even bigger log on top of them. The kindling burned down until the flames were only a foot high, but they curled around the new stuff and started it melting, too, adding its liquid wood to the puddle of fuel.

"It's like plastic or something," Donna said.

Trent wondered what kind of toxic fumes it was giving off. Plastic fires on Earth were usually bad news, but this stuff seemed to be burning clean, with hardly any smoke. And it put out enough heat that a person could stand back a ways. He wasn't sure about cooking meat on a stick over it, but they could sure as hell put a pot of water on and boil it.

He held his hands out and let them warm up for the first time in hours. Oh, yeah, that felt good. Suddenly it was starting to look like a much better day.

They filled an aluminum cook pot with water from the creek and hung it by a wire from a tripod made of the longest arrows that Trent could find. He was afraid they might melt, too, the way the flames came roaring up from the puddle of molten wood, but he learned how to damp the fire down with a flat rock over part of the puddle before the arrows caught. He kept the end of a log sticking over the edge of the rock, providing a constant drip to replenish the pool, and managed to keep a fairly even fire going that way.

They got their folding camp chairs out of the pickup and settled in to soak up the heat. Donna got a box of macaroni and cheese out of the camper, and when the water started to boil, she threw the macaroni in. Stirring it was a trick, until Trent duct-taped a spoon to the end of an arrow so they could do it from a distance. The macaroni took longer to soften than the seven minutes the directions said it would; probably the effect of lower air pressure on the boiling temperature of water. It didn't matter; they were content to just sit and warm themselves by the fire while it boiled.

Donna had brought two mugs and two packets of hot-chocolate mix. When the macaroni was done and Trent had removed the pot from the flames, she dipped the mugs in the pot and filled them with water before she drained the rest of it out and added a squirt of squeeze-butter and the cheese packet to the noodles. She put a little powdered milk in with the cheese and stirred the whole works together, and it came out looking and smelling surprisingly like macaroni and cheese.

She opened the hot chocolate packets and poured them into the mugs of hot noodle-water. Trent wondered how that was going to taste, but balanced against the extra time it would take to boil a fresh pot of water, he agreed with her choice. He hadn't realized how cold he was until he'd started warming up, and he wanted something warm inside him right now.

It tasted pretty good. A little doughy, maybe, but that was probably just the power of suggestion. When Donna was done stirring hers, he raised his mug in a toast and said, "To Katata and Magalak, who gave us fire."

"Hear, hear!" she said, and they clinked their mugs together.

The fire lit up the tree overhead, and a good swath of the meadow beyond. The pickup's chrome bumpers and roll bars and door handles glinted in its light, and even its red paint took on a luster that hid most of the dents and scratches it had picked up in the last couple of days. It was amazing how much better things looked in the right light.

Trent looked for glowing eyes out at the edge of the firelight's reach, but there were so many glistening raindrops on everything that he would have missed anything that didn't move. He imagined he and Donna were being watched, though. As hard as this wood was to light, he figured fire wasn't very common around here. He wished he could believe that the rat-cats would stay away from it, but the one he'd seen this evening had acted more curious than afraid of new things. He made sure his rain jacket didn't cover the pistol, and kept his ears perked for noise. At least this fire didn't crackle and pop the way a normal fire would.

He and Donna ate the macaroni and cheese straight out of the pot. The hot chocolate hadn't killed either of them, so they didn't figure the noodles would, either. Water was water, after all, and ten minutes at a full boil should have killed anything living in it.

The food tasted *wonderful*. "Why is it," Trent said between bites, "that everything tastes better when it's cooked over a campfire?"

Donna shook her head. Her blonde hair was wet and stringy, but it still glowed like gold in the firelight. "I don't know," she said, "but it does. Maybe it's because your taste buds are the only part of your body that's not miserable."

"Hey, come on. We're warming up."

"Thank goodness for that." She turned to toast her left side for a minute, and Trent actually saw steam rising off her jacket.

After they finished off the macaroni, Trent took the pot to the stream and rinsed it out, then brought it back full and hung it over the fire again. "It ain't a whole lot," he said, "but it ought to be enough to wash up with."

"My god, a bath, too!" Donna said. "You're my hero."

They sipped the last of their hot chocolate while the bathwater warmed up, and Trent experimented with various things in the fire, checking to see what would melt and what would burn outright. Arrows worked just the same as the other kind of wood, although the tuft of greenery at the end would burn like a torch if you stuck that end in the flames. It dripped flaming gobs of plastic, though, so you didn't want to hold it upright. The waxy-leaved ground cover was actually wax, by the looks of it; it certainly melted easy enough, and the liquid burned just like the molten wood. The chips that Trent had busted off the slo-mo shells the day before took a lot more heat to melt, but they finally did, and the flame from that was an intense white. He tried leaves from the tree overhead, and he ventured out into the night with a flashlight to gather twigs off the bushes, all to the same effect. Everything he could find except rocks and dirt melted and burned when he gave it enough heat.

"Being rained on all day doesn't seem to affect it a bit,"

he said. "It's like water content isn't even a consideration."

"I wonder if a fish would burn," Donna said.

"Jeez, I don't know. We'll have to try it."

Donna turned to toast her back. She didn't say anything for a while, but when she did, it was a bombshell. "What do you bet we won't be able to eat anything that grows here?" she said.

He hadn't even thought about that, but she was probably right. If life on this planet was made out of plastic instead of protein, there was no way their bodies could digest it. They might as well try to eat a PVC pipe.

"We haven't tested actual meat yet," Trent said. "That might be different."

"It might. You gonna go fishing in the morning, then?"

"I don't have to wait that long," he said. He got up and went over to where he'd dropped the tarp and its cargo of slo-mo shells, and sorted through them for the heaviest one. "This one's still got its innards."

It took him a while with a screwdriver and a hammer to bust open the underside of the shell, and when he did, he wished he hadn't done it on a full stomach. The insides were a gooey mess of slippery organs that stank almost as bad as the alien liquor. He held his breath and cut out a long, stringy slab of something that looked like muscle and speared it with an arrow, then held it out over the fire.

It sizzled at first and stiffened like regular meat would do, and when it got hotter it started to drip the way a steak would drip fat, but these drips looked suspiciously like the ones that came off wood. Trent took a closer look, and sure enough; it was just the end of the meat melting. He held it in the fire until it had completely dripped away, along with the end of the arrow.

"Not good," he said. Not only that, but the odor was still strong in his nostrils, and his stomach was about to rebel. He picked up the ghastly shell and carried it to the creek bank, where he tossed the whole works into the rushing water and wiped his hands clean on the wet weeds, but when he sat back down by the fire, his stomach still felt queasy. "Gah," he said. "That was a mistake."

Donna didn't look very good, either. "We've only got about a month's worth of food," she said.

"A month is a long time," Trent told her. "We'll have power again long before we run out. We can go look for another planet if we have to."

She didn't say anything, but he knew what she was thinking. If she could figure out where they were, then they wouldn't have to look for another planet. They could just go home.

They huddled around the fire for a while longer, soaking up its heat for the long night ahead of them, and Trent's stomach slowly began to settle. When the fire started to burn down, he said, "You want me to put another log on, or should we call it a night?"

"Let's go inside," she said, so they picked up their chairs and the pot of warm water and the bottle of fire starter and carried them in. They turned on the flashlight and set it on the countertop pointing upward, then closed the door and peeled off their wet clothing and took their bath, dipping washcloths in the pot of steaming water and rubbing themselves clean. The warm water felt great on their skin, but drying off with a fresh towel felt even better.

"I hope this rain blows over in the night," Trent said. "I'm about half tired of it."

"Me too." Donna rubbed her hair with the towel, setting her breasts ajiggle. Trent felt himself responding to the sight, but his stomach was still not happy, and Donna didn't seem to be in the right sort of mood, either, so he just toweled off his own hair and helped her set up the bed, piling every blanket they had on it this time.

Donna crawled in first, and he slid in beside her, ready

to sleep, but she said, "I'm still wide awake. Do you mind if I read for a while?"

When they had first gotten married, he couldn't sleep when she did that, but he had long since gotten used to it. "No, that's all right," he said. "Stay up as long as you want."

She reached across him for the computer and woke it up from sleep mode, then switched out the flashlight.

"What are you readin'?" he asked.

"What do you think?" she said, holding the computer sideways so he could see the screen full of equations.

His stomach rumbled again, and he had to fight to keep the macaroni and cheese down. "Good idea," he said.

He couldn't sleep after all. It wasn't Donna's reading; it was his stomach, which had never recovered from the whiff of slo-mo guts. At least that's what he hoped was the problem. They had used the local water for hot chocolate and to boil the noodles. If there was something wrong with that, too, then they were in even worse trouble than if it was just the food.

He struggled for over an hour to keep his stomach in check, but the nausea just grew worse until he finally realized he had about thirty seconds to choose his spot. He tossed off the covers and bolted from the camper, running a dozen steps out into the meadow toward the trench they'd dug for a latrine before the cramps doubled him over and he fell to his knees, heaving his supper all over the ground.

"Trent!" Donna yelled from the doorway. "Are you all right?" The flashlight beam caught him just as he heaved again, then the beam wobbled and he heard her take a couple of steps before she, too, lost her dinner.

For a moment, Trent thought throwing up might be the worst of it, but then he realized that his trouble wasn't just in the front end. He barely had time to get his feet out of the way before his bowels cut loose, too. He heaved and groaned until he was sure he had no insides left, and then he dry-heaved some more. He could hear Donna doing the same behind him. They would both be sitting ducks if there were any night predators out there in the darkness, but at the moment he would have welcomed the release.

The rain was like little ice picks on his back. He finally managed to straighten up and take it on his shoulders, then after a couple of deep breaths he struggled to his feet and staggered back to the camper. Donna was a silhouette on her knees off to the right, the flashlight dropped on the ground beside her.

"Don't come near me," she said.

Trent couldn't help but laugh. "Don't worry, I'm as rank as you are. I'm just getting us something to clean ourselves up with."

"Oh. All right."

He leaned inside without actually going in, felt for the paper towel roll under the cabinet, and tore off a long strip of towels. He tore that in two and gave half to Donna, then went back out into the darkness to clean himself. He felt surprisingly better now, despite the rain robbing the warmth from his body, better enough to get the shovel and bury their mess in the latrine.

Back in the camper, they dried themselves off and crawled into bed again, holding each other close for warmth.

"Do you think it was the water or the smell of that meat?" Donna asked.

"I don't know," Trent admitted. "It could have been fumes from the fire, for that matter."

"I suppose it could have. It's going to be a cold time if we can't start a fire."

"I'm more worried about it bein' the water," Trent said.

He wondered what they could do about it if it was, and he realized there was one thing he should do yet tonight. He sighed and said, "Damn. I've got to go back outside and rig up the tarp and a bucket to catch rainwater while we've still got the chance. We don't have any idea how long this rain will last."

She apparently didn't like the idea of going back outside any more than he did, but after a few seconds she said, "You're right. I'll help you."

They got dressed this time, and Donna carried the light and the pistol while Trent tied two corners of the tarp to the side of the camper that stuck out closest to the edge of the tree's overhang. He angled it downward and tied the other corners to two arrows stuck in the ground, then positioned their five-gallon water bucket under the low end where rainwater would run off the tarp into it.

When he was satisfied that it would actually collect water, they went back inside and crawled into bed again. They were both shivering by now, and Trent's hands were so cold he didn't want to touch Donna with them, but it was pretty hard to snuggle without touching. Her hands were just as bad, so he finally said, "Okay, on the count of three, let's just grab each other and get it over with. One, two—yow!" She had already put her hands on his back and started rubbing.

"Why drag it out?" she asked.

"All right, woman, you asked for it." He laid his cold hands on her back, too. She flinched, but didn't scream, which was a good thing since her mouth was right next to his ear. The relative warmth of her skin under his hands offset the feeling of ice-cold fingers on his own back, and after a minute or so her touch actually started feeling pretty good. That's when she put her feet on his legs.

"Gah!" He jerked away, then forced them back into contact. "Damn, how can you be so warm on one end and so cold on the other?"

"Talent, I guess," she said.

He shivered. "When we get the batteries charged up, let's go someplace warm."

"Deal."

Provided they lived through the night, he thought, but he didn't say that out loud.

He woke ravenous. It was dark as a coal mine in the camper, without even the pale moons of the air vents that had greeted him yesterday morning, but he felt completely slept out. He was warm again, and so was Donna. Whatever had made him sick last night was over. He felt ready to get to work on the generator and start charging the batteries.

He slid out of bed and found his clothes by feel. The stuff he'd worn yesterday was still wet, but he was going to be working in the creek today anyway, so he put on the same things, wincing at the cold shock against his warm skin. He dressed in the dark, patted the counter until he found the flashlight, and slipped outside. There was just enough light to see the shapes of things, but no details. He didn't know if the light was the first glimmer of morning or just starlight behind the clouds, but he didn't care. He was too awake to go back to sleep.

He flipped on the flashlight and swept the beam around in a wide arc, then up into the tree. No wild animals waited to pounce on him.

The temperature couldn't have been over forty degrees. He could see his breath. It was still raining, but he bet there was snow higher up the mountain. He went around to the side of the camper to check on his water collection system and found the bucket tipped over. Dammit. They needed that water. He wondered what had gone for it with the stream right there. The rat-cat, maybe, or a buffaloceros. He didn't see any tracks, so it was most likely the cat.

He looked around once more, righted the bucket and set it under the drip, then went back inside.

Breakfast was an apple and a couple handfuls of Cheerios, found by feel and eaten quietly in the dark so he wouldn't wake Donna. He could have eaten the whole box of cereal, but this was the only one, and he didn't know how much of their other food they were going to be able to eat. They had lots of noodles and macaroni and stuff like that, but only a case of bottled water to cook it in. Until they were sure they could drink the stream water, or could collect enough rainwater to make do, he didn't want to use up the only food they knew they could eat.

He gathered up his tools and slipped back outside. It was growing lighter. He could see the tree trunk now, and the dark spot of ground where they had had their campfire. There were a bunch of slo-mos under the tree, too, or so it looked until he looked for the shells he had gathered yesterday and didn't find them beside the truck where he'd left them. Something had been rooting through them, probably looking for anything edible. He would have bet anything it was the cat.

He swept the flashlight around again, checking out the tree carefully and walking all around the pickup, shining the light outward all the way around. He belatedly thought to check underneath the truck, too, and up on top, but there was nothing there, either. Whatever had checked out their camp, it was gone now.

He sat down on his camp stool and began busting the flat bottoms out of slo-mo shells. It was slow going, but he took his time, prying pieces off a little at a time with pliers and being careful not to weaken the helmet part of the shells. He had done half of them by the time the sky grew light enough to call it morning, and by the time Donna poked her head outside the camper, he was done.

"How long have you been up?" she asked.

"'Bout an hour."

"Did you eat?"

"Yeah. Go ahead and get yourself something."

"All right. Want me to make you something hot to drink?"

A cup of coffee would be great, but she would have to start a fire to do that. "No thanks. I want to get these mounted and get this bugger generatin' power before I take a break."

She gave him a dubious look, but she didn't say anything; just went back into the camper. He got to work boring holes in the slo-mo shells; four each, big enough to pass a parachute shroud line through. That took almost as long as chipping away the shells had, but he kept at it until he got them.

Then he put on his helmet and shoulder armor and rolled the motor out to the logs he'd prepared yesterday. He had to splash across the stream with it, but with the tire taking most of the weight it wasn't that hard. Getting it up the other bank was tougher, but he only had to get it high enough to swing the motor over the logs, then scoot it back out over the pool until he reached the end and could swing the tire around even with the waterfall. He gingerly let the logs take the entire weight, testing to make sure his counterweight of rocks would hold, but the logs barely even flexed, so he tied the motor down and got to work tying arrows and shells onto it. He didn't trust the logs to support the motor's weight plus his own, so he worked from the rocks at the head of the waterfall, leaning out to the tire and running the rope through the slots in the wheel. He made a loop around each arrow shaft, then cinched it tight around the knobby tread so it wouldn't slip, leaving about a foot of arrow sticking out past the tread on either side of the tire, then he tied a slo-mo shell to each pair of arrows so it would hold water when it was on one side of the tire's rotation, then dump it and rise up empty on the other side.

The first ones were easy, but when he got half of them done, he saw the flaw in his plan: he couldn't do the others without the ones he'd already done sticking into the falling water. They were definitely going to work to generate power, because he couldn't keep the wheel from spinning back around every time one of them caught some water.

He had to untie the motor and swing it around so the shells couldn't fill up, tie on all the arrows and shells, then swing it back into place. It immediately started spinning, and he let out a wild "Woo-hoo!" when it did.

Donna came to the camper door and started clapping when she saw what he'd done. "Way to go, cowboy!" she yelled.

"It ain't done yet," he said, but it didn't take much longer to finish. He went back to the pickup and pulled one of the two batteries from its cradle under the hood, unplugged the patch cord between it and the motor he'd removed, and carried them back to the logs, where he mounted the battery next to the motor, tying it down good so curious rat-cats couldn't knock it into the water. Then he plugged the battery into the motor's control box. The wheel slowed and the logs dipped downward a couple inches when he made the last connection, and he thought for a second that they would topple all the way into the pool, but the counterweight held, and the battery's charge light went on.

Donna had come with him to the edge of the stream. "Now you can cheer," he told her.

"Yay!" she said, and she gave him a big hug.

They watched the waterwheel spin. The ammeter was mounted in the pickup's dashboard, so he had no idea how fast the battery was charging, but he counted revolutions of the wheel and figured it was doing maybe thirty rpm, which would be about three hundred feet a minute . . . which was pretty slow. He could walk that fast. Charging a battery that could drive a pickup a couple hundred miles at that rate would take a while.

The motor was waterproof, but he wasn't so sure about the battery, so he got a garbage bag and covered it with that, tying the bag down tight. He couldn't see the charge light now, but he could check it from time to time. It wasn't like he had a whole lot else to do now.

Donna still did. Now the entire weight of their situation rested on her. She went back into the camper and started in on the computer again, grimly determined to solve their navigation problem by the time the batteries were charged.

Trent read over her shoulder for a while, trying to piece together what she was learning, but it might as well have been in French for all the good it did him. He watched her draw circles and triangles on the screen and call up the calculator program to crunch numbers, and he even recognized the numbers, but he couldn't follow what she was doing with them.

He was afraid to distract her with a bunch of questions, but even so she finally said, "Go whittle on a stick or something. You're making me nervous."

It was actually a relief to be let off the hook. He'd felt obliged to help if he could, but he'd known as well as she had that he wasn't going to magically figure out where they were. So he went back outside and watched his waterwheel spin, still pleased with himself about that, at least. The slo-mo shells dipping into the fall made a satisfying *sploosh* when they filled, and when they emptied out at the bottom of their arc they spread little skittering water balls across the pool. The logs supporting the motor flexed a little with each refill, their soft creak adding to the sound of flowing water. After a couple days of non-stop work, it was hard to believe that he could just stand there and watch more work being done without him. This must have been how the first guy to hoist a sail felt, suddenly freed of paddling everywhere.

The rain showed no sign of letting up. It wasn't coming down hard; just steady. He checked on the collection bucket and was happy to see that it already had a couple of inches in the bottom, and while he was at it he pounded arrows into the ground around it to keep animals from knocking it over again.

Then he went out with his camp saw and gathered some more firewood. They might not use it, but they might, and he'd much rather haul wood during the day than after dark.

He spent a while inspecting the dents and scratches the truck had picked up over the course of their travels, and in a what-the-hell mood he went ahead and washed it, using their cook pot for a wash bucket and a sponge from under the sink. It looked pretty good when he was done, if you didn't look too close and ignored the missing wheel.

He found the meteorite in the glove box while he was cleaning out the cab. Holding it in his hand was a surprising comfort. It wasn't from Earth, or even from the solar system, but it was from someplace a lot closer to it than here. So was the pickup and everything in it, but for some reason the meteorite reminded him more of home than any of the man-made stuff. If they ever made it back, he would have a belt buckle or something made from a slice of it.

Donna was still at the computer when he went in around mid-day to check on her, but she wasn't studying orbits anymore. She had a star map program on the screen, and she had a piece of paper on the table beside the computer, on which she had drawn a big circle with little dots scattered around one tiny portion of it.

"What's that?" he asked.

He was half afraid she would tell him to go take another hike, but she just looked up and said, "The galaxy. I decided to hit the problem from another angle. Like you said yesterday, we know what direction we were headed in relation to Earth when we took the big jump, but I didn't know what direction that was in galactic terms, so I mapped it out. I figured I might get lucky and it would turn out to be a direction that didn't require a lot of math to figure out a velocity change."

"It makes a difference?"

She nodded. "As near as I can tell, if we went straight out or straight in or straight along the tangent—that's this line that points the same direction that the galaxy rotates—then it would be fairly easy to guess our distance from the difference in velocity.

"So were you?"

"Was I what?"

"Lucky."

She made a face. "No. We went about nineteen and a half degrees inward from the tangent. That means we went toward the core a little bit as well as across. That's two variables instead of just one."

The lines on her drawing were starting to make sense now. "So how far are we talking, anyway?" he asked. "I mean, if we went straight in or out or across?"

"What difference does it make? We didn't."

"But it might still give us a better idea of how far we came than we've got now."

She sighed theatrically and said, "Well, if Earth is going half a million miles an hour this way," and she pointed to one of the arrows she'd drawn on the galaxy, "then in order to gain another third of a million, which is what we had to make up, we would have to go two-thirds of the way farther out from the core. Or two-thirds closer in, depending on whether we had to speed up or slow down. That's assuming that the galaxy is a solid disk, which it isn't. The outside spins slower than the inside, which is just the opposite of what you'd get if it was."

"So what does that mean?"

"It means my brain hurts. I've got to figure out how to calculate a star's actual orbit around the galaxy, and then I've got to figure out how much difference in velocity there is between two stars partway around it and at different distances from the center."

Trent looked at the drawing. Two-thirds of the way from Earth to the core of the galaxy? That was a long damned ways. The entire region of space that their star map could recognize was probably about the size of one of those dots Donna had drawn. If they couldn't figure out an accurate distance back to that patch of stars, then knowing the right angle to aim for wouldn't help them a bit.

He hated this math stuff. It made him feel helpless. He had always preferred just jumping into things and figuring them out by trial and error until he got 'em right, and most times that was all it took, but that didn't seem to be the way it worked here. It was doubly frustrating because they knew which direction to go. All they really needed was a reasonable guess as to how far, and they'd be in business.

"Can you work it backwards?" he asked.

"Huh?"

"If you can't figure the distance from the velocity, how about picking a distance at random and figuring the velocity you'd wind up with when you got there? It'd give you at least an idea of how far out of the ballpark you were, wouldn't it?"

"It's the damned angle," she said. "I could do it if we stayed the same distance from the center of the galaxy, but it's no easier figuring velocity than it is distance with that angle in there."

He didn't see why not, but then the whole deal was beyond him anyway. If he'd gotten stuck out here on his own, he wouldn't even be trying to learn how to calculate anything; he'd just charge up the batteries and head down that nineteen-and-a-half-degree line until he saw something he recognized or ran out of juice, whichever came first. But interstellar distances weren't like distances back home; his method would probably leave them stranded out in the ass end of nowhere with no more clue where they were than they had now.

"Hey, it's lunchtime," he said. "Let's give it a break and hit it again with some food in our stomachs."

"All right," Donna said. She didn't seem very interested in anything but her math problem, but that was just her usual obsessive focus. If he put food in front of her, she would eat it.

He went outside again to check the rain bucket and decided there was enough in it to boil some more noodles for lunch. The thought of noodles so soon after last night's disastrous run-in with them didn't sound all that good, but they really needed to see if they could use any local water at all, and Trent would rather find out in daylight than after dark again tonight. Maybe chicken-flavored ramen noodles would be enough like chicken soup to taste like comfort food rather than an experiment in alien cooking.

There was no reason why they both had to get sick if the rainwater wasn't drinkable. He got a bottle of Earth water from the camper to use in Donna's noodles, then rinsed out the cook pot with a little of it and dried the pot good with a towel before he poured the rest of the bottled water into it.

He got out the alien alcohol and started a fire, then hung the pot from the wire over the flames. It didn't take long to boil—this plastic wood burned hotter than real wood—but Trent let it boil for a few minutes longer before he added the noodles, just in case he hadn't gotten the pot clean enough.

When her soup was ready, he poured it into a bowl and took it into the camper for her, then made himself another potful with rainwater. He let that boil for a good, long time, but when he realized that he'd boiled off about half of what he started with, he added the noodles and made soup with it.

It smelled good. It tasted good, too. It even warmed up his insides the way it was supposed to. But a couple of hours later he was on his knees out in the meadow again, calling dinosaurs even worse than the first time. Not even rainwater was safe.

They didn't see any animals that day. The rain continued to fall, and the waterwheel continued to spin. Trent checked the battery's charge every couple of hours and watched it nudge upward, until by nightfall it was almost at thirty percent. That was better than he'd expected. A couple more days at that rate and it would be fully charged.

He swapped out that battery with the other one just before dark and installed the partially charged one in the pickup. Might as well have a real light in the camper tonight, and give the fridge a chance to cool off again. Not that it had ever warmed up much in this weather. It was cold enough to see their breath even inside the camper.

They forwent a fire that night even so. Neither one of them felt much like sitting outside in the rain, even by a fire. So they just closed up the camper and let their body heat warm it up as much as it was going to before they went to bed. Donna wanted to stay up and study some more, but Trent challenged her to a game of poker instead, and they wound up drinking beer and playing for matchsticks until they were both tired enough to sleep. They only had one beer each, because the beer and the bottled water they'd brought with them were the only things on this planet that they knew they could drink, but with the waterwheel recharging the batteries, Trent figured they would make another try for home before they died of thirst anyway, even if Donna didn't come up with the distance.

They woke up to snow on the ground. There were just a couple of inches, but it completely transformed the valley, making it seem twice as open as before. It was much brighter, too, even though the sky was still cloudy.

Trent put on his jacket and checked to make sure his generator was still working. There were little knobs of ice on the ends of the arrows holding the slo-mo shells, but the stream hadn't frozen, and the wheel was still spinning merrily. The battery read almost forty percent charged.

There were no paw prints near the camper, but there was a set running uphill along the top of the stream bank. They looked surprisingly like cat or dog prints, with pads and claws in the right places and the same left-right gait as anything you'd expect to see on Earth. They veered toward a clump of bushes and there was a messed-up patch of snow right there, intersecting a smaller set of prints. The small prints didn't continue on.

The sky cleared as the day progressed. Sunlight on the snow was bright enough to make Trent squint even with sunglasses, but the snow didn't last long under its intense rays. By mid-afternoon it was all gone, and the stream was running hard and fast. Trent wouldn't want to cross it now unless he had to. The waterwheel was spinning about twice as fast as it had been that morning, though; he would probably have to swap out a fully charged battery by nightfall.

He kept his eye out for cupids, and it wasn't long before he spotted a couple riding the thermals off the sides of the valley. Most of them already carried arrows in their claws, belying his earlier prediction that they couldn't do that for long. They were either stronger fliers than he'd given them credit for, or they were hungry enough to put out the energy so they could attack at first sight of something edible.

Apparently to them "edible" meant anything in motion. Trent was standing under the tree just across the stream from the waterwheel and watching one circle its way down the valley when it suddenly straightened out and made a bombing run straight toward him. He was at the edge of the tree's canopy, where he'd thought he was safe, but he backed up a couple of steps when he saw the cupid coming. It released its arrow anyway, and he dodged to the side before he realized that the arrow was going to fall way short of him. He watched it fall, then watched it hit what the cupid had been aiming for all along: the waterwheel spinning steadily in the rushing stream.

The arrow struck dead-on in the middle of the motor's cylindrical case, and Trent expected it to bounce off harmlessly, but instead there was a big flash of electricity and the arrow burst into flame.

"Son of a bitch!" he yelled, rushing out from under the tree, but the stream was too high to walk across on the rocks. He had to wade through the tail end of the pool, struggling to keep his footing in the current while he kept watch overhead for a second shot aimed at him.

He made it to the other bank before the cupid came around with another arrow. He wasn't carrying the rifle, but he had the pistol strapped to his hip; he drew that and fired in one fluid motion, but didn't hit anything, so he steadied the gun in both hands and took careful aim, and his second shot hit a wing. Silver scales flew and the cupid dropped the arrow, banking away to glide awkwardly into the tree over the pickup.

Donna came running with the rifle. "Are you okay?" she yelled.

"Yeah, I'm fine," he called back over the rush of water. "But the motor isn't." Then he realized she wasn't wearing her helmet. "Hey, get back under cover! There's cupids out here."

She didn't listen to him, but she kept her eyes on the sky while he climbed up on the rocks above the waterfall and kicked the burning arrow off the motor. It snapped at the edge of the case, and the flaming part sizzled out in the water. The tip was still embedded in the case, and now he was close enough to see what had happened: the cupid had managed to hit a vent hole that led straight to the motor's windings.

A rifle shot made him flinch and nearly fall off the rocks, but he caught himself on the motor and looked up to see Donna just lowering the gun from her shoulder. He looked up in the sky and saw a cupid veering away, a little puff of scales fluttering down below it.

"Got him!" Donna yelled.

"Good shootin'!" Trent yelled back.

He holstered his pistol so he could use both hands, then unplugged the battery and tossed it as gently as he could across the stream to land on the far bank. No way was he going to carry that across. If he slipped and lost it in the stream, they could kiss their escape from here goodbye, even if Donna did figure out the math.

The wheel was still turning. Trent heard the tip of the arrow grinding away at the windings inside the motor. The motor was already ruined beyond repair, but he couldn't bear to let it tear itself apart any worse than it already was, so he started to untie it, intending to swivel it around until the shells tied to the tire no longer caught the falling water, but the rifle cracked again and Donna screamed, "Look out, I missed!" Then it cracked again and Trent looked up just in time to see an explosion of scales and the cupid itself tumbling out of the sky, the arrow beating it to the ground by only a second or two.

There were four or five more cupids coming, all carrying arrows in their claws. Trent abandoned the motor and scrambled across the stream as fast as he could go, picked up the battery, and fled with Donna to safety under the tree closest to the waterwheel.

He heard a metallic *clank* behind him, then another. The new guys were peppering the motor with arrows. One hit the tire and Trent winced as he imagined it puncturing that, too, but it bounced off and clattered onto the rocks.

"Let's see that," he said, reaching for the rifle. Donna handed it over and he walked to the edge of the tree's canopy, sighted on one of the birds, and fired, but he missed and the cupid kept coming, dropping its arrow onto the motor along with the others. It took two more shots to hit another cupid, and two more to get another. That seemed to convince the others that this wasn't a good place to be; they flapped away without dropping their arrows, and disappeared up the valley.

"Valentine, my ass," Trent said. "We ought to call a flock of those bastards a vandalize."

"Did they ruin the motor?" Donna asked.

"Yeah." He handed her the rifle and headed back toward the stream.

"Where are you going?"

"They'll be back. Or other ones will spot the motion. I'm going to stop the wheel while I've got the chance."

He waded across the stream again, climbed up on the rocks, and finished untying the motor, then swiveled it around. The tire came to a fast stop; there was a lot of friction on that axle. Trent wanted to take it back under cover even though it wasn't moving now, but there was no way he could get it across the stream with the water running as high as it was, so he just rotated the motor so its control box was as protected as possible and tied it down again with the wheel out of the waterfall, then he crossed the stream again and carried the battery back to the camper.

He checked the charge level: a shade over fifty percent. That was only one of two batteries, so it was just a quarter of the pickup's full charge, but they could get home on that if they didn't have to make too many jumps.

Right. Considering the trouble Donna was having with the calculations, they were going to need all the power they could get and then some.

Well, there were three more motors. One had a messed-up control box, but the box on the motor that the cupids had just ruined was still good. Trent looked at the pickup, already missing a wheel, then out at the stopped waterwheel. Then with a sigh he got out his tools and set to work unhooking the next motor.

While he was doing that, Donna walked out to the edge of the tree's cover and looked across the stream for a while, then went into the camper and came back out with the parachute and began unfolding it on the ground under the tree.

"What are you doing there?" he asked.

"Looking for a section big enough to hang over the waterwheel and cover it so cupids can't see it," she replied.

He slid out from under the pickup. That was an excellent idea, except they'd cut down the closest trees on that side of the stream. "What can we tie it to?" he asked.

"That tree right across from it, on this side. If we go high enough, we can just stake it to the ground over there. It'll hang at a slant, but there's plenty of parachute. We can cover the whole stretch between the tree and the opposite bank, and that way you don't have to worry about getting bombed when you go out there to check the battery, either."

Trent looked at the parachute, then at the stream, then at Donna. "You're a genius."

She blushed. "Hah. Tell me that when I figure out where the hell we are."

"I don't care if you ever do that," he said, pulling her into a hug. "You just keep figurin' out stuff like this, and you're genius enough for me."

"I don't—"

He stopped her protest with a kiss.

"I just—"

He kissed her again.

When he was sure she felt good and appreciated, he crawled back under the truck, and he found himself actually whistling as he finished unbolting the motor. There were worse things in life than being stranded somewhere exotic with someone like Donna.

While he worked on the motor, she folded the parachute in thirds and stitched it together with one of the shroud lines so the rips wouldn't leave any openings for cupids to shoot through, then she carried the parachute and an arrow up to the tree beside the waterfall, tied a shroud line to the back of the arrow, and tossed it over a branch. It took a few tries to get it looped over the right crook in the branch, but she eventually got it and tied the line to the tree trunk, then she did another line closer to the middle of the tree, and another one on the other side.

"Okay," she said to Trent, who was done with the motor by then and was just watching her with open admiration. "I think it's ready to stretch across the creek."

The only cupids in the sky were a long ways off, but even so, Trent and Donna wore their armor and carried their guns while they unraveled the parachute behind them. When they got to the stream, Trent holstered his pistol and waded across, then Donna tossed him the coiled shroud lines and held the parachute out of the water while he pulled it across and tightened it up. It rose into the air, a glowing white roof leading upward at a gentle slope, clearing the waterwheel by three or four feet while hiding it completely from overhead.

He pounded arrows in the ground and tied the shroud lines to them, then stood back and admired their handiwork. It flapped softly in the breeze, but the stakes held.

"Cupids coming," Donna said. He looked up and saw four of them spiraling closer, no doubt attracted by his and Donna's movement. Or maybe it was the parachute itself that attracted them. That wouldn't be such a good deal if it drew cupids into the area. He splashed back across the stream under its cover and he and Donna waited under the tree to see what they would do.

They were definitely interested in the parachute. They swooped low over it and banked around for closer looks, and one of them tried to land on it until the cupid realized that it wasn't solid enough to support its weight. The cupid croaked indignantly and flapped into the air again, plucked another arrow from a treetop, and flew away, and within a minute the others had lost interest as well.

"I think it's a winner," Trent said as he watched them go.

He was getting tired of slogging back and forth across the stream, so while Donna watched for cupids he sawed down another tree and made a log bridge, positioning it so he could reach the motor while he was standing on the log. Then he carried the new motor across and swapped it for the old one, which was easier said than done since he had to remove the tire with all its arrows and slo-mo shells tied to it, then mount it on the other motor, but with Donna's help he was able to get it with only a couple knuckles bruised and one lug nut dropped in the water. He fished around for it with his hands, but couldn't find it before they started going numb from the cold.

"The hell with it," he said. "Three is enough to hold it. But next time we go star-hopping, remind me to bring some extras."

Donna said, "Who knew that interstellar exploration would require so many lug nuts?"

"It's never the stuff you plan for that gets you," he said. "Well, let's give this a try." He swung the motor around until the slo-mo shells dipped into the waterfall, and smiled when it started spinning again. He went back to the pickup and got the battery they'd used through the night, and when he plugged it in, the wheel slowed under load and the battery's charge light came on.

"All right," he said. "We're back in business."

Trent spent the rest of the day taking the damaged motor apart and fishing out the pieces of arrow and wire. It would never work as a motor again, but with the guts removed it would at least hold a tire and freewheel so they could drive.

Donna went back to work on the computer, and around sunset she came out of the camper with a puzzled look on her face.

"What's up?" Trent asked. He was mounting the motor back on the pickup.

"I've got a number," Donna said. She should have been bouncing up and down with that news, but she just stood there, frowning.

"What's the matter?" Trent asked. He slid out from underneath the truck and got to his feet.

"I don't trust it."

"Why not?"

"It's twenty thousand. Even. What are the odds that a glitch in the navigation program would send us exactly twenty thousand light-years away?"

"Sounds pretty likely to me," Trent said. "One digit and a bunch of zeros. A bit gets flipped in the ten-thousandth place, and here we are."

"But that's not what it looks like in binary. It's nowhere near an even number in binary."

"Maybe the part of the program with the bug in it isn't written in binary."

She shook her head. "None of it's actually written in

binary, but that's how the numbers are stored. If something went wrong with one of them, it would show up as an even number in binary, not decimal."

"So maybe the bug's not in the numbers."

"What else could it be? We know from looking at the log file that it's not in the part that actually calculates the jump, because those numbers were right. That doesn't leave much room in the program for a bug in the numbers while they're still in decimal form. The navigation module hands them off to the hyperdrive control module, and that's it. Even the handoff is probably done in binary."

"Hmm." Trent was beginning to see what she was getting at. He wiped his hands on his pants and said, "So how did you come up with the number? This morning you were just as stuck as ever."

She said, "I kept thinking about what you said about working the problem backwards, picking a distance at random and seeing what the velocity would be at that point. There were only a couple of spots in the galaxy where I could do that with what little I've learned about orbits, but I got to thinking about the simulator program that we used when we were first learning how to navigate. It only simulates solar systems, but they're kind of like little galaxies with just a few stars in 'em, so I figured I could set up a simulated solar system and jump around from place to place in it and see how much velocity difference I picked up."

"I didn't know you could do that," he said.

"You can't tell it where to put the planets, but you can tell it how many planets you want, so I gave it a hundred, plus a big asteroid belt. That gave me plenty of targets, so I just picked one to start with and set up the same angle of jump that we took to come out here, and checked the relative velocities of all the planets and asteroids along that line until I got the right number."

"I didn't think planets moved that fast."

"They don't. Everything's about ten times slower, but all

the angles are the same, and the distances are proportional. I was even able to account for our initial velocity when we left Mirabelle, and the orbital velocity of the planet we landed on before we came here."

"But you don't trust the result, because it's an even number."

"It's just too pat. There's got to be something wrong with my calculations."

He didn't know what to say to her. She was probably right, but this was the one time in their lives when telling her she was right would be the wrong thing to say. He looked out at the waterwheel, hard at work charging up their batteries, and said, "We can go have a look easy enough in a day or two."

She looked at him as if he'd lost his mind. "We can't just jump twenty thousand light-years and hope I'm right. What if I'm not?"

"Then we look for another planet wherever we wind up. We can't stay here anyway. We'll be out of water in a week."

She said, "We can make a still."

"Rainwater's about as close to distilled as it gets, and that didn't settle any better than creek water. There's something funky in it. And even if we could get it pure enough, we're going to run out of food in a month anyway."

She ran a hand through her hair. "We don't know that we can't eat anything here."

"You *want* to play Adam and Eve?"

"I don't want to be the one who gets us killed!" She turned away, her arms crossed and her fists clenched.

He reached out to put a hand on her shoulder, but she shrugged him off. He waited a second, then said, "Doing nothing is what'll get us killed. You may not trust your numbers, but I do, at least enough to go see if they're right."

She took a few deep breaths before she turned around and said, "Let me go run the simulation again."

"Sure."

She went back inside the camper, and he crawled underneath to finish mounting the motor.

The sun was down by the time he finished. The day had warmed up pretty well when the sun was out, but it started to cool off again pretty quickly as the stars came out. Trent was tired of being cold, and tired of wearing wet boots, so he lit another campfire and he and Donna sat beside it in their stocking feet while they dried out their clothes. Trent amused himself by tossing the tiny little darts off the leafy ends of arrows into the flames and watching them flare up, while Donna just stared out into the night. They heated up a can of chili over the fire and had another beer, and neither of them got sick on it or on the smoke, which pretty much hammered the last nail in the water coffin as far as Trent was concerned.

It didn't matter. They were leaving anyway. In another day, maybe two, the batteries would be charged, and they would be off to face another problem somewhere else. Trent didn't have any doubt that the universe would serve them up another one. Even if they made it home without incident, there were problems enough waiting there to last a lifetime.

Trouble was like an onion, he decided, only you peeled it from the inside out. Instead of working your way down to smaller and smaller ones, you worked your way out to bigger and bigger ones, and they kept going forever. There didn't seem to be any shortcut through them, either. Simply bailing out for another life didn't work. The very trouble they were trying to escape had followed them to Mirabelle. He didn't suppose he could blame the United States government for the programming glitch that brought them here, at least not directly, but their refusal to let people develop better software and sell it on the open market had definitely contributed to Donna's picking this version to download.

That was something else to worry about. Would the software take them back to Earth? It had worked fine jumping around out here in the middle of nowhere, but if they did wind up in familiar space again, could they just pick Earth off the menu and jump to it, or would they wind up another twenty thousand light-years away? Maybe they should try for Onnescu again. The program had at least taken them there okay.

He supposed he and Donna would have to hash that out before they left, but he didn't feel like getting into it tonight. Not while she was so unsure of her calculations to even get them back to familiar space.

The alien wood didn't leave much in the way of coals, so they had to keep feeding fresh wood into the flames to keep it going. After a while it became more trouble than it was worth, so Trent suggested they turn in, and Donna just shrugged and said, "Why not?"

The long days and long nights were really messing with Trent's sleep patterns. He had no trouble sacking out, but it was still pitch black when he awoke, and he just lay there for hours afterward, waiting for daylight. When it finally came, he was tired again, but he got up and went outside to check the waterwheel.

It was still spinning, though not as fast as yesterday. The stream was back down to the level it had been when they first arrived. The battery was fully charged, though, so he swapped it out for the other one and installed the charged one in the pickup.

He spent the rest of the day going over everything he could think of, making sure that it was ready for space. He used the foot pump to refill the air tanks under the seat and the tanks in their Ziptite suits. He could have used the compressor, but the battery was fully charged now and he didn't want to draw it down even a little bit if he could help it. Besides, he was beginning to see how long and boring a day could be with nothing to fill it, and refilling the tanks by hand was at least something he could do.

Donna alternated between double-checking her logic on the computer and battening down the hatches in the camper for zero-gee. By nightfall, the pickup was as ready to go as the day they'd left Earth, except for the second battery, which was still at only three-quarters of a charge. It would be ready by morning, though.

Trent had an even harder time sleeping that night. Tomorrow they would be in space again, for better or for worse. They would either find their way home, or have to find another planet that would be more hospitable than this one.

It occurred to him that they'd never named the place. They'd named its creatures, but not the planet itself. What would be appropriate? Plasticland? That sounded more like a shopping mall than a planet. Styrohome? Better, but it wasn't actually home. He tried to come up with a play on polystyrene or polyurethane or PVC, but he never came up with anything he liked. Unless Donna had a bright idea, he guessed it would just have to be "that place with the cupids where we stopped to recharge the batteries and figure out where we were." Kind of a shame to discover a planet and not name it, but he didn't think they'd be back, and this wasn't the sort of place he wanted to name after himself or Donna. He wanted their planet to be habitable, at least.

What would his ideal planet be like, he wondered? He and Donna had gone out looking, but they hadn't really defined their terms ahead of time. He tried to think about it now, and decided that it would probably look a lot like this one, with mountains and streams and trees, only without the risk of getting an arrow through the top of your head. He would opt for a spot that was a little more open, though. Close to the mountains, but not *in* them. He was already getting tired of looking at the same old valley day after day.

As he drifted off to sleep, he realized that the picture forming in his mind was of the red buttes around Rock Springs.

The other battery was fully charged in the morning. Trent installed it in the truck, then dismantled the waterwheel and re-mounted the motor, too. The sun hadn't even cleared the mountain by the time they were ready to roll.

They put on their Ziptites and sealed the doors, then overpressurized the cab to make sure it was tight. There was no radio to listen to this time, and neither one of them felt like playing the stereo. Donna held the computer on her lap and ran one more time through what they were going to do.

"I calculated the exact spot in the sky where we want to go," she said, "based on the position of the stars after the big jump and all the jumps we made after that. It's about five degrees off from where we were aiming when we did that trick with the map, but I think it's more accurate."

"I'd be surprised if it wasn't," Trent said.

He looked out at the meadow that they'd called home for five days. There was a path worn from the pickup to the stream, and the logs were still there, too. There was a pile of arrows and slo-mo shells on the bank where he'd cut them loose from the waterwheel. Closer at hand, there was a smudge of plastic residue under the tree beside them where they'd had their fire. Other than that, there was nothing to indicate that humans had been here. They'd undoubtedly left some bacteria behind, but the odds of that thriving here were slim to none. Intestinal bacteria were just as specialized as people; they would have little better chance of surviving here than Trent and Donna would.

Still, he could reduce the odds of that down to practically nothing. He shifted the pickup into forward and drove out into the meadow, stopping right over the spot where they'd dug their latrine. He'd filled it with dirt, but this would be even better. Pack out what you pack in, and all that.

He looked at the pressure gauge. Steady as a rock. "Ready to do it?" he asked.

"Not really," Donna said, "but I'm probably as ready as I'm going to get."

"Good enough for me," he said. He opened the stopcock in his door and listened to the excess air rush out until the gauge steadied out at eleven and a half pounds—atmospheric pressure here—then he closed it off again and said, "Let's go."

"Hang onto your hat, cowboy."

He reached up and did just that, glad to be wearing it again. He'd stowed their helmets and shoulder guards in the camper for posterity, but if he never wore them again, it would be too soon.

Donna hit the "enter" key, and the valley blinked out of existence. Sunlight blasted in the driver's window, casting stark shadows across the cab, at least until the usual cloud of debris rose up to mask it. The pickup rocked a little as the wet ground boiled away beneath them, but Trent let it go without correction until they were quite a ways away from the biggest mass of it and they weren't getting bumped much any more. He didn't want to waste a single puff of air that they didn't have to.

Zero gee reminded him all too clearly how his stomach had felt a couple days ago, but he held it down. He wasn't sick this time; just light.

Donna set the computer in its spot on the dashboard and let it get a look at the stars. After a few seconds the red arrow appeared on the top right corner of the screen, so Trent used the right-rear jet to tip the truck that direction until the arrow became a circle that drifted down with the stars. He stopped their motion with the front-left jet, and looked out at the patch of stars that the computer was flagging. "That's where home is, eh?"

"That's where I'm prayin' it is," Donna said. "Nineteen thousand, five hundred and thirteen light-years from here."

"I thought you said it was twenty thousand even?"

"From where we first showed up. We made five more hundred-light-year jumps before we gave up looking for home and then backed up thirteen looking for a good planet."

"Oh. Sure," he said, feeling dumb. He'd totally forgotten that little detail. That's why Donna was the navigator.

"So are you ready for the big jump?" she asked.

"Do it."

She had already keyed in the figures on the ground. Now she just double-checked that they were right, then hit "enter."

There was the same long moment of disorientation that they'd felt when they made their other big jump, and the starfield completely changed. The bright sun was gone.

"Okay, baby," Donna whispered, "find something familiar."

They waited, hardly breathing, for the computer to lock on, but after thirty seconds or so, it made the Homer Simpson "D'oh" sound and flashed "Unable to orient" on the screen. Trent didn't recognize anything, either, but that didn't mean anything. The computer was programmed for it; he wasn't.

"Let's give it a full picture to work with," he said, hitting the buttons for both front jets. The nose tilted down, and more stars streamed up from behind the hood, but none of those proved familiar, either. He hit the side jets and let the odd corkscrew motion of rotation in two planes twist them around ninety degrees so the computer could see what had been to their sides, too, but still no luck.

Donna was biting her lip and making little hand motions toward the computer as if she wanted to help it out somehow, but didn't know how.

Trent brought the pickup to rest with the point they'd been aimed at before out his window. "Okay," he said, "so we didn't hit it the first time. We've got plenty of power; let's try jumping to the side a ways. Maybe our angle was off a little."

"We could jump all day and never find it," Donna said.

"We could. But at least we'll have tried."

She reached for the computer. "A hundred light-years?"

"Five hundred," Trent said.

"That's farther than—"

"—the star map is good for, I know. But we've got a lot of space to cover. Let's cover some of it."

"It's going to be like jumping from hole to hole in a piece of Swiss cheese," Donna said.

"Yeah, well, the holes are what makes it Swiss," Trent replied.

"Huh?"

He shrugged. "That was supposed to be profound."

"Oh." She narrowed her eyes. "It wasn't."

"I gathered that. So let's jump already."

"Any place in particular look good to you?" she asked.

"An even ninety degrees to the side of where we were pointing when we got here," he said. "Might as well make the math easy if we have to calculate how far we've gone."

"Okay. Here goes." She moved the cursor until the numbers in the popup display were right, typed in 500 light-years in the distance box, and hit "enter."

The stars shifted again. The disorientation that went with the jump was less than last time, but that was the only indication that they'd gone only 500 light-years instead of 20,000.

They let the computer look for familiar stars, but it didn't find anything this time, either. "Where to now?" Donna asked. "Ninety degrees away from the last time?"

"Sure, why not?" Trent said. It didn't really matter, but they might as well be consistent.

They jumped again, and let the computer have a look at the entire sweep of sky. It found nothing familiar, but Trent felt his heart suddenly start to pound when he saw three stars in a row with another three at an angle above them. They looked just like the belt and sword of Orion. There were even two more bright stars where one shoulder and the opposite knee would be. The constellation was way smaller than Orion was from Earth, but it sure looked right to him.

"There," he said, hitting the jets to bring the pickup to a stop before it slid out of sight. In his excitement, he overshot and had to correct twice more before he got it, but that left the stars still visible just to the right of center. "Isn't that Orion?"

"Where?"

"On its side. Right there." He tapped the computer screen; it was easier to point to a spot on that than at something outside.

"It . . . certainly looks like it," Donna said, "but it must not be, or the computer would recognize it. I mean, it's not like it can't see it."

"Tell it to try again," Trent said.

She pulled down a menu and selected "Orient," but the computer made the Homer "D'oh" sound again.

"Damn it, I know that's Orion. I mean, what are the odds of there being another one just like it somewhere else?"

"I don't know," Donna said, "but what are the odds of the computer not recognizing something that obvious? It must see something we don't, like the stars are the wrong distance apart or the wrong spectrum or something."

"This is the same program that sent us twenty thousand light-years off course."

"Well, yeah, but—"

"No 'but.' That's Orion."

She ran a hand through her hair. It stayed put when she let go, but she didn't seem to notice. "Okay," she said slowly. "If that's Orion, then let's see if I can figure out where we are myself."

She called up the star map as seen from Sol and found Orion on that. "It's a hell of a lot bigger from the Sun, that's for sure," she said.

"Wait a second," said Trent. Something didn't look right. He looked from the screen image to the one out the windshield. He had to cock his head sideways to get the same orientation on it, but when he did, the sword was pointing the wrong way, and the belt was hanging to the right instead of to the left.

"Shit, it's not the same. It's backward."

She looked from one to the other, back and forth, and finally said, "What if we're behind it?"

"Is that possible?" he asked. "I thought the stars in a constellation were all different distances away. That's why they get all messed up when you go very far. There *isn't* a 'behind' to a constellation, is there?"

"I don't know." She pointed the cursor at one of the belt stars on the computer's image of Orion as seen from Earth and read the distance figure that popped up beside it. "Wow. Fifteen hundred light-years. That's a ways." She pointed at the next one. "Fifteen hundred to that one, too." She hit the third belt star. "Same." She pointed at the left shoulder and said, "Not that one; it's only four hundred. The right shoulder is only four hundred, too, but that star right next to it is fifteen, and the sword and the left knee are, too. That's bizarre. They're all the same distance from Earth. I had no idea."

"So they *would* still look like they went together from the other side," Trent said. "But are those the right ones to make it look like this?"

"Left knee and belt and sword," she said, "and this one here next to the right shoulder. We've got a left shoulder and a right knee and a belt and a sword. I think that's it."

"Hot damn. How far away do you figure?"

She looked at it, then closed her eyes and said, "It looks about half the size that I remember it. Is that about what it looks like to you, too?"

"About that," he admitted.

"Then we're twice as far away as Earth is, which would put us about—jeez, three thousand light-years? Could we be that far off?" She answered her own question. "Of course we could. My calculations were about as accurate as a shotgun."

"Hey," Trent said, "shotguns hit stuff, too."

"Well, we seem to have hit something this time. Let's go around to the other side and see if the computer recognizes it from there." She brought up the real-time image on the screen and pointed the cursor at the middle star in the backward Orion's belt, then keyed in 3,500 light-years. "That ought to make it nice and bright," she said.

She hit "enter" and the stars shifted. The computer tried to orient itself, but after thirty seconds it made the Homer "D'oh" and gave up.

"Okay, it can't see anything familiar up ahead," Donna said, "but neither can I. Orion should be behind us. Turn us around and let's see."

"Here goes," Trent said. He hit the front jets and the nose tilted down. He watched stars sweep up into view, some of them pretty bright. A really bright one popped over the hood, then just as it was about out of sight overhead, another one rose up to replace it. There was a big halo of light around it, and Trent was just starting to wonder if this and the one before it could possibly be the belt stars when Donna gasped and he looked over at her.

And past her, to the gorgeous blue nebula that rose up above the right fender. There were four or five more bright stars embedded in it, clearly the source of the light that made it glow like a neon cloud. There were wispy filaments of dark dust scattered throughout, and distant stars shone through the edges of it.

Then the big one rose into view. Much larger than the blue nebula, this one was reddish, and filled half the windshield. It was brighter on the left side, lit by four stars in a squat diamond buried in the densest part of the nebula, and trailing off into long wisps on the right. A little to the left, a smaller puff of red glowed by the light of another star embedded in the middle of it.

"Where's the camera?" Trent managed to ask.

"In the back, of course," Donna said.

"Of course." Not that he would need a photo to remember this. All he would have to do, even if he lived to be a hundred, was close his eyes and this image would be there.

He brought the pickup's motion to a stop and leaned close to the windshield. There were the three belt stars, and these two nebulas and that third bright star had to be the sword.

"We're practically on top of it," he said.

"Too close for the computer to figure it out," Donna said. "We've got to back off a ways."

Trent nodded. "Not just yet, though." They had air enough for hours, and they weren't lost anymore. He couldn't imagine a place he'd rather be.

He glanced at the pressure gauge. Steady, but it had been twenty minutes or so since they had sealed up, so he opened the stopcock in his door and let half their air out, then closed it and refilled the cab from the tank under the seat. He smiled when he saw the little puff of steam that drifted away from the truck. Air that he and Donna had breathed was now part of Orion. Every time he looked into the sky at night and saw the constellation shining up there, he would think, *I am part of that.*

They finally realized that they could kill two birds with one stone. They had a lot of velocity to shed, and that would take some time, so they hunted down a nearby star and found a gas giant planet whose gravity they could use to bring them back into the same ballpark as the local stars. They had plenty of time to look at the nebulae while they let the planet do its thing. It was even better with binoculars. The gas clouds held detail that you couldn't see by naked eye; folds and filaments and subtle variations of color on every scale.

At last the navigation program told them that they were moving at roughly the same velocity as the gas giant, so Trent aimed the pickup away from Orion and Donna set the distance for 1,500 light-years. They jumped, and Trent didn't even have time to turn them around again so the computer could get a look at behind them before it flashed the "locked on" message on the screen. It had obviously recognized something else.

"Woo hoo!" Donna yelled. "We're home free."

Trent flipped the truck over anyway. Maybe the computer didn't need to see Orion, but he did.

There it was, glittering just the way he remembered it. Bright as hell, even this far away. He took a deep breath and let it out, feeling days of tension flow out of him with the air. "Man, that's a sight to behold."

"It is."

He pulled his eyes away from it and looked over at Donna. "I've been thinking about where to go when we got back to familiar territory, and I'm wondering if Galactic Federation headquarters might not be the smartest bet."

"Yeah?"

"Yeah. Earth has a nasty habit of shootin' at people who drop in uninvited, and we've only got one parachute left."

"That's a good point. You think we could get another one from the Feds?"

"Probably. I wouldn't mind talking to Allen and Judy about what to do once we get home, either. They might have a better idea than I do."

"They might." Donna pulled up the destination menu and found "Gal. Fed. HQ" on the list. When she selected it, all the stats popped into place in the target window.

"It's only eighty light-years away," she said. "Practically in our back yard."

"Everything on that list is practically in our back yard compared to where we've been," said Trent. He looked at the computer and saw the red arrow pointing straight up, so he used the rear jets to tilt the truck upward until the targeting circle started sliding down the screen. He stopped their motion when it was as close to dead center as he could get, and said, "Okay, let's see if this damned program will take us there."

Donna hit "enter," but instead of the familiar shift of stars and light disorientation of a short jump, they felt the major lurch of a big jump and the stars completely changed.

"Son of a bitch," Trent said. "It did it again."

"It did." Donna swallowed hard. "I'm starting to take this kind of personally."

"Me too. Let's get us turned around and head right back." They had to do the edge-of-the-map trick again to find the opposite direction of where they were pointed, but Trent had been careful to note the exact star that had traded places with the targeting circle on the computer screen, so they were able to get a pretty good one-eighty from that. They set the targeting circle on their reverse course and set the distance for 20,000 light-years, and Donna hit the button.

Another big jump, and all the stars changed. The computer didn't get a quick lock this time, but when Trent set the pickup spinning slowly, he picked up Orion just about the same time the computer did. The constellation was squashed quite a bit head-to-toe, which meant they were a long ways to the north or south of where they had started, but the computer claimed it knew where they were.

"Federation headquarters is now three hundred and thirty-two light-years away," Donna reported. "I'm setting up this jump in explorer mode."

"Good idea."

She copied the distance figure and the coordinates from the automatic targeting window, double-checked to make sure she'd typed everything right, and hit "enter." The stars did a pretty good shift this time, but a few of them stayed put, and one off to the right was close enough to show a disk.

"That looks promising," she said. "Let's triangulate." She set up another jump of just a few light-hours. When she hit "enter" the star shifted quite a ways behind them, and the computer popped up a window with its position and distance. "Okay, we've got a lock, and it claims it knows where Gal. Fed. is in its orbit. I'm setting that up in explorer mode, too . . . and here we go." She hit the button, and the star became a bright sun. And off in the distance, a winking light drew their eyes toward a space station.

It was a long, flattened-football-shaped thing, with stuff sticking out of it at all angles. It looked a little like a pile of scrap metal, but Trent had seen pictures of it in magazines, and he knew that some of those booms were over a mile long, and the whole body was at least fifteen miles from end to end. It was impressive as hell, fitting for a seat of government. It was also receding at several thousand miles an hour.

"Looks like we're in for a long vector translation," Trent said. "Let's at least let them know we're here first, and find out where to go." He turned on the radio and switched to channel 19. He didn't hear any traffic, so he keyed the microphone and said, "Break one-nine for anybody at Galactic Federation headquarters. This is Trent Stinson requesting permission to come aboard."

He let off the button and waited a few seconds, and a voice responded, "Welcome, Trentstinson. You are welcome to come aboard, but please don't attempt the docking yourself. Too many pilots have miscalculated, with unfortunate results. If you'll shift to channel twenty-nine and transmit a ten-second signal, we will locate you and send a tug out to get you."

"Hot damn," Trent said to Donna. "Valet service." He keyed the microphone and said, "That sounds good to me. Shifting to twenty-nine." He tuned up ten channels and said, "Trent Stinson on channel twenty-nine, saying sure, come get us. We've had more than our share of trouble with this damned navigation program anyway. It took us twenty thousand light-years out of our way, and we spent damned near a week tryin' to figure out how to get back home. We'd *love* a ride in." He let off the microphone and asked Donna, "Was that ten seconds?"

"I think—"

"We have your position," the voice responded, "and we're sending the tug now. It'll take us a few minutes to match your velocity. In the meantime, if you'll tell us your species, we'll determine which part of the station to take you to."

"We're human," Trent said. "From Earth," he added, somewhat reluctantly.

There was a pause, then, "You are Trent Stinson, of Rock Springs, Wyoming?"

Trent raised an eyebrow. Donna smiled and said, "You're famous."

"Infamous, more likely," Trent said. He keyed the microphone and said, "That's me. Do I know you?"

"You know part of me," said the voice. "Several of my units once belonged to the being you knew as Tippet."

Tippet was the alien butterfly that Allen and Judy had met on their first trip, who had turned out to be just one member of a vast hive mind on board an interstellar starship. Tippets were all more or less interchangeable units in the same being, so talking to any of them was like talking to them all. Trent and Donna had met the original on their last trip into space, and they had gotten along famously, after the initial exchange of death threats.

"Well hells bells," Trent said, "Howdy, old buddy! How've you been?"

"Divided," said the alien. "Tippet's experience was too valuable to keep to itself, so it shared half of its members with other hives. I am mostly Potikik, a governor hive from our home planet, but I have Tippet's memories and some of its temperament now. I remember meeting you aboard Tippet's ship several months ago. Are you still travelling in the same red pickup?"

Trent laughed. "Yep. It's a little worse for wear these days, but it's the same one. Are Judy and Allen still hanging out with you guys?"

"They're here," said Potikik. "They'll no doubt want to see you, but their time is limited. They have no extra units to divide their labor, and running the galaxy is hard work."

"No doubt. I apologize in advance, but I'm afraid we're going to make that job even harder."

"Oh? In what way?"

"I don't know if you realize what the United States is up to, but they're bombing the shit out of anybody they don't agree with, and generally making life unpleasant for everybody else. We've got to put a stop to that."

"Ah, yes. Human internal politics. I'm sure they would be happy to discuss it with you." There was a crackle, then the same voice said, "This is your transfer pilot. Please disengage your hyperdrive engine and refrain from maneuvering while I adjust your velocity for docking."

Trent saw a flicker of motion out his side window and turned to see a spherical framework of metal beams just a few dozen feet away. It was maybe five feet across, with six arms and six big bell-shaped rocket nozzles evenly spaced around its surface. It drifted closer, and one of the arms reached out and the grapple at its end closed around the roll bar just behind the cab. Trent could see a little glass bubble about the size of a softball in the middle of the framework, with an iridescent blue butterfly floating in its midst, its legs manipulating tiny control levers. Potikik, or one of its hive-mates.

Donna quit the navigation program and unplugged the hyperdrive connector from the back of the computer.

"We're ready," Trent said through the radio.

There was a brief moment of disorientation, and they popped out close to a gas giant planet. It was icy blue and dimly lit. Where the sun had been a moment ago, now just a bright star glowed.

"Long ways to go for a vector translation," Trent said.

The butterfly didn't reply for a second, but then it said, "Excuse my delay. My mind needs a moment to reset itself after a hyperspace jump, and now that we are away from the hive, my higher functions are mostly artificial. But in answer to your implied question, we have no planets closer in. They have all been eaten by the space stations."

"Eaten?" Trent wondered if it was his turn to reset his brain, because he couldn't have heard that right.

"The stations are biological," said the butterfly. "Engineered, we believe, by a civilization long gone, but they are self-sustaining. They live on sunlight and reproduce by feeding on any matter they encounter. They long ago filled this solar system as far out as sunlight would power them."

"Oh."

Donna said, "There must be a hell of a lot of them, if they ate the *planets*."

"How many of these space stations are there?" Trent asked their tug pilot.

"Millions," the butterfly replied.

"All just waiting for people to come live in 'em?"

"Who knows their purpose? But we have colonized several without incident."

"Huh. They've got breathable air in 'em and everything?"

"We import it. We've pressurized different sections with different mixtures for different species."

It was mind-boggling. Millions of space stations, just waiting for anybody who came along. Somebody was thinking ahead.

They fell outward from the gas giant for another couple of minutes, then their pilot said, "Translation will be complete in ten seconds," and ten seconds later they jumped to within spitting distance of Federation Headquarters.

The station did look organic up close. The long booms visible from a distance looked more rounded, with habitat modules sticking out like mushrooms from their surfaces, and long vine-like tubes connecting them. The core of the station was lumpy and peppered with round ports and windows, like eyes peering out through holes in a blanket.

The tug pilot fired one of his attitude jets and the pickup swung around until the station was to their right, then he fired another jet and they felt the thrust pushing them sideways toward it. It grew bigger and bigger, one of the huge booms sweeping past only a few hundred feet away, until a tiny black dot became a yawning cavern mouth.

"If I see teeth in there, I'm hitting the bugout button," Donna said.

"You're not hooked up," Trent pointed out.

She gave him the look, but spared him the words.

The tug pilot spun the pickup partway around and corrected their approach, then spun them around the rest of the way and slowed them down so they drifted into the docking bay at just a few feet per second. It was an oddly shaped chamber, almost rectangular but with walls that bulged inward in the middle. Glowing circles in the walls provided illumination when the door irised closed behind them, then air rushed in to fill the vacuum and the walls straightened out.

The tug pilot reoriented the pickup so its wheels were near one of the walls, then reached out with two arms and gripped protruding knobs in the adjacent wall, holding the pickup in place. "It's safe to exit," he said.

Trent popped his door latches, but the door wouldn't budge. There was more pressure outside than in. He opened the valve in his door and it hissed for a few seconds, and then he was able to open the door.

The air was warm, and rich with the smells of life. Not unpleasantly so, but you could tell that people—and lots of other creatures, too—lived here. Trent and Donna pushed themselves out of the cab and gripped the sides of the pickup to keep from drifting away, and their tug pilot popped open his control bubble and flew out to hover next to his craft. Without the radio, Trent wasn't sure how to communicate with him, but a voice spoke from the side of the tugboat: "These mobile transceivers will allow you to hear us, and we you. They also allow us to function as translators for beings who don't speak English. Please take one and strap it to a convenient body part."

Trent heard Donna trying to suppress a giggle. He just smiled and said, "Okay." There were four little gray boxes about the size of matchbooks clipped to the framework next to the alien; he pulled loose two of them and reached across the top of the truck to hand one to Donna. The strap was an inch-wide piece of black nylon long enough to go around his thigh if he'd wanted to put it there, but he decided on his upper arm instead.

"How's that?" he asked. "Can you hear me?"

"Yes, that's fine," the speaker replied. The butterfly flapped its wings and the speaker said, "If you will follow me, then, I'll give you the tour."

Trent and Donna pulled themselves around to the front of the pickup and were about to push off after the butterfly when a slit in the docking bay's inner wall spread apart and Allen Meisner and Judy Gallagher floated through.

"Trent! Donna!" Judy yelled, and she launched herself toward them, her arms held out wide.

Judy was a medium-tall, dark-haired woman with a big smile. She wore a blue coverall and brown socks with individual toes in them so she could use her feet as well as her hands to grip things. Trent got a good look at the socks on their way past as Judy tumbled in the air and landed feet-first against the windshield of the pickup, leaving her in perfect position to wrap her arms around Trent and Donna's waists and give them both a big sideways hug.

"How *are* you?" she asked.

"Doing okay," Trent said automatically.

"Better now than we were, that's for sure," Donna added.

Allen was tall and blonde and wore the same smile and the same basic clothes as Judy, only his coveralls were bulging with pockets full of science-geek equipment. "Hey," he said, hanging onto the doorframe.

"Hey yourself," Trent said.

"So what brings you here?" Judy asked.

"Long story," Trent replied.

"It's the United States problem," the speaker on Trent's arm said, and it took him a second to realize that it was the tug pilot—presumably just a different extension of the same Potikik they had talked to earlier—who had spoken.

Judy shook her head, and her short black hair flipped from side to side. "Oh, man. What isn't?" she said. "What did they do this time?"

"Dropped a meteor on us, for one thing," Trent said.

"What for?"

"Visiting a French colony."

"Oh. Well. They are at war, you know. At least the Americans think so."

"But these were civilians. The U.S. is bombing civilians."

"That's not surprising. They've been doing that in other countries for decades." Judy straightened up and said, "Come on, let's show you around a little, and then we can meet up with some of the other Federation delegates and you can tell us what happened."

She pushed off toward the doorway, carrying Trent and Donna with her, and Allen caught them when they got there. The corridor behind him was smaller, just the right size for two people to move through side-by-side and let each be able to touch a wall. It was oval in cross section and had a rough surface, like tree bark, with lots of knobs sticking out for gripping. Doors opened off either side at irregular intervals; marked only by the seam where the two sides would pull apart when you pressed their edges. They did that to a few. Some of the chambers behind the doors were huge; several had big windows looking out into space, with sunlight streaming in on green parks and lush gardens.

"This was all just waiting here, empty?" Trent asked. "Along with maybe a million more of them?"

"Yep," said Allen. "And to answer your next question, no, we don't know who designed 'em. Near as we can tell, they died out or just packed up and left over a million years ago. None of the original stations have survived that long, as far as we know, so we haven't found any artifacts, other than the stations themselves. That tells us plenty, though. For instance, they were about our size, breathed air, lived in groups, liked open areas with lots of light, and came and went in spaceships."

"And they thought big," Donna said.

"That, too."

They came to a door that opened into the biggest chamber they'd seen yet, a bubble at least five hundred feet across with three big skylights that poured sunlight into a spherical park filled with trees and bushes and flowers. Dozens of unfamiliar animals floated among the vegetation, some browsing on it, others just hanging onto it for support, and after a minute Trent realized that most of them were engaged in conversation. These were aliens.

"Let's introduce you around," Judy said, leading them into the park. "These aren't all of our delegates, not by a long shot, but they're enough to start with."

Even so, there were more names and body types than Trent could remember. The reptilian guy with the big yellow gills was Kasak, and the fuzzy snowball with the sticks for arms was Menaripal, but the others went by too fast for him to do more than nod and say, "Pleased to meet you." Most of them didn't speak English, but when they used their own language, the speakers on Trent's and Donna's arms would translate, using different voices for each.

Judy led them all to a sunny patch of bushes where they could nestle in and not drift around while they talked, and she had Trent and Donna tell everyone what had happened to them. When they got to the bit about going 20,000 light-years too far, and figuring out how to get back only to have the program do it again when they tried to jump to Federation headquarters, Allen said, "That doesn't sound possible if they're using the control software I wrote for the core code. Can I have a look at that program?"

"Be my guest," Donna told him. "I was going to ask if I could download one that's more reliable. And we should warn people not to use this version."

"Certainly. On both counts."

There were a few seconds of silence, then a shiny green bug about four feet long chittered something, and the speakers on Trent's and Donna's arms said, "Go on with your story."

"That's pretty much it," Trent said. "Donna figured out how to find our way back, and here we are."

The bug chittered some more, and the speakers said, "So let me make sure I understand your complaint. Your government is suppressing personal freedoms within its own borders, and attacking other humans it disagrees with outside its borders. But it is not to your knowledge attacking other species?"

"Not that I know of," Trent admitted.

"This sounds like an internal matter to me."

"And to me," said several of the other aliens.

"The Federation stopped the war that broke out when Allen invented the hyperdrive," Trent pointed out. "That was an internal matter, too."

"It was," said the arm speakers in a high-pitched voice. Trent didn't know who was talking, but the voice went on to say, "It was the Federation's first act, entered into when there were only four member species, and it was entirely a bluff. There would have been no retaliation if humanity had destroyed its homeworld. I believe your governments knew that, but perhaps welcomed the excuse to withdraw from the brink of disaster. I doubt if we would be so lucky a second time."

"You don't have to threaten them with war," Trent said, addressing the entire group for lack of a specific target. "There are lots of other ways to make people back down."

"All of which require the Federation to interfere in a species' internal affairs, solely to improve conditions for certain members of that species," the speakers said. "That is not our purpose."

"So you're just going to let the U.S. keep killing people it doesn't like?"

"That is what humans seem to do," said the yellow-gilled reptile, Kasak, using English directly. "You aren't the first of your species to come to us with this request. We've investigated the matter thoroughly, and we've concluded that humans kill one another when they disagree. That is your way of solving problems. If we impose our own moral code on you, we would be forcing you to do something unnatural for your race."

Donna hadn't said much, but she spoke up now. "We're not all the same. Peace is the natural state for most of us. It's just the kind of people who go into government who like to fight wars."

"And the kind of people who go into military service," said Kasak. "You have the highest proportion of your populace devoted to military service of any species we have encountered."

"They're still a minority!"

"But they are the ones who run things."

She looked over at Judy and Allen. "Come on, you two. Help us out here. You helped set up this federation. You can't believe it's right to let something like this go on, can you?"

Judy said, "Of course it's not right, but think for a minute what you're asking. You want us to go in and overthrow a government because it's gotten out of control. But how did the United States become what it is today? By overthrowing governments that were out of control. They thought they were the world's policeman."

"That's not why they did it," Trent said. "They were after oil."

"Maybe at first," Judy said. "I could argue otherwise, but even if that was their motive at first, they had all the oil they wanted after Iraq, and they didn't stop there. They got locked into a foreign policy of bullying other nations to get their way, and they're still doing it."

"And you're saying that's okay?"

"No it's not okay! But if the Federation starts doing the same thing, where do you think we're going to wind up in twenty years?"

Trent didn't have an answer to that, probably because the answer was so obvious.

"What can we do, then? Start bombing Washington ourselves?"

"That would be the natural way for humans," Kasak said.

"*Some* humans," Trent said. "Idiot humans. We're not all like that."

"Yet you carry a weapon in your vehicle," said the arm speakers. That had to be Potikik, the only one who had seen their pickup.

Trent looked up to the butterfly, who floated over the middle of the group and kept itself in place with gentle flaps of its wings. "That weapon saved our lives a time or two. There's a difference between self-defense and murder."

"It is perhaps a more subtle difference than you believe," said the speakers.

Trent almost said, "Tell me that when they're dropping shit on *your* head," but he knew that wouldn't gain him anything. Instead, he said, "So what would you do, then, if you were in our shoes?"

"Speaking only for my species, we would exchange members with the minds opposed to us until we achieved consensus. In extreme cases, we would swarm the offensive mind and force it to disband."

"Killing it," Trent said.

"Redirecting it," the butterfly said. "Or you might say outvoting it. None of the individual members would be sacrificed."

That didn't seem particularly helpful. "How about you?" Trent asked Kasak.

"We eat the eggs of those we oppose. The next generation is descended from the winners."

"And that's not murder?"

"The eggs are purchased, and the seller knows what they will be used for."

Donna made a puzzled face. "Why do they sell them, then?"

"Because they believe that they can out-breed their opponents."

Trent snorted. "So your solution is to make love, not war."

"Precisely."

"My grandparents' generation tried that. It didn't work."

"Perhaps they weren't rich enough."

Hah. That was probably closer to the truth than they had wanted to believe. Love and compassion were great in theory, but it seemed like the rich were the ones who called the shots in practically every political system humanity had ever invented.

"Any other bright ideas?" Trent asked, looking from alien to alien around the circle.

The fuzzy snowball squeaked and shivered, and the arm speakers said, "Educate the warmongers. My species learned long ago that those who preferred violent solutions to their problems were simply ignorant of better ways."

That was probably true of anybody, Trent thought, but one guy couldn't very well educate an entire nation. Not Trent, anyway.

The green bug chittered, and the speakers said, "Your species' belief in religion offers a possibility. If you start a new religion based on pacifism—"

"Been done," Allen interrupted. "The religion gets subverted, and before you know it, you've got crusades."

There was an embarrassed silence. Trent felt sorry for the bug, who was just brainstorming, but then he realized that the embarrassment wasn't for it, but for humanity.

"Your first instinct was perhaps the wisest," the speakers said in Potikik's voice. "Remove yourself from the violence, and seek a better life elsewhere."

"That would be fine if it didn't follow us," Trent said, "but there's no escaping it. Not if we want to stay in contact with civilization, such as it is. And besides, I promised André I'd try to stop it."

Judy said, "I don't imagine he expects you to turn around twenty years of hostile foreign policy by yourself."

"No, but he expects me to do what I can, and I'm going to do it."

Kasak said, "An admirable attitude, but the execution is between you and your government. We wish you success, but we can't interfere."

"Don't say 'can't' when you mean 'won't,'" Trent said.

"Very well; 'won't,' then."

The snowball started chittering, and a moment later the arm speakers followed along behind it, saying, "We can do one thing. I have long felt that we should undertake a mapping project of the entire galaxy. Your experience with inadequate star maps underscores the need for a more comprehensive survey, and this is a task that falls directly in the Galactic Federation's purview."

"Better star maps," Trent said. "People are gettin' killed, and you're going to make better star maps."

"Yes," said the snowball. "Those maps will save lives, too."

That was probably true. They would certainly have helped him and Donna find their way home. But it was a far cry from the help they had wanted.

"Knock yourself out," he said. Then he turned to Donna and said, "I think we're done here. Let's go home."

They didn't leave right away. They still needed to install a better navigation program on their computer, and Judy wouldn't let them go without at least having a meal with them and catching up on old times. Donna wouldn't have a meal with anybody without a bath first, so she and Trent wound up in a guest room just off the docking bay, trying to figure out how to use the plumbing.

They identified the bathroom easily enough by the mirror and the sink and the medicine cabinet, though the sink had a clear bubble over it with holes in the front to stick your hands through so water wouldn't come flying out all over the place, and the medicine cabinet had clips and pockets instead of shelves to hold everything. The toilet was either disgusting or amazing; Trent couldn't decide which. The seat was soft enough to seal around his butt when he sat down, and then the air pressure went down inside, sucking everything down to the bottom of the bowl before it could make a mess. It took a minute to get used to the steady breeze blowing down between his legs, but he eventually relaxed enough to get the job done.

The shower turned out to be a separate room beside the bathroom, an oblong big enough for two or three people at once, with lights at either end and little round bulges with holes in the ends of them sticking out of the walls every foot or two. Those had to be nozzles, but there was no obvious way to turn them on. Trent grabbed one and gave it a twist, then pushed on it, then pulled on it and a jet of warm water sprayed him right in the face. He shoved it in again and it stopped.

"Success!" he said, scraping the water off his face. It drifted away in fat globules, which Donna, watching from the open door, batted back inside the shower. She slipped on in and the door closed behind her, and Trent tugged the nozzle on again.

Water sprayed against his chest and bounced everywhere, dancing in the air all around them; then a soft breeze began to pull it up through an opening above their heads.

"I think that's where our feet are supposed to go," Donna said. She curled into a ball and turned over, stretching out again with her legs next to Trent's face.

He wasn't quite as limber, but he managed to turn around, too, and open another nozzle on that end so they had water flowing at both ends of the shower.

There was a bar of soap in a little mesh bag hanging right where they needed it. They had fun lathering one another up and washing each other's hair and rinsing off, then they had even more fun experimenting with how other things worked in zero-gee. It was a long shower by the time they turned off the water jets and chased all the loose globs of water into the drain before they opened the door again, but they both felt a lot better about life by then.

They toweled off and put on fresh clothes that they'd brought from the camper, then set out to find Judy and Allen's apartment. Trent wore his hat and boots, even though he wasn't likely to need either inside a space station. He just felt naked without them.

Potikik guided them through the space station with instructions through their mobile speakers, leading them to a huge open atrium lined with shops and filled with airborne aliens—with a guy-line along the walls that they hung onto so they wouldn't become airborne, too—and into a more conventional corridor that led past several more parks before ending at an unassuming slit in the wall.

"You're there," said Potikik. "Enjoy your dinner."

There was no doorbell. There was no door to knock on, either. Trent rapped a knuckle on one of the lips, but it made practically no noise, so with a "what the hell" shrug, he pushed the two sides apart the way he'd learned to open all the other doors on the station.

This one didn't open, but it did make a loud hum, like a singer warming up his voice. Nothing more happened for a few seconds, but just when Trent was wondering if he should make the door hum again, it opened to reveal Allen floating there with his arms out wide.

"Come in!" he said, reaching out and pulling them into the living room beyond. At least that's what Trent assumed the place was; it had paintings on the walls, and bookshelves with little elastic webs across them to keep the books from drifting loose, and potted plants and some kind of twisted abstract sculpture that had to be alien. There was no furniture, but in zero gee there didn't seem to be any need for it.

Allen didn't even pause in the living room. He led them right on through, and through a video room with a six-foot screen on the wall, past archways that led to bedrooms—with hammocks rather than beds, just like in their guest room—on through a dining room that had a table with attached chairs and seatbelts to hold people to the chairs, and into a kitchen, where Judy was busy chasing vegetables through the air.

"We had a little accident with the salad spinner," she explained, fielding a baby carrot and popping it into a yellow plastic tub with a lid full of flexible slots. Trent and Donna and Allen joined in the hunt, and they quickly brought the salad under control again.

"Cooking without gravity is a different experience,"

Judy said. "I'm still not very good at it. Allen is much better."

"I use the microwave a lot," he said. "Heat transfer without physical contact is the key. Do you like rabbit?"

Trent laughed, somewhat ruefully. "Last time we were asked that, dinner got interrupted by a meteorite."

"That was on Mirabelle?"

"Yeah."

"Then we'll have salmon."

Trent said, "No, rabbit's okay. I just—it just reminded me, that's all."

Allen nodded. Then a moment later he brightened and said, "Hey, I've invented something I think you'll appreciate." He opened a very ordinary looking refrigerator at the back of the kitchen and said, "Budweiser, right?"

"Absolutely," Trent said.

"Here you go." He handed over a regular can of beer, but it had a little plastic cap on it like a water bottle with a push-pull stopper. "You shove down on it like this to pop the top," he said, demonstrating, "and then when you want a drink, you just stick the cap in your mouth and pull it open with your teeth. Internal pressure squirts beer into your mouth, and you push it closed when you've got enough. No foam flying all over the place."

Trent gave it a try, and it worked like a charm. "Hot damn," he said. "I hope you got a patent on this."

Allen shrugged. "Eh. Managing a business is a pain. I just like to invent stuff."

"How's your alternate dimension thing going?" Donna asked, accepting another beer from him.

"Huh?"

"Last time we saw you, you were working on something that you said would let you see into alternate dimensions."

"Oh, that," he said. "It . . . kind of got put on a back burner."

"I convinced him it was a bad idea to open too many frontiers at once," Judy said. "Hand me that knife." She pointed at a paring knife stuck to a magnet on the wall, and Allen handed it over to her.

While she sliced radishes, Trent said, "How about antigravity? That would come in pretty handy on landing. Be a lot safer than parachutes."

Allen laughed. "It would, if I had a clue how to do it, but I'm afraid that's not my area of expertise."

Donna asked him, "Did you have a chance to look at that navigation program yet?"

He lost his smile. "Yeah. Turns out it wasn't a bug so much as a deliberate bomb. The basic code is the same program that I gave out with the hyperdrive plans, but there's an added module that looks for any visits to planets on the United States's interdict list, and after you visit any of them, it resets the navigation module to add twenty thousand light-years to any destination you choose off the menu."

Trent felt a cold chill run down his spine. "Then that's twice our own government has tried to kill us."

"Looks like," Allen said.

"I don't suppose the Federation is going to do anything about that, either?"

"No, but I will."

"What?"

"I've got a couple of ideas," said Allen. "Don't worry, the government will wish they hadn't tried this."

Trent wondered what he could do. Allen had a considerably higher profile than Trent did, but Allen was a criminal in the eyes of the U.S. He'd been branded a terrorist, and could legally be shot on sight. Under the Patriot laws, he had no rights whatsoever. He couldn't take anyone to court for messing with his software, even if he had patented it, which he no doubt hadn't. Whatever he did, he would have to do it from outside, and unless he wanted to declare all-out war, Trent was willing to bet it would have no more effect than the myriad other economic and political sanctions the U.S. had endured over the years. The U.S. wouldn't change its tactics until it changed its politics, and now that the dissidents were leaving for more tolerable lives elsewhere, the odds of that happening were practically nil.

They changed the subject after that, and by dinnertime they were laughing and joking as if everything was all right. They learned why there was a dining table—it was much easier to strap yourself down and stick your plate to a solid surface than to chase it around the room—and they learned how to pass dishes around without spilling them. Judy and Allen told stories about some of the more interesting aliens who had been discovered in the last few months, and Trent and Donna told about being stranded on the plastic planet and how they had built a generator out of a wheel motor and slo-mo shells to recharge their batteries. After dinner they moved into the living room and talked for a couple more hours, but eventually Trent realized Judy had yawned about half a dozen times in as many minutes, and Allen was starting to space out even more than usual.

"Hey," he said. "We're keeping you guys up. What time is it around here, anyway?"

"Past midnight, for us," Judy admitted.

"Holy cow. Sorry about that! We've only been up for a few hours."

"The station never sleeps," Allen said. "You can find plenty of things to do at any hour."

"Thanks," Trent said, "but I think Donna and I are about done sightseeing for a while. I'm kind of thinking it's time to go on home. How about you, kiddo?"

Donna nodded. "I'd kind of like to sleep in my own bed tonight."

That wasn't likely, given that they would have to land in Canada and drive home from there, but Trent didn't say anything. Just setting down on Earth again would be close enough for starters. Thinking of which . . .

"Hey," he said, "we're going to need our computer if we're going to go anywhere."

Allen slapped himself on the forehead, then got the computer from his workshop and gave it to Donna. They spent another fifteen minutes at the door the way people always seem to do when they know they won't see one another again for a while, but Judy yawned again in the middle of a story about a cat that loved to set itself adrift in the commons and let the birds fly all around it, and Donna laughed and said, "Will you people go to bed so we can go home?"

"Right," Judy said. "Bedtime it is. You guys take care, and keep in touch."

They said their goodbyes, and Trent and Donna pushed off down the corridor. When they got to the central atrium, Trent saw the shops and said into his arm speaker, "Hey, is there someplace we can buy a spare parachute around here? We're down to just one, and I get nervous trying to land without a backup."

Potikik guided them to a shop right next to the corridor that led to the docking bay, where they found hyperdrives, plasma batteries, portable solar cells, air tanks, and all the other equipment a person might need to build or repair a hyperdrive spaceship, including parachutes. The proprietor was a spidery yellow bug about nine feet tall who didn't speak a word of English, but Potikik helped translate for them and they found a cargo chute big enough for a loaded pickup.

"How much?" Trent asked.

"How much do you have?" the bug replied through Potikik.

"No, that's not the way it works," Trent said. "You tell me how much you want, and I tell you whether or not I want to pay it."

The bug spoke at length, and the shoulder speakers said,

"Peculiar. Basic economic theory predicts the development of class stratification if goods are priced without regard to the user's ability to pay. It would lead to excess and oppression, possibly even war."

Trent looked over at Donna, who said, "He's got you there."

"Okay," said Trent. He fished out his wallet and opened it up. The five orange twenties that Greg had given him on Onnescu were right up front. "I've got a hundred bucks Australian, and about sixty American."

"And how badly do you need the parachute?" asked the bug.

"We can live without it," Trent said.

"How many other purchases do you need to make before you replenish your money?"

"God only knows," Trent said. "I'm still lookin' for work."

The bug turned to an abacus-looking gadget on the counter beside him and flipped a couple of colored balls around its wire loops, then said, "For you, then, seventy-two Australian will do."

That was actually a lot cheaper than he could buy a cargo chute at home. "Okay," Trent said. He handed over eighty, and the bug handed him back three oblong yellow coins with little swirly galaxies stamped on them.

"Federation currency," the bug said. "Good anywhere."

"Right," Trent said. He somehow doubted that they would be worth much in the good old US of A, but they were certainly worth no less than his remaining Australian twenty.

He picked up the parachute and followed Donna out into the atrium and down the corridor toward their docking bay. They stopped to collect their clothes from the guest room, and Donna packed those in the camper while Trent made sure the parachute was folded right and packed it into its pod.

The tug pilot showed up while he was doing that, so

they clipped their mobile speakers to the tug's framework again, then donned their Ziptite suits and climbed into the pickup. Trent closed the door, then looked out at the mirrors still pointing backward for driving. "This time," he said, opening the door again and adjusting his mirror so it pointed straight down.

"My god, we remembered," Donna said, opening her door and adjusting her mirror, too.

They closed up again and Trent turned on the radio. "Give us a few minutes to make sure we're airtight."

"Certainly," said Potikik. "Take your time."

Trent pressurized the cab and they watched the air gauge for a few minutes while Donna connected up the computer and loaded the new program that Allen had put on it. When the pressure had remained steady after ten minutes, Trent let the excess air out and said into the microphone, "Okay, we're ready to roll."

Potikik didn't say anything, but they saw several holes open up in the walls and the air rushed out of the docking bay. The holes were in the inner wall, so Trent supposed the air was being held somewhere, maybe in a big set of lungs, to be exhaled into the bay again when the next ship docked.

The outer door opened and the tug disengaged its clamps from the inner wall, letting the last puff of air send them out into space. The pilot pushed them out past the protruding booms—one of which no doubt held Judy and Allen's apartment—and when they were well into clear space, he released the tug's hold on the roll bar and backed away.

"You're clear for launch," he said. "And you're welcome back any time."

"Thanks for the hospitality," Trent replied. "We'll be seeing you around." He put the microphone back in its clip and said to Donna, "Anytime you're ready."

"Okay," she said, pulling down the destination menu and selecting "Earth" from the list. Not just "Sol" like the other program, but "Earth." She double-checked the numbers that popped into the "details" window, then said, "Looks good. Here goes."

She hit the "enter" key, and the space station vanished, to be replaced in almost exactly the same spot by the sunlit Earth.

"Holy cow," Donna said. "He's got the targeting down cold."

The planet was about the size of a basketball held at arm's length; far enough to put them outside the range of the United States's laser satellites, but close enough to see the continents so they could pick a preliminary landing site.

Provided they could recognize the continents. Trent squinted against the glare of sunlight on clouds, and finally managed to see a patch of brown beneath the white. There was a curved edge over to the left with a big bite taken out of it, and a big triangular island kind of below and to the left of that. There was a big white area to the left of that, too smooth to be clouds, but what clouds there were did seem to be kind of sticking out of it in big curls. Trent turned his head sideways to put them at the top of the picture, then the other way to put them at the bottom, and everything clicked into place. That was the south pole over there to the left, and the brown continent with the island to the south was Australia.

Which meant North America was on the night side of the planet.

"Dammit," Trent said. "I don't want to make a night landing."

"You want to go back to Federation headquarters and try again in twelve hours?" Donna asked.

"Not particularly."

"I don't think we have enough air to wait it out here."

"Probably not." Trent didn't have the patience, either.

He looked at the brown continent, ringed with cloud and bare in the middle. Somebody was having a nice, sunny day down there. After all the rain and cold he and Donna had been through in the past few days, a little desert sun would be more than welcome. "Hell with it," he said. "We've always wanted to go to Australia. Looks like now's a pretty good time for it. We've even got twenty bucks left. What do you say we spend the rest of the day there and *then* go home?"

Donna smiled. "That actually sounds kind of fun. Anyplace in particular you want to go?"

"I don't know Australia from a hole in the ground. Just pick a spot and let's see what we get."

"Okay, here goes."

She put the target circle dead square in the middle of the continent and pushed "enter." Earth vanished, to appear much larger and only half-lit off to the right, then after a couple minutes it shifted again so they were directly over a huge expanse of red desert. There was still some sideways motion; apparently the program had only killed part of their velocity so they could fly over their target area and pick a specific landing site more carefully.

Donna looked over at Trent, but he just shrugged and said, "Anywhere," so she left the targeting circle right where it was and pressed "enter."

The program took them halfway around the planet again to kill the rest of their velocity, then put them back where they were, only much closer to the ground. One more jump downward, and Donna said, "That's it. We're at the top of the atmosphere already." Trent used the air jets to orient the pickup wheels-down while Donna said, "Get ready with the parachute in five . . . four . . . three . . . two . . . one . . . now."

He flipped the switch for their new chute. No time like the present for testing new equipment. It streamed upward and tugged gently on the pickup, but not nearly as hard as their other chutes did. Was it fouled? Trent leaned forward and looked up just in time to see a series of cords break away from where they held the canopy closed, and the chute blossomed open a little at a time until it was fully deployed. There had been hardly a lurch through the whole sequence.

"Now that was a neat trick," Trent said. "I'll have to learn how they did that."

There were big black letters on the chute. They were backwards from underneath, and in various languages including several that weren't human, but Trent could read one set of block letters easily enough: Galactic Federation. He wasn't sure whether that was a good thing or a bad thing, but it was too late to worry about it now.

They drifted down through clear skies, watching the desert rise up to meet them. The ground was red, just like it was around Rock Springs, and they could see big swirls and arcs of rock outcrops from where it had folded and then been eroded flat over millions of years. Off toward the horizon were a couple of white patches that looked like salt pans.

"Looks like we're in the outback," Trent said. So much for spending that last twenty.

As they drew closer to the ground, they realized it wasn't nearly as barren as it looked from higher up. Around each of the rock outcrops there was a light brown ring the color of dry grass, and between the rings were specks of green that turned out to be trees. There were actually lots of trees, just spaced a ways apart, and big tufts of grass or bushes or something growing between them.

Trent looked in the downward-facing mirror as they approached the ground, and he saw a group of twenty or thirty animals moving out in a circle around where they were going to come down. They were up on two legs—kangaroos? But their arms flailed as they ran, and brightly colored cloth billowed out behind several of them.

"People!" he said. "There's people down there."

"Oh, shit!" said Donna. "Should we jump?"

"They're gettin' out of the way." Trent kept his eyes on the mirror just to make sure, but the runners on the ground were well clear now.

"Jeez," Donna said. "What are the odds we'd land right on top of the only group of people for miles around?"

"Pretty slim, but we managed it. Hang on."

They leaned back in their seats, and a moment later there was a hard jounce as the tires hit the red dirt. The pickup skidded to the left a little, but it didn't feel like it was in danger of going over. A cloud of red dust rose up around them and drifted slowly to the left, rising to meet the parachute as it draped itself over a couple of bushes and several of the people who had watched them land.

They were aborigines. Dark skinned, dark-haired, except for the ones who had gone gray, with wide noses and big smiles. That was a good sign.

Trent popped the latches on his door and opened it, to be hit with a wall of heat. He had intended to apologize for landing right in the middle of their get-together, but instead the first words out of his mouth were "Wow, it's hot."

"You get used to it," said one of the group in surprisingly good English.

Trent squinted in the bright sun. This guy didn't look like the others. He looked like a lobster that had been boiled too long, bright red and peeling even though he wore a big floppy hat and a loose-fitting gray robe.

Trent remembered what he'd meant to say. Stepping down to the red ground, he said, "I'm sorry we dropped in right on top of you. We didn't—"

"We were expecting you," said one of the aborigines, an older man with dreadlocked hair and a wispy brown beard shot with gray. His English was good, too, with just a little of the accent Trent would have expected from a native Australian.

"You were expecting us? How? We didn't even know we were coming here ourselves until a few minutes ago."

"The universe knows," the aborigine said. He was wearing a leather thong around his neck with an irregular lump of black rock tied to it; he reached up and touched the rock as he spoke.

The red-faced man said, "We started walking here five days ago. He wouldn't tell me why; just said I'd know when it was time. I thought we were headed for a town or a ranch or something, but we wound up here this morning and he says, 'Now we wait.' So we're standing here in the middle of nowhere in the middle of the day, and I'm about out of patience, when here you come. My hat's off to you, old man." He lifted his hat, but dropped it right back on his head. Trent didn't blame him; the sunlight felt like liquid fire.

He peeled out of his Ziptite and tossed it in the cab. Donna had already shed hers; she came around the front of the pickup, saying "Hi" to everyone on the way, until she stood next to Trent. "Hi," she said to the aboriginal leader. "I'm Donna Stinson, and this is Trent."

"They call me Billy when I need a name," the aborigine said.

"And I'm Dale," said the other man. "Dale Larkin."

It took a moment for the name to register, but when it did, it hit like a load of bricks. "The bank robber? You stole the whole damned—how did you wind up *here*?"

"Long story."

"I brought you here to tell it," said Billy. "So tell it."

"Here? Now?"

"The heat makes him a little crazy," Billy said. "Of course here. Of course now. This is where we are, and these people are only here for the day."

"How do you know that?" Trent asked.

Billy laughed softly. "Would you stay any longer in this heat?"

That was a good point. But Trent wasn't going to stand around in it and listen to a story all day, either. "Why don't we find some shade before we roast?" he said.

Billy laughed again and waved toward the bushes with the parachute draped over them. "You have already provided it."

That was a good point, too. "Fair enough," Trent said. "Want a beer?"

"That would be fabulous," Dale said.

"Yes, thank you," said Billy.

Trent looked out at the other people and realized he didn't have enough for everyone, but he and Donna went into the camper and brought out what they had, and the rest of their bottled water as well. The water proved to be a bigger hit than the beer; when the picking and choosing was over, the water was gone and there was a six-pack of beer left.

About half the tribe settled in under the parachute. The others spread out into the bush, digging for roots and who knew what else. Trent and Donna sat on the red dirt between two tufts of spiny grass, and Billy and Dale sat facing them. It was surprisingly more pleasant in the shade, even though the ground was still hot. Trent scooped up a handful of dirt and let it trickle through his fingers, and when he looked up at Donna, he saw that she was watching him and smiling.

"Earth," he said.

"There's no place like home, eh babe?"

"Nope." He popped open his beer and took a swig. Nice and cool. No need for a nipple to drink it through, either.

Billy nudged Dale in the ribs. "So tell your story."

Dale shifted uncomfortably. "What if they don't want to hear it?"

"Too bad. The Dream brought them here, and we walked a long ways to meet them. Your lives are connected. From what Trent said a minute ago, I think it started before today, hmm?"

"He bankrolled the guys who invented the hyperdrive," Trent said. "Donna and I helped them build their spaceship. But we haven't met before." He looked straight at Dale and added, "Then he robbed a bank right after I got some money out of the cash machine. I mean took the whole building and everything. The backwash blew me into the hole."

"Sorry about that," Dale said. If he blushed, it was impossible to tell behind his already-red skin. "I thought you were far enough away."

"You miscalculated a little."

"That wasn't the only mistake I made, believe me."

"Robbin' banks is generally a mistake," Trent said.

Dale shrugged. "We all fight the system in our own particular way. But I was out of cash, and almost out of options. After the Feds traced the money I gave to Allen and Judy, I had about ten minutes to grab what I could and get out of town. I holed up at my sister's place in Granger and finished turning my van into a spaceship, but I didn't want to go live on some frontier planet. I was getting pretty tired of living in the States, though, with all the anti-this and anti-that going on, so I figured I'd knock off one last bank and then go to Rio or something. But it didn't turn out quite the way I expected."

"What happened?" Trent asked, growing interested despite himself.

Dale laughed. "Jesus, what didn't? When I jumped, I expected the cloud of air that went with me to push me away from the building a little when it expanded, but I didn't stop to think that the building would be full of air, too, and all of that would be rushing away from the other side of the wall. So the entire bank came *at* me instead of away, and it slammed into the van like a runaway train. It smashed the whole right side and busted the passenger window, so all the air rushed out and sent me corkscrewing away like a wobbly football. I had to use an entire fire extinguisher to stop the motion, and another one to push me back to the bank."

"Fire extinguisher?" asked Donna.

"Yeah, I had a bunch of CO_2 fire extinguishers for

maneuvering around. They work great for that; they've got those bell nozzles and everything. But you wouldn't believe how hard it is to steer a van with one when you're leaning out the door and spraying it into space.

"I managed to push the van back toward the building, but the building was tumbling, too, so I had to use another extinguisher to stop before I bumped up against it and got knocked away again. I'd planned to tie the van to the bank with a rope, but I couldn't do that with the building spinning around, either, so I had to cross over the last few feet on my own, wearing just my Ziptite suit.

"And that's when I realized that I hadn't set the jump field tight enough. I'd figured it would cut the vault in half and I could just go in and throw the loot into the back of the van and be done, but it was still locked tight. There was a little nick out of one corner, maybe big enough to reach an arm through, but the edges looked *sharp*, and that Ziptite suit was starting to feel awfully fragile. And cold. Nobody told me how cold it would be! Or how scary. All that loose dirt and rocks and stuff that came along for the ride kept whacking into me, and the air regulator kept making that little popping sound when I breathed—I thought it was the suit getting ready to blow."

Trent laughed. "Man, I know that feeling. So what did you do?"

"I went back to the van and made another jump. I was about ten feet away from the building, so I waited until it rotated around the way it was to begin with and sliced off a ten-foot chunk of it. It worked, too. When the interior spun around again, the vault was spilling its guts out into space."

Dale ducked his head sheepishly when everyone laughed. "Yeah, it's funny now. At the time, though, man I was pissed. Coins and jewelry and paper money was flying out in a big spiral, whacking into the van's windshield—"

"Sounds pretty," Donna said.

Dale snorted. "Oh yeah, it was pretty. Some of it was Krugerrands. I opened the door and tried to catch some of it, but it just bounced off my gloves before I could grab it, and then I lost my grip on the door and almost slipped out into space again myself. And of course by then my breath was condensing inside my helmet, so I couldn't see, and I was panting like crazy and the air regulator was popping away, and I got this sudden image from *Butch Cassidy and the Sundance Kid.* You ever see that movie?"

Trent and Donna both shook their heads, but surprisingly, Billy nodded and said, "Robert Redford and Paul Newman. Their best work."

"You're kidding," said Dale.

"Yes, of course I must be. Their names must have come to me in a dream."

Dale shook his head and said, "This guy's a constant source of surprise. So in the movie, Butch and Sundance are robbing a train, but they use way too much dynamite to blow the safe, and when they touch it off it blows up the entire boxcar, safe and all. It throws all the cash up into the air, and it's fluttering down like leaves around the Hole-in-the-Wall gang, who're grabbing it and stuffing it into their hats. But the posse is already closing in on them, so they jump on their horses and ride, all but one of them, who can't leave all that money behind. He keeps gathering it up even when Butch shouts at him to leave it and ride for safety, and a second later, the posse shoots him dead."

He took a drink of beer and said, "I decided right there that maybe money wasn't the most important thing in life, so I slammed the door and headed for home. Only it was the middle of the night at home, and the cops were no doubt hotter on my ass than ever before. I took a look at the sunny side of the planet and decided I'd always wanted to see Australia, so here I am."

"He had a little trouble landing, too," said Billy. "He

came down on a big rock. It shorted the battery and started a fire."

Dale said, "I barely got out before the whole van went up. So there I was in the middle of this, with just the clothes on my back." He waved his arms to encompass the brilliant sunlit landscape beyond the shade of the parachute. "I would have died if these people hadn't showed up when they did."

Trent shook his head. "Man, it sounds like you've had more than your share of trouble. If it hadn't started out with you robbin' a bank, I'd almost feel sorry for you."

Donna poked him in the side, but Dale said, "No, he's right. I brought it all on myself."

"So what are you going to do next?" she asked.

"I don't know. I just know that I won't be robbing banks anymore."

"Do you want a ride home?"

Dale shook his head. "No, thanks. I don't think North America is a good place for me. I'm not sure if the Australian outback is my place, either, but it's refreshingly uncomplicated out here. And it's right in the middle of the continent, so people are dropping in all the time. If I want a ride anywhere, one's bound to come along in a few days."

Trent wasn't sure what to think about this guy. By all rights, he should be locked up. He'd stolen a couple of million dollars in cash and who knew what else in people's safe deposit boxes, and he'd ruined an entire bank building in the process. The fact that he didn't get to keep any of the money was something, but even so, just letting him walk free didn't seem quite right. Except Trent couldn't see how putting him in jail was going to help anybody else. He'd decided to stop robbing banks on his own. Locking him up now would just be an act of vengeance, and would ultimately cost people more than just letting him go.

He realized that Billy was looking at him with an amused expression on his face.

"What?" Trent asked.

"Life is complicated," said Billy. "Even out here." Then he stood up and walked out into the sunlight.

Trent and Donna and Dale stayed under the parachute, swapping stories about their travels and about Rock Springs and the things that had happened to them there. Trent told Dale about meeting Judy and Allen on their space station, and how the Galactic Federation had refused to get involved in human politics.

"Makes sense, in a way," Dale said. "You start micro-managing everybody else, and you just wind up like the U.S., fighting wars on a dozen different fronts and not doing anybody any good."

"That's fine, in principle," Trent said, "but it doesn't do *us* a whole lot of good, either. We're still stuck with the government from hell."

"So change it," said Dale. "It's designed to let us throw the rascals out every four years. Do you vote?"

"Yes, I vote, for all the good it does. There isn't a candidate on the ballot who's any better than the people in office."

"So run for office."

Trent snorted. "Yeah, right. I can just imagine how well that would go over."

"You'd get my vote," Donna said.

"And I'd get laughed out of the country," Trent said.

Dale examined his empty beer can as if there was some hidden truth in its side. "You don't have to start at the top, you know."

"Dogcatcher," Trent said with a laugh. "Now there's a race I could probably win."

"It's a start," said Dale.

"Sure. And it would do the country a whole lot of good to have me out there with a net, goin' after loose poodles."

Dale shrugged. "Hey, we do what we can. I bought into the instant success idea for so long, the best I can do now is take myself out of the picture. Be glad you can do more than that."

Trent was starting to get embarrassed by the way the conversation was going, so he was actually kind of relieved when there was a cry of alarm from out in the open. He jumped to his feet and rushed out from under the parachute to see everyone looking upward, where a big meteor was drawing a fiery line across the sky.

His first thought was that the U.S. had decided to bomb Australia, too, but this was coming in at much too shallow an angle for a meteor-bomb.

"I wonder if that was somebody trying to land," he said quietly.

Whatever it was, parts were breaking off and burning in separate little chunks, spreading apart until there were a whole swarm of pieces streaking across the sky side by side.

Then another one flared up way in the north, moving at a wide angle to the first. Two people making bad landings within seconds of one another? That didn't seem likely.

Trent climbed into the pickup and turned on the radio, but there was only static. Way out here in the middle of nowhere, he hadn't expected much else, but it had been worth a try.

The meteors burned themselves out high in the atmosphere, leaving thick smoke trails behind them that persisted long after the fireballs were gone. Billy walked over to where Trent and Donna and Dale were standing and said, "That looked like the time Skylab came down."

"Skylab?" Trent asked.

"Before your time," said Billy. "It was a space station that fell out of the sky." He held up his rock-on-a-thong necklace and said, "My father made us walk for days so we could watch it. He was a little too accurate in his dream. This piece hit him on the head."

Donna said, "Did it . . . did it kill him?"

Billy laughed. "No, it was moving too slowly by the time it found him. But the centrifuge gave us all a scare." He let the rock—more likely a fire-blackened bolt or piece of a solar panel or something—fall back to his chest and said, "The dream is never clear. I had no idea there would be more than one good omen today."

"You think that was a good omen?" Trent said.

"Undoubtedly, for someone," said Billy. "This one, I think, is good for you."

Trent couldn't see how. After Mirabelle, he didn't think meteors were good luck at all. But he held his tongue.

He and Donna could feel themselves already starting to sunburn, so they retreated under the parachute and had another beer, waiting out the rest of the day until they could jump around to the other side of the planet and land in the light. The aborigines came and went from the shade, listening to their conversation with Dale and Billy or just napping in the long, lazy afternoon.

When the sun went down, Trent and Donna folded up their parachute and packed it away, but the computer's atlas said it was still too early for daylight in North America so they helped gather wood and started a fire, roasting hot dogs over the flames and sharing whatever else they had left in the camper that didn't require water to cook. The temperature dropped fast in the clear night air, and it wasn't long before they were putting on sweatshirts and sitting close to the fire.

Fire time was the aborigines' turn for storytelling. Billy talked about the Dreamtime when the world was created, and how the beings that shaped the land lived on in spirit form, lending their knowledge to anyone who knew how to listen. Trent listened out of politeness at first, but he gradually realized he was interested in what Billy was saying.

It was religion, certainly, but it made a lot more sense than the selfish gods and angry battles of the religions he had grown up with. Its central message, if he understood it right, was that human beings were a part of nature, inextricably linked with all other living things on Earth, which included the Earth itself. You didn't have to appease anyone or anything, just live in harmony with it.

"I just realized something," Trent said. "You guys aren't going to colonize other planets, are you?"

"Does the fish move onto the land?" Billy asked. Then he laughed and said, "Yes, as a matter of fact, it does if you give it enough time. And so will some of us, I'm sure. But not today. Right now we belong here." He threw a branch onto the fire and bright red sparks shot up into the night sky, but they winked out before they could settle on anything and catch it on fire.

At last, when the sky was pitch black and the stars were as bright as they were from deep space, Donna figured it would be morning over central North America. She and Trent said goodbye to Dale and Billy and the others, put on their Ziptite suits, and climbed into the pickup. They drove a few hundred feet out into the bush, swinging once around to make sure that nobody was sleeping where they intended to launch from, then they sealed up and jumped into space.

Donna took them around to the sunlit side of the planet, then dropped them a few thousand miles out over northern Canada. "I wonder how close to the border we can go before we get shot at?" she asked.

"I don't know," Trent said. "Theoretically we should be able to land just north of Montana, but I wouldn't bet my life on it. Let's see if anybody down there can tell us." He turned on the radio again and tuned to channel 19, but there was too much traffic to get a word in edgewise. He tuned up and down the dial, but it was the same everywhere. Every channel was packed with voices. At last he went back to 19 and called out, "Break one-nine. Break one-nine for information. Can anybody tell me how close to the U.S. border a guy can land these days?"

There was a moment of static when he let up the microphone, then a dozen voices tried at once to respond, so he waited for them to die down and said, "Too many of you! Just one, try again."

Of course everybody broadcast again. "One guy!" Trent said.

"There were five or six voices this time, but one of them cut through the others. "Haven't you heard? The laser satellites are down. Something dropped them all out of orbit about eight hours ago."

"The laser satellites are gone?" Trent asked. "You mean it's safe to land in the U.S.?"

"Well, that's a matter of opinion," said the voice with the strong signal. "It's still the bloody States, after all. But they won't be zapping you with a laser today, that's for sure!"

"Holy shit," Trent said to Donna. "That's what we saw over the outback."

Donna said, "I'll bet you anything it was Allen. He said he was going to do something to get back at the U.S. for that navigation software."

"But killing every laser satellite! How could he do that?"

"He's part of a whole group of scientist geeks. They probably hacked into the guidance program months ago, and were just waiting for the right time to trigger it. What better message than to turn the whole country's navigation software against them?"

"Damn. Remind me never to get him mad at me." He put the microphone back in its clip and turned down the radio. "Well, hell, I guess we might as well take advantage of it. I'll bet you anything the military's too busy shittin' their pants to worry about people landing in Rock Springs."

Donna took them in closer so they could find it, then she slid the targeting circle to the east of Salt Lake and just past the pincer-shaped Flaming Gorge Reservoir. It was rising pretty fast to meet them, but she was quick about it. "That ought to do," she said, hitting "enter."

The computer took them around to the other side of the planet for a few minutes, then set them back where they had started and dropped them down to the edge of the atmosphere in two more quick jumps. "Ooh, I like this program," Donna said. "Get ready on the parachute."

Trent reached for the switch, deciding at the last moment to use their original parachute this time. It might not be a good idea to have "Galactic Federation" written across their chute today. He flipped the toggle when Donna called "zero" and they endured the lurch and the few seconds of worry afterward that they would somehow be shot down even now, but they descended peacefully through the atmosphere, watching the ground slowly rise to meet them. It looked a lot like the outback down there; the same red soil and spotty vegetation, but with much more varied terrain. Trent couldn't help smiling when he saw the flat-topped buttes with their sheer cliffs and the talus slopes of shale at the base.

Then he realized that they were coming down right on top of one. Worse, they were going to hit on the edge. "Get ready to bail out," he said. "This doesn't look good."

Donna was already holding her hand next to the keyboard. Trent waited until the last moment to be sure, but when there was less than two hundred feet between the pickup and the rocks, he yelled "Bail out!" and Donna hit the "enter" button, throwing them a hundred thousand kilometers back into space.

She had widened the jump field enough to include their parachute, but now it hung out there in the vacuum, twisting itself up in its shroud lines and getting in the way of the other one.

"Shit," said Trent. So close. But it was only a matter of time before they had to do a bailout, and they'd been lucky so far. "Button up," he said, sealing his suit.

Donna did the same, and when he was sure they were both okay, he let the air out of the cab, tying the rope around his waist and the other end to the steering wheel while the pressure dropped. When it was down to zero he opened his door and unbuckled his seatbelt, then stood up in the doorway and reached over the top of the cab, pulling the parachute down one-handed and wadding it into its pod while he hung on with his other hand. There was no way he could get the parachute folded right in space, so he didn't even try.

The fabric tried to get away like something alive, but he wrestled it into the pod and managed to latch the cover with only a few puckers of it sticking out the edges. Good enough. Then it was back inside, close the door, latch it tight, and refill the cab with air and open his helmet.

"Okay, let's try this again," he said.

They already had the right velocity relative to their landing site, so it was a simple matter to pop back to the edge of the atmosphere and give it another shot. Donna used the arrow keys to scoot them sideways a few miles, putting them over flatter terrain, and when they hit the air, Trent popped the other chute.

It yanked them hard, too, now that it didn't have its special rigging, but it held, and they descended without incident until they were just a couple of miles above the ground, when a fighter jet roared past just a few hundred feet away.

"Son of a bitch," Trent said. "Now what?"

The pickup bounced through the turbulence while the plane banked around and came back for another pass. "Get ready to jump again," Trent said, but he picked up the microphone and turned the radio to channel 9, the emergency channel, and said, "Hey, what the hell do you think you're doing?"

He didn't really expect a response, but the radio crackled to life and a voice said, "You're in restricted airspace. Leave immediately or be shot down."

"Restricted, my ass," Trent said. "Near as I can tell, I'm

right over my own goddamned house. I'm an American citizen and I'm going home. You gonna shoot down a civilian?"

"It says 'Galactic Federation' on your parachute," said the fighter pilot. "That doesn't look like an American chute to me."

"Why don't you check the license plate on my pickup, then?" Trent said. "You're flying goddamned close enough!"

The plane roared straight toward them, banking at the last second and peeling away to the side. "County four," the pilot said. "Well, I'll grant you that much, but I can't let you land."

"The hell you can't," Trent said. "You want to arrest us for possession of a hyperdrive, you go right ahead and do that, but it's sure as hell legal to parachute for recreation around here, and that's what we're doing."

"Nobody lands," said the pilot. "We're in a state of national emergency."

"Fuckin' right we are," Trent said. "We've been in a state of national emergency for twenty years. Well it's time to decide whose side you're on, buddy, because I'm an American citizen and I'm landing on American soil. You want to shoot me for buildin' a spaceship in my back yard, you go right ahead, but you just try looking in the mirror when you get back home tonight."

The plane banked around again, and Trent watched it come toward them, his heart pounding. How much time would they have if he fired a missile? Time enough to jump away? He glanced over at Donna, saw her hand shaking over the keyboard, and he opened his mouth to say "Jump," but she shook her head and said, "Not yet."

The plane swooped toward them, nose to nose again, but it roared beneath them without shooting and then it banked around and began to circle. "I'm gonna lose my damned commission for this," the pilot said, "but welcome home, cowboy."

Trent could barely hold the microphone in his shaking

hands, and he had to swallow twice before he could say, "If you do, you come on around to my place and I'll build you a spaceship of your very own."

"We're almost there," Donna said.

He looked out and down, suddenly realizing that they had dropped nearly to the ground. He had just long enough to look in the mirror and see that they weren't aimed for a cliff this time, then shoved himself back against the seat for the impact. The pickup bounced over a big sagebrush and the steering wheel spun crazily, but Trent fought it back around and steered into the slide before they turned over. They skidded to a stop, and the parachute slid down in front of them to hang up in the sagebrush.

"I think that was about as much fun as I want to have in one day," Trent said. "Let's go home."

The house was still there, just as they had left it. The mailbox was full of ads and catalogs, the answering machine was blinking its attention light, and when Donna logged on to check their email, they had over a hundred messages, not counting spam. Life had clearly gone on without them.

They turned on the TV long enough to confirm the news that the entire system of laser "defense" satellites had simultaneously de-orbited and burned up in the atmosphere. Homeland Security was already screeching that it was the prelude to an alien invasion and was promising a new, more vigorous program of "incursion deterrence" just as soon as they could figure out what had happened to the old one. Never mind that the only aliens who even seemed interested in Earth were xenobiologists, and those mostly out of morbid curiosity. HomeSec had never seen a news story that couldn't be turned into a reason to boost public paranoia, and this was a golden opportunity for that.

Trent dismantled the hyperdrive and stowed the pieces in their hiding places in case the cops paid a visit, and he and Donna cleaned out the camper. They put their slo-mo-shell armor on the mantel, and Donna printed the photo of Trent wearing his to set behind them. Trent wanted to drill a couple holes in his helmet and run an arrow through it, but Donna said that would look too tacky, so he just leaned a couple of arrows up against it. They put the meteorite on the mantel, too, and Trent wished they had a photo of André's house with the crater behind it, but like the view of Orion from up close, they would just have to remember that.

They finished unpacking and cleaning up by noon. It felt a lot later in the day to them, but the Sun was still high in the sky, and it didn't seem right to go to bed now. Donna had heard that the best way to beat jet-lag was to force yourself to stay up until bedtime, and they were too wound up to sleep anyway, so they just settled into their regular routines, Donna puttering around the house and Trent puttering around the garage. He had plenty of work to do on the pickup, pounding out dents and touching up scratches. He would eventually have to repaint it if he wanted it to look right, but he needed a new wheel motor first, and even that would have to wait until he got a job.

He checked the classified ads in the paper to see if any construction jobs had miraculously come up while he was gone, but there weren't any. The front page from three days ago had an article about the new civic center, which the city council had voted down by the same one-vote margin that they'd had when they failed to reject the ban on hyperdrives. Bunch of short-sighted wimps with their heads in the sand, Trent thought. Give people in this town something to do on a Saturday night, and make it friendlier to come and go, and it might not look like a ghost town. Hell, start standing up for people's rights and they'd be moving in by the busload.

He tossed the paper in the trash and went back to polishing the truck, but he kept thinking about the newspaper article, and how close the vote had been. One vote, and he would have a job. One vote, and he wouldn't have to hide his hyperdrive in a boombox and an old motor case. It wouldn't stop the federal government from harassing people on their way home, but it would at least be a step in the right direction. It would call attention to the cause, and show that not everybody in America was happy with the way the country was being run. Hell, it might spark a movement that would turn things around and make the United States a place to be proud of again.

He snorted. Yeah, right. Like that was going to happen. The only people left in the country were people who didn't know or didn't care that they didn't have any civil rights anymore. The government had been whittling away at the Constitution since Trent was born, and they'd done it so slowly and deliberately that most people hadn't even noticed. Who would vote for a person who wanted to upset the whole applecart in one big shove, especially now when the world was in such turmoil anyway?

He made himself grasp the thought he'd been nibbling around the edges of: Who would vote for him, Trent Stinson?

Donna would. And he guessed it wasn't bad form to vote for yourself, so that was two. At least he wouldn't get skunked.

But if he was on the council, he couldn't vote for the civic center. It would be a conflict of interest to vote for that and then make money building it. On the other hand, if he was on the council then he would already *have* a job, wouldn't he? And of all the things he could think of to pay off his promise to André, this was the one that actually stood a chance of making a difference.

It was ridiculous. Trent wasn't a politician, and never would be. He didn't know a thing about running a city. But obviously neither did a one-vote majority of the people on the council right now.

And it was just about the right time to start campaigning. It was spring, and elections were in November.

He laughed out loud at the absurdity of it and focused on polishing up the truck, but the idea kept coming back, and finally he tossed his rag onto the workbench and started rooting around in his lumber scrap for some lath and a piece of foam-core. If he'd learned anything from this trip, it was that there was no better way to scare yourself away from something than to take a step toward it.

He was just finishing up when Donna came out to see what he was doing. To her credit, she didn't laugh. She just looked at the sign, and then at Trent, and finally said, "Let's go stick it in the yard."